EXTRAS

SCOTT WESTERFELD

SIMON AND SCHUSTER

To everyone who wrote to me to reveal the secret definition of the word "trilogy".

SIMON AND SCHUSTER
First published in Great Britain in 2007 by Simon & Schuster UK Ltd,
1st Floor, 222 Gray's Inn Road, London WC1X 8HB

This edition published in 2014

Originally published in the USA in 2007 by Simon Pulse,
an imprint of Simon & Schuster Children's Division, New York.

A CIP catalogue record for this book is available from the British Library

ISBN 978-1-47112-397-9

10 9 8 7 6 5 4 3

Printed and bound by CPI Group (UK) Ltd, Croydon, CR0 4YY

Part I

WATCH THIS

You all say you need us. Well, maybe you do,
but not to help you. You have enough help, with the
millions of bubbly new minds about to be unleashed,
with all the cities coming awake at last. Together, you're
more than enough to change the world without us.
So from now on, David and I are here to stand in your way.
You see, freedom has a way of destroying things.
—Tally Youngblood

DOWN AND OUT

"Moggle," Aya whispered. "You awake?"

Something moved in the darkness. A pile of dorm uniforms rustled, as if a small animal stirred underneath. Then a shape slipped from among the folds of spider silk and cotton. It rose into the air and floated toward Aya's bed. Tiny lenses gazed at her face, curious and alert, reflecting starlight from the open window.

Aya grinned. "Ready to go to work?"

In answer, Moggle flashed its night-lights.

"Ouch!" Aya squeezed her eyes shut. "Don't *do* that! It's vision-wrecking!"

She lay in bed another moment, waiting for the spots to fade. The hovercam nuzzled against her shoulder apologetically.

"It's okay, Moggle-chan," she whispered. "I just wish I had infrared too."

Lots of people her age had infrared vision, but Aya's parents had this thing about surge. They liked to pretend the world was still stuck in the Prettytime, when everyone had to wait until they turned sixteen to change themselves. Crumblies could be so fashion-missing.

So Aya was stuck with her big nose—definitely ugly—

and her normal vision. When she'd moved out of her home and into a dorm, her parents had given her permission to get an eyescreen and skintenna, but that was only so they could ping whenever they wanted. Still, it was better than nothing. She flexed her finger and the city interface flickered to life, layering across her vision.

"Uh-oh," she said to Moggle. "Almost midnight."

She didn't remember dozing off, but the tech-head bash must have already started. It was probably crowded by now, packed enough with surge-monkeys and manga-heads that nobody would notice one ugly extra snooping around.

Besides, Aya Fuse was an expert at being invisible. Her face rank was proof of that. It sat unmoving in the corner of her vision: 451,396.

She let out a slow sigh. In a city of a million, that was total extra-land. She'd had her own feed for almost two years now, had kicked a great story just a week ago, and was still anonymous.

Well, tonight was finally going to change that.

"Let's go, Moggle," she whispered, and slipped out of bed.

A gray robe lay in a shapeless puddle at her feet. Aya pulled it over her dorm uniform and tied it at the waist, then perched on the windowsill. She turned to face the night sky slowly, easing one leg, then the other, out into the cool air.

She slipped on her crash bracelets, glancing at the ground fifty meters below.

"Okay, that's dizzy-making."

At least no monitors were skulking around down there. That was the kick thing about a thirteenth-story room—no one expected you to sneak out your window.

Thick clouds hung low in the sky, reflecting worklights from the construction site across town. The cold tasted of pine needles and rain, and Aya wondered if she was going to freeze in her disguise. But she couldn't exactly throw a dorm jacket over the robe and expect people not to notice.

"Hope you're all charged up, Moggle. It's drop-time."

The hovercam drifted past her shoulder and out the window, settling close against her chest. It was the size of half a soccer ball, sheathed in hard plastic and warm to the touch. As Aya wrapped her arms around Moggle, she felt her bracelets trembling, caught in the magnetic currents of the hovercam's lifters.

She squeezed her eyes shut. "Ready?"

Moggle shivered in her arms.

Clinging to the hovercam with all her strength, Aya pushed herself into the void.

Getting out was much simpler these days.

For Aya's fifteenth birthday, Ren Machino—her big brother's best friend—had modified Moggle. She'd only asked him to make it quick enough to keep up with her hoverboard. But like most tech-heads, Ren took pride in his mods. The new Moggle was waterproof, shockproof, and powerful enough to carry an Aya-size passenger through the air.

Close enough, anyway. With her arms wrapped around the hovercam, she fell no faster than a cherry blossom twirling toward the ground. It was much easier than stealing a bungee jacket. And except for the nervous-making moment of jumping, it was kind of fun.

She watched the windows flicker past—dreary rooms full of standard-requisition squalor. No one famous lived in Akira Hall, just loads of face-missing extras wearing generic designs. A few ego-kickers sat talking into their cams, watched by no one. The average face rank here was six hundred thousand, despair-making and pathetic.

Obscurity in all its horror.

Back in the Prettytime, Aya vaguely remembered, you just asked for awesome clothes or a new hoverboard and they popped out of the hole in the wall like magic. But these days, the hole wouldn't give you anything decent unless you were famous or had merits to spend. And getting merits meant taking classes or doing chores—whatever the Good Citizen Committee commanded, basically.

Moggle's lifters connected with the metal grid beneath the ground, and Aya bent her knees, rolling as she hit. The wet grass squished beneath her like a sodden sponge, soft but shivery cold.

She let go of Moggle and lay for a moment on the rain-soaked earth, letting her heartbeat slow down. "You okay?"

Moggle flashed its night-lights again.

"Okay . . . that's *still* blind-making."

Ren had also modified the hovercam's brain. True AI might still be illegal, but the new Moggle was more than just a wedge of circuitry and lifters. Since Ren's tinkering, it had learned Aya's favorite angles, when to pan and zoom, and even how to track her eyes for cues.

But for some reason, it didn't get the whole night-vision thing.

She kept her eyes closed, listening hard as she watched the spots across her vision fade. No footsteps, no whir of monitor drones. Nothing but the muffled thump of music from the dorm.

Aya rose to her feet and brushed herself off. Not that anyone would notice the wet grass clinging to her; Reputation Bombers dressed to disappear. The robe was hooded and shapeless, the perfect disguise for party-crashing.

With a twist of a crash bracelet, a hoverboard rose from its hiding place in the bushes. Stepping on, Aya faced the glittering lights of Prettyville.

Funny how everyone still called it that, even if most of the residents weren't pretty anymore—not in the old sense, anyway. Prettyville was full of pixel-skins and surge-monkeys, and plenty of other strange new fads and fashions. You could choose among a million kinds of beauty or weirdness, or even keep your natural-born face your whole life. These days "pretty" meant whatever got you noticed.

But one thing about Prettyville was still the same: If you hadn't turned sixteen, you weren't supposed to go there. Not at night, when all the good stuff happened.

Especially if you were an extra, a loser, an unknown.

Gazing at the city, she felt engulfed by her own invisibility. Each of its sparkling lights stood for one of the million people who had never heard of Aya Fuse. Who probably never would.

She sighed, urging her hoverboard forward.

The government feeds always said that the Prettytime was gone forever, freeing humanity from centuries of bubbleheadedness. They claimed that the divisions among uglies, pretties, and crumblies had all been washed away. That the last three years had unleashed a host of new technologies, setting the future in motion again.

But as far as Aya could see, the mind-rain hadn't changed everything. . . .

It still pretty much sucked, being fifteen.

TECH-HEADS

"Are you getting this?" she whispered.

Moggle was already shooting, the shimmer of safety fireworks reflecting from its lenses. Hot-air balloons swayed over the mansion, and revelers screamed down from the rooftops in bungee jackets. It looked like a party back in the old days: self-indulgent and eye-kickingly radiant.

At least, that was how Aya's older brother always described the Prettytime. Back then everyone had gotten one big operation on their sixteenth birthday. It made you beautiful, but secretly changed your personality, leaving you brain-missing and easily controlled.

Hiro hadn't been a bubblehead very long; he'd turned sixteen only a few months before the mind-rain had arrived and cured the pretties. He liked to claim that those months had been awful—as if being shallow and vain was *such* a stretch for him. But he never denied that the parties had been awesome.

Not that Hiro would be here tonight; he was way too famous. Aya checked her eyescreen: the average face rank inside was about twenty thousand. Compared with her older brother, the people at this bash were total extras.

Compared to an ugly ranked at half a million, though, they were legends.

"Be careful, Moggle," she whispered. "We're not wanted here."

Aya flipped up the hood of her robe, and stepped out of the shadows.

Inside, the air was full of hovercams. From Moggle-size

all the way down to paparazzi swarms, each cam no bigger than a champagne cork.

There was always plenty to see at tech-head parties, crazy people and kick new gadgets. Maybe people weren't as beautiful as back during the Prettytime, but parties were a lot more interesting: serious surge-monkeys with snake fingers and medusa hair; smart-matter clothes that rippled like flags in a breeze; safety fireworks skittering along the floor, dodging feet and sizzling incense as they passed.

Tech-heads lived for new technologies—they loved showing off their latest tricks, and kickers loved putting them on their feeds. The endless cycle of invention and publicity bumped everyone's face rank, so everyone was happy.

Everyone who got invited, anyway.

A hovercam buzzed close, almost low enough to peek in at Aya's face. She lowered her head, making her way toward a cluster of Reputation Bombers. Here in public they all kept their hoods up, like a bunch of pre-Rusty Buddhist monks. They were already bombing: chanting the name of some random member of the clique, trying to convince the city interface to bump his face rank.

Aya bowed to the group and joined the blur of name-dropping, keeping her ugly face covered.

The whole point of bombing was to dissect the city's reputation algorithms: How many mentions of your name did it take to crack the top thousand? How quickly did you drop if everyone stopped talking about you? The clique was one big controlled experiment, which was why they all wore the same anonymous outfits.

But Aya figured most Bombers didn't care about the math. They were just cheaters, pathetic extras trying to talk themselves famous. It was like how they'd manufactured celebrities back in Rusty days, a handful of feeds hyping a few bubbleheads and ignoring everybody else.

What was the point of the reputation economy, if someone was *telling* you who to talk about?

But Aya chanted away like a good little Bomber, keeping her attention on her eyescreen, watching the view from Moggle's lenses. The hovercam drifted over the crowd, picking out faces one by one.

The secret clique Aya had discovered *had* to be here somewhere. Only tech-heads could pull off a trick like that. . . .

She'd spotted them three nights before, riding on top of one of the new mag-lev trains, traveling at insane speeds through the factory district—so fast that all the shots Moggle had taken were too grainy and blurry to use.

Aya had to find them again. Whoever kicked a crazy trick like mag-lev riding would be instantly famous.

But Moggle was already distracted, watching a gaggle of NeoFoodies underneath a pink blob floating in the air. They were drinking from it with meter-long straws, like astronauts recapturing a spilled cup of tea.

NeoFoodies were old news—Hiro had kicked a story about them last month. They ate extinct mushrooms grown from ancient spores, made ice cream with liquid nitrogen, and injected flavors into weird forms of matter. The floating pink stuff looked like an aerogel, dinner with the density of a soap bubble.

A small blob broke off and floated past. Aya grimaced, smelling rice and salmon. Eating strange substances might be a great way to bump your face rank, but she preferred her sushi heavier than air.

She liked being around tech-heads, though, even if she had to hide. Most of the city was still stuck in the past, trying to rediscover haiku, religion, the tea ceremony—all the things that had been lost in the Prettytime, when everyone had been brain-damaged. But tech-heads were building the future, making up for three centuries of missing progress.

This was the place to find stories.

Something in her eyescreen sent a flicker of recognition through her.

"Hold it, Moggle!" she hissed. "Pan left."

There behind the NeoFoodies, watching with amusement as they chased down stray bloblets, was a familiar face.

"That's one of them! Zoom in."

The girl was about eighteen, classic new-pretty surge with slightly manga eyes. She was wearing a hoverball rig, floating gracefully ten centimeters above the floor. And she had to be famous: A reputation bubble surrounded her, a cohort of friends and groupies to keep extras away.

"Get close enough to hear them," Aya whispered. Moggle eased to the edge of the bubble, and soon its microphones caught the girl's name. Data spilled across Aya's eyescreen. . . .

Eden Maru was a hoverball player—left wing for the Swallows, who'd been city champions last year. She was also legendary for her lifter mods.

According to all the feeds, Eden had just dumped her boyfriend because of "a difference in ambition." Of course, that was just code for "she got too famous for him." Eden's face rank had hit ten thousand after the championship, and what's-his-name's was stuck at a quarter million. Everyone knew she needed to hook up with someone more face-equal.

But none of the rumors mentioned Eden's new mag-lev riding clique. She must be keeping that a secret, waiting for the right moment to reveal the trick.

Kicking it first would make Aya famous overnight.

"Track her," she told Moggle, then went back to chanting.

Half an hour later, Eden Maru headed out.

Slipping away from the Bombers was bliss-making—Aya had chanted the name "Yoshio Nara" about a million times. She hoped Yoshio enjoyed his pointless face rank bump, because she never wanted to hear his name again.

From Moggle's midair view, Eden Maru was slipping through the door—alone, no entourage. She *had* to be headed off to meet her secret clique.

"Stay close to her, Moggle," Aya croaked. All that chanting had left her throat dry. She spotted a drinks tray hovering past. "I'll catch up in a minute."

Grabbing a glass at random, Aya guzzled it down. The alcohol sent a shudder through her—not exactly what she needed. She snatched another drink with lots of ice and pushed her way toward the door.

A gaggle of pixel-skins stood in her way, their bodies rippling through colors like drunken chameleons. She slipped among them, recognizing a couple of their faces from the surge-monkey feeds. A little reputation shiver went through her.

Out on the mansion steps Aya spilled the drink out through her fingers, saving the ice cubes. She tipped the glass back into her mouth and started crunching. After the sweltering party a mouthful of ice was heavenly.

"Interesting surge," someone said.

Aya froze . . . her hood had fallen back, revealing her ugly face.

"Um, thanks." The words came out muffled, and Aya gulped down cold shards of ice. The breeze hit her sweaty face, and she realized how fashion-missing she must look.

The boy smiled. "Where did you get the idea for that nose?"

Aya managed to shrug, suddenly word-missing. In her eyescreen she could see Eden Maru already flying across town, but tearing her gaze from the boy was impossible. He was a manga-head: eyes huge and glistening, his delicate face inhumanly beautiful. Long, tapered fingers stroked his perfect cheek as he stared at her.

That was the weird thing: *He* was staring at *her*.

But he was gorgeous, and she was ugly.

"Let me guess," he said. "From some pre-Rusty painting?"

"Uh, not really." She touched her nose, swallowing the last few shards of ice. "It's more, um . . . randomly generated?"

"Of course. It's so unique." He bowed. "Frizz Mizuno."

As Aya returned the bow, her eyescreen displayed his face rank: 4,612. A reputation shiver went through her, the realization that she was talking to someone important, connected, meaningful.

He was waiting for Aya to give her own name. And once she did that, he'd know her face rank, and then his wonderful gaze would turn somewhere more interesting. Even if in some logic-missing, mind-rain way he liked her ugly face, being an extra was simply pathetic.

Besides, her nose was *way* too big.

She twisted a crash bracelet to call her hoverboard. "My name's Aya. But I kind of . . . have to go now."

He bowed. "Of course. People to see, reputations to bomb."

Aya laughed, looking down at the robe. "Oh, this. I'm not really . . . I'm sort of incognito."

"Incognito?" His smile was eye-kicking. "You're very mysterious."

Her board slipped up next to the stairs. Aya stared down at it, hesitating. Moggle was already half a kilometer away, trailing Eden Maru through the darkness at high speed, but part of her was screaming to stay.

Because Frizz was still gazing at her.

"I'm not trying to be mysterious," she said. "It's just working out that way."

He laughed. "I want to know your last name, Aya. But I think you're purposely not telling me."

"Sorry," she squeaked, and stepped onto the board. "But I have to go after someone. She's sort of . . . getting away."

He bowed, his smile broadening. "Enjoy the chase."

She leaned forward and shot into the darkness, his laughter in her ears.

UNDERGROUND

Eden Maru knew how to fly.

Full-body lifter rigs were standard gear for hoverball players, but most people never dared to wear them. Each piece had its own lifter: the shin and elbow pads, even the boots in some rigs. One wrong twitch of your fingers could send all those magnets in different directions, which was an excellent way to dislocate a shoulder, or send you spinning headfirst into a wall. Unlike falling off a hoverboard, crash bracelets wouldn't save you from your own clumsiness.

But none of this seemed to worry Eden Maru. In Aya's eyescreen, she was zigzagging through the new construction site, using the half-finished buildings and open storm drains as her private obstacle course.

Even Moggle, who was stuffed with lifters and only twenty centimeters across, was finding it tricky keeping up.

Aya tried to focus on her own hoverboarding, but she was still half-hypnotized by Frizz Mizuno, dazzled by his attention. Since the mind-rain had broken down the boundaries between ages, Aya had talked to plenty of pretties. It wasn't like the old days, when your friends never talked to you after they got the operation. But no pretty had ever looked at her *that* way.

Or was she kidding herself? Maybe Frizz's intense gaze made everyone feel this way. His eyes were so *huge*, just like the old Rusty drawings that manga-heads based themselves on.

She was dying to ask the city interface about him. She'd never seen him on the feeds, but with a face rank below five thousand, Frizz had to be known for something besides eye-kicking beauty.

But for now Aya had a story to chase, a reputation to build. If Frizz was ever going to look at her that way again, she couldn't be so face-missing.

Her eyescreen began to flicker. Moggle's signal was fading, falling out of range of the city network as it followed Eden underground.

The signal shimmered with static, then went dark. . . .

Aya banked to a halt, a shudder passing through her.

Losing Moggle was always unnerving, like looking down on a sunny day to find her shadow gone.

She stared at the last image the hovercam had sent: the inside of a storm drain, grainy and distorted by infrared. Eden Maru was curled up tight, a human cannonball zooming through the confines of the tunnel, headed so deep that Moggle's transmitter couldn't reach the surface anymore.

The only way to find Eden again was to follow her down.

Aya leaned forward, urging her hoverboard back into motion. The new construction site rose up around her, dozens of iron skeletons and gaping holes.

After the mind-rain, nobody wanted to live in fashion-missing Prettytime buildings. Nobody famous, anyway. So the city was expanding wildly, plundering nearby Rusty ruins for metal. There were even rumors that the city planned to tear open the ground to look for fresh iron, like the earth-damaging Rusties had three centuries ago.

The unfinished towers flashed past, their steel frames making her board shudder. Hoverboards needed metal below them to fly, but too many magnetic fields made them shivery. Aya eased back her speed, checking for Moggle again.

Nothing. The hovercam was still underground.

A huge excavation came into sight, the foundation of some future skyscraper. Along its raw dirt floor, puddles of afternoon rain reflected the starlit sky, like jagged slivers of mirror.

In a corner of the excavation she spotted a tunnel mouth, an entry to the network of storm drains beneath the city.

A month ago, Aya had kicked a story about a new graffiti clique, uglies who left artwork for future generations.

They painted the insides of unfinished tunnels and conduits, letting their work be sealed up like time capsules. No one would see the paintings until long after the city collapsed, when its ruins were rediscovered by some future civilization. It was all very mind-rain, a rumination about how the eternal Prettytime had been more fragile than it seemed.

The story hadn't bumped Aya's face rank—stories about uglies never did—but she and Moggle had spent a week playing hide-and-seek through the construction site. She wasn't afraid of the underground.

Letting her board drop, Aya ducked past idle lifter drones and hoverstruts, diving toward the tunnel mouth. She bent her knees, pulled in her arms, and plunged into absolute blackness. . . .

Her eyescreen flickered once—the hovercam *had* to be nearby.

The smell of old rainwater and dirt was strong, trickling drainage the only sound. As the worklights behind her faded to a faint orange glow, Aya slowed her board to a crawl, guiding herself with one hand sliding along the tunnel wall.

Moggle's signal flickered back on . . . and held.

Eden Maru was standing upright, flexing her arms. She was someplace spacious and dead-black in infrared, extending as far as Moggle's cams could see.

What was down there?

More human forms shimmered in the grainy darkness. They floated above the black plain, the lozenge shapes of hoverboards glowing beneath their feet.

Aya smiled. She'd found them, those crazy girls who rode mag-lev trains.

"Move in and listen," she whispered.

As Moggle drifted closer, Aya remembered a place the graffiti uglies had bragged about finding—a huge reservoir where the city stored runoff from the rainy season, an underground lake in absolute darkness.

Through Moggle's microphones, a few echoing words reached her.

"Thanks for getting here so fast."

"I always said your big face would get you into trouble, Eden."

"Well, this shouldn't take long. She's just behind me."

Aya froze. *Who* was just behind Eden? She glanced over her shoulder. . . .

Nothing but the glimmer of water trickling down the tunnel.

Then her eyescreen faded again. Aya swore, flexing her ring finger: off/on . . . but her vision stayed black.

"Moggle?" she hissed.

No flicker in the eyescreen, no response. She tried to access the hovercam's diagnostics, its audio feed, the remote flying controls. Nothing worked.

But Moggle was so close—at most twenty meters away. Why couldn't she connect?

Aya urged her board forward slowly, listening hard, trying to peer through the darkness. The wall slipped away from her hand, the echoes of a huge space opening around her. Trickles of rainwater chorused from a dozen drains, and the damp presence of the reservoir sent chills across her skin.

She needed to *see*. . . .

Then Aya remembered the control panel of her hoverboard. In this absolute darkness, even a few pinpricks of light would make a difference.

She knelt and booted the controls. Their soft blue glow revealed sweeping walls of ancient brick, patched in places with modern ceramics and smart matter. A broad stone ceiling arched overhead, like the vault of some underground cathedral.

But no Moggle.

Aya drifted slowly through the darkness, letting the subtle air currents carry her board, listening hard. A smooth lake of black water spread out a few meters below her board.

Then she heard something nearby, the slightest catch of breath, and turned. . . .

In the dim blue glow, an ugly face stared back at her. The girl stood on a hoverboard, holding Moggle in her arms. She gave Aya a cold smile.

"We thought you might come after this."

"Hey!" Aya said. "What did you do to my—"

A foot kicked out from the darkness and sent Aya's hoverboard rocking.

"Watch it!" Aya shouted.

Strong hands pushed her, and she took two unsteady steps backward. The hoverboard shifted, trying to stay under her feet. Aya stuck her arms out, wobbling like a littlie on ice skates.

"Knock it off! What are you—"

From all directions, more hands shoved and prodded her—Aya spun wildly, blind and defenseless. Then her board was kicked away, and she was tumbling through the air.

The water struck her face with a cold, hard slap.

AUDITION

Blackness boiled around her, its watery roar like thunder stuffed into her ears. The shock of impact stripped away any sense of up and down, leaving only the tumbling, freezing cold. Her arms and legs flailed, the water filling her nostrils and mouth, squeezing her chest . . .

Then Aya's head broke the surface. She gasped and sputtered, hands clawing at the water, searching for something solid in the dark.

"Hey! What's your *problem*?"

Her cry boomed through the vast space, echoing in the blind emptiness. But no answer came.

She paddled water for a moment, catching her breath, trying to listen.

"Hello . . . ?"

A hand grabbed her wrist, and Aya found herself pulled into the air. She hung there, feet dangling, her shivers sending water cascading from her soaking robe.

"What . . . what's going on?"

A voice answered. "We don't like kickers."

Aya had figured as much: They wanted to kick their own story about how they rode the trains, and keep all the fame for themselves.

Maybe it was time for some truth-slanting. "But I'm not a kicker!"

Someone snorted, then a closer voice said, "You followed me here from that party—or your hovercam did, anyway. You were looking for a story."

"Not a story, I was looking for *you*." Aya shivered again, fighting to keep her teeth from chattering. She had to convince them not to drop her into the black lake again. "I saw you guys the other night."

"Saw us where?" the closer voice said, and the grip on her wrist adjusted. That one had to be Eden; nobody could hold her up like this without help from a hoverball rig.

"On top of a mag-lev train. You were riding it. I tried to find out who you were, but there was nothing on the feeds."

"That's the way we like it," the first voice said.

"Okay, I get it!" Aya said. "Um, are you just going dangle me here like this?"

"Would you prefer I drop you?" Eden asked.

"Not really. It's just that this is kind of . . . wrist-hurting."

"Call your board, then."

"Oh . . . right." In her panic, Aya had forgotten all about her hoverboard. She reached up with her free hand and twisted her other crash bracelet. A few seconds later the hoverboard nudged her feet, and the iron grip released her.

She wobbled for a moment on the board, rubbing her wrist. "Thanks, I guess."

"Are you telling us you're not a kicker?" It was the first voice again, maybe the ugly woman she'd glimpsed. It echoed through the darkness low and growly, like she'd surged her throat to sound scary.

"Well, I've put a few things on my feed. Same as everyone."

"Pictures of your cat?" someone said, then snickered.

"So do you always go to parties disguised as a Bomber?" Eden asked. "With a hovercam in tow?"

Aya wrapped her arms around herself. The soaked robe was clinging to her skin, and her teeth were going to start chattering any minute. "Look, I wanted to join up with your clique. So I had to track you down. Moggle's good for that."

"Moggle?" the mean voice asked.

"Uh . . . my hovercam."

"Your hovercam has a *name*?"

Laughter echoed from every direction. Aya realized that there were more of them than she'd thought. Maybe a dozen hidden in the darkness.

"Hang on a second," Eden's voice said. "How old are you?"

"Um . . . fifteen?"

A flashlight flicked on, blindingly bright in the total darkness.

"Ouch!" She squeezed her eyes shut.

Whoever was holding the flashlight added, "Thought that nose looked big. Even in infrared."

As Aya's eyes adjusted to the flashlight, she began to make out faces. They looked like Plain Janes, the clique for girls who didn't want to be pretty or exotic, just normal—as if that concept still existed. Except for Eden Maru's padded and muscular form, the hovering figures around Aya all looked the same—generic bodies, designed to disappear in a crowd. All of them were girls, as far as Aya could tell, just like the night she'd seen them hitching a ride on the mag-lev train.

"So you like to sneak around at night?" Eden said.

"I guess so. Beats sitting in my dorm room."

"Easily bored?" The other girl drawled the words in her growling voice. "Then maybe you *should* have a surf sometimes."

"A surf?" Aya swallowed. "You mean I can ride with you?"

A few grumbles came from the darkness.

"But she's only fifteen," the girl holding the flashlight said.

"Are you still back in the Prettytime?" said the growly-voiced girl. "Who cares how old she is? She crashed Prettyville and came down here all alone. Got more guts than most of you, probably."

"What about the hovercam?" Eden said. "If she kicks a story, we'll have wardens all over us."

"She could still call the wardens if she wants to." The mean-voiced girl slid closer on her board, until her nose was only a few centimeters from Aya's. "So we either leave her down here for good, or get her on our side."

Aya swallowed, glancing down at the shimmering black lake.

"Um, do I get a vote?"

"No one but me gets a vote," the girl said, then smiled. "But how about this? You *do* get to make a choice."

"Oh?"

The girl held Moggle at arm's length, and Aya saw the lock-down clamp against its skin. It was frozen, brain-dead until someone removed the clamp.

"You can either take your hovercam and go away. Or I drop it right now, and you get to come surfing with us."

Aya blinked, listening to the cold water still trickling from her robe. Ren claimed he'd made Moggle waterproof, but could she find her way back to this exact spot?

"How important is it to you, getting out of that boring little dorm room?"

Aya swallowed. "Very."

"Then choosing should be easy, right?"

"It's just . . . that cam cost me a lot of merits."

"It's a toy. Like face ranks and merits, it doesn't *mean* anything if you don't let it."

Face rank didn't mean anything? This girl was brain-missing. But she was right about one thing: Nothing was more important than getting out of boring, pathetic Akira Hall.

Maybe Ren could help her find the way back here. . . .

Aya closed her eyes. "Okay. I want to come with you. Drop it."

The splash echoed like a slap.

"Good choice. That toy isn't what you really need."

Aya opened her eyes. They stung with hidden tears.

"I'm Jai," the girl said, bowing low.

"Aya Fuse." She returned the bow, her eyes falling to the widening ripples beneath them. Moggle was really gone.

"We'll see you again soon," Jai said.

"See me *soon*? But you said—"

"I think you've had enough fun for one night, for a fifteen-year-old."

"But you promised!"

"And you said you weren't a kicker. I want to see if you were truth-slanting about that."

Aya started to protest, but the words faded in her mouth. There was no point in arguing now—Moggle was already gone.

"But I don't even know who you are."

Jai smiled. "We're the Sly Girls, and we'll be in touch. Come on, everyone—we've got a train to catch!"

They spun their hoverboards into motion, swirling around Aya, filling the underground chamber with echoing whoops and hollers. The flashlights flickered out, and she heard them shooting away one by one, their cries swallowed by the storm drain mouths.

Aya found herself alone in the dark, swallowing back tears.

She'd given up Moggle for nothing. Once the Sly Girls checked her feed, they'd know all about her stories. And if they realized that her brother was one of the most famous kickers in the city, they'd never trust her again.

"Stupid Hiro," she murmured. If it wasn't for Mr. Big Face, being an extra wouldn't be so hard. She wouldn't have so much to prove.

And she wouldn't have traded Moggle . . . for nothing.

Aya squeezed her fists tight, letting her board descend until she heard the light slap of its lifters against the water. Kneeling, she stretched out one hand in the darkness, lowering her palm and resting it gently on the surface. She could still feel the ripples spreading from where Moggle had splashed.

"I'm sorry," Aya whispered. "But I'll be back soon."

BIG BROTHER

Vast mansions zoomed past Aya, huge and brightly lit with torches. In the early morning light, bonfires burned everywhere: massive carbon allowances on display. Overhead drifted swimming pools, hovering bubbles of water shaped by invisible lines of force. As she flew beneath them, Aya glimpsed the outlines of people lounging on floaters, gazing at the dawn.

Hiro's mansion rose three hundred meters into the air, a spindly tower of gleaming glass and steel. To keep the gorgeous views from getting stale, the entire building rotated at the speed of an hour hand. Its mass held up by hoverstruts, only a single elevator shaft touched the ground, like an enormous and glacial ballerina spinning on one toe.

In this neighborhood, all the buildings moved. They hovered and transformed and did other flabbergasting things, and everyone who lived here was legendarily bored by it all.

Hiro lived in the famous part of town.

As Aya's hoverboard approached the mansion steps, she remembered what her brother had been like in those months during the Prettytime: beautiful, contented, respectful. Sure, he'd gone to all the bashes, but he'd come home for every holiday, always bringing Aya and the crumblies presents.

The mind-rain had changed all that—except for his pretty face.

For the first year after being cured, Hiro had jumped from clique to clique: Extreme Surge, the city hoverball team, even a tour in the wild as a Ranger trainee. He hadn't stuck with anything, shifting aimlessly, unable to make sense of freedom.

Of course, in that logic-missing first year a lot of people were confused. Some actually decided to reverse the mind-rain—not just old crumblies, but new pretties, too. Even Hiro had talked about turning back into a bubblehead.

Then two years ago came the news that the economy was in trouble. Back in the Prettytime, bubbleheads could ask for anything they wanted: Their toys and party clothes popped out of the hole in the wall, no questions asked. But creative, free-minded human beings were more ravenous than bubbleheads, it turned out. Too many resources were going to random hobbies, new buildings, and major projects like the mag-lev trains. And nobody was volunteering for the hard jobs anymore.

Some people wanted to go back to Rusty "money," complete with rents and taxes and starving if you couldn't pay for food. But the City Council didn't go that crazy; they voted for the reputation economy instead. From now on, merits and face ranks would decide who got the best mansions, the most carbon emissions, the biggest wall allowances. Merits were for doctors, teachers, wardens, all they way down to littlies doing schoolwork and their chores—everyone who kept the city going, as determined by the Good Citizen Committee. Face ranks were for the rest of culture, from artists to sports stars to scientists. You could use all the resources you wanted, as long as you captured the city's collective imagination.

And to keep the face ranks fair, every citizen over the age of littlie was given their own feed—a million scattered threads of story to help make sense of the mind-rain.

The word "kicker" hadn't even been invented yet, but somehow Hiro had understood it all instinctively: how to make a clique huge overnight, how to convince everyone to requisition some new gadget, and most of all how to make himself legendary in the process.

As Aya landed outside the mansion's elevator door, she sighed quietly. Hiro had been so *smart* since they'd fixed his brain. . . .

If only all that fame hadn't turned him into such a self-centered snob.

"What do you want, Aya-chan?"

"I need to talk to you."

"Way too early."

Aya groaned. Without Moggle to float her back up to her window, she'd had to wait till dawn to get back into her dorm. And Hiro thought *he* was tired?

He couldn't have had a worse night than she'd had. She

kept imagining Moggle at the bottom of the underground lake, lying cold and lifeless.

"Please, Hiro? I just spent a bunch of merits to switch my morning classes, so I could come see you."

A grumbling noise. "Come back in an hour."

Aya glared at the elevator door. She couldn't even go up and pound on his window; the mansions in the famous part of town didn't let you fly close to them.

"Well, can you at least tell me where Ren is? His locator's off."

"Ren?" A chuckle came from the door. "He's on my couch."

Aya breathed a sigh of relief. Hiro was a million times easier to deal with when his best friend was around. "Can I talk to him, then . . . *please*?"

The door went silent for so long that Aya wondered if Hiro had gone back to sleep. But finally Ren's voice came on.

"Hey, Aya-chan. Come on in!"

The door opened, and Aya stepped inside.

Hiro's rooms were garlanded with a million cranes.

It was an old custom from pre-Rusty days, one of the few that had survived the Prettytime: When a girl turned thirteen, she made a string of a thousand origami birds with her own two hands. It took weeks of folding little squares of paper into wings and beaks and tails, then stringing them together with an old-fashioned needle and thread.

After the mind-rain, a few girls had started a new trend: sending their finished strings to reputation-crushes, new-pretty boys with big face ranks. Boys like Hiro, in other words.

Just seeing them made Aya's fingers ache from the memory of her own thousand cranes. The chains of paper birds were draped everywhere in the apartment, except for Hiro's sacred feed-watching chair.

He was slumped there, wearing a hoverball sweatshirt and rubbing his eyes. Green tea was swirling from the spigots of the hole in the wall, filling the air with the scents of cut grass and caffeine.

"Could you get those?" he asked.

"Good morning to you, too." She gave him a sarcastic bow and went to fetch the tea. Two cups, of course—for him and Ren, not her. Aya couldn't stand green tea, but still.

"Morning, Aya-chan," Ren called groggily from the couch. He sat up, a flock of squashed cranes unpeeling from his back. Empty bottles were strewn everywhere, and a cleaning drone was vacuuming up the remains of food and spilled bubbly.

She handed Ren his tea. "Were you guys celebrating something, or just reliving bubblehead days?"

"You don't know?" Ren laughed. "Well, you better congratulate Hiro-sensei."

"Hiro-*sensei*? What?"

"That's right." Ren nodded. "Your brother finally cracked the top thousand."

"The top thousand?" Aya blinked. "Are you kidding?"

"Eight hundred and ninety-six, at the moment," Hiro said, staring at the wallscreen. Aya saw the number on it now: 896 in meter-high numerals. "Of course, my own sister ignores me. Where's my tea?"

"But I didn't . . ." Aya's exhaustion turned dizzy-making for a moment. This morning was the first in ages that she hadn't checked Hiro's face rank. And he'd hit the top *thousand*? If he could stay there, he'd be invited to Nana Love's Thousand Faces Party next month.

Hiro, like most boys, had a major crush on Nana Love.

"I'm sorry . . . last night was really busy. But that's fantastic!"

He lazily stretched out a finger, pointing at the teacup in her hand.

She brought it to him, offering a real bow. "Congratulations, Hiro."

""Hiro-*sensei*," he reminded her.

Aya just rolled her eyes. "You don't have to call your own brother 'sensei,' Hiro, no matter how big a face he is. So what was the story?"

"You wouldn't be interested. Apparently."

"Come on, Hiro! I watch all your stories . . . except for last night."

"It was about this bunch of crumblies." Ren lay back across the couch. "They're like surge-monkeys, except they don't care about beauty or weird body mods. Just life extension: liver refits every six months, new cloned hearts once a year."

"Life extension?" Aya said. "But stories about crumblies never go big."

"This one has a conspiracy angle," Ren said. "These crumblies have a theory that the doctors secretly know how to keep people living forever. They say the only reason anyone dies of old age is to keep the population steady. It's just like the bubblehead operation back in the Prettytime: The doctors are hiding the truth!"

"That's brain-kicking," Aya murmured, a shiver traveling down her spine. It was so easy to believe in conspiracies, after the government had made everyone brain-missing for centuries.

And living forever? Even littlies would pay attention to that.

"You forgot the best part, Ren," Hiro said. "These crumblies are planning to sue the city . . . for *immortality*. Like it's a human right or something. People want an investigation! Check it out."

Hiro waved his hand. On the wallscreen his face rank disappeared, replaced by a web of meme-lines, a huge diagram showing how the story had kicked through the city interface all night. Vast spirals of debate, disagreement, and outright slamming had splintered from Hiro's feed, over a quarter-million people joining the conversation.

Was immortality a bogus idea? Could your brain stay bubbly forever? And if nobody died, where on earth would you *put* everyone? Would the expansion wind up eating the whole planet?

That last question made Aya dizzy again. She remembered that day at school when they'd showed satellite pictures from the Rusty era, back before population control. The sprawling cities had been huge enough to see from space: billions of extras crowding the planet, most of them living in total obscurity.

"Look at that!" Hiro cried. "Everyone's already going off the story. My rank just dropped to nine hundred. People can be so shallow!"

"Maybe immortality's getting old," Ren said, grinning at Aya.

"Ha, ha," Hiro said. "I wonder who's stealing my eyeballs."

He flicked his hand again, and the wallscreen broke into a dozen panels. The familiar faces of the city's top twelve tech-kickers appeared. Aya noticed that Hiro had jumped to number four.

He was leaning forward in his chair, devouring the feeds to find out where his ratings had gone.

Aya sighed. Typical Hiro—he'd already forgotten that she'd come up here to talk to him. But she stayed quiet, curling next to Ren on the couch, trying not to crumple too many sad little paper birds. It probably wouldn't hurt, letting Hiro get his feed fix before admitting she'd left her hovercam at the bottom of a lake.

And Aya didn't mind a little feed-time. The familiar voices soothed her nerves, washing over her like a conversation with old friends.

People's faces were so different since the mind-rain, the new fads and cliques and inventions so unpredictable. It made the city sense-missing sometimes. Famous people were the cure for that randomness, like pre-Rusties gathering around their campfires every night, listening to the elders. Humans needed big faces around for comfort and familiarity, even an ego-kicker like Nana Love just talking about what she'd had for breakfast.

In the upper right corner, Gamma Matsui was kicking a new tech religion. Some history clique had applied averaging software to the world's great spiritual books, then programmed it to spit out godlike decrees.

For some reason, the software had told them not to eat pigs.

"Who would do that in the first place?" Aya asked.

"Aren't pigs extinct?" Ren giggled. "They seriously need to update that code."

"Gods are so last year," Hiro said, and Aya smiled.

Resurrecting old religions had been kick right after the mind-rain, when everyone was still trying to figure out what all the new freedoms *meant*. But these days so many other things had been rediscovered—family reunions and crime and manga and the cherry blossom festival. Except for a few Youngblood cults, most people were too busy for divine superheroes.

"What's the Nameless One up to?" Hiro said, switching the sound to another feed.

The Nameless One was what the two of them called Toshi Banana—the most brain-missing big face in the city. He was more of a slammer than a real tech-kicker, always attacking some new clique or fashion, stirring up hatred for anything unfamiliar. He thought the mind-rain had been a disaster, just because everyone's new hobbies and obsessions could be unsettling and downright weird.

Ren and Hiro never said his name, and changed his nickname every few weeks, before the city interface could figure out who they meant—even mocking people helped their face stats. In the reputation economy, the only real way to hurt anyone was to ignore them completely. And it was pretty hard to ignore someone who made your blood boil. The Nameless One was hated or loved by almost everybody in the city, which kept his face rank floating around a hundred.

This morning he was slamming the new trend of pet owners and their ghastly breeding experiments. The feed showed a dog, dyed pink and sprouting heart-shaped tufts of fur. Aya thought it was kind of cute.

"It's just a poodle, you truth-slanting bubblehead!" Ren shouted, tossing a cushion at the wallscreen.

Aya giggled. Giving dogs funny hairdos wasn't exactly Rusty, like making fur coats or eating pigs.

"He's a waste of gravity," Ren said. "Blank him!"

"Replace with next highest," Hiro told the room, and

the Nameless One's angry face disappeared.

Aya's eyes drifted across the screens. Nothing looked remotely as kick as surfing a mag-lev train. The Sly Girls *had* to be more famous-making than poodles, pig eating, and rumors of immortality. Aya just had to make sure that she was the first kicker to put them on her feed.

Then she saw who had supplanted the Nameless One in the top left of the wallscreen, and her eyes widened.

"Hey," she murmured. "Who's that guy?"

But she already knew the gorgeous, manga-eyed boy's name. . . .

It was Frizz Mizuno.

FRIZZ

"*That* bubblehead's the thirteenth-most-popular tech-kicker now?" Hiro groaned. "That was fast."

"Turn his sound on," Aya said.

"No way!" Hiro said. "He's so gag-making."

He waved his hand, and Frizz's face was replaced by yet another feed.

"Hiro!"

Ren leaned closer to her on the couch. "He's the founder of this new clique—Radical Honesty. Hiro's just mad because Frizz decided to kick the clique himself, instead of letting one of us help out."

She frowned. "Radical what?"

"Honesty." Ren pointed at his temple, his eyescreens—like a true tech-head, he had one in each eye—spinning. "Frizz designed this new brain surge. Like back in the

Prettytime, except instead of making you a bubblehead, they change your mind so you can't lie."

"Yeah, it's supposed to be the brave new horizon of human interaction," Hiro muttered from his chair. "But they just babble about their feelings all day."

"Friend of mine tried it for a week," Ren said. "He said it's very boredom-killing. Turns out if you never lie, there's *always* someone mad at you."

Hiro and Ren laughed, and the two of them went back to analyzing the other feeds, watching the kickers' ranks rise and fall. The software religion was a flop—Gamma-sensei had lost face all morning. But the poodle was working, as funny-looking animals usually did, sending the Nameless One all the way up to sixty-three, one notch above the mayor.

Aya kept silent, staring at the corner of the screen Frizz had briefly occupied. She was trying to remember every word he'd said to her—that he'd liked her randomly generated nose, thought she was mysterious, and wanted to know her full name.

And he hadn't been lying about any of it.

Of course, when he found out that she didn't have such great taste in randomly generated noses—that she'd just been born with it, because she was an ugly and a party-crashing extra—what would he say then? He wouldn't even be polite about it. The honesty surge would *make* him show his disappointment about their difference in ambition. . . .

Unless she wasn't an extra by then.

"Hey, Ren," she asked quietly. "Have you ever snuck footage of anyone?"

"You mean like fashion-slammers? No way. That's totally unkick."

"No, I don't mean shots of famous people. More like going undercover for a story."

"I'm not sure," Ren said, looking uncomfortable. He was a tech-kicker; his feed was filled with more hardware designs and interface mods than people stories. "The City Council keeps changing their minds about it. They don't want to get all Rusty, with people owning information and stuff. But nobody likes all those feeds that just show people cheating on their partners. Or fashion-slammers making fun of clothes and surge."

"Yeah, everyone hates those feeds. Except the zillions of people who *watch* them."

"Hmm. You should probably ask Hiro. He keeps up with that stuff."

Aya glanced at her brother, who was deep in a feed-trance, absorbing all twelve screens at once, no doubt plotting his big follow-up to immortality. Not the right moment to mention her new story, especially since that would mean bringing up a certain missing hovercam.

"Maybe not right now," she said. "So what are you working on?"

"Nothing huge," he said. "This middle-pretty science clique asked me for a kick. They've got some merits but no face. They're trying to recreate all those species the Rusties erased, you know? From old scraps of DNA and junk genes."

"Really?" Aya said. "That sounds totally kickable!"

"Yeah, till it turned out they're starting with worms and slugs and insects. I was like, 'Worms? Let me know when you get to tigers!'" He laughed. "I saw your underground graffiti story, by the way. Good work."

"Really?" Aya felt herself blush. "You thought those guys were interesting?"

"They will be," Hiro murmured from his chair, "in about a thousand years, when their work gets unburied."

Ren smiled, whispering, "See? Hiro watches your feed too."

"Not that she returns the favor," Hiro said, his eyes never leaving the wallscreen.

"So what are you kicking next, Aya-chan?" Ren asked.

"Well, it's kind of a secret right now."

"A secret?" Hiro said. "Ooh, mysterious."

Aya sighed. She'd come here to ask for Hiro's help, but he obviously wasn't in a help-giving mood. He was going to be insufferable now that he'd reached the top thousand.

Maybe it was pointless anyway. She wasn't even sure that the Sly Girls would keep their promise and contact her, or how to find them again if they didn't.

"Don't worry, Aya-chan," Ren said. "We won't tell anybody."

"Well . . . okay. Have you guys ever heard of the Sly Girls?"

Ren glanced at Hiro, who turned slowly in his chair to face her. A strange expression had appeared on both their faces.

"I've heard of them," Hiro said. "But they're not real."

Aya laughed. "Not real? Like, they're robots or something?"

"More like a rumor," he said. "The Sly Girls don't exist."

"What do you know about them?" she asked.

"Nothing. There's nothing *to* know about them, because they aren't real!"

"Come on, Hiro," she said. "Unicorns aren't real, and I

know stuff about them. Like . . . they have horns on their foreheads. And they can fly!"

Hiro groaned. "No, that's Pegasus that flies. Unicorns just have a horn, which makes them a lot more real than the Sly Girls, who I can't tell you *anything* about. It's just a random phrase kickers use. Like last year when someone was jumping off bridges wearing homemade parachutes, and no one ever figured out who. Everyone just said, 'The Sly Girls did it.' Because *sly* in English means clever or sneaky."

Aya rolled her eyes. "My English is a lot better than yours, Hiro-sensei. But what if they really exist?"

"Then they wouldn't be secret, would they? I mean, some cliques start off underground, and a lot of people pull tricks on the sly, but nobody stays anonymous forever." He swept his gaze around the apartment—the huge wallscreen, the garlands of paper cranes, the floor-to-ceiling window with its slowly shifting view. "Thanks to the reputation economy, they'd rather be famous. Did you know that every real criminal since the mind-rain has wound up confessing?"

Aya nodded. *Everyone* knew that, and how they'd all hit the top one thousand for at least a few days. "But what if—?"

"It's not real, Aya. Whatever it is."

"So if I bring you some shots of the Sly Girls?" she said. "What are you going to say then?"

Hiro turned back toward the wallscreen. "The same thing I'd say if you stuck a plastic horn on a horse and started kicking unicorns: Quit wasting my time."

Aya clenched her fists, her eyes stinging. The doubts she'd had about sneaking footage of the Girls were gone now. She was going to make Hiro eat his words.

She turned to Ren. "What's a good cam to requisition? One that's small enough to hide." She fingered a button on her dorm uniform. "This big."

"That's easy," Ren said, then frowned. "Where's your hovercam, anyway? You never used to go anywhere without Moggle."

"Oh . . . well, that's sort of why I was looking for you, Ren."

He grinned. "What, did you break another lens? You've got to stop jumping out your window."

"Um, it's kind of worse than that," Aya said softly, but she could see that Hiro was listening. Why was she always invisible to him, until she made a mistake? "You see, I kind of . . . lost Moggle."

Ren's eyes widened. "But how . . . ?"

"You *lost* it?" Hiro turned to them, a glare set on his pretty face. "How do you lose a hovercam? They just fly home when you leave them behind!"

"It's not like I *left* it somewhere," she said. "I mean, I would never—"

"Do you know how long Ren spent on those mods?"

"Look, Hiro, I know where Moggle is, sort of," Aya said, a lump rising in her throat. "I just need a little help finding it and . . . getting it back to the surface."

"The surface of *what*?" Hiro cried.

"There's this sort of underground lake, and . . ." Her throat closed up around the words, and Aya shut her eyes. If Hiro kept yelling at her, she'd burst into tears.

She felt Ren's hand on her shoulder. "It's okay, Aya-chan."

"I'm sorry," she managed.

"Well, it sounds like a pretty famous-making story." He exhaled slowly. "I think I've got some time tomorrow. Maybe I can help you dredge up Moggle from this . . . underground lake?"

She nodded, eyes still closed. "Thanks, Ren-chan."

"She'll just lose it again," Hiro said.

"No I won't!" she shouted. "And I'm going to prove that you're wrong about the Sly Girls, too!"

But Hiro didn't answer . . . he just shook his head.

Aya made her way home, still trying not to cry.

She was exhausted, Ren hated her, and her stupid brother was getting more famous and horrible every second. If Ren couldn't find Moggle, there was no way she could scrape together enough merits for a new hovercam.

All Aya wanted to do was sleep until tomorrow morning, when Ren had promised to meet her at the new construction site. But this afternoon was already stuffed with classes—the ones she'd rescheduled from this morning on top of the dreaded Advanced English. She couldn't skip: Schoolwork was the quickest way to build up merits when you were an ugly—all the good jobs went to pretties and crumblies.

When she reached Akira Hall, she went down to the basement and found an empty wallscreen.

"Aya Fuse," she told it.

It popped to life, listing her pings and assignments, and displaying her miserable face rank of 451,441.

She was dying to look up Frizz Mizuno and Radical Honesty, but not until schoolwork was out of the way. As she scanned the list for any new assignments, her eyes froze on one. . . .

It was anonymous and spitting animations, like the fluttering hearts that littlies decorated their pings with. But these weren't hearts, or exclamation points, or smilies.

They were eyes—dull, unsurged, Plain Jane eyes—and they kept winking at her.

Aya opened the ping. . . .

> Saw your story about the graffiti. Not bad, for a kicker. Meet us at midnight, where the mag-lev line leaves Uglyville.
>
> But don't bring a cam, or we won't let you play.
>
> —your new friends

SLY GIRLS

"Can't I use my own hoverboard?"

Jai snorted. "That toy? Too slow. The train will be doing a hundred and fifty by the time you jump on."

"Oh." Aya stared down at the long, shimmering curve of the mag-lev line. It cut through the low industrial buildings, an arc of white through dull orange worklights. The Sly Girls had brought her to the city's edge, where the greenbelt faded into factories and new expansions. "I just assumed you guys got on the train while it was standing still."

"The wardens would be *expecting* that, wouldn't they?" Jai swung her feet casually, as if there weren't a hundred-meter drop below them. "They have monitors all over the train yards."

"But isn't a hundred and fifty kind of fast?" Most boards were safety-capped at sixty kilometers an hour.

"That's nothing for a mag-lev," Eden Maru said. "We're catching it when it slows down on the bend." She pointed toward the wild. "The trains do three hundred once they hit the straightaway outside town."

"Three hundred klicks? And we'll still be riding it?"

"Let's hope so." Jai smiled. "Considering the alternative."

Aya glanced down at the magnetic bracelets strapped to her wrists. They were like the crash bracelets everyone wore for hoverboard falls, just much bigger. But were they really powerful enough to fight a three-hundred-kilometer head-wind?

She wrapped her arms around herself, trying not to look down at the nervous-making drop. The three of them were balanced atop a tall transmission tower, high enough to see darkness on the horizon, the place where the city stopped.

Aya had never glimpsed the wild before tonight, except on nature feeds. Somehow the thought of venturing out into that lightless, barren expanse was even scarier than jumping on a speeding train.

Moggle's absence made her doubly uneasy. It was eerie knowing that none of this was being recorded. Like a dream, whatever happened would all be gone tomorrow morning. Aya felt cut off from the world, unreal.

"The next train passes in three minutes," Jai said. "So what's the most important thing to remember once we're surfing?"

A cold trickle squirmed down Aya's spine. "The decapi-tation signals."

"Which work how?"

"When anyone in front of me flashes a yellow light, that means duck. Red means a tunnel's coming, so lie flat against the train."

"Just don't get too excited." Jai giggled. "Or you'll lose your head."

Aya wondered if the Sly Girls had ever considered lying flat for the whole ride, which would make decapitation much less of an issue. Or realized that not surfing mag-levs *at all* would keep head-losing safely in the realm of the unimaginable, where it belonged.

"Sounds like you've got it down," Jai said.

Eden snorted. "Yeah, she's practically an expert."

"Relax, face-queen," Jai said. "Not all of us are hoverball stars."

"Not all of us are fifteen, either. Or kickers."

"She doesn't even have a cam anymore."

Aya listened to them argue, wondering how high Jai's face rank was. Lots of people who avoided the feeds were famous, of course. In fact, the most famous person in the city—in the whole world—didn't have a feed of her own. But people talked about her every time they mentioned the mind-rain.

"You don't have to worry about me," Aya said. "Just because I'm an ugly doesn't mean I'm stupid."

"Of course not," Jai said. "In fact, I find your ugliness enchanting."

"I've been getting a lot of that lately," Aya said, thinking of Frizz Mizuno.

"One minute to go!" Eden called, and jumped from the tower. Her hoverball rig caught her fall, and she pirouetted in midair to face them. "Just be careful, Aya."

"She will be." Jai pushed off, stepping onto her waiting board. "They're always careful the first time!"

She laughed and spun away, the two of them sweeping down toward the tracks together.

Aya stepped gingerly onto the high-speed board they'd given her. It gave a little under her weight, like a diving board, but she could feel the power surging beneath her feet.

The approaching train was visible now, just crawling out from the yards, loaded with trade bound for other cities. She couldn't hear its rumble yet, but Aya knew that three hundred tons of speeding metal would shake the earth like a suborbital launch as it passed.

She followed Jai and Eden across the factory belt, down to the hiding place where the others waited—the rooftop of a low industrial building next to the tracks. A few driverless trucks rumbled along the streets below, tending the factories and building sites. No people anywhere.

As Aya swept in for a landing, loose gravel crunched under her hoverboard. She slid to a hiding spot behind a ventilation tower spitting exhaust from the underground depths of the factory. A smell like sulfur and hot glue tinged the air.

Crouching there, listening to the train rumbling in the distance, Aya found herself thinking of Frizz Mizuno again. He seemed to cross her mind every few minutes—how had one random conversation been so brain-rattling?

The teachers always warned about getting too involved with pretties. Since the mind-rain, they weren't as innocent as they looked. They could mess with your head so easily, just by gazing at you with those huge, gorgeous eyes.

Of course, Frizz wasn't like that. She'd checked the city interface after classes, and Ren had been right about Radical Honesty: They couldn't lie, or even *imply* a falsehood. The whole truth-slanting part of their brain had been switched off, just like bubbleheads were missing willpower, creativity, and despair.

But the fact that Frizz had been truthful just made him more nerve-jangling. As did the fact that his face rank was going up every hour. He'd only been pretty a few months, and he was headed for the top thousand.

"Nervous?" a voice came from the darkness.

It was one of the other Sly Girls, crouching beside the next air vent. She looked younger than Jai and Eden—with the same Plain Jane surge and hole-in-the-wall rejects they all wore.

"No, I'm okay."

"But surfing's more *fun* if you're scared."

Aya laughed. With her mousy brown hair, the girl looked almost like an ugly. Her eyes were so lusterless and dull that Aya wondered if she'd surged them that way.

"This should be plenty of fun, then."

"Good." The girl grinned. "It's supposed to be!"

She certainly looked like she was having fun. As the rumble of the train built, her smile gleamed like a pretty's in the darkness. Aya wondered what made her so thrilled to be risking her life like this. How many people even knew that she was a Sly Girl?

"Hey, aren't you in my dorm?" Aya asked. "What's your name?"

The girl laughed. "You going to check my face rank later?"

"Oh." Aya looked away. "Is it that obvious?"

"Fame's always obvious—that's the point of it." She glanced back toward where Jai was hiding. "I know you kick stories once in a while. We'll have to break you of that habit."

"Sorry I asked."

"No problem. Listen, if it makes you feel better, my first

name's Miki. And my face rank's about nine hundred and ninety-seven thousand."

"You're kidding . . . right?"

"Pretty sly, huh?" Miki said with a grin.

Aya shook her head, trying to think through the building rumble of the train. It didn't make sense. Anyone who pulled tricks like this should have cracked a hundred thousand, whether they'd been kicked or not. The city interface picked up any mention of your name, especially gossip, tall tales, and rumors.

And 997,000 was almost a *million*! That was the land of extreme extras, like newborn littlies and crumblies who'd never taken the mind-rain pills. Non-people, practically.

Miki just laughed at her dumbfounded expression. "Of course, Jai's even slyer. That's why she's the boss."

"You mean slyer . . . as in *less* famous?"

Miki winked. "As in kissing a million."

"Get ready!" Eden Maru called, barely audible above the growing roar of the train.

"Surf's up!" Miki yelled, kneeling.

Aya grabbed her hoverboard's forward edge, trying to focus. This story was suddenly much stranger than just surfing a mag-lev. For some reason, the Sly Girls had turned the reputation economy upside down.

They *wanted* to disappear. But why?

Her crash bracelets snapped against the board, locking her down tight. The factory roof itself was shuddering now, the gravel strewn across it dancing like hailstones hitting grass.

She could finally kick a story like one of Hiro's: long, dizzy-making interviews, a dozen background layers tracing the Girls' histories, wild footage of train rides and underground meetings. If she could just shoot it without them finding out . . . and with her hovercam at the bottom of a lake.

Aya glanced over her shoulder at Jai, feeling a cold smile creep onto her face. Finally she knew how to take the perfect revenge for Moggle's watery burial. She was going to kick this story big, and make the Sly Girls famous beyond their wildest nightmares.

She'd make sure *everyone* knew their names.

"Hey, you look a little funny," Miki called above the roar. "Not finally getting scared, are you?"

Aya laughed. "No. Just getting ready!"

The thunder built louder and louder, finally exploding as the train arrived, a solid blur of lights and noise shooting past. A dozen whirlwinds of dust swirled to life across the rooftop.

Then the train leaned into the curve, and Aya heard a chorus of humming slowly build, like an orchestra of wineglasses tuning up. Three hundred tons of levitating metal and smart matter were bending into a new shape, slowing down just a little bit.

"Now!" Eden screamed.

And they rose into the air.

SURFING

The board shot forward, dragging Aya along by her wrists.

It wrenched and twisted like a bad spinout, when crash bracelets could almost jerk a rider's arms from their sockets. But spinouts never lasted this long. Aya's hoverboard was still accelerating, faster and faster along the slow curve of the mag-lev line.

She squeezed as flat as she could against the board, her feet dangling off the back end, her dorm jacket snapping like a flag in a gale.

Squinting against the wind, Aya could hardly see anything. Only a few meters ahead, Miki was nothing but a teary blur. Luckily, the board was programmed to fly itself until it matched the speed of the train.

Sneaking out the night before to look for Eden and her friends, Aya had never expected to wind up riding the train *herself*. She'd imagined zooming along at a safe distance, with Moggle closer in, capturing images for her feed.

Yet here she was, taking the most brain-kicking ride of her life, and it wasn't even being recorded!

The ground flashed by below, but the train beside her seemed to be gradually slowing down. The hoverboard was really catching up.

Soon she'd have to climb aboard.

For a second, she thought about veering off, shooting away into the night. She could still kick a secret clique bent on wild tricks and avoiding fame.

Of course, she'd have nothing to prove her story but two crash bracelets, a high-speed board, and a waterlogged hovercam. Except for Eden Maru, she didn't even know any full names. No one would believe her—especially not Hiro.

To get the footage she needed, she had to make the Sly Girls think that Aya Fuse was one of them. And to do that, she had to surf this train.

In the howling wind, she could feel the awesome physical forces all around her, waiting for any mistake.

The mag-lev seemed to drift into place beside Aya as her board matched its speed.

The hoverboard's autopilot flashed once—it had done its job.

Now Aya was in control.

Jai had warned her about this part. Any sudden shift of weight could send the board crashing against the train, or spinning away into a passing building.

Ahead of her, Miki was swaying back and forth, testing her control.

Aya held her breath . . . and lifted the fingers of her right hand. The wind bent them back painfully, and her board shuddered, veering away from the train.

She dragged her fingers back into a fist, and the stabilizers kicked in, steadying the hoverboard. Her whole hand throbbed.

This was fast. . . . If only Moggle were watching.

Ahead, Miki was only a meter from the train—another girl farther on was already reaching out a hand toward the roof. Aya had to get onboard before the mag-lev line straightened out.

"Here goes," she said through gritted teeth.

She crooked her left thumb, barely lifting it from the hoverboard's front edge. The board responded more evenly this time, angling toward the steady expanse of the mag-lev's roof. She drifted closer in cautious stages, like handling a kite with minute tugs on its strings.

A few meters from the train, her board began to jump and shudder again. Jai had warned her about this, too: the shock wave, an invisible boundary of turbulence stirred up by the train's passage.

Aya fought the tumult with twitches and gestures, every

muscle straining. Her ears popped with pressure changes, and her eyes streamed tears into the wind.

Suddenly she pulled free of the turbulence, sweeping across the remaining space to bump softly against the metal flank of the train. Aya felt the mag-lev's vibrations buzzing in the board beneath her as its magnets firmed up the connection.

The wind was muted now—she was inside a thin bubble of calm surrounding the train, like the eye of a hurricane.

Aya demagnetized her left crash bracelet, then slowly slid her hand across the board's grippy surface to the roof of the train.

It smacked down hard and secure.

But it was nervous-making, disconnecting her other crash bracelet. The hoverboard was Aya-size, the mag-lev inhumanly huge and powerful. She was like a rat hitching a ride on a stampeding dinosaur.

Shutting her eyes, she pulled her right hand free, then hauled herself up onto the roof and slapped her wrist down.

She'd done it! The train rumbled below her like an unsettled volcano, and the half-muted wind still tore at her hair and clothes. But Aya was onboard.

The humming rose up around her—the train's smart-matter joints pulling it back straight. She'd made it just in time.

The train's roof stretched out dead straight ahead of her, dotted with nine Sly Girls along its length. Glancing back, the wind whipping handfuls of hair into her mouth, she saw the other three—everyone had made it.

The wind built as the train accelerated, and most of them were already surfing, standing with their arms out to catch the wind. Just like flying, Eden had said.

Aya sighed—as if riding on top of a mag-lev wasn't risky enough without *standing up*!

But if the Girls were going to accept her, she'd have to be as crazy as they were. And it wasn't really surfing if you were lying down.

She unthreaded the straps on her right bracelet, pulled it off, and curled up to wrestle it over her foot. It was all very clumsy, but after a minute's fumbling, she had the bracelet strapped tightly around her ankle.

She magnetized it, and felt her shoe plant hard against the metal roof.

Gingerly she released her other wrist . . . the wind didn't whip her away.

Time for the scary part.

Aya pushed herself up gradually, feet planted wide apart and arms out, like a littlie standing on a hoverboard for the first time. Up ahead, Miki's body was angled sideways into the wind, like a fencer presenting the smallest possible target. Aya imitated her as she stood up.

The higher she got, the fiercer the wind grew. Invisible, chaotic whirlwinds buffeted her body, twisting her hair into knots.

But finally Aya was fully upright, every muscle straining.

All around her, the world was a wild blur.

The train had reached the outer edge of the new expansion, where the city grew every day. Banks of work-lights shot past like bright orange comets, earthmovers the size of mansions flitting by. The wild lay just ahead, its dark mass the only steady shape in the maelstrom of lights and noise and rushing wind.

Then the last glow of construction streaked past, and the train plunged into a sea of darkness. As the city network fell behind, Aya's skintenna lost its connection with the city interface. The world was quickly emptied: no feeds, no face ranks, no fame.

As if the screaming wind had stripped everything away.

But somehow Aya didn't miss it all—she was laughing. She felt huge and unstoppable, like a littlie on horseback galloping at breakneck speed.

The train's awesome power flowed across her hands. Angling her palms flat, she felt the airstream lift her up, pulling her against the straps around her ankle, like a bird straining to fly. Every gesture whipped her body into a new stance, as if the wind was an extension of her will.

But just ahead, Miki's dark outline was crouching. Something was in her hand. . . .

A yellow light.

"Crap!" Aya angled her palms down and bent her knees.

As she crumpled to the train's roof, something huge and invisible sliced the air overhead, hissing like the blade of a sword whipping past. Its shock wave rang through her body like a blow.

Then it was gone. Aya hadn't even seen what it was.

She swallowed, squinting into the wind. Ahead, a string of yellow lights stretched away toward the front of the train. They flicked off one by one, the danger past.

How had she missed them?

"Don't get too excited," Jai had warned. *"Or you'll lose your head."*

Trembling, she rose slowly from her crouch, her momentary sense of giddy power vanished. The darkness stretched out ahead as far as she could see.

Suddenly Aya Fuse felt very small.

TUNNEL

There were four things Aya was realizing about the wild.

It was formless. The forest rushing by on either side blurred into one impenetrable mass, a roiling void of speed.

It was endless, or maybe time had broken. Whether she'd been surfing for minutes or hours, she had no idea.

Third, the wild had a huge sky, which didn't make sense—it seemed like the sky would be the same size everywhere. But the blackness overhead sprawled out—unmarked by the city's jagged skyline, unstained by reflected light—starlit and vast.

And lastly, it was cold. Though that was probably thanks to the three-hundred-klick wind in Aya's face.

Next time, she was bringing two jackets.

Some time later, Aya saw Miki's outline drop into a crouch. She looked worriedly at the other girls ahead, but no decapitation warning lights were showing.

Miki seemed to be playing with the bracelet around her ankle—then suddenly she was untethered, sliding backward across the train's roof on the seat of her pants, carried by the fierce headwind.

"Miki!" Aya screamed, kneeling and sticking out a hand.

As she slid within Aya's reach, Miki slammed a crash bracelet down, spinning to a halt. She was laughing, the wind whipping her hair in a frenzy around her head.

"Hey, Aya-chan!" she shouted. "How's it going?"

Aya pulled her hand back. "You scared me!"

"Sorry." Miki shrugged. "The wind always carries you straight down the train. Enjoying yourself?"

Aya took a deep breath. "Sure. But it's kind of icicle-making."

"No kidding." Miki pulled her standard-requisition shirt up, revealing Rangers' silks. "These work, though."

Aya rubbed her hands together, wishing Jai had warned her about the cold.

"I came back because we're almost in the mountains," Miki shouted, rising to one knee. "That's where the train slows down again."

"And we jump off?"

"Yeah. But the tunnel comes first."

"Oh, right." Aya shivered. "The red-light warning. I almost missed that first yellow."

"Don't worry. It's hard for a mountain to sneak up on you." Miki put her arm around Aya. "And it's not as windy in there."

Aya shivered, huddling closer. "Can't wait."

The mountain range rose slowly from the horizon, black outlines against the starlit sky.

As they grew nearer, Aya realized how big the mountains were. The one straight ahead looked wider across than the city's soccer stadium, and much taller than the central tower in town. It ate the sky as they approached, like a wall of blackness rolling toward them.

By now Aya was getting used to the unexpected size of everything out here. She wondered how anyone had managed to cross the wild back in pre-Rusty days, before mag-levs or hoverboards or even groundcars. The scale was enough to drive anyone crazy.

No wonder the Rusties had tried to pave it over.

"Here we go," Miki said, pointing.

At the front of the train, a red light was flickering. Another appeared behind it, a string of seven more igniting like a chain of sparklers.

Miki pulled a flashlight from her pocket and flicked it on. She twisted it to red, then waved it toward the tail of the train.

Aya was already unlacing the bracelet from her ankle. She wanted both wrists magnetized by the time they reached the tunnel.

"You okay?" Miki asked. "You look funny."

"I'm fine." Aya shivered. Suddenly she felt small again, the way she had after the train had first plunged into the wild.

"It's okay if you're not sure yet," Miki said. "I don't just surf because it's fun, you know? It also changes me. And that part takes a while to settle in."

Aya shook her head. She hadn't meant to sound unenthusiastic. The Sly Girls had to believe she was one of them, that she'd embraced their insanity keenly enough to give up kicking for good.

But it was true—something had shifted inside Aya, something she didn't quite understand yet. The ride had whipped her so quickly from terror to elation, then just as suddenly to insignificance. . . .

She stared out across the dark landscape, trying to untangle her emotions. This feeling was nothing like the obscurity-panic that consumed her when she saw the lights of the city, the horrible certainty that she would never be famous, that all those people would never care about her at all.

Somehow, staring into the darkness, she felt contented that the world was so much bigger than her. Overwhelmed, but calm.

"I know what you mean . . . it's sort of brain-shifting, being out here."

"Good." Miki smiled. "Now get your head down."

"Oh, right. Tunnel."

They lay flat on the train, snapping their crash bracelets down hard. The mountain grew closer and closer, until it towered over them like a huge wave rolling out of a black sea.

Squinting ahead, Aya watched the red warning lights disappearing one by one, gobbled by the tunnel's maw along with the front half of the train.

Then, with a vast shudder of the air, darkness swallowed them. The roar of the train redoubled with echoes and reverberations. Aya's whole body felt the difference in the train's vibrations.

The tunnel's blackness was a hundred times heavier than the starlight outside, but Aya could feel the tunnel roof sliding past—close enough to reach up and touch, if she wanted to lose a hand.

She felt the megatons of rock overhead pressing down, an infinite mass, as if the sky had turned to stone. Seconds ago the mag-lev had seemed huge, but instantly the mountain had dwarfed it, squashing her into the narrow sliver of space between the two.

"Do you feel that?" Miki called.

Aya turned her head. "What?"

"I think we're slowing down."

"Already?" Aya frowned. "Isn't the bend on the other side of the tunnel?"

"It is. But listen."

Aya focused on the tumultuous roar around them. Gradually her ears began to tease apart the sounds. The rumble of the train had a rhythm inside it, the steady beat of some imperfection in the track.

And that beat was slowing down.

"You're right. Does the train ever stop in here?"

"Not that I ever heard. Whoa! Feel that?"

"Um, yeah." Aya's body was sliding forward; the train was braking faster now. Her feet spun in a half circle around the bracelets, carried by her own momentum.

The roar and rumble died slowly around them, the train gliding to a graceful, silent stop. The stillness sent tremors across Aya's wind-burned skin.

"Something must have gone wrong with the train," Miki said softly. "Hope they get it fixed fast."

"I thought cargo trains didn't have crews."

"Some do." Miki let out a slow breath. "I guess we wait and—"

A light glimmered across the tunnel roof. It came from the right side of the train, flickering unsteadily, like a carried flashlight. For the first time, Aya saw the inside of the tunnel, a smooth cylinder of stone wrapped around the train. The roof was perhaps twenty centimeters from her head. She reached up and touched the cold stone.

"Crap!" Miki hissed. "Our boards!"

Aya swallowed. The hoverboards were still clinging to the right side of the train, a few meters above head height. If whoever was out there looked up and saw one, they'd definitely wonder what it was.

"Let's see what's going on," Miki whispered. She unlocked her wrists and pulled herself toward the roof's edge.

Aya released her bracelets and crawled after Miki. If the hoverboards had been spotted, they had to warn the others right away.

At the edge of the roof, she and Miki peered over. A group of three figures had crowded into the narrow space between train and stone, flashlights lengthening their shadows into distorted shapes. Aya realized that they were floating, wearing hoverball rigs like Eden's.

But they hadn't seen the boards. They weren't looking at the train at all. All of them stared at the tunnel wall. . . .

It was moving.

The stone of the mountain was transforming, undulating softly and changing colors, like oil floating on top of rippling water. A sound like a humming wineglass filled the tunnel. The air suddenly tasted different in Aya's mouth, like in the wet season when a downpour was about to start.

One by one, thin layers of the liquid stone peeled away, until a wide door had opened in the tunnel wall.

The figures' flashlights lanced into its depths, but from atop the train Aya couldn't see inside. She heard echoes from a large space, and saw an orange glow from the doorway playing among the flashlight shadows.

A panel in the train slid open, matching the gap in the tunnel wall. The train settled slightly on its levitation magnets, descending until the two openings were aligned.

One of the figures moved, and Aya jerked her head back into the shadows. When she peeked out again, all three of them had stepped aside to watch a massive object drift from the opening in the train.

It looked like a cylinder of solid metal, taller than Aya and a meter across. It must have been heavy: The four lifter drones clamped to its base trembled unsteadily, carrying it across the gap with the measured pace of a funeral transport.

Before the object had disappeared into the mountainside, another followed, exactly the same. Then a third emerged.

"Do you see them?" came Miki's soft whisper.

"Yeah. But what are they?"

"Not human."

"Not . . . *what?*"

Aya glanced at Miki's face and realized that she wasn't watching the metal objects floating past. She was staring wide-eyed at the people down below.

Aya peered through the darkness, and finally saw that the flashlights weren't distorting the figures' shapes as she'd thought. The people hovering in the gloom were simply *wrong*—their legs absurdly stretched and gangly, arms bending in too many places, fingers as long as calligraphy brushes. And their faces . . . the large eyes were set too wide, the skin hairless and pale.

As Miki had said: not human.

Aya let out a shallow gasp, and Miki pulled her back from the edge. They lay there side by side, Aya's eyes squeezed shut, her heart pounding as she imagined one of those spindly hands reaching up onto the top of the train and grasping her.

She forced herself to breathe slowly, clenching her fists until the panic subsided.

Finally she slid to the edge of the train once more and looked down, wishing for the hundredth time tonight that Moggle was hovering at her shoulder. But she had only her own eyes and brain.

The inhuman figures still floated there, watching a procession of lifter drones glide from the tunnel door into the train. They carried chairs and wallscreens, food synthesizers and industrial water recyclers, countless garbage canisters. Even a full aquarium balanced between two lifters, the bubbler still rumbling, fish darting around unhappily inside.

Someone was obviously moving out of the hidden tunnel space . . . but what were those metal things they'd moved *in*?

At last, the train slid shut, and the air began to hum again. Dark strands wove across the opening in the tunnel wall, like a time-lapse of a spider building a web. Then rippling layers began to roll across them, until the gap was completely covered.

"Smart matter," whispered Miki beside her.

As Aya nodded, the surface shivered one last time, then turned into a perfect imitation of stone. The flashlights flickered off, dropping the tunnel back into absolute darkness.

"Come on," Miki whispered, pulling her back toward the centerline of the train. Soon it shuddered into motion, and the wind began to swirl around them again. "We'll be jumping off soon, and we can tell the others."

"But who were those people, Miki?" Aya said.

"I think you mean, *what* were they?"

"Yeah." Aya lay there exhausted in the rumbling darkness, trying to replay in her mind what she'd seen. She needed time to think; she needed the city interface. And most of all, she needed Moggle.

This story had just gotten much more complicated.

RESCUE

"You know, when I waterproofed Moggle, I didn't think you'd ever *need* it."

"Sorry," Aya sighed. She'd said "sorry" about a thousand times since meeting up with Ren this morning; even she had to admit it was getting old. "Um, I mean, it won't happen again."

Ren dropped his gaze back to the motionless black water. "You still haven't told me how it happened in the first place."

"They must have snuck up on Moggle. They used a lock-down clamp, I'm pretty sure." Aya stepped to the front edge of her hoverboard, peering down. She wasn't even certain if she had the right spot. Her memories of that night were all shadows and chaos, and now Ren's hoverlamps were illuminating the underground reservoir with a cheery glow. Nothing matched the images in her mind. "They dropped it here, I think."

"They . . . the Sly Girls, you mean?"

"Yes, Ren, they're real. You just haven't seen them because they don't like kickers very much." She pointed at the black surface. "Hence my hovercam under water."

He snorted, thumbs twiddling with the instrument in his hands, his eyescreens spinning. Ren made his own trick-boxes, gadgets that could talk to any machine in the city. "Well, they used a serious clamp. Moggle isn't showing up at all: no city signal, no private feed, not even battery flicker."

Aya groaned, and the sound glanced across the still surface of the water, echoed off the ancient brick walls in a chorus of defeat. The reservoir was even bigger than she remembered, vast enough to store the whole rainy season. Finding one little hovercam down here would be impossible.

"What are we going to do?"

"Well, us tech-heads have a saying: If you can't use the

kickest new technology, just use your eyes." He fiddled with his gadget's controls, and one of the little hoverlamps focused into a blinding spotlight straight down into the water. The hoverlamp flew toward Aya, sliding to a stop beside her, illuminating the depths of the reservoir.

Aya eased her hoverboard down to the water's surface and knelt to peer into its depths.

"Whoa . . . we actually drink this stuff?"

"They filter it first, Aya-chan."

The water was murky, speckled with suspended dirt and debris carried down by the storm drains. It smelled like damp earth and rotten leaves.

"Does this light get any stronger?"

"Maybe this will help." He flicked his hand, and the hoverlamp descended until its nose broke the surface.

The spotlight grew in intensity, and a half sphere of luminous water bloomed beneath Aya, as if she was hovering above an upside-down sunset in shades of green and brown.

She could finally see the bottom of the reservoir: a fine layer of silt, twigs, and construction rubbish with a few spots of ancient brickwork showing through.

But no Moggle.

"Hmm, this might be the wrong spot."

"Too bad." Ren lay back and stretched out on his hoverboard, staring at the arched ceiling. He raised his arms out in front of him, gesturing through the start-up sequence of some thumb-twitch game. "Let me know when you find the right one."

"But Ren-chan—"

"See you later, cam-loser."

She started to protest again, but Ren's eyescreens

started blinking a full immersion pattern, his fingers flexing and twitching—he was deep in the game.

Aya let out a sigh, stretching out facedown on her board, her chin resting on the front end. She let herself drift slowly across the water, peering down through the luminous muck.

Ren had been right about one thing: This was definitely boring. Every time the hoverlamp obediently followed her, its nose rippled the surface, and Aya had to wait for the water to settle before she could see again. She spotted a few surprising bits of rubbish—a boomerang, the remains of a crumpled box kite, a broken warbody sword—but still no Moggle. She could see why Ren would rather play games than stare into the bottom of a garbage-filled lake.

At least all her test scores yesterday had been aces, and her littlie-watching duty after lunch would build up the last few merits she needed for some black camo paint for Moggle.

When this story finally kicked, she'd be famous enough to never worry about merit-grubbing again.

As Aya peered into the underground lake's mysterious depths, her thoughts returned to what she and Miki had seen last night. What was so secret that you had to hide it in a mountain? And why had those people looked so strange? Even the most serious surge-monkeys never bent their bodies *that* far out of shape.

The Sly Girls were headed out again tonight to look for clues. Ren had given Aya a spy-cam the size of a shirt button, but it was only good for grainy close-ups. To capture the Girls in all their eye-kicking glory, Moggle had to be sneaking along behind.

Down in the depths, a small silt-covered bump rose from the reservoir floor.

"Moggle?" she murmured, rubbing her eyes.

It was the perfect shape and size, like a soccer ball cut in half.

"Hey, Ren," she cried. *"Ren!"*

His immersion blinker sputtered to a halt, the eye-screen glaze slipping from his face.

"Moggle's down there!"

He stretched his arms, swinging his legs over the side of his hoverboard. "Great. Time for stage two, which is *much* more kick."

"Good. I was kind of getting bored."

He smiled. "Believe me, you won't find this boring."

Stage two turned out to involve a tank of compressed helium the size of a fire extinguisher, with a limp weather balloon hanging from its nozzle.

Aya stared at the contraption. "I don't get it."

Ren tossed her the tank, and Aya grunted under its weight. Her board dipped for a moment before the lifters compensated, smacking flat against the water.

"Feel how heavy that is?" he said.

"Um, *yes*." Water trickled across the board's riding surface, getting her grippy shoes wet.

"That's to solve your floating problem," he explained.

"I have a floating problem?"

"Yes, Aya-chan: Like most people, you float," he said. "It's all that pesky air in your lungs. That tank's heavy enough to carry you straight to the bottom."

She blinked. "Ren, wait a second . . . I *like* my floating problem. I like the air in my lungs! I'm not going down there!"

He laughed. "How else are you going to get Moggle?"

"I don't know," she said. "I thought maybe you'd make some sort of . . . little submarine?"

"Like I don't have better things to spend my merits on?" He pointed at the helium tank. "There's a magnet on the bottom. Just balance the tank upright on top of Moggle, and it should stick."

"But how do I get back up? This thing weighs a ton!"

"That's the clever part: Just turn this." He drifted closer and gave a valve on the tank a turn. It hissed for a second before he twisted it back. "The balloon fills up, and that carries you and Moggle back to the surface! Pretty kick, huh?"

"Okay. But I can't breathe helium. Where's my underwater mask?" She looked at the open cargo compartment on his hoverboard.

"Just hold your breath."

"Hold my *breath*?" Aya cried. "That's your awesome tech-head solution?"

Ren rolled his eyes. "The bottom's only five or six meters down—like the deep end of a high-diving pool."

"Oh, thanks for bringing up high-diving, Ren. My favorite panic-making activity." She frowned. "And it's *cold* down there!"

"Good." He nodded. "Maybe next time you'll think about that *before* you lose your hovercam."

Aya stared at Ren, realizing that Hiro must have put him up to this. If the two of them only knew how kick this story was, they'd understand why sacrificing Moggle had been worth it. But she couldn't explain yet, not until she found out what was hidden in that mountain.

"Fine." She clutched the helium tank closer to herself, glaring down into the luminous water until she spotted

Moggle again. "Anything else I need to know?"

He smiled. "Just be careful, Aya-chan."

"Whatever."

She sucked in a deep breath . . . and jumped.

The splash rumbled in her ears for a moment, but the weight of the tank carried her swiftly through the turbulence to the still waters deeper down. The hoverlamps glowed through her closed eyelids, and it was freezing cold.

Her feet bumped against the reservoir floor, grippy shoes skidding for a moment on loose dirt. The heavy tank threatened to drag Aya to her knees, but she managed to stay upright.

She opened her eyes. . . .

Rotten leaves and twigs swirled around her head, a mini whirlwind thrown up by her landing. Depth had turned the light dull green, and spinning shadows danced across the reservoir floor.

A flash caught her eye—one of the shiny stickers on Moggle's cover, shimmering in the lamplight like the eye of some bottom-dwelling beast.

She walked in slow motion toward the hovercam, feet skidding on the slippery bricks. Every step stirred up whirligigs of silt and slime, dark clouds billowing around her. Moggle almost disappeared among them.

But there was no time to let the muck settle. Her heart was beginning to hammer against her rib cage, demanding more oxygen, and her fingers and toes were going numb in the freezing cold. The pressure of the water was dizzy-making, like two hands squeezed around her head.

Squinting through the murk, she maneuvered the helium tank over Moggle and let it drop. The *clank* carried straight to Aya's eardrums, a certain and final sound.

She fumbled for the nozzle of the air tank, lungs screaming, heart pounding, but her frozen fingers managed to give it a twist. A rumbling filled the water, and the weather balloon began to expand.

Aya let go and pushed away, shooting up from the reservoir floor. She kicked hard, propelling herself toward the blinding suns of the hoverlamps.

With one last glance down, she saw the balloon growing, straining against the tank's weight as it gained buoyancy. Slowly the whole contraption began to rise.

Aya broke the surface gasping, sucking in welcome lungfuls of air.

"You okay?" Ren was kneeling on his hoverboard.

"It's right behind me!" she sputtered, paddling water.

The weather balloon exploded from the water, sending hoverlamps scattering in all directions. Momentum carried it up into the air, cascading water like the head of a breaching whale. Then it crashed back against the surface, splashing them once more before coming to a bobbing halt.

"You actually did it!" Ren said.

"What did you think?" she asked, twisting a crash bracelet with cold-numbed fingers. "That I was going to *drown*?"

He shrugged. "I was expecting it to take a couple of tries."

The weather balloon was rising again, carried by its helium into the air. Moggle still clung to the bottom of the tank, dripping like a wet dog.

Ren slid his board closer, reached out, and shut off the flow of helium.

Aya pulled herself onto her hoverboard, shivering with cold.

"I still can't believe that worked," Ren murmured.

Aya coughed water into a fist. "Rope would have been simpler."

"*Simpler?*" Ren said. "That word's not in the tech-head language."

"Just check if Moggle's okay."

He chuckled, detaching the hovercam. As it fell into his hands, the balloon shot up to bounce against the ceiling. "Hey, did you know your lips are turning blue?"

"Great." Aya wrapped her arms around herself, trying to squeeze the water from her dorm uniform. She sat there shivering and watching Ren.

He pulled the lock-down clamp from Moggle, his eye-screens flickering to life. "My waterproofing held! I'm a genius!"

Aya let out a sigh of relief, which turned into a full-body shudder; her teeth were chattering now. She held herself tighter, promising never to sacrifice Moggle to a watery grave again.

But she had a hovercam. This story was going to kick.

RADICAL HONESTY

Flying home to Akira Hall, Aya wondered if she was catching a bug.

The sun was shining, but shivers kept rolling through her body. Last night had been so exhausting, and it didn't help that her uniform was wet and covered with reservoir gunk.

"Remind me to drink some meds when we get home."

Moggle flashed its night-lights, and Aya smiled. Even slimy and shivery cold, the world felt better with a hovercam flying beside her. All she needed now was a hot shower and things would be back to normal. Well, as normal as they could be after her midnight ride through the huge and brain-shifting wild. Everything looked so sedate here in the city.

In the perfect weather, the parklands were crowded—parents out with littlies, an ugly baseball team playing against crumblies. The soccer fields beside Akira Hall were roped off for a bunch of littlies fighting a mech battle. They clanked around in robot warbodies, clobbering each other with plastic swords, shooting foam missiles and safety fireworks. It was all very silly—even the best mech players never got famous—but it still looked like fun.

As she and Moggle skirted the soccer fields, a spinning war wheel escaped from the roped-off battle zone, bouncing past them into the trees. Moggle went after the trail of safety sparks, and Aya followed, laughing, descending to where it had rolled to a stop in the grass.

Stepping from her board, she hefted the war wheel in her hands. It was sizzling harmlessly, the fireworks not yet expended.

Aya grinned, turning back toward the battle and taking aim.

"Watch this!"

Her throw was clumsy, but as it flew through the air the war wheel sputtered back to life, gaining speed from its spinning jets of safety fire.

It careened through the battle, hopping like a flat stone across water, and finally hit one of the mech warriors smack in the middle of his back. It was a clean kill, and his warbody went into wild death throes, flailing its arms and gushing sparks before crumpling to the ground. The littlie inside crawled out and looked around in annoyance, trying to figure out who'd made the kill.

Aya giggled at the lucky throw, stepping back onto her board. It felt as though fate was finally taking her side, and fame couldn't be far away.

"Good shot," a voice said. "But not entirely rule-abiding."

She turned and finally saw a boy sitting cross-legged on a hoverboard, his shape concealed by the dappled shadows of the trees. He smiled a radiant smile.

Frizz Mizuno, appearing out of nowhere again.

"What are you . . . doing here?" she said softly.

"I came to see you," he said, bowing. "And when you weren't home, I thought I'd watch the battle. I haven't seen any mech combat since I turned sixteen. Which is very Prettytime of me—I used to *love* mechs."

Aya returned his bow, trying to imagine Frizz doing anything as face-missing as wearing a warbody. Sometimes it was hard to remember he was only a year older than she was.

"Plus, I was hoping you'd come home," he said. "It's rather mysterious, turning off your locator. It makes you hard to find."

"Oh, I didn't turn off my locator. I was just sort of . . . underground."

He frowned. "You don't feel stalked, do you? I'd go away if you did."

"Um, no. I don't feel stalked. Just sort of . . ."

"Damp?" Frizz asked. "And covered with muck?"

Her arms wrapped around her shoulders, as if that would hide her wet, bedraggled uniform. "Um, yes. Muck-covered."

"As looks go, it's even more mysterious than your Reputation Bomber robe."

She stood there, trying to think of something to say, but it seemed as though the cold of the reservoir had leaked into her brain and frozen it. It didn't help that Frizz's eye-kicking gaze was raining down on her, tangling her tongue in her mouth. The bigness of her nose suddenly loomed in the bottom of her vision.

"I was doing some . . . underwater rescue."

"Underwater *and* underground?" He nodded again. "That would explain wetness. And yet I'm still mystified."

Another shiver went through her; her head felt hot now. "Me too. I didn't tell you my last name. How did you find me?"

Frizz smiled. "Now that's an interesting story. But I think you should change."

"Change?" Her hand went to her nose.

"Into dry clothes—you keep shivering. Maybe some meds?"

Moggle's night-lights flashed.

He waited outside, watching the battle while Aya went upstairs.

She stood under a hot shower for a solid minute, dizzy from watching twigs and slime swirl down the drain, wondering how he'd found her. This was all so shaming. Frizz had figured out her last name, which meant he knew she was an ugly and a party-crashing extra.

And yet he'd come to see her anyway. . . .

What was *wrong* with him? Had the honesty surge broken his brain? His face rank had been steadily climbing—it was under three thousand now—and Aya was practically invisible!

Clean and dry, she faced the hole in the wall. Nothing but dorm uniforms, and no merits to waste on disposable clothing. Of course, Frizz had already seen her covered with slime—a clean uniform wouldn't be that much worse.

She dressed quickly and turned toward the door.

Moggle barred her way, flashing its lights once.

"Oh, right," she said, and told the room, "Meds, please. I was underwater and I'm all shivery and hot."

The wall's hand-plate flashed, wanting to feel her temperature and taste her sweat. Aya lay her palm on it, and soon the hole was coughing up something murky into her favorite teacup. Drinking down its orangey sourness, she stared at her standard-requisition furniture and face-missing clothes, the smallness of the room, the obscurity of everything about her.

At least medicine didn't cost any merits. And there must have been nanos in the drink—by the time the elevator reached the ground floor, her dizziness had mostly gone.

"Finding you was easy," Frizz said. "I knew your first name, after all."

She frowned. "But the city must have a thousand girls named Aya."

"More like twelve hundred." Frizz chuckled as another warbody exploded into death throes. The battle was gathering intensity, littering the soccer field with casualties. Moggle was flitting along the edges, practicing tracking shots on rubber missiles and looking completely recovered from being submerged in ice-cold water.

Aya couldn't say as much. Sitting next to Frizz in the dappled shade, she still felt tremors playing on the surface of her skin, as if the medicine had transformed her fever into reputation shivers. At least his tongue-tying manga gaze was focused on the battle instead of her.

"But I knew you'd been reputation bombing," he continued. "So I checked the face rankings for that night. Someone named Yoshio Nara became Yoshio-sensei out of nowhere."

Aya flinched. Even hearing Yoshio's name again sent a sharp little ping through her brain. "But how did you get from him to me?"

"I went through his meme-lines, looking for the name Aya."

"You can do that? I thought conversations were private! Not that it was a real conversation, just me saying the same name for an hour. But still!"

"No, you're right. The city interface won't reveal what you say." He shrugged. "But our city isn't designed for privacy; it's designed for *publicity*, to spawn connections and debates and buzz. So you're allowed to trace face-hits back to the source, especially if it's a *lot* of hits. And you were the only Aya to mention Yoshio Nara three thousand times that night."

"Ouch. Quit saying that name," Aya said, then sighed. "I guess I didn't know that. My brother studies his meme-lines for hours, but my stories never get enough feedback to bother with."

"He's famous, isn't he?"

Aya nodded. "Very. That's probably why he's such a snob. He thinks my stories are stupid."

"They're not. That underground graffiti you kicked was beautiful."

"Oh, um, thanks." Aya felt a blush spill across her cheeks, astonished that Frizz had actually looked at her feed. "But that's just kid stuff. I'm working on something much bigger. Totally famous-making! It's about this secret clique, and they—"

Frizz held up his hand. "If it's a secret, you'd better not tell me. I'm not very good at keeping secrets."

"Right, because of your . . ." She resisted the urge to point at his head. It was strange—bubbleheads were the only brain surgers Aya had ever known, and Frizz didn't seem like a bubblehead at all. "But what does honesty have to do with keeping secrets?"

"Radical Honesty gets rid of all deception," Frizz recited, like he'd explained this a million times before. "I can't lie, truth-slant, or pretend not to know something. You can't even invite me to surprise parties, or I'll give it all away."

A laugh bubbled up in Aya. "But doesn't that make everything less . . . surprising?"

"You'd be surprised how often it makes things *more* surprising."

"Huh." She stared at the battle, wondering how many things she kept secret every day. "You can't hide yourself at all. That must be scary-making."

He turned to her. "Scary-making for me? Or everyone else?"

His gaze sent Aya's shivers scattering across her skin, and she felt a flush returning to her cheeks and a tingle in her spine. His honesty *was* scary-making! Her head spun with all the questions she was dying to ask, but wasn't sure she could stand the answers to. About why he was here, and what he thought of their difference in ambition.

"You like me, don't you?" she said.

He laughed. "Was I being too *subtle*?"

"No, I guess not. But it doesn't make sense . . . because you're so famous and I'm an extra! Plus I'm an ugly and you keep seeing me wearing stupid robes or covered in slime and when we met I lied about my nose!"

Aya sputtered to a halt, wondering where all those words had come from. They'd just gushed out of her, like bubbly from a shaken bottle, fizzing and undrinkable.

"Wow," she said. "Is Radical Honesty contagious or something?"

"Sometimes." Frizz was grinning. "It's an unexpected benefit."

Aya felt herself blushing and tore her eyes from him, staring out at the soccer fields. Only a handful of warbodies remained standing, battering each other with plastic swords and battle-axes. "But *why* do you like me?"

He reached out and took her hand, and the reputation shivers became a tightness in Aya's chest, as if she were underwater again, holding her breath.

"When I first saw you outside that party, you were on a mission—very intense. And then your hood fell back, and I thought, 'Wow, she's pretty brave to wear that awesome nose.'"

Aya groaned. "But I'm not brave—I was just *born* with it. So it was a kind of truth-slanting for me to say it was randomly generated."

"True. But by the time I realized that, I knew other things about you."

"Like I'm an extra and live in an ugly dorm?" she said. "And mislead people about my huge nose?"

"That you sneak into tech-head parties and go on underwater rescue missions. And that you kick great stories, even though they don't bump your face rank."

She sighed. "Yeah, my stories are *really* good at doing that."

"Of course they are." He shrugged. "They're too interesting."

"That doesn't even make sense." She looked at him. "If they're so interesting, why isn't anyone interested?"

His eyescreen flickered. "Have you seen Nana Love's feed lately? She's been picking her outfit for the Thousand Faces Party. Today it's: 'This hat? Or *this* hat?' Seventy thousand votes so far, and there's a hundred other feeds running commentary."

Aya rolled her eyes. Nana was a natural-born pretty, one of the vanishingly rare people who wouldn't have needed surgery even back in the Prettytime. Which was why she was the second-most-famous person in the whole city. "That doesn't count. Nana-chan can be interesting without trying."

He smiled. "And you can't?"

She stared into his huge eyes, and for once they didn't tangle up her brain, as if some barrier between them had disappeared.

Suddenly Aya knew what she really wanted to ask him. "What's it like, being famous?"

Frizz shrugged. "Pretty much the same, except a lot more people joining my clique—and then leaving after a week."

"But before Radical Honesty got so big, didn't you ever feel like something was missing? Like looking at the city and feeling invisible? Or watching the feeds and almost crying, because you know all their names and they don't know yours? Feeling like you might disappear, because no one's heard of you?"

"Um, not really. Do you feel that way?"

"Of course! It's like that koan they tell in littlie school. If a tree falls and nobody's watching, then it doesn't make a sound, like one hand clapping. You have to be seen before you really exist!"

"Um, I think that's *two* koans, actually. And I'm not sure that's the point of either."

"But come on, Frizz! You haven't been famous that long, you must remember how horrible it was to . . ." Aya stammered to a halt, trying to read the look on his face. His radiant smile was gone.

"This is an odd conversation," he said.

Aya blinked. Ten minutes of Radical Honesty and already she'd been *too* honest.

"I'm being a total extra, aren't I?" She sighed. "Just sign me up for Radical Stupidity."

He laughed. "You're not stupid, Aya. And you're not invisible to me."

She tried to smile. "Just mysterious?"

"Well, not so much anymore. Verging on obvious."

"Obvious?"

"You know, about fame, and the way it makes you feel."

Aya swallowed. *Obvious*. That's what she was, in his radically honest opinion. Way too late, she remembered another thing they taught in littlie school: Complaining about your face rank to other extras was okay, but you didn't talk this way in front of anyone famous.

She turned away, staring out at the soccer fields, knowing that if she looked into Frizz's eyes again she'd say something else stupid. Or he'd blurt out more about what *he* was thinking, which would probably be worse. Maybe the feeds were right about differences in ambition, that big faces and extras should never get too close. There was too much opportunity for embarrassment.

The mech battle was over, and lifter drones were carting

off the last few warbodies. Littlies were lining up in front of Akira Hall for their next activity.

"Oh, crap," she said. "What time is it?"

"Almost noon."

"I have to go!" She jumped up. "Littlie-watching duty. I'd skip it, but . . ." *I need the merits*, she thought.

Frizz still sat cross-legged on the hoverboard, his face clouded. "It's okay. You shouldn't break promises."

Aya bowed good-bye, wondering if this time he was glad to see her running away. She tried to think of something to say, but it all sounded too embarrassing in her head.

So she called for Moggle and dashed toward the dorm, hoping she wasn't late.

INITIATION

Something was pinging. . . .

Aya emerged from a deep and sticky sleep, fighting dizzy-making waves of exhaustion. A noise was poking at her ears again and again, demanding her attention.

Even with her eyes closed, she could see a wake-up signal flashing in her eyescreen. It was blinking and making an earsplitting sound, warning her that it was almost midnight.

Aya squeezed a fist to silence the alarm, groaning. She'd meant to nap this afternoon, but thanks to her brain-damaging conversation with Frizz, the littlie-watching shift, and an hour spent spraying Moggle with black camo paint, she hadn't crawled into bed till ten.

Less than two hours' sleep.

But she forced herself to sit up, remembering how famous

tonight could make her. For a reminder, she glanced at her pathetic face rank of 451,611 in the corner of her vision.

Moggle rose from the floor, and the hovercam's point of view delicately overlaid her vision, a ghostly second sight perfectly balanced with her own.

Aya smiled. She wouldn't miss any eye-kicking shots tonight.

"Ready to go?" she whispered.

Moggle flashed its lights, and Aya winced. Thirty-six hours underwater hadn't cured the hovercam's bad habits.

She felt her way to the window, blinking away spots, and climbed onto the sill. Her eyes adjusted slowly, until the city lights made her throat tighten—the usual obscurity-panic, much worse now that she'd embarrassed herself in front of Frizz. All she'd meant to say was he didn't have to worry, because *she* was going to be famous too. But she'd wound up sounding as face-missing as a new ugly with her first feed. *Obvious,* he'd said.

It was pointless getting depressed about it, though. Fame wasn't like beauty, where you had to wait till you were sixteen, or get lucky like Nana Love and be born with it. Fame you could make yourself.

Once this story kicked, face rank wouldn't be an issue between her and Frizz anymore. She was certain of it.

Moggle drifted out the window, brushing against her shoulder, and Aya smiled as she wrapped her arms around the hovercam. She was glad to be headed somewhere away from the city lights. Someplace mysterious enough that Frizz would go back to being amazed at her, once he found out all the things she'd done.

She pushed out herself out into the cold night air.

*

"Before we get started," Jai said, "we have some business. First item is my name; someone's been talking about me where the city interface can hear."

A few of the Sly Girls looked down sheepishly.

Jai clicked at them with her tongue. "That's right. I woke up this morning and my face rank was almost out of the bottom thousand. That means the city's starting to track my nickname again. Time to change it."

Aya raised an eyebrow. So that was how they kept their face ranks down, by changing nicknames—the same way Ren and Hiro concealed their obsessive hatred of the Nameless One.

"From now on, my name is Kai. Everybody got that? Good. And now for item number two."

Kai turned toward Aya, who felt a tingle roll down her spine.

"Our new friend is with us again," Kai said. "Anybody got a problem with that?"

A nervous-making silence fell, and Aya heard the distant rumble of a train on its way. On either side of her, the rails glowed a soft warning, looking hot to the touch, like the elements inside the hole in the wall after it fabricated something big. But none of the Sly Girls seemed to notice, as if the middle of the mag-lev tracks was where they always held their business meetings.

Aya couldn't even use Moggle to keep watch for the train. The hovercam was somewhere out among the industrial buildings, stalking her, but she had its point of view turned off to keep telltale flickers from her eye.

"Isn't she a kicker?" someone muttered.

Kai looked at Aya, waiting for an answer.

She cleared her throat. "I used to be. But I was never a big face. I didn't feel like kicking what Nana Love was wearing." A few of them laughed.

"But you still go around with a hovercam?" someone else said. Her name was Pana, Aya remembered. With their generic faces, she had trouble telling the Sly Girls apart—but Pana was taller than the rest of them, nearly Eden's height.

"I let you drop it in a lake—you all saw that. Had some pretty awesome lifters on it, too."

"No cams tonight?" Kai said.

Aya shook her head. She was wearing the dorm uniform from the underwater rescue, which looked as scruffy as the Girls' reject clothing. She hoped its shabbiness made the spy-cam in its top button less obvious.

Moggle was more likely to give her away. She wasn't certain the hovercam's tiny brain understood the whole staying-hidden concept. Moggle could only track Aya's skintenna signal up to a kilometer, and it had never operated independently for hours at a time before, especially while chasing speeding mag-levs.

The distant rumble was audible now, the train a few minutes away.

"Aya-chan was pretty brave when we saw the freaks," Miki said. "And you all saw her surf. I trust her."

When Miki smiled, Aya felt her first unpleasant ping of deceitfulness. When she kicked this story, Frizz would know she'd lied to them all. She wondered if he'd understand.

"How about we hear from you, Aya-chan?" Kai asked. "Tell us why you want to be a Sly Girl."

Aya cleared her throat, nervous under Kai's plain-Jane stare, as brain-freezing as the train's rumble growing under her feet. What did they want her to say, anyway?

Suddenly, the words she'd said to Frizz that morning came back to her.

"Like you said, I was a kicker. Since I was a littlie, I wanted to be famous. I didn't want to watch other people on the feeds—I wanted them watching *me*. Because if they didn't, I was invisible."

A murmur went through the group, and Aya saw cold expressions everywhere. She kept talking, trying to ignore the tremors underfoot and the trickle of sweat rolling down her back.

"Don't get me wrong. I wasn't some ego-kicker, sitting in my room with a cam pointed at myself, talking about what my cat ate for breakfast." Someone laughed at that, and Aya managed a smile. "I was trying to find stories that mattered. People who were using the mind-rain to do something really kick . . . I mean, really interesting. That's how I found you."

Aya was looking back at them now, meeting their stares one by one.

"And here's what I realized: You Sly Girls don't cry when you watch the big-face parties on the feeds, just because you weren't invited. You don't stay friends with people you hate, just to bump your face rank. And even though nobody knows what you're doing out here, you don't feel invisible at all. Do you?"

No one answered, but they were listening.

"Fame is radically stupid, that's all. So I want to try something else."

There was a silent, nervous-making moment . . . and then the tension broke. A few girls clapped, only half-sarcastically, and Miki was grinning, nodding slowly. Aya had somehow found the right words.

The strange thing was, it hadn't even felt like lying.

They didn't bother with a vote, and no one congratulated her. Kai just slapped Aya on the back and jumped onto her hoverboard, shouting, "Surf's up! Let's go find out what those freaks are hiding!"

Then the thirteen of them were spinning into the air, rushing to reach their hiding places before the train thundered into view.

Just like that, Aya Fuse was a Sly Girl.

She wondered if Moggle had gotten the shot.

TURBULENCE

Catching the mag-lev was easier the second time.

She slipped through its shock wave like a needle, as if her body had learned to roll with the bumps and shudders of the air. Once inside the calm slipstream, she was on the roof and standing before the mag-lev line began to straighten.

The city fell behind, and as the darkness of the wild wrapped itself around the train, Aya began to realize how many sights she'd missed on her first panicked ride. Huge old trees shot past, as gnarled as some immortal crumbly. Silhouetted flocks of birds rose up against the sky, scattered by the train's thundering passage. Once Aya recognized a snow monkey's scream in the roar of the wind—hardly dangerous and person-eating, but the thought of untamed animals out here sent a nervous shudder through her. Or maybe that was just the cold. Even wrapped inside two dorm jackets, a three-hundred-klick wind was shiver-making.

The ride was all contrasts: the dead-straight mag-lev

line bisecting the knotted shapes of the forest; her fierce speed under the stillness of the sky; the mountains rising at a stately pace, punctuated by the nervous-making glimmer of decapitation warnings. But Aya felt the strange contentment again, as if her own troubles were an afterthought in the vastness of the wild.

The only worrying thing was Moggle. Even tracking her skintenna signal, the hovercam had to be falling farther behind with every minute. Ren's lifters couldn't fly more than a hundred klicks an hour—a third of the train's speed. Moggle would catch up once they jumped off, but Aya wasn't sure how long its little brain could function without her instructions. If it got confused enough, the hovercam might forget all about staying out of sight, and that would end Aya Fuse's career as a Sly Girl.

Of course, there was nothing she could do about that now—she was stuck with deception. She wondered if that was why Frizz had come up with Radical Honesty. If you never lied, you'd never feel this trickle of dread in your stomach, the worry of being unmasked.

The mountains grew closer, until Aya could see that their black peaks were marbled with snow, like slivers of pearl glistening in the moonlight. A red flicker came from the front of the train, then a string of decapitation warnings. Aya pulled out her own flashlight and twisted it red, waving to the Girls behind her.

She knelt to strap a crash bracelet around her ankle, then lay flat, waiting for the sudden darkness of the tunnel to swallow her.

This time there were no unscheduled stops.

The train shot straight through the mountain, in and

out in a roaring fury that made Aya's ears pop like a quick hovercar descent. The hidden doorway must have flashed past in a fraction of a second, utterly invisible.

She remembered from her first ride that the next bend came up quickly. Ahead of her, Miki was already crawling toward the side of the train, readying to dismount. Aya headed toward where her hoverboard was stuck.

Getting off the train was trickier than getting on. In the city the grid was everywhere, but out here you had to stay close to the tracks. Too far out and magnetic lifters lost their grip on the metal, making boards and crash bracelets useless.

At two hundred klicks an hour, that would be deadly.

The train was slowing, a hum filling the air as it angled into the turn. Aya pulled her right wrist free, reaching out to slap it against her hoverboard.

The night before, she'd dismounted too cautiously, winding up much farther down the track than the rest of the Girls. This time she'd decided to be the first one to a dead stop.

Aya tugged at her board, and it released itself from the train, slowly turning from sideways to level. It fought the wind, steadying as the mag-lev slowed into the bend, and she slid her weight across onto the riding surface.

As the humming reached its crescendo, Aya angled gently away from the train, staying within arm's reach, inside the bubble of relative calm that flowed around it. Two meters out was the deadly shock wave zone.

The rushing wind thrashed at her hair, whipping the jackets into a frenzy, but Aya didn't lie flat—she let her body slow her down. The Sly Girl who'd been surfing just behind her shot past on her board, then another went by, then a third.

She was braking faster than all of them!

To her left the train's flank was thundering past now, its magnetic field sending shudders through the hoverboard. Aya fought to keep steady, keeping close to the flashing metal wall of the train.

But maybe she was braking *too* quickly. . . .

The rear of the train shot past, its wake yanking Aya into the suddenly empty space over the tracks now. Her board spun, earth and sky whirling around her.

She tried to pull herself flat, but the board bucked and twisted in her grip, like a kite in a gale.

"Let go!" someone shouted.

Aya obeyed—the board tumbled away from her. She fell toward the blur of metal tracks. . . .

The magnets in her crash bracelets kicked in, yanking her up by both wrists. She flipped once head over heels, like a gymnast swinging from two rings, her feet barely missing the ground. She hover-bounced down the mag-lev tracks that way until her momentum was expended.

The bracelets set her down gently, facing the receding lights of the train. She rubbed her wrists, dizzy from spinning.

"You okay?"

Aya looked up to find Eden Maru floating beside her, an amused expression on her face.

"I think so," Aya said.

"You shouldn't brake that fast."

"I noticed." Aya sighed. The night before, she'd watched Eden dismount from the train. In her full hoverball rig she made it look easy, like rolling off a building in a bungee jacket. "Thanks for telling me to let go, I guess."

"You're welcome, I guess." Eden glanced down the tracks toward the receding train. "Your board will be back soon, along with the others. Slowing down takes longer if you don't wipe out."

Aya glared back at Eden's smile. She was so beautiful, and the only one of the Sly Girls with a big face rank. What did someone so famous get out of skulking around with a secret clique?

Maybe now was the time to find out. Aya straightened her uniform, angling the spy-cam toward Eden. "Can I ask you a question?"

"If it's not too nosey."

"You're not like the rest of them . . . I mean, the rest of *us*. You're a big face in the city."

Eden did a slow midair spin. "That's not a question."

"I guess not." Aya remembered the rumors about Eden's ex-boyfriend. "But don't you and the Sly Girls have sort of a . . . difference in ambition? You're a hoverball star, and they work so hard to be extras."

Eden snorted. "You would ask something lame like that. I bet you don't even know where that word comes from."

"Extras?" Aya shrugged. "It just means extra people, like superfluous."

"That's what they teach at littlie school. But it had a different meaning back in Rusty times."

"Well, sure," Aya said. "They had billions of extras back then."

Eden shook her head. "It had nothing to do with overpopulation, Aya-chan. You've seen old wallscreen movies, right?"

"Of course. That was how Rusties got famous."

"Yeah, but here's a weird thing: Rusty software wasn't smart enough to make backgrounds, so they had to build everything in the movie. They had whole fake cities for the actors to walk around in."

"Fake *cities*?" Aya said. "Wow, talk about waste."

"And to fill these fake cities, they hired hundreds of real people to walk around. But they weren't in the story *at all*. Just in the background. And they were called extras."

Aya raised an eyebrow, not sure if she believed any of this. It all sounded so crazy and out of proportion . . . which was, of course, very Rusty.

"Isn't that how you feel sometimes, Aya-chan?" Eden said. "Like there's a big story going on, and you're stuck in the background?"

"Everyone feels that way sometimes, I guess."

"And you'd do *anything* to make yourself feel bigger, wouldn't you? Even betray your friends?"

Aya set her jaw. "I'm a Sly Girl now, Eden. Didn't you hear?"

"Yeah, I head your little speech." Eden floated higher, looming over her like a giant. "I just hope you were telling the truth, because real life's not like some Rusty movie, Aya-chan. There's not just one big story that makes the rest of us disappear."

Aya narrowed her eyes. "But you're not in the background. You're famous!"

"You can disappear in front of a crowd, too, you know. Once they start telling you what to do, who to be friends with." Eden spun head over heels, a graceful version of Aya in her crash bracelets. "Out here with the Sly Girls, I get to keep something for myself."

Aya heard a burst of laughter—the other Sly Girls were gliding toward them down the tracks. She only had time for one more question.

"So if you don't care about face rank, why did you break up with your boyfriend?"

"Who says I broke up with *him*?"

"A hundred or so feeds, last time I looked."

"Don't always believe the feeds, Aya. He's the one who couldn't stand people talking about our 'difference in ambition.' So the little moron ran away."

Eden floated a few centimeters lower, reaching out one finger till it was almost touching Aya's nose.

"And that, my Nosey-chan, is what being an extra *really* means."

THE MOUNTAIN

As they approached the tunnel mouth, a few of the Sly Girls pulled out flashlights. Beams of red played across the opening, barely piercing the darkness within.

At least Aya wasn't the only one without infrared.

"What happens if a train comes while we're in there?" Pana asked.

Kai shrugged. "Just lie flat on your board, up by the ceiling."

Eden shook her head. "That won't work. The train's wake would pull you down." She hooked her thumb at Aya. "Sort of like what happened to Nosey-chan here."

A few of them laughed. On the way back to the mountain, Eden had demonstrated Aya's hover-bounce down the tracks. Several times.

"Well, it doesn't matter anyway," Kai said. "There aren't any more trains scheduled tonight."

"Don't they run *unscheduled* trains sometimes?" Pana said.

Kai rolled her eyes. "Maybe once a month. Hardly nervous-making, compared to what we do most nights. Come on!"

She and Eden shot forward into the tunnel mouth. A few of the other Sly Girls stood motionless for a moment, staring after them unhappily.

Aya twisted her flashlight on and urged her board forward. Eden Maru was suspicious of her already; she wasn't about to give the rest of them any reason for doubt.

A one-in-thirty chance wasn't *that* bad.

In the red light of her beam, dust swirled across the tracks, still unsettled from the train's passage. A low moan filled the blackness, and her skin prickled. A steady breeze moved through the tunnel, as if the stone walls themselves were breathing.

Aya wondered how they were supposed to find the hidden door. Last night it had looked exactly like the tunnel wall. Maybe surged eyes or Moggle's fancy lenses could tell smart matter and stone apart, but Aya doubted that her normal human vision would be much help.

Miki was already drifting down the tunnel, a flashlight in one hand. She slid her fingers across the wall's surface, peering closely at the stone.

Aya brought her hoverboard alongside. "No infrared, huh?"

"No," Miki sighed. "How about you?"

Aya shook her head. "My crumblies won't let me. But you're sixteen, aren't you?"

"Yeah, but I like my eyeballs."

"They can make them look exactly the same, you know."

"But I like *my* eyeballs, not an imitation of them. I know that's sort of pre-Rusty."

Aya shrugged. "My brother kicked this natural-body clique who never surge. Some of them have to wear these things like sunglasses just to see, even when they're not out in the sun!"

Miki narrowed her eyes. "Your brother's famous, isn't he?"

"I guess," Aya said, suddenly wishing she hadn't brought up kicking.

"That's why you became a kicker, isn't it? Because of him?"

"That's what Hiro thinks, like I worship him or something. But he's actually an advertisement for *not* being famous. It turned him into a big snob."

Miki laughed. "You don't have to run your brother down, Aya-chan, just because he's a big face. We don't hate kickers—we just don't want anyone kicking *us*."

"Yeah, I get it." Aya shifted on her board, aligning the button camera again. "But a lot of people would love to see us surf, wouldn't they?"

"Yeah, but then *everyone* would start mag-lev surfing, and the wardens would get involved." Miki shook her head. "We have to keep this trick ours. You understand that, right?"

"Of course!" Aya insisted, but Miki was still frowning. Maybe it was time to switch gears. "By the way, thanks for sticking up for me."

"No problem. Like I said, I trust you."

Aya turned to study the wall closely, the nervous trickle starting in her stomach again. "Yeah. But I still owe you one."

A tapping sound came from ahead, and they both looked up.

It was Kai, striking the wall with her flashlight as she

slid through the air. Her blows echoed down the tunnel, the stone sounding as solid as a mountain.

"So that's our plan for finding the secret door?" Aya said softly. "Banging on the wall?"

"Do you think they could program smart matter to *sound* like stone?"

"Probably," Aya answered. Ren always said you could program smart matter to do practically anything. It was one of the big inventions since the mind-rain, like AI and internal eyescreens, innovations that the Prettytime had postponed for centuries. "But why would they bother? Whoever made that door wouldn't expect anyone to walk around down here looking for it."

Miki tapped her own flashlight against the stone—it sounded like solid rock. "So if it hadn't been for us mag-lev surfing, no one would ever have found that door." She smiled. "Maybe it's like the Youngblood cults say: Being crim can change the world."

Aya turned toward her, making sure the button cam had a shot. "And how does finding this door change the world?"

"Well . . . I guess that depends on what's inside." Miki tapped the stone. "I mean, what if there's something really scary hidden down here?"

"Like a secret toxic waste dump?" Aya smiled. "Think how many merits the Good Citizen Committee would give us for uncovering it."

"Don't say that too loud, Aya-chan. Kai hates merits even more than fame." Miki tapped the wall again. "But thanks for mentioning toxic waste. That should distract me from the unscheduled train I've been imagining."

"Hey, Eden!" someone called. "Come here!"

Ahead, a small cluster of Girls had gathered around a section of the wall, all tapping with their flashlights. Aya and Miki glanced at each other, then urged their boards farther into the tunnel.

As they grew closer, Aya listened hard. Was there was something hollow about the echoing blows?

"Let me past, Nosey," Eden Maru's voice came from behind her.

As Aya slid aside, she saw the device in Eden's hands and her heart began to race. It was a matter hacker.

This wasn't just tricks; this was really illegal. Matter hackers could reprogram smart matter any way you wanted—there were whole *buildings* you could hack to the ground if you were crazy enough.

And all she had was this stupid button camera. Shots of an illicit matter hacker would be a total eye-kick.

Aya peered ahead into the darkness, hoping that Moggle was lurking somewhere close. She was dying to check for a signal, but her eyescreen's flicker would be a dead giveaway in the blackness of the tunnel.

The cluster of Sly Girls parted for Eden, all eyes on the small device in her hands. She pressed it against the wall, fingers running over the controls.

After a moment, she nodded. "This is it. Stand back—there could be anything behind there."

"Or any*one*," Miki murmured.

Aya thought of the inhuman figures again, their strange faces and long, thin fingers. "But those body-crazy freaks were just storing something down here," she said. "Nobody *lives* in this place."

Miki shrugged. "I guess we're about to find out."

A humming filled the tunnel as the clever molecules

of smart matter began to rearrange themselves—the wall rippled, its texture changing from rough stone to the pearly sheen of plastic. The door's shape came into focus, a rectangle the exact size of a mag-lev cargo door.

Then the wall began to peel aside, one layer after another, like water sliding across a flat surface. Just as it had the night before, the air tasted tremulous, like a thunderstorm was coming.

The tremors traveled along Aya's skin, as if the matter hacker was changing her as well. . . .

The last layer slipped away, and the door stood open wide before them. A long hallway stretched out ahead, lit with an orange glow.

"Now this is *very* sly," Kai said, and stepped inside.

THE HIDDEN

The Sly Girls dashed ahead into the mountain hideaway, everyone wanting to be the first to discover what wonders were hidden here. Calls and laughter filled the air, echoing from the bare stone walls.

Aya couldn't see a single right angle, just arches and rounded corners. Every few meters, oval doorways led away to more winding halls, an undulating maze cut into stone.

"Well, whoever lives here is definitely moving out," Miki said.

Aya nodded. The main hallway was crowded with equipment and storage containers, a disorganized jumble covered with a fine layer of dust.

"Maybe we should look for those big metal cylinders,"

she said. "Those were the only things they were moving *in* last night."

"As long as whatever we find isn't alive." Miki gestured toward a bunch of work chairs crammed together in the hallway. They were the wrong shape—too high and narrow, suited for some inhuman form.

Aya shone her flashlight down at her feet. A meter-wide path of metal studs glistened from the stone floor, leading straight down the middle of the main hallway. "That's to give hover-lifters something to push against. Anything heavy would have to go this way. Come on."

The two of them followed the metal path with careful, silent footsteps. The arched doorways revealed empty rooms, dust patterns on the floor showing where furniture had been removed.

As they went deeper into the mountain, the echoes of the other girls' voices grew faint around them. Aya wondered how so many tons of rock had been carried away to make this place. Whoever had built it must have tricked the automatic mag-lev trains into taking a lot of cargo for them. Or maybe one of the city governments was involved—this all seemed too big to do on the sly.

Every city had expanded since the mind-rain, pulling the Rusty ruins apart for scrap, scrambling to get more metal.

"Who has the resources to build something like this?" Aya murmured.

"Maybe this was one of those Rusty places where they dug up metal. What were they called . . . mines?"

Aya realized that they were whispering. Noises reverberated sharply against the bare stone walls, making her conscious of every sound she made.

The long, sleep-missing day was finally catching up with her, a brain-fogging exhaustion erasing the excitement that had propelled her through the mag-lev ride. The dim orange lighting was playing tricks on her eyes. Long shadows leaped from the beams of their flashlights, and Aya doubted her button cam was getting any decent shots.

Suddenly Miki spun around. "Did you see that?"

"See what?"

"I don't know." Miki pointed her flashlight down the hall behind them. "The shadows were moving funny. Like something's following us."

"Some*thing*?" Aya said, turning to stare into the darkness. She felt totally awake now.

"Maybe I'm just imagining it."

Aya sighed. "Great. Now I'm imagining it too."

"Come on," Miki said. "I feel like we're getting close to something."

"Is that the same something that's following us? Or a different something?"

Miki shrugged, and moved ahead.

In the next room, the path of metal studs led to a large opening in the wall and a set of stairs leading down. There were no orange worklights below, only blackness.

Aya came to a halt. "Maybe we should call the others."

"You want Kai to think you're scared of the dark?" Miki snorted, and headed down the stairs.

Aya sighed, then followed.

As they descended, the echoes of their footsteps began to lengthen, a larger space opening up around them. Aya's flashlight played across high arches, like the stone roof of the giant reservoir below the city. For a moment she wondered if the entire mountain had been hollowed out to capture runoff during the rainy season—but why would people building a storm drain look so weird?

Then her flashlight found the cylinders. The room was full of them, in neat ranks like hulking metal soldiers on parade, stretching into the darkness.

"Okay, we found them," Miki whispered. "But what *are* they?"

Aya shook her head. She walked up to the closest cylinder and pressed her palm against it: cold metal, its surface seamless. When she stood on tiptoe to look at its top, she found no sign of any seal.

"Looks like solid steel to me."

Miki walked past her, a host of shadows wheeling in unison to avoid the beam of her flashlight. Aya followed her deeper into the army of cylinders, looking for any clue as to what they might be. But the metal forms were unmarked and featureless, like giant pawns in an endless chess set, all exactly the same.

But wasn't there a metal *shortage* going on? This was enough steel to double the size of the city.

Miki came to a sudden halt. "There it is again."

"What?"

Miki turned and pointed her flashlight past Aya. "I saw a reflection in the metal. Someone's back there!"

Aya spun around, sweeping her flashlight across the ranks of cylinders. Shadows leaped and darted from its beam, but she saw nothing except the reflection of her own half-lit face, warped across the cylinders' smooth sides.

"Are you trying to scare me?" Aya hissed.

"No, I mean it," Miki whispered, her eyes wide in the red glow of their flashlights. "I'm going to get some help."

"Are you sure? Maybe we should . . . ," Aya started, but

Miki was already dashing toward the stairs, calling for the others.

Aya squinted into the darkness. Something flickered in the corner of her eye, but when she spun to face it, she saw nothing but shadows scattering from her wavering flashlight.

She took a few quick steps to the side, peering down the next row of metal cylinders. Still nothing.

Cries echoed down the stairs—the other girls answering Miki's shouts. They were coming, but not fast enough for Aya.

She began to walk back toward the stairs, checking nervously over her shoulder. Her flashlight swept from side to side, but that only made the long shadows dance and swivel around her, filling the room with furtive movements.

Then she saw it reflected in a row of smooth metal sides: a black silhouette smeared across them, darting through the shadows.

Aya froze, trying to work out which way the shape was moving, but it was like playing tag in a hall of mirrors.

"Miki!" she called. "I think it's . . ."

Her voice faded. The hovering shape had floated into view directly before her, the red flashlight reflecting a familiar pattern of tiny lenses.

It was Moggle.

ESCAPE

"Miki!" she shouted. "It's okay! I don't think there's anything—"

“Don’t worry, Aya-chan,” Miki’s voice called from halfway up the stairs. “They’re almost here!”

“Crap,” Aya muttered. She knelt, beckoning to the little hovercam. “Come here!”

It wavered for a moment—this new command contradicted its old orders to stay hidden. But when Aya called again, it scooted down the row of cylinders and shot into her arms.

“Hey, Moggle!” she whispered, stroking its sprayed-black plastic shell. “Good job finding me. But you need to be more careful.”

“Are you okay?” Miki’s shout came from above.

“I’m totally fine! But I don’t think anything’s down here!” Aya called back, then hissed, “We have to find a place to hide you.”

She switched off her flashlight and shoved it into a pocket, looking around for another exit. But the rows of featureless cylinders stretched endlessly into the darkness.

More shouts came from the top of the stairs. Miki was headed back down, a gaggle of flashlights bobbing behind her.

Aya ducked lower and headed away. The only light came from the Sly Girls descending the stairs, their red and yellow flashlights reflected in the smooth metal curves of the cylinders. Aya covered Moggle with the loose folds of her open jacket.

“When I let you go, find a place to hide. Understand?”

In answer, Moggle flashed its night-lights right into her face.

“Stop *doing* that!” Aya hissed, stumbling blindly to a halt.

“What was that?” Miki called. “Aya, where are you?”

Aya blinked away spots, standing up to peer across the

cylinder tops. The Sly Girls were fanning out randomly across the room.

But Eden Maru was rising into the air, her hoverball rig using the metal cylinders for lift. She flew swiftly across the ranks of cylinders, arms outstretched like the wings of a bird of prey. She would have serious infrared, of course—most intercity hoverball games were at night.

Aya swore, ducking lower and running as quickly as she dared. She had to get into another room.

But was there any way out of here?

Suddenly Moggle was tugging at her grip.

"Not yet!" she whispered, but the hovercam yanked itself free, pulling Aya off balance. It shot away through the ranks of cylinders like a cannonball.

Aya stumbled to a halt, squinting into the darkness, trying to see where the hovercam had disappeared.

"Lose your flashlight, Nosey?"

She looked up to find Eden Maru hovering just above her.

Aya tried to think of some excuse for putting her flashlight away, but failed. "Yeah, I sort of dropped it."

"Nice going." Eden's eyes scanned the darkness. "So what are we chasing, anyway?"

"Beats me." Aya shrugged, careful not to look in the direction Moggle had fled. "I think maybe Miki's seeing things."

"That doesn't sound like Miki," Eden murmured, her surged eyes scanning the cylinders. Her gaze came to rest in the direction Moggle had flown. "What's over there?"

Aya squinted into the darkness. The other Sly Girls' flashlights were growing closer now, and her unsurged eyes could just make out where the ranks of metal cylinders ended. She took a few steps closer, and saw a meter-wide circle of blackness—the mouth of a passageway.

Aya let out a silent sigh. Moggle must have decided to hide in there. Eden Maru was already on her way, gliding through the air.

"Maybe we should wait for the others," Aya called, jogging after her. "Whatever it is could be dangerous."

"I thought you said Miki was seeing things," Eden said. She landed in front of the circular hole and crawled inside.

As she ran to catch up, Aya realized that the opening was exactly the right size for one of the cylinders to pass through endwise. At its mouth, she felt the familiar pattern of inlaid studs beneath her palms, metal to carry the cylinders on hover-lifters.

Aya crawled after Eden as fast as she could. "Find anything?"

"Yeah. But it doesn't make sense."

A few of the Sly Girls had reached the tunnel entrance behind Aya. Flashlight beams flickered down the tunnel, revealing what Eden had discovered.

A thick metal door stood open, one small window glinting in its center.

Aya frowned. "That's the only door I've seen down here."

"You mean airlock," Eden said, pointing ahead. "There's another one up there."

"An *airlock*?" Aya shook her head. "Why would anyone have an airlock inside a mountain?"

But as they crawled farther, she saw more metal glinting ahead—another heavy door, standing open just like the first. She swallowed. If this really was an airlock, this tunnel *had* to be a dead end.

Which meant that Moggle was trapped.

"I better go first!" she said, pushing past Eden.

"But you can't even see!"

Aya ignored her, scrambling down the tunnel. At least she could warn Moggle that someone—judging from the echoing voices behind her, *everyone*—was coming.

"Moggle!" she said with the barest hiss of sound.

She slowed a little, trying to listen. Somehow the air felt different in here.

A step later Aya's foot twisted beneath her, coming down wrong on an uneven stretch of floor. She grunted, reaching her hands out ahead to steady herself. . . .

They touched nothingness.

And then Aya was rolling forward, falling into a void.

SHAFT

Aya dropped in absolute darkness, spinning head over heels into the mountain's depths.

She reached for her crash bracelets, hoping they would find enough metal to keep her from splattering. At the first twist, the bracelets found purchase, jerking her upright with a shoulder-wrenching snap. Her feet swung out with unspent momentum, and one cracked against solid stone.

Aya hung there stunned for a moment, pain sparkling against the solid blackness. As her head cleared, the echo of her own breathing pressed close around her. She swung her feet out—they connected with stone, pushing Aya backward into a wall of rock. The impact prized a cry of pain from her lungs.

"Quit kicking!" came Eden's voice from the darkness just above. Seconds later strong arms wrapped around her waist, lifting her up. The agony in her shoulders lessened a little.

"You okay, Nosey?" Eden said.

"I'll live. But maybe no more falling tonight."

"I hope you don't keep trying to get killed just to impress me."

Aya only grunted. As Eden carried her back up through the formless darkness, she felt the tingle of blood rushing back into her hands.

Eden set her down firmly on a ledge—the one she'd just plummeted off. "Maybe you should leave the exploring to people who can see in the dark. And can fly."

"Sure," Aya said, gingerly rubbing her shoulders. "And thanks."

"Thanks *again*, you mean."

Voices echoed around them—the other Sly Girls were headed down the tunnel.

"Slow down!" Eden shouted. "It's a trap . . . or something."

"Yeah, something," Aya muttered, pulling out her flashlight and leaning carefully over the shaft. It was circular, big enough across for the cylinders to travel down. The walls were striped with copper coils as thick as Aya's arm, laid into the stone under clear plastic.

The shaft also continued upward, past where her flashlight faded in the distance.

Moggle had certainly found an odd place to hide.

Eden grunted. "I see you found your flashlight, Nosey."

"Oh, yeah." Aya shrugged. "I guess it was in my pocket all the time."

Eden nodded slowly.

"You found something?" Kai's voice called. She pushed her way past the other Sly Girls crowding the tunnel, crawled to the edge of the shaft, and peered into its depths. "Wow. What *is* this?"

"I guess we're not sure," Eden said. "Are we, Nosey?"

"No clue," Aya said, rubbing her wrists. "But take it from me—don't jump down it."

Kai crouched there, her hands tracing the metal studs in the tunnel floor. She glanced back toward where the cylinders stood waiting in their rows.

"This must be where those big metal things wind up."

"I guess so," Aya said. "Maybe it's some kind of elevator."

"An elevator with an airlock?" Kai shook her head. "Not likely. Can you see the bottom?"

"No, but I can go there." Eden stepped off into the void, her hoverball rig's lifters catching before she fell even a centimeter. "Sorry to steal all the glory, Kai." Eden smiled as she dropped out of sight.

Aya watched her fall into the depths, hoping that Moggle had gone up rather than down. . . .

Kai turned to her. "What were you and Miki chasing, anyway?"

Aya shrugged, which sent a twinge of pain through her shoulders.

"You okay?"

"I've been using my crash bracelets a lot tonight."

"I noticed that." Kai chuckled. "I knew you were one of us, Aya-chan."

"Thanks." Aya smiled weakly—another dizzy-making wave of exhaustion was hitting. "But maybe I'll rest a minute. My adrenaline needs a recharge."

"No problem." Kai leaned out to peer down the shaft and sighed. "This could take a while."

*

Aya crawled past the other Sly Girls in the tunnel, waving off their questions, saying she needed a rest. She climbed out and made her way through the cylinders and to the stairs. Halfway up, she crouched down, booting her eyescreen.

"Moggle?" she whispered.

The hovercam's point of view appeared against the darkness. It took Aya's tired brain a moment to adjust to infrared, but Moggle was looking down.

The cluster of body-heat blobs below were the Sly Girls crowded at the shaft's edge. Eden Maru was a pinprick of light farther down, the lifters of her hoverball rig shimmering against cold stone.

Moggle had lucked out so far. Of course, Eden would explore the upper part of the shaft eventually.

"Keep climbing," she whispered. "And look for a way out."

The sides of the shaft passed by unchanging—thick copper coils every meter or so, no way in or out. But a subtle infrared glow came from directly over Moggle, a sliver of heat at the top of the shaft.

"Find out what's up there. But *don't* use your night-lights!"

Aya dimmed her eyescreen for a moment, checking to make sure no one had followed her. The room full of cylinders was still empty.

As Moggle climbed, its signal began to fritz, shimmers of static dancing across her eyes. The connection was punching through a lot of stone, and Aya wondered how long the shaft was. Her skintenna could only reach a kilometer without the city network helping.

By the time Moggle reached the top, Aya could barely see through the clouds of interference. The hovercam seemed to be in a transparent bubble; soft lights shone down through the rounded plastic walls.

They looked like . . . stars.

Aya moved a few steps up, and the static cleared for a moment. It was true: Moggle was looking out from the top of the mountain.

Suddenly the whole mountain range was laid out around her. Sharp peaks cut into the starry sky, and down in the valley the mag-lev's solar collectors glimmered with reflected starlight. Aya could even see the lights of the city glowing faintly in the distance.

But what was the point of carrying the cylinders up to the top of the mountain? There were simpler ways to move big hunks of metal, after all—lifting fans and heavy vehicles.

And why do it all from inside a mountain?

The signal fritzed again, and Aya shifted on the stairs until she found a better spot. When the image cleared, she frowned. Something glittered in the corner of her eye.

"Turn left a little, Moggle."

The view rotated to bring the mag-lev line in front of her, and Aya swallowed. The warning lights along the expanse of tracks were blinking. . . .

Then she saw it in the distance, a string of lights crawling silently from the city. An unlikely, maybe-once-a-month, unscheduled train was headed toward the tunnel.

And Kai had left the hidden door wide open.

AIR PRESSURE

"Stay up there until I call you," she whispered. "But be ready to move!"

Aya ran down the stairs, wondering what would happen if the train shot past the open doorway. Equipment and furniture were piled up around the entrance, along with a big stack of the Sly Girls' hoverboards.

Aya had felt with her own body what the wake of a speeding mag-lev train could do.

She ran through the cylinders, her reflection a blur in their smooth metal sides, her mind spinning. How was she supposed to explain how she *knew* a train was coming?

The mouth of the tunnel glowed with the Sly Girls' flashlights. They were sprawled around its entrance and down its length, crowding the narrow space.

"Out of my way!" She dove into the tunnel, crawling straight across the Girls, ignoring their annoyed shouts. "Everyone, listen! A train's coming!"

Silence fell, and Kai turned to peer at her. "What do you mean?"

"You know those unscheduled trains you weren't worried about? Well, one's headed toward us! It'll be here in a few minutes!"

Kai narrowed her eyes. "What makes you think that?"

"I was heading back toward the main door . . . to get a hoverboard. I thought maybe some of us could go down the shaft on one."

"You got all the way there and back in five minutes?"

"No . . . but halfway there I could feel the ground rumbling. Come *on*, Kai. We don't have time to lose!"

Kai hesitated, and a murmur of disbelief traveled through the tunnel.

Aya groaned, scrambling over more bodies and up to the edge of the shaft. "Eden . . . *a train's coming!*"

A few seconds later Eden Maru shot up into view. "A train? We didn't seal the door!"

"So what?" Kai said. "At that speed, who'll notice anything? Most mag-levs don't even have crews."

"But our boards! They'll get sucked into the slipstream, along with anything else that's not tied down!"

"And you didn't mention this before?" Kai cried.

"*You* said there wouldn't be any trains!"

"I said *probably*!"

"Just get out of my way!" Eden put her hands together like a diver, and shot down the crowded tunnel.

Instantly the narrow tunnel was full of scrambling bodies. The Sly Girls were shouting and shoving past one another, tumbling out to follow Eden back toward the entrance to the mountain.

Kai hesitated for a moment, her eyes fixed on Aya. "You sure you didn't just imagine this?"

Aya nodded, still breathless.

Kai swore and rose into a half crouch, scrambling after the others.

Aya waited until the sounds of pursuit faded away, then booted her eyescreen again. She lay against the stone floor, staring straight up into the blackness of the shaft.

There was nothing but air between her and Moggle now, the view from the mountain top crystal clear. The train was much closer, a bright string of pearls crawling along the flashing mag-lev line, only minutes away.

"Get down here fast, Moggle!" she said. "Don't hover—just drop!"

Moggle angled its lenses downward, and Aya watched the fall from the hovercam's point of view. The hot yellow infrared speck of her own head grew, faster and faster as

Moggle accelerated down the shaft, until she could see her own wide-eyed expression.

"Stop!" she shrieked.

The hovercam came to a perfect halt a few centimeters from her nose, and flashed its night-lights happily.

"It's nice to see you too. And ouch, blinded, etc." Aya scuttled down the narrow tunnel. "Follow me, but not too close. If we run into anyone else, remember to hide!"

Aya dashed through the stone warren of the hideout, following the metal studs back toward the entrance. That was how Moggle had found her, of course. Just like the cylinders, a hovercam could only travel along the metal path.

By the time she reached the main hallway, Aya was breathless from running, her heart pounding. Straight ahead, the crowd of Sly Girls was silhouetted by the entrance to the mag-lev tunnel.

Staggering to a halt, Aya felt the train's rumble beneath her feet.

"Any time now," Kai was saying.

"I'm *trying*!" Eden knelt by the doorway, the matter hacker clutched in one hand, the other flitting across its controls.

But the smart matter of the door wasn't moving.

Aya glanced over her shoulder and caught Moggle peeking out to get a shot. She smiled. Whether the door closed or not, whatever happened next was going to be very kickable.

"Everyone get set," Eden said. "Just in case."

Ahead of her, the Sly Girls linked crash bracelets to form a human chain. Not that it would help—if this loose furniture and equipment started flying around, they were all in trouble anyway.

Finally Eden Maru let out a grunt of triumph. The smart matter was rippling to life, its black tendrils beginning to weave across the opening.

But the train was already in the tunnel—Aya could *feel* it, her ears popping as the air squeezed toward them at three hundred klicks an hour. The rainy scent of the changing smart matter washed over her.

The rumble was building quickly now, whirlwinds of dust spinning madly in flashlight beams. The first layer of the door had stretched across the entrance, but it bulged out toward Eden, like a toy balloon squeezed between two hands.

If the door blew out, Aya wondered what would happen to the train. Would the sudden change in pressure be enough to blow it off its tracks?

Next to the bulging expanse, Eden was still twisting at the hacker's controls, yelling something drowned out by the roar of the train.

More layers slid into place. . . .

The thundering peaked, the piles of equipment all around Aya dancing across the floor. The smart-matter surface of the doorway was vibrating too fast to see, shimmering like a plucked guitar string.

After a long moment, the roar began to fade as the train slipped away.

The door hadn't collapsed; now that the train had passed, Aya couldn't even tell the smart matter apart from the stone.

As Eden slumped to the floor, Kai turned to the rest of them, a weary smile on her face. "Maybe that was enough fun for one night."

A tired murmur went through the others; maybe Aya wasn't the only one who'd gone sleep-missing the last couple of nights. The Sly Girls started sorting out their hoverboards, getting ready to head for home.

The only problem now was sneaking Moggle out.

"Hey, Kai," Aya called. "Can we borrow a few things?"

Kai looked around at the equipment cluttering the hall. "I suppose so. But don't make it too obvious someone's been here."

"In this mess?" Aya laughed. "They're stripping the place, not taking inventory."

Adding their assent, a few of the Sly Girls started poking through the equipment. With no face rank or merits, Aya realized, they couldn't do much requisitioning. The wallscreens and workstations lying around were tempting targets.

She walked quickly back to where Moggle was hiding, and picked a storage carton at random. Dumping the contents out—light pens and drawing tablets—she waved the hovercam inside. The plastic top sealed with an airtight *pop*, hiding Moggle completely.

At a twist of her crash bracelets, Aya's hoverboard made its way down the hall to her. She pressed the container against its riding surface, and felt the snap of Moggle's lifters gripping through plastic.

She was ready to go, carrying one hovercam full of very kickable shots.

"Pretty tricky, you knowing that train was coming."

She looked up to find Eden Maru floating above her.

Aya shrugged. "Not what I'd call tricky. The floor was rumbling."

"Funny thing, though," Eden said. "When I first got here,

I couldn't feel anything. Not till the train was much closer. But you noticed it from way back inside the mountain."

"Maybe it's that hoverball rig you're always wearing." Aya smiled. "You're not used to walking the Earth like us extras."

"Yeah, that must be it." Eden glanced down at Moggle's hiding place. "Find anything interesting?"

"Just light pens, stuff like that. Want one?"

Eden hesitated, then shook her head. "No thanks. I don't have to steal stuff. I'm famous, remember?"

"Sorry, I forgot."

Eden finally smiled. "Don't be sorry, Nosey-chan. It shows you're coming along."

She slapped Aya on her sore shoulder, then flew back to the matter hacker and began reopening the door.

SLIME QUEEN

Aya slept through her alarm the next morning, missing Advanced English and two kinds of math.

By the time she awoke, the sun was streaming into her window, a despair-making sight. Missed classes meant stacks of merits gone missing, enough damage to keep her at zero for a month.

But as she lay in bed, staring at the ceiling and rubbing the aches and bruises of last night's adventure, it occurred to Aya that merits wouldn't matter much longer. Once her Sly Girls story hit the feeds, she'd be too famous to bother with exams, dorm chores, and littlie-watching jobs—they'd all be as worthless as the moldy displays of Rusty money in the city museum.

A big face rank meant you didn't have to worry about impressing the Good Citizen Committee. All you had to do was stay famous, which, as ego-kickers liked to say, was much easier than getting that way in the first place.

Aya rubbed her eyes. She'd fallen asleep reviewing shots downloaded from Moggle and her button cam: hours of mag-lev surfing, mysterious tunnels, and hard-edged Sly Girls spilling the secrets of their clique. All of it very kickable.

It was almost too much to work with, more complicated than any story Aya had ever attempted before. Hiro always said that no matter how eye-kicking the shots, people got bored after ten minutes. How was she supposed to squeeze secret hideouts, skinny aliens, and crazy Sly Girl stunts down to that? She could do ten minutes on mag-lev surfing alone!

Of course, most shots of any story wound up in the background layer, so other kickers could use them later, or check to see if you were truth-slanting, like Rusty feeds always had. But if Aya was going to betray the Sly Girls, she owed it to them to show how amazing they really were, not hide their best tricks where only a few feed-addicts would ever see them.

Lying there, she wondered about breaking the story up into a series. Last summer Hiro had kicked a ten-part cycle about people hurting themselves to become famous: cutters, self-starvation, the people trying to grow tobacco to smoke. But the thought of creating something that intricate—weaving characters in and out, recapping themes without being repetitious—was too overwhelming.

The inhuman-looking figures were the worst part. Aliens were totally unbelievable, especially since Aya didn't have any shots of them. She might as well put unicorns in the story.

She turned her eyescreen on, and saw that Ren was at Hiro's. He'd know what to do, and maybe Hiro would even help, now that Aya could prove that the Sly Girls were real.

She was about to call Ren when her voice caught—hundreds of messages were spilling across her vision, almost all of them from strangers. For some reason she'd been ping-bashed the night before.

Then a familiar name caught her eye—Frizz Mizuno.

Aya hesitated. What if he was writing to say something radically honest, like he'd made a terrible mistake in liking her? Or that Aya Fuse was a face-missing extra that *nobody* would want to hang out with, much less someone famous and beautiful?

There was only one way to find out. She opened the ping.

> Swarmed by hovercams today!
> And I just figured out why.
> Oops . . . I'm so sorry.
> —Frizz

Aya frowned. Why was he apologizing, when she'd been the totally brain-missing one yesterday? And what did he mean about hovercams? Then she noticed that the ping ended with a feed kick, and a trickle of nerves started in her stomach.

She followed the kick, and one of the fashion-slammer feeds blossomed across her vision. . . .

The shot had been taken yesterday, right after she'd rescued Moggle. There she was in her dorm uniform, covered with muck and slime and talking to Frizz beside the Akira Hall soccer fields. Even through the grainy minicam lens he was as beautiful as ever, sitting cross-legged on his hoverboard. But Aya looked like she'd just crawled out of a sewer.

The caption read: *Who's the ugly making slime with Frizz Mizuno?*

Aya closed her eyes. Not this . . . not *now*.

The worst thing was, she should have known this would happen. Frizz had just started a new clique and was rocketing up the face ranks. Paparazzi cams probably trailed him everywhere, but she'd been so addled by his attention that being careful had never occurred to her.

Just when she was trying to stay incognito, here she was burning up the feeds.

Aya watched the shot again; at least you couldn't hear what she and Frizz were saying, and Moggle had been off chasing plastic missiles and war wheels.

And it was just a stupid slammer feed, the kind of story that Aya glanced at, laughed about, then promptly forgot every day. She should just ignore it. . . .

But for some reason Aya couldn't stop herself. She glanced through the shots in the background layer, dozens of them, all just as hideous. Of course, whoever had kicked them hadn't bothered to show her *after* she'd taken a shower. Where was the fun in that?

And the worst part was reading the web of conversations flowing outward from the images, a thousand joking captions and slams and stupid theories: that Radical Honesty surge had given Frizz some kind of brain damage, that he had a thing for big noses, that a new species of girlfriend had crawled from the sewers.

Late last night, an anonymous resident from Akira Hall had recognized Aya and rekicked to her feed, but by then the fact that she had a name hardly mattered. Everyone was having too much fun calling her "Slime Queen."

Aya lay back on her bed, wondering how people could be so integrity-challenged, sending hovercams to sneak shots of people. Like Ren had said yesterday, slammer feeds were for unkick idiots. Most of them were probably just jealous, annoyed that Frizz liked her, an ugly extra, instead of some other big face.

But no matter how much Aya dismissed them in her mind, it didn't help that they all were brain-missing and petty. For some reason, what they said still hurt.

A soft chime sounded in her ear, and she groaned—probably more ping-bashing from one of Slime Queen's new fans. But when the sender's name appeared, she sat bolt upright.

"Frizz?"

"Hey, Aya-chan. Um, have you seen the feeds this morning?"

She lay back down and sighed. "Yes. Slime Queen at your service."

"I'm so sorry, Aya. I haven't gotten used to this whole paparazzi thing yet. It didn't occur to me that—"

"It's not your fault, Frizz. *I* should have known better." She sighed. "Hiro's been famous since his first story. I knew the rules. I just forgot them when I saw you waiting for me."

There was a moment of silence, then he said, "That's happy-making, I suppose."

For the first time since waking up, Aya felt something besides the awfulness of being ambushed. At least Frizz wasn't calling to say how lame she was. "Yeah, I guess so."

"Why don't you come over? We can go on a picnic or something."

"I thought you were cam-swarmed."

"Totally, but so what?" Frizz said. "It's a chance for

people to see you without the, you know, slime factor." He giggled.

"But I can't. Remember that story I'm working on? It's still a secret."

"So we won't talk about it. It's not like I know anything."

"But the clique I'm kicking, they have this crazy brain condition about fame—they hate any whiff of it. If they see me out cam-grubbing with you, they're going to get suspicious."

"Suspicious of what? That you like picnics?"

"Frizz," Aya groaned. "I'm incognito, remember? The clique doesn't *know* I'm doing a story on them."

There was a long pause. "Wait a second . . . I thought it was just secret from other kickers, but it's secret from the clique, too?"

"Yeah. They don't know I'm a kicker."

"You mean you're doing the same thing to them that just happened to us? Taking shots without telling them?"

Aya's mouth opened, then shut again, her words tangling in her head. Finally all she managed was, "It's *completely* different!"

"How is it different?"

"I'm not slamming them, Frizz—I'm showing how kick they are! This story's going to make them famous!"

"But I thought you said they hated fame."

"They do but . . . ," Aya started, but her words got snarled again. Frizz's Radical Honesty was crazy-making! Sometimes it was like he was from some face-missing city.

"I need to think about this, Aya," he said softly.

"You need to . . . what?"

"Sorry, but it's strange for me, all this incognito stuff.

But it sounds like you have to stay clear of me anyway. So maybe we should back off a while."

For a moment Aya wanted to argue, or even to rush out and see him, hovercams or not. But she couldn't just blow her cover. Things were already bad enough with her name all over the feeds.

Maybe he was right about holding off for a few days, even if it was very unhappy-making to admit it.

"Are you sure, Frizz?"

"Yes. I need to think about this. It's hard to know what kind of person you are sometimes."

Aya clenched her fists, grasping for something to say. Now Frizz thought she was some brain-missing slammer! If only she could explain to him that this story was more important than the Sly Girls' privacy; whatever was hidden in that mountain could be dangerous.

But thanks to his Radical Honesty and his fame, anything she told him would be on the feeds the next day. She didn't dare.

Finally they said good-bye, and the connection went dead.

Aya lay there, deleting mocking pings, growing more miserable every second. Maybe avoiding Frizz was already pointless. What if one of the Sly Girls stumbled on the Slime Queen story? Would they blame Aya for her sudden spurt of fame? It wasn't her fault that Frizz was famous and beautiful and a total hovercam-magnet. . . .

Exactly the sort of boyfriend she would've killed to have a week ago.

Aya frowned, realizing that this was the first morning since littlie days that she hadn't checked her face rank—and for once it might have risen. She blanked the fashion-slammer feed, clearing away the meme-lines and gossip threads that cluttered her eyescreen, until she could see her little corner of shame.

She sat there for a moment, staring at it, not sure what to think.

Her face rank hovered at 26,213—much higher than she'd ever been before. At long last, Aya Fuse was famous.

For being slimy.

MASS DRIVER

There were hovercams lurking in front of Akira Hall.

The Slime Queen story was already fading—there were much bigger faces to slam in the city, after all—but Aya decided to be careful. A few more days of obscurity and she'd be happy with all the cam-swarming she got.

Arms wrapped around Moggle, she jumped out a fifth-story back window, landing hard in the dorm's new chrysanthemum garden. A monitor drone chirped at Aya angrily—she'd crushed a flower flat into the mud.

This wasn't going to be a good day for merits, it seemed.

"Get my board, Moggle," she said. "But don't let any of those cams see you."

Moggle spun away toward the hoverboard racks, pausing to peer around the corner. After last night's adventure, it was finally getting the hang of sneaking.

Aya scanned the forest as she waited, wondering if any paparazzi cams were hidden among the trees. Her skin prickled as she imagined being watched. Was this what it felt like being Kai? Skulking around all the time, nervous of any whiff of a reputation? It seemed like a paranoia-making way to live.

Moggle reappeared with her board in tow, and Aya jumped on.

"See you at Hiro's," she ordered.

Moggle flashed, then shot ahead into the forest, toward the famous part of town.

"Hey, Slime Queen!"

Aya groaned. "Let me in, Hiro. Someone might recognize me."

"But how could they? You're not wearing your raiment of slime."

"Hiro!"

More laughter, but finally the elevator door slid open, and she and Moggle slipped inside.

Hiro and Ren were still laughing when the door opened again. The two were splayed across the couch, playing a thumb-twitch game on Hiro's giant wallscreen. Explosions and the chatter of gunfire were making the strings of paper cranes rattle and dance.

"What are you two doing?" Aya shouted over the noise.

"The Nameless One just kicked some story slamming thumb-twitch games," Ren yelled. "So we've devoted ourselves to a day of war!"

She rolled her eyes. Hiro was still annoyed at the Nameless One for slamming the crumblies in his immortality story, calling them freaks and world-wreckers. "Isn't it kind of loud, though?"

"Sorry, Slime-sensei," Hiro yelled. "Nice work on your face rank, by the way. A few more appearances as Slime

Queen, and you'll get an invitation to the Thousand Faces Party!"

She scowled. "Aren't you the one who always says there's no bad fame?"

"No, that's the city interface," Hiro cried. "I'm against slime-fame!"

Ren giggled, falling to one side to coax his thumb-twitch character through some perilous maneuver.

"What are *you* laughing at, Ren?" Aya shouted. "You're the one who made me go underwater!"

"I didn't know you were going to talk to some big-face pretty boy on the way home."

"Neither did I!" Aya screamed over the explosions.

"Sure you didn't," Hiro answered. "Just like when we saw Frizz Mizuno's feed yesterday, and you had *no idea* who he was."

"I didn't know him yesterday. I didn't know his name, anyway. I'd just met him the night before . . . at this party."

Hiro frowned, then made a gesture. The wallscreen images froze, the sound abruptly shutting off. "Since when do *you* get invited to the same parties as Frizz Mizuno?"

"I wasn't exactly invited," Aya said. One of Hiro's eyebrows rose, and she groaned. "I crashed this tech-head bash, okay? I was looking for the Sly Girls."

"Oh, the imaginary Sly Girls again." Hiro let out a long sigh. "Why are you wasting your time with unicorns, Aya-chan?"

"They're not imaginary. Actually, I joined up with them last night."

"You joined the unicorns?" Hiro asked.

"The Sly Girls, you bubblehead. I even went surfing with them."

"What do you mean?" Ren asked.

"You guys haven't heard of mag-lev surfing?" Aya gestured, and Moggle started loading a stack of shots into Hiro's wallscreen. "Then you need to watch this."

Hiro started to say something, but the wallscreen was already flickering to life. He crossed his arms, staring in silence as Aya's night as a Sly Girl began to unfold.

When it was over, the first thing Hiro said was, "Mom and Dad will kill you."

Aya couldn't argue. Her parents didn't even approve of bungee jumping. She couldn't imagine what Mom was going to say after watching her mag-lev surf.

"Crumblies are the least of your worries," Ren said. "After you kick this, the wardens are going to visit."

"I know." Aya sighed. "That's the bad part about kicking this story. Nobody's ever going to mag-lev surf again."

"That's not what I mean," Ren said softly. "The wardens will forget all about surfing once they spot that mass driver."

Aya glanced at Hiro, but he looked as puzzled as she was.

"What's a mass driver?" she asked.

Ren stood and crossed to the wallscreen, rewinding the images with a twirl of his finger. He froze the shot where Moggle was climbing up the shaft, reached out, and pointed at the glint of metal embedded in the stone. "That's a copper coil, right?"

"I guess," Aya said. "Like in an electric motor?"

"Or a train track," Ren said. "Mag-levs have two kinds of magnets. The ones that levitate the train and the mass drivers."

"Which do what?" Aya asked.

"They move the train. As it glides along, the mass

drivers switch from negative to positive—pulling from in front, pushing from behind, sending it faster and faster. You can do the same thing straight up."

"So this shaft is like a mag-lev train that goes up and down?" Aya shrugged. "You mean it *is* an elevator?"

Ren shook his head. "This could accelerate a thousand times faster than any elevator. You saw that airlock, right? If you suck all the air out of the shaft, you're accelerating through a vacuum. No friction at all—pure speed. With enough juice, a mass driver could throw you into orbit."

"But what's the *point*?" Hiro asked. "Why hide it in a mountain?"

Ren stared at the image of the copper coil. "That depends on what those cylinders are."

Aya shrugged. "They just looked like big hunks of metal."

"What if there's smart matter inside? They could change shape as they fly, make fins and wings to guide themselves to a target. Maybe even whip up a heat shield as they fall."

"No way, Ren." Hiro sat up straight. "The Nameless One is actually right—our thumb-twitch games have made you war-crazy!"

"Very funny, Hiro." Ren moved the image to a close-up of a cylinder. "Let me do some math. How big are they, Aya?"

"Um . . . maybe a meter across the top? And a little taller than me." Aya frowned. "What are you getting so excited about?"

"He's delusional," Hiro said.

"Let's say two meters tall." Ren's fingers twitched and spun, and numbers began cascading across the wallscreen image of the cylinder. "So the radius squared is a quarter of a meter, times pi is about point seven-five. Times two meters tall is one and a half. Hey, room? How much would one-and-a-half cubic meters of steel weigh?"

"What kind of steel?" the room asked.

"I don't care. Just round it off."

"Almost twelve tons."

"Twelve *tons*?" Ren took a step backward and fell into Hiro's feed-watching chair, staring wide-eyed at the screen.

"What's the big deal?" Aya asked softly.

Hiro leaned forward, the amused expression fading from his face. "Hey, room? How much energy would twelve tons of steel have if you dropped it from orbit?"

"From how high in orbit?" the room asked.

Hiro glanced at Ren, who shrugged and said, "Two hundred kilometers? Forget about air resistance and round it off."

The room hardly paused. "The object would land at two thousand meters per second, releasing twenty-four gigajoules, equal to six tons of TNT."

"Okay . . . that's not good," Hiro said.

"What's TNT?" Aya asked.

"These days, it's a unit of energy," Ren said. "But a long time ago, it was a chemical that Rusties used to make bombs."

"Bombs?" She swallowed. "Like when they used to shoot missiles at each other?"

"Wow, Slime Queen," Hiro said. "You catch on quick."

Ren nodded slowly. "This could be some kind of city killer."

"You're not serious." Aya remembered the Rusty weapons that had destroyed whole cities in seconds, burning the sky and leaving the ground poisoned for decades. "But city killers had warheads. Those cylinders are just solid steel!"

"Yeah, Aya, and the dinosaurs were wiped out by iron," Ren said. "Iron *falling from space*. These things wouldn't come down randomly. The smart matter could split them into slivers, one for every building in a city. How many of those cylinders did you say there were?"

"There were hundreds, Ren," she said softly.

"Thousands of tons?" he said. "With the metal shortage going on?"

Aya shook her head. "But aren't you guys jumping to conclusions? We don't even know if there's any smart matter inside."

"Maybe I can get you something to test them," Ren said.

"Would a matter hacker work?" Aya asked, and they both turned to stare at her. "Because the Sly Girls sort of, um . . . have one."

"Aya," Hiro said slowly. "Don't tell me you've been playing around with matter hackers."

"I never even touched it!"

"Aya! Matter hackers aren't just merit-losing illegal; they're going-to-*jail* illegal!"

"It's perfect, though," Ren said. "Just send a basic run command to one, and watch what it does."

"Ren!" Hiro shouted. "No way is my little sister spending another second with those Sly Girls. Do you want my mom and dad to kill me?"

Ren turned to her. "If you don't want to go, Aya, I'll try to get in there. But it's your story. . . ."

Aya didn't answer at first, staring at the tangle of math on the screen, remembering when she was ten years old. Her entire littlie class had been loaded into hovercars and taken to an ancient ruin from the Rusty's second global war.

A burned-out shell of a dome rose up from shattered walls with empty windows, marking where a hundred thousand people had died in one quick flash. She hadn't believed it possible, not even of the Rusties.

But it looked like someone was following in their footsteps.

"Sorry, Hiro, but I have to," she said. "The end of the world isn't something we can kick halfway."

Part II

CITY KILLERS

Lurking behind every chance to be made whole by fame is the axman of further dismemberment.

—Leo Braudy, *The Frenzy of Renown*

BANNED

The Sly Girls were not pleased with Slime Queen.

It turned out that Kai watched the others' face ranks as closely as her own. Aya's sudden jump from obscurity to mild fame hadn't escaped her notice. After several pings back and forth, Kai admitted that *maybe* it wasn't entirely Aya's fault, but it was still a problem.

No hovercam-magnets allowed.

So Aya was banned from the Sly Girls, at least until her face rank fell back into six figures.

At first Aya thought the delay would drive her crazy. Here she was, a huge story finally in her grasp, and she had to wait for a bunch of nobodies to stop making fun of her about nothing.

On top of that, Aya didn't dare hang out with Frizz until this was all over. If anyone spotted them together, another wave of Slime Queen slamming would erupt, driving her face rank back up.

But as the days passed, waiting turned out not to be so bad.

Aya stayed in her room, avoiding classes by claiming that her underground lake chill had worn her out. She took all her old stories down from her feed for a week, and only answered pings from Hiro, Ren, and Kai. And gradually Aya Fuse (and her alter ego, Slime Queen) began to disappear, her face rank dropping thousands every day.

The strangest part was not having a feed. For the last two years, everything important to Aya had been stored there: images, stories, class schedules, and grades. Lists of everything she did and thought and wanted, and of all her friends and enemies. Even if hardly anyone ever looked at it, blanking her own feed was like erasing part of herself.

Fortunately Aya had plenty to keep her occupied.

It took a whole week to edit a rough draft, making sure to conceal the awful truth until the end, yet still revealing enough to keep people watching. It was the longest story she'd ever kicked—almost twenty whole minutes. Hiro told her to shorten every version he saw, but Aya wasn't worried about anyone getting bored.

The story had everything: eccentric outsiders, mysterious technology, eye-kicking shots of the wild, even a near miss with a mag-lev train. And of course, good old humanity trying to wreck the planet once again—all the promise and danger of the mind-rain wrapped up in one big kick.

The only thing she left out was the trio of inhuman figures she and Miki had seen. There weren't any shots of them, after all. And surely city-killing weapons were enough, without adding implausible aliens to the mix. She didn't even mention them to Hiro and Ren, who would probably just say she was believing in unicorns again.

She left a blank space at the end for the truth about the cylinders, once she'd proved Ren's theory about smart matter. But Aya was already convinced: The math all checked out, and she'd found out that the Rusties had also hollowed out mountains, places for their leaders to survive while the rest of the world crumbled. This was all an awful flashback to the ancient wars that had killed millions.

Maybe once they saw the truth, the Sly Girls would forgive her for kicking the story. Even Kai could understand that the safety of the world was more important than keeping a few tricks secret.

So Aya waited patiently, editing and reediting, putting up with Hiro's annoying comments, and giving Ren a whole minute to fill with the math of orbital mechanics and kinetic energy. That part was boring at first, but it ended with explosions—the perverse eye-kicks of buildings tumbling after their hoverstruts were ripped apart by slivers of half-molten metal.

And finally, after a long week, her face rank slipped back across a hundred thousand. Slime Queen was no more, and Aya Fuse became a Sly Girl one last time.

TESTING

"You're sure nothing followed you?" Kai called.

"Very," Aya said, skidding her hoverboard to a halt. Just to be certain, Moggle had stalked her all the way from Akira Hall, watching for any hovercams left over from Slime Queen's short reign. And to make doubly sure, Ren had sewn six spy-cams into her dorm jacket, facing in all directions, and none had spotted a thing.

"Where's everyone else?" asked Aya. Eden and Kai were the only Sly Girls waiting here at the edge of town.

"Taking the night off," Eden said. "It's a little windy for

surfing. But we thought you'd be game, since you've been on parole."

"Really?" Aya frowned. She'd noticed the wind on the way out, but it hadn't seemed that strong. "Thanks, I guess. I was getting pretty bored of my dorm room."

"That's what you get for hanging out with big faces." Kai laughed. "Maybe if you got that nose trimmed down, you wouldn't attract so many pretty boys."

Aya rolled her eyes. Her nose was too *pretty* now? "Whatever, Kai. I just want to get inside the mountain again. I've been doing some research, and I've got a theory about those cylinders."

"Can't wait to hear it," Eden said. "But I'm afraid you're a little behind."

"You mean you already know about them?" Aya asked softly.

Eden grinned and shook her head. "No, I just mean that Kai is *Lai* these days."

"It's a never-ending battle, staying obscure," Lai said. "But you know all about that now, don't you, Slime Queen?"

"Sure, Lai." Aya hid her relief with a glance over her shoulder. The rumble of the train was just beginning to build beneath her feet.

"Don't worry about being out of practice, Nosey," Lai said, smiling. "Mag-lev surfing's just like riding a hoverboard. You never forget."

The slipstream was worse than ever.

The wind grew stronger as the train neared the city's edge, and lying flat against her board, Aya could feel every tug and shudder in the air. The breeze was blowing straight across the arc of the turn, its energy blending with the turbulence of the train's passage, like two swift rivers merging into boiling rapids.

Her first contact with the slipstream knocked Aya into a barrel roll, spinning earth and sky around her. Only Eden's souped-up crash bracelets kept her hanging on, her fingers white-knuckled around the board's front end.

She struggled for control, wrestling the board level again. But every time she edged it toward the train, the tumult knocked her into another spin.

No wonder Lai and Eden had told the other Girls to stay home!

The train began to hum—it was straightening again, speeding up—and Aya gritted her teeth. No way was she spending another day locked in her dorm room, sitting on the biggest story since the mind-rain. . . .

She leaned hard to the left, yanking her hoverboard toward the train, willing it through the slipstream's barrier.

The board spun into another set of barrel rolls, but this time Aya didn't fight the spins. She let the world twist around her a dozen times, until the pattern of the track lights steadied. Then, letting the board's gyrations carry her, she rolled across the tumult.

In the calmer air, Aya wrestled her board back to level flight. Her head was still spinning, but the train stretched out beside her, as steady as a house.

She slipped up against its metal flank and climbed aboard.

A few meters ahead Lai and Eden were already standing, watching with amusement.

"Not bad," Lai called. "Maybe you're ready to learn some new tricks!"

The train was still speeding up, and Aya didn't answer,

scrambling to shift a crash bracelet to her ankle. She stood just as the train hit cruising speed, and the three of them rode in silence together, ducking decapitation hazards, the wild shooting past on either side.

Soon the mountains rose into view, their dark bulk a hundred times more ominous now that Aya knew what was inside.

Ren had sent her more math today: Only a mountain could hide a mass driver large enough to hurl a projectile into orbit. Conveniently, the atmosphere was thinner up around mountaintops—less air resistance for the cylinders once they left the shaft. Whoever had built this had thought long and hard about how to destroy the world.

As the dark peaks grew before her, Aya wondered for the first time if mind-rain slammers like the Nameless One were right. Maybe humanity really was too dangerous to be free. It was only three years since the cure, and already someone had built a weapon that would have made the Rusties proud.

At least the discovery made one thing easier: Once they realized what the mass driver was for, the Sly Girls would *have* to understand that they couldn't keep it secret anymore.

"So what's this theory of yours?" Lai asked.

"Well, it has to do with that stuff." Aya pointed her flashlight at the hidden door.

Eden Maru was kneeling beside it, the matter hacker in her hands, her fingers jumping across the controls. The tunnel was pitch-black except for Aya's flashlight—the other two had infrared—and the darkness around them came to life as the door began to hum.

"You mean smart matter?" Lai asked.

"Exactly." Aya swept her light across the surface, watching it ripple and undulate, smelling the scent of rain. "What if those cylinders are laced with it?"

Eden glanced over her shoulder at Lai, but neither said anything.

"That shaft Eden found looks like a mass driver to me," Aya continued. "And if the cylinders can change shape, they must be missiles of some kind."

For a moment there was no sound except the hum of smart matter, then Lai said, "You mean this whole mountain is a weapon?"

"Exactly. An old-fashioned, Rusty sort of weapon."

"Interesting theory." Eden watched the last layers of the door slip aside, revealing the orangey glow of the tunnel. "How sure are you about this?"

"Almost positive. I can prove it when we get to the cylinders."

They stepped inside, and Eden turned to close the hidden door again. As expected, Moggle would be trapped on the other side tonight. At least Aya had her spy-cams.

"Clever," Lai said. "But you're not the only one who's been clever this week."

Aya frowned. The two of them didn't even seem surprised. "This is serious, Lai. Those cylinders could take out a whole city. They're much deadlier than anything used in the Diego War."

"Maybe so, Nosey. But wait till you see what we've cooked up."

"But this could mean—"

"Aya, I said *wait*!"

The door rippled closed, and Aya fell silent. She'd

forgotten that Eden Maru was also a tech-head, a much more famous one than Ren. What had she and the Sly Girls been up to for the last week?

The three of them made their way down the stone hallways, through clutter and equipment. When they reached the cylinder room, Aya paused at the top of the stairs, letting her spy-cams take in the ranks of metal missiles.

"What's the matter, Nosey?" Eden said.

"If I can borrow the hacker for a minute, I'll show you something."

"It's not a toy," Eden warned.

"I know that. Just let me try something."

"Let her," Lai said. "This could be interesting."

Eden sighed, then handed Aya the device. It was heavier than it looked, its topside thick with controls and readouts. Ren had warned that it was one of the few machines deliberately designed to be tricky to use—no voice help, no handy instruction screen, as opaque and interface-missing as the Rusty gadgets in the city museum.

Aya made her way down the stairs and chose a cylinder at random. She pulled Ren's memory strip from her pocket and slid it into the hacker's reader.

"*You* wrote code for a matter hacker?" Eden snorted. "You're full of hidden talents, aren't you?"

Aya shrugged. She was tired of lying.

The hacker sprang to life, and she pressed it against the smooth metal flank of the cylinder. A hum filled the air, much lower than the sound of the hidden door. Like the rumble of a train approaching, but as smooth as a bow drawing across a cello string.

A scent filled the air. Just like when the door opened, she tasted rain and lightning.

The cylinder began to change, rolling slowly into another shape, like metal syrup poured into an invisible mold. First it transformed into a cone, its point rounded and colored pale white. Ren had said that would happen—the white part was made entirely of smart matter, a heat shield to protect it from burning up on the journey into orbit. Four stubby wings protruded from the sides, one reaching toward Aya like the pseudopod of some metal bacteria.

She stepped back, fascinated by the undulating shapes.

The wings shifted and turned, designed to use the upper atmosphere to guide the missile into the right orbit. Then the transformations came to a halt, like a liquid suddenly freezing in the cold, and the metal sat in front of them unmoving.

Maybe it was waiting for specific instructions, something beyond the simple command Ren had programmed.

"Is that it?" Lai said.

"I guess." Aya frowned. "But you saw those wings. That means it's a missile, right?"

Eden smiled. "That's what we figured. Nice proof of concept, though."

"You *knew*?" Aya cried.

Lai shrugged. "Once we'd realized the shaft was a mass driver, the rest was obvious. But I'll hand it to you, Aya, we didn't think of testing the cylinders. We were looking at the other half of the equation."

"What other half?"

"Come and see, Slime Queen."

Eden took her hand firmly, pulling her toward the entrance to the mass driver. The three of them clambered along the tunnel, through both airlocks, and to the edge of the shaft. Lai pointed down into the blackness.

"Notice anything new?"

Aya's flashlight faded before it reached the bottom. "I can't see a thing, Lai. I don't have infrared, remember?"

"Oh, right. Take a closer look then."

Lai placed one hand firmly in the middle of Aya's back, and pushed her off into the void.

SHAFTED

Eden Maru's crash bracelets must have been reprogrammed. They didn't jerk Aya to a halt this time, just slowed her fall, lowering her gently through the darkness.

For a panic-making moment, she wondered if Eden and Lai had discovered what she was, and were planning to leave her down here. Then she heard their giggles following her down the shaft.

"Very funny!" she called up.

Eden drifted past her, saying, "I hope you're not afraid of falling, Aya. That might be a problem."

"What's that supposed to mean?"

Eden didn't answer, just grabbed Aya's feet and guided her downward till they settled on a stone floor.

Aya rubbed one sore shoulder, pointing the flashlight with her other hand. The shaft was roomier down here, and a strange contraption stood in the center. It was four long-distance hoverboards crudely bound together with strips of metal, a tangle of industrial lifters crowding the space inside them.

"You didn't find this thing down here, did you? You built it."

“Of course. It’s my little sled.” Eden stroked the nearest hoverboard. “Bet you can’t wait to ride it.”

“Ride it? *Where?*”

Eden tugged on the chain around her neck, pulling a whistle from inside her hoverball rig. Puffing her cheeks, she blew a long, ear-kicking blast.

“Ouch!” Aya said, covering her ears too late. “A little warning, please?”

Lai settled to the ground next to her, giggling as she swung from her crash bracelets. An answering whistle blast came from above.

Aya looked up, and saw a tiny glimmer overhead. Moonlight.

“The opening was sealed, so they can pump the air out,” Lai said. “Of course, those cylinders can blow straight through plastic. But since *we’re* the projectile, I sent the Girls up to clear the way.”

“We’re the . . . ?” Aya started, then frowned. “But you said the others were taking the night off.”

“I lied,” Lai said with a sigh. “And lying is wrong, isn’t it?”

Aya looked at the sled. “Hang on, you haven’t gotten the mass driver to work, have you?”

“No way,” Eden said. “With juice in those coils, the acceleration would kill us. But there’s enough steel in the mass driver for hoverboards to push off. My little sled can go pretty fast.”

“Us? But what happens when we reach the end?”

“Inertia happens,” Lai said. “Flight happens. *Fun* happens.”

Aya’s jaw dropped. “What about when *gravity* happens? We could wind up hundreds of meters in the air!”

Eden shook her head. "Oh, much higher than that, Nosey-chan."

"But how's your little sled supposed to land? There's no grid out here. Those hoverboards will fall like rocks."

Lai smiled. "Don't you listen to the gossip about us, Nosey?"

She pointed at the floor. Aya's flashlight revealed four heavy bundles there, like backpacks full of laundry, bungee straps dangling from them.

Then Aya remembered Hiro's story about the Girls. The rumors of them jumping off bridges . . . wearing parachutes.

Homemade parachutes, because the hole in the wall wouldn't give you real ones.

"Oh, crap."

"Just don't pull the cord before you count to thirty," Eden said. "Night like this, the wind could carry you for hours if you pop your parachute too high."

"But I don't—"

"First time I did it," Lai said, "I wound up halfway to the ocean. Took me *hours* to hike back to the tracks."

Aya's head was throbbing. "You mean you've done this before?"

"Five times!" Lai announced, holding up a handful of outstretched fingers. "We've been practicing all week, getting it ready just for you!"

Aya stared up at the tiny glimmer of moonlight. "What do you mean, getting ready for *me*?"

Suddenly her crash bracelets booted, slamming her wrists against the contraption. She twisted and pulled, trying to demagnetize them, but they held firm.

"What are you doing?" she cried.

Eden lifted one of the backpacks and held it behind

Aya. Its straps came to life, coiling like snakes around her thighs and shoulders.

"Just making sure your story has a brain-rattling ending," Eden said.

Lai laughed. "We wouldn't want to disappoint your fans!"

"But I'm not a . . ." Aya's voice trailed off, and she slumped against the sled, all out of arguments. In a strange way, it was a relief that they'd learned the truth. "How did you know?"

"You think we're completely stupid, Nosey?" Eden said. "That we hadn't noticed you pumping me and Miki for information?"

"Or that we really believed you heard that train when it was fifty kilometers away?" Lai added. "What was that, a hovercam posted on the tracks?"

Aya shook her head, tears stinging her eyes. "No. Moggle was hiding at the top of the shaft."

"Oh, yes, Moggle." Lai laughed. "That was the final proof. Those slam shots of you and Frizz Mizuno."

"Me and Frizz? But Moggle wasn't anywhere near us!"

"Maybe not near you. But your little friend was off in the background in one, chasing plastic missiles and war wheels while you two made manga eyes at each other. I didn't even realize it was Moggle at first, till Eden noticed those big lifters on the bottom. Then we all started wondering why that particular hovercam wasn't at the bottom of a lake where it belonged."

"Okay, I'm a kicker, all right?" Aya swallowed. "What are you going to do to me?"

"Isn't it obvious?" Eden pulled the parachute straps tighter. "We're taking you on a joyride."

JOYRIDE

Lai and Eden strapped on backpacks of their own, then fastened the fourth parachute to the sled. They stood across from Aya, equally spaced around the contraption, facing each other like three littlies holding hands.

Aya felt a trickle of relief. At least they were coming with her on this joyride.

"How does that parachute feel, Nosey? Secure?"

Aya twisted her wrists; they didn't budge. "Very."

The parachute's straps were definitely borrowed from a bungee jacket; they adjusted as she moved, but stayed reassuringly tight around her arms and thighs. Still, Aya couldn't make herself forget that the jacket's lifters—useless out here in the wild—had been replaced with a big wad of silk.

Her life depended on a piece of *fabric*.

She vaguely remembered the theory: Parachutes had a much bigger surface area than you did, so you fell like a feather instead of a stone. *If* you didn't panic and forget to pull the cord, and *if* the homemade mechanism opened up without tangling. . . .

"You've really done this before?"

"Twenty-seven trips up the shaft altogether," Eden said. "Only one broken leg."

"That's comforting."

"Try to relax." Lai smiled. "One thing we learned from bridge-jumping: Only the nervous ones die."

"Are you . . . ?" Aya started, then realized she didn't want to know if Lai was kidding or not. Maybe that was the real reason why the Girls hated to be kicked: Tricks like this could go very, very wrong.

She tugged her crash bracelets one more time, but they felt welded to the frame of the sled.

Eden was already counting down. "Three . . . two . . . one . . ."

Aya had expected a jolt, but the launch was as smooth as any hoverboard takeoff. Soon, though, the sled was picking up speed, the copper rings blurring past them.

Aya squinted up at the tiny dot of moonlight. As the walls of the shaft shot past, a panic-making thought began to grow inside her. What if this was the Sly Girls' idea of an amusing way to get rid of her forever? What if she wasn't really wearing a parachute, but a backpack full of old laundry?

"You know why I had to lie to you, right?" she pleaded. "Can't you see how important this story is?"

"You were truth-slanting from the start, Nosey," Eden yelled over the wind. "Not trying to save the world, just trying to get famous."

Aya opened her mouth, but no words came. Whatever she'd told herself this last week, one truth remained: Her career as a Sly Girl had started as a lie.

Finally she managed, "I was mad at you for dropping Moggle."

"That was your choice," Lai said.

"Okay, I lied! But this is still important. People need to know about it."

Neither of them answered. The wind had torn her words away.

"This weapon could reach anywhere in the world!" she cried. "You have to let me—"

"Here we go!" Lai screamed.

Suddenly the world grew bright . . . they'd burst out

into moonlight! Aya's ears popped, her head ringing. She caught a split-second glimpse of cheering Girls on the mountaintop, but they streaked past in an instant, the whole horizon expanding around her.

"How's this for eye-kicking?" Lai yelled, her insane smile as radiant as any pretty's. "I hope you brought spy-cams!"

Aya squinted against the wind, astonished at how high they were climbing. Above them she saw a wisp of white catching the moonlight. It seemed to dissolve as they approached, turning to vague tendrils on every side.

She swallowed, looking around. They were actually climbing through the lowest clouds. . . .

The view was suddenly huge—an entire mountain range stretched around them, the mag-lev line cutting through it like a seam of silver.

Lai disconnected one hand and pointed down at the glimmer of solar panels on either side of the tracks. "That's where the mass driver gets its power, steals it from the mag-lev's solar array. Just pause all the trains, and you've got enough juice to toss a cylinder every minute."

Aya angled the spy-cam on her left shoulder to get the shot. This sequence would be more amazing than anything so far, as long as her parachute actually worked. . . .

Their ascent was slowing, the sky turning lazily overhead as the sled began to spin. A momentary dizziness passed over her.

"You're really going to let me kick this?" she asked.

"Of course," Eden said.

"But you'll never be able to come here again."

Lai laughed. "We Sly Girls happen to *like* the world, lucky for you. We may not be merit-grubbers, but death machines are bad for tricks!"

Aya looked down at the city lights on the horizon, trying to imagine countless tons of steel, aerodynamically shaped and precisely targeted, streaking from the outer reaches of the atmosphere.

Something shifted in her stomach. Suddenly, the sky seemed still around them except for the slow spin of the sled.

The wind had died completely.

"Um, are we falling now?"

"We're going down," Eden said. "But you're about to learn a new definition of falling, Aya-chan."

"Oh." Her stomach rebelled again, as if something were trying to push its way out—something that *didn't* want to be several kilometers up in the air with nothing but a backpack full of silk, two crazy people, and four useless hoverboards for company.

"Pay attention now, Aya," Eden shouted. "When you land, hike back to the mag-lev line, then call for a hoverboard with your bracelets. We left one waiting for you by the tracks."

Aya nodded, trying to stay focused. This was the brain-kicking ending her story needed, and she had only a few more seconds to wrap up loose threads.

"So what will you do, now that you're going to be famous?"

"We're leaving the city tonight," Lai said. The wind was building again, her hair streaming straight up, making her look even more deranged than usual. "We'll change our faces. That's why we gave you this ride, to give ourselves a head start."

Aya found she still couldn't believe it. "But don't you realize how much face you'll get for uncovering this? How many merits?"

"It's going to stir up more than merits." Lai pulled one

bracelet free, reached across the sled, and took Aya's hand in a firm grip. "You be careful."

"Don't worry. I'll count to thirty."

"No, I mean be careful *after* you kick this."

The sled was starting to spin faster as it fell, the sky and earth twisting around her. "Careful with *what*?"

"With everything and everyone!" Lai shouted over the wind. "Whoever built this monstrosity is dangerous!"

The sled was starting to tip now, rolling onto its side, the spin turning into a wild tumble.

"Speaking of dangerous, shouldn't we get off?" Aya asked, twisting at her crash bracelets.

"Just be careful!" Lai yelled. "And enjoy your fame!"

She planted a boot on Aya's chest, and shoved her away

Aya spun head over heels away from the sled, her breath knocked out of her. She was suddenly all alone, falling helplessly through the air. Even if it was just a bunch of useless hoverboards, at least she'd had *something* to cling to a moment ago.

Now it was just her and the rushing air.

Spreading out her arms, Aya tried to get control of her fall. She was supposed to count to thirty before pulling the cord. But was that from the top of the climb . . . or from when Lai had pushed her off?

And how many seconds had already passed?

Gradually Aya's descent steadied. But her eyes were streaming from the wind, the Earth a dark blur beneath her. If she popped the parachute too soon, she had no idea how far the wind might carry her.

She looked frantically around for the others and saw them ten meters away, clinging to the sled, Eden reaching inside to pull its chute cord. The two kicked away from it, and a rippling stream of fabric burst from the top.

The chute blossomed into shape, and the whole contraption shot upward into the darkness away from Lai and Eden.

The Earth below was growing visibly—Aya could see the Sly Girls now, their flashlights a circle around the mass driver's mouth.

Lai and Eden were a dozen meters away, still screaming their heads off, reveling in every second of their final jump. Aya realized that waiting for them to pull their cords might not be the best idea.

She stared down at the spinning Earth. It was growing faster now, trees and rocks and bushes shimmering into focus. She imagined herself hitting at full speed. . . .

And pulled the cord.

The parachute bloomed over her head, fluttering for a moment, then snapping into shape with an ear-kicking *pop*. The straps jerked her upright, like a puppet yanked from the floor by its strings.

A brief moment of violence . . . then suddenly the air was still around her.

The moon glowed hazily through translucent silk, and Aya could see the rectangular outlines of silk sheets and pillowcases that the Girls had sewn together. The mountainous panorama around her steadied.

Lai and Eden had already zoomed past, tendrils of their screams trailing behind. They dropped farther and farther away, arms outstretched as if rushing to embrace the mountain below.

Were they trying to kill themselves?

At the last second, chutes blossomed from their packs, pouring out in long streams, then billowing into shape.

Lai and Eden were still moving fast, though. The wind carried them sideways across the top of the mountain, the other Sly Girls scrambling behind. They coasted for a moment a few meters high, then dropped again, boots scraping through the dust and scrub, skidding to ungainly halts.

The other Girls reached them, swarming to gather the crumpled folds of their parachutes.

But Aya was still more than a hundred meters up. The wind seemed to strengthen, pulling her away from the opening of the mass driver. She passed over Lai and Eden, the parachute carrying her like a silken sail. The mountain's edge slipped past to reveal the valley below, and Aya realized she still had a very long way to fall.

This was why they'd picked such a windy night. It would be long minutes before she touched down, maybe hours before she could hike back to the mag-lev tracks. Plenty of time for them to make their own escape before she could even think of kicking the story.

Aya fixed her gaze on the bright silver streak of the mag-lev line. She swung her feet and pulled on the straps, trying to guide herself toward the tracks. But the parachute puffed up overhead, caught by another updraft.

It was going to be a long hike. For the moment, though, there was nothing to do but let her spy-cams take in the scenery and—slowly, slowly—fall.

Lai's final warning echoed in her ears, but Aya wasn't afraid. Once the story went to feed, none of this was her problem. Since the Diego War, the world had very strict rules about stockpiled weapons. The Global Concord Committee would swoop down within hours, pulling the mountain apart.

Someone was in big trouble.

But not Aya Fuse. Her biggest problem now was what to wear to Nana Love's Thousand Faces Party. Because with an ending like this, the City Killer story was going to make her *that* famous.

Maybe for the rest of her life.

KICKING IT

"You are *not* wearing that!"

"Why not?" Aya twisted the ringlets in her hair, which was puffed up like a manga-head's and dyed bright purple. Her dress was spattered with sparkle lights, and her shoes were variable-friction platforms—she'd skidded into Hiro's apartment like the floor was made of ice. She took two handfuls of the dress and spread it out, looking down at herself. "This outfit is totally kick!"

"Maybe if you're fifteen," Hiro muttered.

Aya rolled her eyes. "Well, I happen to *be* fifteen. And you can't tell me how to dress for this party. My story's the whole reason we're going!"

"Yeah, but I'm the one with the invitation, remember? You're just tagging along."

"For now," Aya said softly.

Tonight wasn't *the* party—the Thousand Faces was still a week away—this was just a monthly tech-head bash. But Ren had said Aya should be there tonight when her City Killer story kicked. Full of physics-heads and mag-lev spotters, the bash would spawn the interviews, feed wars, and rampant rekicking that every big story demanded.

"Whatever, Aya-chan. Just *please* don't visit Mom and Dad till those flash tattoos fade."

Aya stuck her tongue out at him, which made the spirals on her cheeks spin. The temporary tattoos still tickled when they moved, and she let out a giggle.

"Ren Machino," Hiro told the room, then asked, "Where *are* you?"

"Almost there," he pinged back.

"Just wait downstairs. We're almost out the door."

"What's the rush?" Ren sounded amused. "City Killer doesn't kick for an hour."

"I know. I've been staring at the clock all night."

"Clock-staring makes him grumpy," Aya cut in, spinning in place on her platforms. "It's *my* story, you know, and you don't see me getting all shaky."

Hiro sighed. "She refused to hide the sled sequence in the background layer, Ren. It's going to give my parents brain damage."

"And Hiro keeps forgetting whose story this is!" Aya said. "But don't worry. I keep reminding him."

Ren's laughter boomed. "I'll remind him too, Aya-chan!"

Hiro snorted, cut the connection with a snap of his fingers, and turned the giant wallscreen into a mirror. He'd borrowed one of their father's old formal jackets: black spider silk and real bamboo buttons. He didn't look half bad.

Aya skated across the room on her platforms, watching her dress trail sparkles in the wallscreen, Moggle tracking the motion. She'd paid for the dress with Hiro's reputation, but paying him back was going to be a cinch.

She didn't get why Hiro was so nervous. Tonight felt long overdue to Aya, more real than all the merit-grubbing and obscurity of her life so far. All that had merely been preparation for this . . . for fame.

Best of all, Frizz was coming to the bash. He still felt bad about the Slime Queen story, but tonight would banish all that awkwardness. Though Frizz didn't know it yet, Aya and he were finally going to be face-equal, not to mention headed to the Thousand Faces Party together next week.

"Stop skating around like that!" Hiro said. "You look like an ugly about to kick some pictures of your cat!"

She skidded to a halt. "Oh, no!"

"What? Did you forget an edit?"

"No, it's just that . . . maybe this story *would* be better with a cat!"

Hiro finally cracked a smile, then turned back to the mirror. "Actually, it's pretty much perfect, Aya-chan. Even if it does give Mom and Dad a heart attack."

"Perfect?" she asked, hoping Moggle was getting this. "Really?"

"Really." He shrugged. "If it wasn't, I wouldn't be rekicking it. Want to see something?"

He flicked his finger, and the screen changed—a schematic of an apartment. It was huge, with walk-in closets and smart-matter windows, and a hole in the wall that could grind out almost anything.

"What's that?" she asked.

"An apartment in Shuffle Mansion. It just opened up."

Aya blinked. Shuffle Mansion was where the absolute biggest faces in the city lived. It had the best views and the strongest privacy, and even its walls were profoundly status-conscious. Every few weeks they moved a little, giving the mansion its name, every square centimeter reflecting the latest updates in the face ranks.

"Shuffle Mansion? You think I'll be *that* famous?"

He shrugged again. "You may have stopped a war, Aya-chan. That means merits on top of fame. Ready to go?"

Aya felt heat on her cheeks, not just from the new flash tattoos. She glanced into the wallscreen one last time and gestured, changing the view back to her profile. Tonight, somehow, she almost looked like a pretty. Even her nose seemed perfect.

She nodded. "Yeah, I'm totally ready."

It was time.

Ten hovercams were drifting overhead, and dozens more waited over the mansion's steps. Their lenses flickered with torchlight as they swiveled to focus on Hiro, Aya, and Ren.

Everyone knew that Hiro Fuse's new story was going up tonight, and rumors were flying that it was even bigger than immortality. What nobody knew was that the story was blank except for a rekick to his little sister's feed. Piggy-backing on Hiro's face rank annoyed Aya, but she had to admit it was the quickest way to spread the news.

As they reached the mansion's steps, she pushed her dress's sparkling into overdrive.

"Don't run down your batteries," Ren whispered, smiling for the cams.

"But Hiro said I needed to make a big entrance!" Her own smile faltered a little as she climbed the stairs. Her right ankle was still sprained from being dragged across rocks and brush by that stupid parachute. "Maybe I shouldn't have worn this," she mumbled.

"You look fantastic," Hiro said. "Just keep the friction on those shoes turned up—falling on your face is the wrong kind of famous-making."

"And remember," Ren added quietly, "one hour from now, you'll have the biggest face in the room."

Aya glanced nervously at Hiro, and he took her hand.

She checked her eyescreen: The average face rank of the party was already at two thousand, much higher than the one she'd crashed ten days ago. And that number would only climb as the big faces arrived, the popular tech-kickers who could explain mass drivers in terms that extras could understand.

Inside, the air was so thick with hovercams that Aya wondered how any of them could get a clear shot. Whole swarms moved together, like minnows in an overcrowded fish tank. Moggle joined the dance overhead, looking oversize and clumsy amid the finger-size cams.

The funny thing was, she'd watched a million parties like this on the feeds, and she'd never once noticed all the hovercams. But now their flitting forms were as distracting as mosquitoes in the rainy season.

But she could understand why they were here. The surge-monkeys alone were eye-boggling. Dozens of new skin textures abounded: fur, scales, strange colors, and translucent membranes—even a stony crust, as if living statues had joined the party. Aya spotted face-types based on animals, historical figures, and she-didn't-know-what, all vying for the attention of the swarming cams.

With Nana Love's party only a week away, everyone was pulling out all the stops, trying to eye-kick their way into the top one thousand.

Somehow, though, none of the surge-monkeys here was as unnerving as the figures she and Miki had glimpsed in the mag-lev tunnel. This party was all about fashion and eye-kicks, but those freaks were something . . . inhuman.

She took a deep breath, banishing body mods from her mind. Not everyone here was a surge-monkey. There were also the geniuses: math-heads playing with puzzle cubes and airscreen mazes, science cliques in lab wear, all blended together in a tech-kicker's paradise.

Aya scanned the crowd for Frizz, but extraordinary sights kept arresting her gaze.

"Look at those pixel-skins!" she cried. Across the room a couple stood half naked, blurry images moving across their backs. Somehow they were changing their skin cells' colors fast enough to show a feed channel, like chameleon lizards clinging to a wallscreen.

"It's rude to point," Ren said. "And that's old news. Check out those four in the corner."

Aya followed his gaze. "What do you mean? I don't see anyone."

"Exactly. That's the latest generation of pixilated skin—almost perfect camouflage."

"Very funny, Ren. You're totally full of . . ." Her voice trailed off. The corner had just *moved*, a barely perceptible shift, like a wrinkle passing through the wallpaper. The motion left a shape in her vision—a human body. She whispered, "Moggle, are you getting that?"

"Big deal," Hiro said. "Octopuses can do the same thing."

"That's where the idea came from," Ren said. "Octopus skin cells have these little bags of pigment inside, which they control with—"

"Hang on," Aya interrupted. "Why can't we see their clothes?"

Hiro chuckled, and Ren said, "What clothes?"

Aya's eyes widened. "Oh. That's . . . interesting."

"One problem, though," Hiro said thoughtfully. "Isn't invisibility the *opposite* of fame?"

"Hiro!" Ren hissed. "Nameless One Alert!"

Aya looked up to see Toshi Banana making his way across the room, his famous shark-shaped hovercam slicing through the air overhead. An entourage of wannabe kickers and fame groupies trailed in his wake.

"What's *he* doing here?" Hiro said. "He's way too famous for this party, and he hates tech-heads!"

"And, um, is he coming toward us?" Aya asked softly.

"No way," Hiro said.

But Toshi's wide-shouldered frame was headed straight at them, shoving his way between a leopard-pelted surge-monkey and a bunch of manga-heads.

The entourage swept to a halt around the three of them, a small armada of hovercams sliding into place overhead. Aya suddenly remembered all the slam interviews Toshi had pulled over the years—he was an expert at making his opponents look like idiots.

"Hiro Fuse? Is that you?" Toshi's voice sounded just liked it did on his feed: low and gravelly, threatening to shift into outrage at any moment. Aya noticed that he didn't bother to bow.

"Um . . . ," Hiro began.

"Not sure? Well *I* think it's you, and I'm seldom wrong." Toshi chuckled, and his groupies broke into laughter. "*Loved* your immortality story."

"Oh, thank you, Toshi-sensei." Hiro cleared his throat. "I appreciate that."

Aya rolled her eyes. One compliment from the Nameless One, and Hiro was already face-grubbing.

"Cloned hearts! Disgusting!" Toshi glanced back at the

leopard girl and rolled his eyes. "Some people love to pervert the natural order, eh?"

"You mean those crumblies?" Hiro shrugged. "I think they were just afraid to die."

"Fear, exactly! That's what the mind-rain has given us."

"You keep slamming the mind-rain," Ren said. "So why not go back to being a bubblehead?"

Toshi turned his huge frame and sized Ren up. "Do I know you?"

Ren bowed a fraction of a degree. "I doubt it."

"Well, contrary to popular belief, not everyone was a bubblehead back in the Prettytime. Some people had to run the city." Toshi turned back to Hiro. "Your face rank seems to have slipped since that story, Hiro-chan. Maybe it's the company you're keeping."

"Hey!" Aya cried, doing a little frictionless spin. "His company is standing right here!"

Toshi looked down at her. "An extra? Dating downward, Hiro-chan?"

"Dating? That's my . . . ," Hiro started, but under the stares of Toshi's entourage, his voice faded.

The Nameless One exhaled a slow breath, his gaze drifting over Hiro's shoulder, as if looking for someone more important. "Well if your effort tonight is interesting, perhaps you can guest on my feed. It might help you break into the big leagues."

"Forget it!" Aya said. "After tonight, we'll both be a zillion times famouser than you!"

The entourage's hovercams swiveled, all suddenly focusing on Aya. Toshi stared down at her like he'd found a cockroach between his chopsticks.

"Is this *ugly* in your story, Hiro-chan? If so, I don't get it."

As Aya started to reply, a troubling realization crossed her mind. To mind-rain slammers like the Nameless One, the city killer would be more evidence that humanity threatened the planet, just more proof that everyone had to be controlled again.

With his dozen hovercams, Toshi was already gathering material to spin her story his way. He'd already used Hiro's immortality kick to stir up fear of overpopulation. How much more could he do with a *city killer*?

"Don't worry, Toshi-*chan*," Ren said. "You'll get it soon enough. Everyone will." He turned to Aya. "Let's kick it early. Let's kick it now."

"Really?"

"Good idea, Ren," Hiro said. "A little surprise for everyone."

Aya looked up at the Nameless One. Anything that threw him off balance was fine with her. She bowed. "Excuse us. We have something important to do."

He started to sputter a reply, but the three of them were already walking away. Unlock codes tumbled across Aya's eyescreen, and Hiro's fingers were already twitching. She shot a quick ping to Frizz, just to make sure he caught the story the first time around.

Hiro's hands settled, and he turned to her. "Ready, little sister?"

She nodded slowly, and felt her flash tattoos spinning. "Ready."

"Kick in three . . . two . . . one . . ."

They mouthed their final codes together, then stared at each other.

The City Killer story was on the feeds.

Ren pushed straight through the crowd, stepping into the middle of the room beside a manga-head with meter-tall sparkling hair. He clapped his hands together twice.

"Ladies and gentlemen, a brief announcement!" He paused for a moment while the chatter settled down. Even the Reputation Bombers were silenced by his audaciousness, but Ren looked unashamed, fixing everyone with his gaze.

He gave the room a low bow.

"Forgive me for interrupting, but Hiro and Aya Fuse's new story is up and running. And it concerns something you may be interested in . . . the end of the world!"

TRUTH-SLANTING

Fifteen minutes later, it was starting to build.

Of course, most of the partygoers had gone back to their conversations after Ren's announcement. A few handhelds flickered, but the mansion's big public wallscreen stayed dark. Why interrupt a bash to watch one feed out of a million? Especially once it turned out to be Hiro Fuse's little sister kicking tonight, and not Mr. Big Face himself.

In one corner, Toshi Banana was making a show of ignoring the rest of the party, telling jokes to his entourage and basking in their laughter. But Aya noticed one of his groupies lost in her eyescreen. As the story reached the truth about the city killer, she rose on her tiptoes to whisper in the Nameless One's ear, and a thoughtful look crossed his face.

Out in the city it was building faster—friends pinging friends, feeds rekicking it, the story spreading like a brushfire in the dry season. Aya watched her feed ratings slowly climb, her face rank crawling upward, already back under a hundred thousand.

"Just caught a ping-blast on the wardens' feed," Ren said. Both his eyescreens were on, his expression lost in scribbles of light. "They're scrambling hovercars."

Aya smiled. Like a good little citizen, she'd put a security flag on the story to make sure the city government watched it right away. They'd have wardens out there tonight, securing the site from thrill-seekers and paparazzi, making sure nobody got smashed into mag-lev paste. Of course, this wasn't just about personal safety—by tomorrow, the Global Concord Committee's suborbitals would no doubt be headed here from every continent.

Staring into his eyescreens, Ren burst out laughing. "This is hilarious! Gamma Matsui is slamming you: She thinks you faked the sled footage! She says you couldn't have stayed up in the air that long—so the whole story's a hoax."

Aya's jaw dropped open. "That's so mean! What does she know, anyway?"

"It doesn't matter *what* she knows, Aya," Ren said. "What matters is that she's the most famous kicker to notice you so far."

Aya growled in frustration, but it was true: Her feed ratings had just bumped again. She brought up Gamma on her eyescreen, struggling to hear over the music and babble of the party.

"I'd kill for your wallscreen right now, Hiro," she said, her eyes suddenly itching for twenty feeds to follow the story's spread. "Why did I let you guys talk me into coming here?"

Ren placed a hand on Aya's shoulder, giving her a glass. "Hush, and drink some champagne. See that extra-looking woman playing with the puzzle cube? She can calculate the sled's terminal velocity off the top of her head, just by watching. When it comes to physics, she'll eat Gamma for breakfast. *That's* why we're here."

"But she's not even watching my feed!" Aya cried. "Should I go explain to her?"

"Don't you dare," Hiro said. "No one else is talking about hoaxes yet. Don't poke a dead fire."

Aya groaned, putting the champagne aside. Sometimes, the hardest thing was doing nothing.

"Well, there's some good news," Hiro said. "The Nameless One's leaving."

Aya looked up in time to catch Toshi Banana and his entourage heading out the door. They looked like they were in a hurry.

Ren chuckled. "Probably wants to get back to his wall-screens and start slamming you before this gets too big."

"Shouldn't *we* be slamming him first?" Aya asked.

Ren blinked away his eyescreen squiggles and turned to face her. "We don't need to. This is a city killer, remember? It's way too big for that bubblehead to make his own."

Five minutes later the story went massive, ballooning out across the feeds, reaching past the city interface into the global network. It seemed to happen all at once, in one of those explosions of kick that was inexplicable—or at least *way* too fast for Aya's little eyescreen to make sense of.

Here at the party people were starting to glance in her

direction, aware that something big was roiling the city interface. They pulled out handhelds, gathering in corners to watch together.

"So far so good," Hiro announced. "Your face rank just hit the top ten thousand. You're beating tonight's Reputation Bomber!"

"Glad to hear that." She flinched—her alert tone had just gone crazy, like a tiny jackhammer ringing a bell in her ear. "Something's wrong with my eyescreen!"

"Nothing's wrong, Aya," Ren said. "Those are pings rolling in. Better turn off your sound."

She squeezed her fists shut, silencing the noise, then rubbed her ear. "Ouch. Being famous is so brain-shattering!"

"Aya Fuse, complaining about fame?" someone said. "Talk about brain-shattering."

Aya turned to find Frizz standing there, huge-eyed, beautiful, and grinning.

"Frizz!" she cried, gathering him into a hug. "Did you see my story?"

"Of course." He squeezed her hard, then took a step backward and bowed to Hiro and Ren. "Frizz Mizuno."

Hiro smirked as he returned the introduction. "So you're the famous Slime King?"

"And you're Aya's famous older brother," Frizz said, then frowned. "But probably not so famous anymore, compared to her."

Hiro's eyes widened, and Aya grabbed his arm.

"Go do something else, Hiro," she commanded. Radical Honesty was anxiety-making enough without her older brother around.

Smiling, Ren dragged Hiro away toward a group of kickers waiting for interviews.

"I've only got a minute, Frizz. I'm supposed to answer questions soon. But I'm glad you came!"

"I missed you." He stepped closer, his eyes locked on hers. "I never got to say sorry in person for getting you slammed."

Aya looked away, trembling a little under his manga gaze. "It wasn't your fault, Frizz—I should have been more careful. And being Slime Queen was kind of . . . interesting."

"After tonight they won't call you that anymore." He took her arm. "But I never thought of you as slimy."

She dared his gaze again, speaking too softly for the buzzing hovercams to hear. "But remember what you said that day? That you weren't sure what kind of person I was? Do you see now why I had to lie to get this story?"

It was Frizz who looked away this time. "It sounded awful, betraying friends like that. But I get it now." He sighed. "I guess sometimes you have to lie to find the truth."

He looked so sad saying those words that Aya wrapped her arms around him again, squeezing tight. She didn't care how many hovercams were watching, or how many slammer feeds compared her ugliness to Frizz's beauty.

"But I'll never lie to you, Frizz." She felt his muscles tighten.

"Then tell me one thing," he said.

"Anything."

"If you hadn't found the city killer, if this story was just about the Sly Girls and their mag-lev surfing, would you have kicked it anyway?"

Aya pulled away. Frizz wasn't stupid; he'd noticed that her truth-slanting had started long before she'd known about the city killer.

But *would* she have betrayed them, just to get famous?

Like Miki had said, surfing through the wild had been so brain-expanding, and the more time Aya had spent with them, the more the Sly Girls had started to feel like friends. She could have changed her mind . . . maybe.

Was it lying if you weren't certain about the truth?

She cleared her throat. "When I joined the Sly Girls, I was just looking for a story, *any* story. But after talking to you that day, I was starting to wonder."

He nodded. "So you'd already changed your mind?"

Aya looked up into his manga eyes—he wanted to believe her. It would be so easy just to agree.

And why make Frizz sad? It wasn't like she could ever be incognito again. After tonight everyone would know Aya Fuse was a kicker—no more lying for stories. So what did it matter if she was a truth-slanting Slime Queen just one last time?

"It all happened so fast," she said. "First it was just tricks, then suddenly the whole world was at stake." She looked away. "But no . . . I couldn't have done that to them."

Frizz pulled her close again. "That's a relief."

Aya squeezed her eyes shut, hiding from her own doubts. Frizz had believed her, just like that. Maybe it wasn't such a stretch—the whole question was hypothetical, after all.

It would be crazy to throw Frizz away forever, when the price of keeping him was one little stretch of the truth.

"Um, Aya?" Frizz whispered in her ear. "I think your brother wants you."

She grasped him tighter. "I don't care."

"Actually, it's not just Hiro. It's sort of . . . lots of people."

Aya sighed and pulled away, glancing over his shoulder. When she saw them all, her jaw dropped open.

The feeding frenzy had begun.

FEEDING FRENZY

There were dozens of people waiting. Ren was arranging them on the mansion's main staircase, with the most famous closest to the bottom. About half were tech-heads with crazy surge and smart-matter clothes, the rest looking out of place here at the bash—ego-kickers, newsies, a handful of city officials. Some big faces, some not.

But all of them were here to see *her*.

Hiro took Aya's arm and gently propelled her toward an empty spot at the bottom of the stairs. Several hundred hovercams were focused on her now, in constant motion as they jostled for the best angles, shadowing her every step. Aya felt strangely small under their collective gaze, as insignificant as that first night she'd surfed into the wild.

But this was the opposite of obscurity, she reminded herself. This was what she'd always wanted—for people to watch her, to pay attention to every word she said.

"Eyescreen off," Hiro whispered. "You'll need your whole brain for this."

Aya nodded and flexed her ring finger. But as she stared up at the attentive faces before her, all suddenly crystal clear, the answers she'd practiced the night before started flying from her head.

"Um, this is kind of paralyzing," she said softly.

Hiro squeezed her arm. "I'll be right here."

She nodded and cleared her throat. "Okay, let's start."

The questions came hard and fast.

"How did you find the Sly Girls, Aya?"

"Just lucky, I guess. I just saw them surfing one night, and tracked them down at a party like this one."

"Why are some shots in the background layer altered?"

Aya cleared her throat, wondering how anyone had watched all those hours so quickly. "The Sly Girls wanted anonymity. So I scrubbed a few faces. That's all."

"You're not hiding anyone else?"

"Like who?"

"The builders of the mass driver."

"Of course not!"

"So you don't know anything about them?"

Aya paused, wishing she'd mentioned the inhuman-looking figures in her story. But it was such a crazy claim, and she didn't have a single shot to back it up. Alien builders would be a million times more implausible if she brought them up now.

"Why would I protect *them*? Whoever built the city killer is crazy. Or did you miss the city-killing part?"

"Isn't that title a little hype-making, Aya?" another kicker asked. "A few tons of falling steel can't really destroy a city, can it?"

Aya smiled. Ren had made sure she was ready for this one. "At reentry velocities, it only takes a small projectile to knock out a hoverstrut-supported building. So if a cylinder splits into thousands of pieces . . . well, you do the math. Or better yet, ask that woman over there to do it. The one with the puzzle cube."

"Couldn't we stop the cylinders? Like the Rusties used to shoot down rockets?"

She'd looked this one up herself. "The Rusties never got very good at intercepting city killers—except in their own propaganda. And rockets trail big plumes of smoke. Slivers of metal would be tiny and invisible."

"Why do you think they left the mountain empty?"

"Ren Machino, who helped me with all this, thinks the mass driver was designed to be completely automatic."

"Do you think there could be more of these things in the world?"

She blinked. "I sure hope not."

"With the metal shortage going on, where do you think they got all that steel?"

"I have no idea."

"What made you want to be a kicker, Aya?"

"Um . . ." She paused, unready for this one, though Hiro had warned her that there was always some bubblehead asking personal questions, no matter how important a story was. "After the mind-rain I was having trouble figuring out the world. And telling other people's stories is a good way to do that."

The kicker smiled. "Isn't that the same answer your big brother always gives?"

"Oh, crap . . . no comment," Aya said. At the sound of their laughter, she smiled and finally relaxed a little.

"What kind of face do you want when you turn sixteen?" a fashion-kicker shouted from the back.

"I don't know yet. I'm sort of partial to manga-heads."

"So we noticed, Slime Queen!"

"Okay. No comment again."

"Do you worry that you're glorifying dangerous tricks, Aya?"

She shrugged. "I'm just telling the truth about the world."

"But you didn't tell the truth to the Sly Girls. . . ."

Aya glanced at Frizz and said, "Sometimes you have to lie to find the truth."

"Why do you think a big face like Eden Maru hangs out with the Sly Girls?"

Aya shrugged. "Like she said in that interview: to get away from you guys."

"Do you think *our* city built the mass driver?" someone in the back row asked—one of Toshi Banana's groupies, Aya realized.

"Why would we do that?"

"We're the closest city to the mountain. Wouldn't that make you a traitor?"

"Make me a *what*?"

"What if we need the mass driver to defend ourselves?"

She looked at Hiro, who said, "If this is about defending us, then shouldn't we *know* about it?"

"So, Hiro?" a tech-kicker interrupted. "What's it like to be upstaged by your little sister?"

"Pretty vex-making," Hiro said, then smiled. "But much better than watching my mansion getting bombed."

The questions kept coming: Aya's childhood, her favorite kicker, plans for follow-up stories. Endless talk about math and missiles, Sly Girls and spy-cams, parachutes and paparazzi. Every time one kicker peeled off to prepare their story for the feeds, another joined the fray, and soon the questions began to repeat. Aya tried to come up with fresh answers, but eventually found herself mouthing the same words again and again.

Finally Frizz dragged her away into a corner, promising she'd be back soon. Hiro kept going without losing a beat.

"Water," she croaked.

Frizz thrust a glass into her hand, and Aya drank deep.

"Thanks," she gasped when it was empty, taking a look around. The air was thick with hovercams pointed at her, but people were keeping their distance, trying not to stare. For the first time in her life, a reputation bubble had formed around Aya.

On the other side of the room, a bunch of tech-heads had gathered at the mansion's big public wallscreen, watching Ren demonstrate the grim math of ballistic weapons and collapsing buildings. For a moment she was alone with Frizz.

"How'd I do?" she asked softly.

"Amazing." He grinned. "So what does it feel like, being famous?"

She groaned, remembering her radical stupidity the last time they'd been together. "Very funny."

"No really," he said, "what's it like hanging out with someone as face-missing as me?"

"Cut it out! What happened to your radical honesty?"

"Teasing isn't lying," Frizz argued. "And besides, I'm really wondering how you see me now."

Aya rolled her eyes. "But it's not like you're some extra. There's no difference in ambition between us!"

"Yes there is."

"What do you mean?"

"You went for an hour without checking your face rank?" He laughed. "That's pretty jaw-dropping. Take a guess, before I blurt it out."

Aya swallowed. She'd hardly breathed since the story'd kicked, much less tracked her face rank. And somehow she was afraid to boot her eyescreen and check. "You mean I'm more famous than you? Am I under a thousand?"

"Don't be brain-missing, Aya! Immortal crumblies got your brother under a thousand. This is a city killer! Take a *real* guess."

Aya shrugged, not wanting to sound ego-kicking. "Um, five hundred?"

"Still brain-missing!" A pained expression twisted Frizz's face. "Not telling you is killing me."

"Then tell me!" Aya cried.

"You're the seventeenth-most-famous person in the city!" Frizz spat out, then rubbed his temples. "Ouch. That hurt."

Aya stared at him—even if Frizz couldn't lie, he had to be mistaken. "Seventeen?"

"Nana Love kicked you."

"No way!" Aya cried. "What does *she* care about Rusty weapons?"

"Nana-chan cares about all humanity." He shrugged. "Which is nice of her. Maybe she pinged you."

"No way!" Aya turned her eyescreen on, heart pounding as it came to life. "You really think so?"

"Probably. She pinged me when I hit the top thousand."

Aya's interface appeared, stuffed with an enormous stack of pings, tens of thousands of them stretching off into the invisible distance. She'd *never* have time to read them all!

"You should see yourself, Aya," Frizz said, laughing. "You look like a littlie who just ate too much ice cream."

"Too much is right. You should see all these messages!" She remembered Hiro's trick after big stories, when he was always ping-bashed with tips. Her fingers began to twitch. "Hang on, let me sort them by face rank. Pings from extras go to the bottom and the important ones rise to the top. If Nana-chan really is in here, she'll be right at the . . . *whoa*."

There were so many pings, Aya could actually see them moving, the city interface straining as it checked each one against the constantly updating face ranks. Gradually a few bubbled to the top—big-face kickers, politicians, a note of thanks from the Good Citizen Committee. . . .

"I am totally going to score some merits out of this," she murmured. "Shuffle Mansion, here I come."

Then she saw it . . . a glowing ping rising on angel's wings.

"Oh, Frizz. You were right . . . Nana-chan *was* watching!"

He laughed. "I told you so!"

Aya was about to open it, but suddenly the ping slid down. She stared at the new message in disbelief. It carried no decoration at all, its black text as bare as an automatic reply.

"Um, Frizz, there's another one above it."

"Another what?"

"I think someone more famous than Nana Love just pinged me."

"But there isn't anyone who's . . . except . . ." Frizz let out a strangled sound. "You mean *Tally Youngblood just pinged you*?"

Aya nodded slowly. It was right there, painted in laser light on her eyeball. A ping from the world's most famous person—the girl who'd made the mind-rain fall. The name prayed to by the Youngblood cults every morning, cursed by Toshi Banana as he slammed the latest mind-rain clique, repeated countless times whenever the story of the Diego War was taught to littlies . . .

"How could she know so fast?" Aya murmured. "Isn't she hiding in the wild somewhere?"

"The story went global two hours ago," Frizz said. "She must have friends checking the feeds for her."

"But since when does Tally Youngblood just *ping* people?" Saying the name made her throat go dry again.

"Who cares? *Open* it!"

Aya twitched her finger, and the ping expanded. It was tagged by the global interface, guaranteed authentic. But as she read the message, Aya wondered if Tally's English was confusing her somehow.

"What does it say?" Frizz cried.

"It's only seven words."

"*What* words? 'Thanks'? 'Congratulations'? 'Hello'?"

"No, Frizz. It says, '*Run and hide. We're on our way.*'"

PINNED

"This is stupid," Hiro hissed. "We should go back to the party. Running off like this is making us look like idiots!"

"You're telling me to ignore Tally Youngblood?" Aya said. "Her ping said run and hide!"

"You call this hiding?" Ren asked.

Aya glanced into the sky. A hundred or so hovercams had trailed them out of the party, probably wondering why the seventeenth-most-famous person in the city had suddenly abandoned her first interview ever. The swarm was silhouetted against the night sky, a host of lenses glinting down at them like the eyes of predators.

"That's a good point," Frizz said. "We have to find somewhere private."

"I'm *trying*." Aya sighed.

The four of them had left the bash by a side door and headed randomly across a darkened baseball field. Safety fireworks were still shooting up from the mansion's roof. Flickering across the grass, they sent Aya's huge, jittering shadow stretching out in front of her.

She remembered Lai's last warning on the sled: "*Whoever built this monstrosity is dangerous.*"

"What's the point of privacy?" Hiro snapped. "If you think someone's coming after you, shouldn't we stay where *everyone can see us*?"

Aya came to a halt, stopping so quickly that Moggle bumped her from behind. Maybe the safest place was in full view. No one would dare do anything at a crowded party—or with a hundred hovercams directly overhead, for that matter.

She sighed. "I guess we could go back in."

"Exactly," Hiro cried. "We can kick Tally Youngblood's ping. If everyone finds out she's on her way here, it'll be massive!"

Frizz cleared his throat. "This probably isn't the best time to worry about face ranks, Hiro."

"This isn't about face ranks, you bubblehead!"

"Technically speaking, I'm not a bubblehead," Frizz said calmly. "Which is why I'm not shouting our plans where *everyone can hear them*."

Aya glanced up. There was still a fair-size reputation bubble around her, but a few cams were close enough to have caught Hiro's outburst.

"Whatever we do, let's keep our voices down," she said. "Somehow, I don't think Tally-sama wants the whole city to know she's coming."

Ren shook his head. "She's not from here, Aya, so she doesn't understand how the reputation economy works. About half a million people are watching right now. Your fame will protect us."

"You *can't* hide, Aya," Hiro said. "Everyone knows exactly where you are. Wasn't that the *point* of tonight?"

Frizz frowned, looking at her. "I thought the point of tonight was to save the world."

Aya sighed. "There may have been several points, okay? Everyone just be quiet for a second while I think!"

The other three fell silent. Aya stood there, feeling their eyes on her, and the lenses of a hundred hovercams, and another half a million people watching through them. Even Moggle was staring at her.

It wasn't the best spot for thinking.

Frizz drew closer, putting an arm around her shoulder. "If we go back to the party and someone comes after you, who's going to stop them? A bunch of pixel-heads?"

Hiro shrugged. "The wardens, just like any other crime."

"Do we trust the wardens?" Frizz asked. "Remember what that kicker said? Our city might have built this thing!"

"The guy who called her a traitor?" Hiro laughed. "He was totally brain-missing!"

"Well, maybe not totally," Ren said. "The mass driver was built using mag-levs that started here. Someone from our city must have been part of it."

"Someone with a lot of authority," Frizz added. "To use all that steel with nobody knowing."

Aya swallowed. The city killer was so huge—whoever had built it wielded enough power to hollow out mountains. Could a few wardens really stop them? Would half a million witnesses stay their hand, when they had the audacity to destroy whole cities?

Gazing into the dark ring of trees around the baseball field, she remembered Eden Maru's words. . . .

"You can disappear in front of a crowd, too."

"Moggle, go as high as you can and look around." She

turned to Hiro. "I'm going to do what Tally-sama says . . . and hide."

She started walking again—away from the mansion's lights, away from everything.

Hiro followed, still arguing. "You're thinking like an extra. You *can't* hide! All anyone has to do to find you is turn on the feeds!"

A dizziness washed over Aya as she walked—the hovercams were moving overhead now, shadowing her every step, as if she was on a treadmill going nowhere. She felt trapped under their lenses, like a butterfly fixed with a hundred pins.

"Can you do something about those things?" she asked Ren.

"Well, maybe." Ren pulled out a trick-box. "When the big tech-kickers want an industrial-size reputation bubble, they jam everything for a hundred meters or so. I might be able to arrange a couple of minutes out of sight."

"Please." Aya glanced up at the cams overhead. "A little obscurity looks pretty good right now. Safer, anyway."

"But *why* would anyone want to come after you?" Hiro kept arguing. "Everyone in the world already knows this weapon exists. What more can you do to them? You didn't hide anything, did you?"

Aya shook her head. "Of course not. You and Hiro always say burying shots is totally truth-slanting. So it's all in there. Well, except . . ."

She paused, thinking of the inhuman-looking figures she and Miki had seen.

"Except what?" Frizz asked softly.

"There's one thing I sort of left out." She looked at Hiro. "But I didn't even have any shots of them."

His eyes narrowed. "Shots of who, Aya?"

"Well, that first night I surfed . . . What does it matter, anyway?"

Hiro took a step closer. "Because if you don't put everything on the feeds, someone can *silence* you! What did you leave out?"

"Well, in the tunnel that first night, I saw some people who weren't quite, um . . . human."

There was a pause. The three of them stared at her, dumbfounded.

A thump came from the darkness nearby, and they all jumped. A few meters away, a hovercam lay on its side, its running lights dark. Another thump came from farther away, then a third. Aya looked up.

The hovercams were starting to fall.

She smiled. "Wow, Ren. How'd you do that?"

Ren lowered the trick-box, a puzzled expression on his face. "Here's some bad news. I'm *not* doing that—someone else is."

The thudding came from every direction now, like a slowly building hailstorm. Raising her arms over her head, Aya saw that the sky was already half empty.

Soon she would be invisible again. And then, once no one was watching, Aya Fuse might disappear forever.

She started running.

RUN AND HIDE

"Get us four hoverboards," Hiro was yelling. "Property override! I don't care who owns them, this is an emergency!"

Aya led them back toward the bash—at this point, a

crowd seemed better than darkness. The last few hovercams trailed them doggedly, tumbling from the air one by one.

"Moggle, are you still up there?" she hissed. The hovercam's view appeared—she saw herself and the others from a distance, specks against the vast expanse of the baseball field. No one else was in sight. "Stay up high, Moggle! Someone's jamming everything around us."

On cue, another hovercam crashed to the ground in front of Aya. She jumped over it, her party dress threatening to tangle around her ankles.

"There they are!" Hiro shouted.

Four hoverboards were shooting across the field toward them, silhouetted by the lights from the tech-head party.

"Won't they just crash?" Aya asked. "Like the cams?"

"I think I can block the lifter jamming," Ren said, poking at his trick-box as he ran. "Just stick close to me."

"But is anyone chasing us?" Frizz asked.

Aya scanned the darkness between mansions. Still nobody in sight—nothing but the motionless remains of cams littering the ground.

Then she heard the whoosh of a hovercar.

It shot overhead, drowning out the thudding of their footsteps, whipping her hair with its passage. For a moment Aya thought it was the wardens, but then she heard the scream of lifting fans—the car was designed to work outside the city, where wardens never went.

And somehow she doubted it was Rangers overhead.

The car wheeled violently, dropping in front of them. The grass shimmered underfoot, roiling in the tempest of the lifting fans. Whirlwinds of dirt rose from the baselines of the baseball diamond.

Through the windshield, two drivers gazed back at her

with a strange calm—their eyes set too wide apart, their skin pale and hairless, just like the ghastly faces in the tunnel.

She stumbled to a halt. Like Miki had said that night, they didn't look human.

Frizz pulled her back into a run, angling around the hovercar. Flying dust forced her eyes half-shut, and her dress billowed like an open parachute around her.

As the car settled to the ground, its side split open, spilling a wedge of light across the field. Two more figures stood silhouetted inside, visible for a moment among rolling clouds of dirt.

Then Aya heard a cry—Ren and Hiro zooming out of the dust storm, two empty hoverboards following them.

"I've never ridden one of those before!" Frizz shouted.

"Just stick with me!" Aya leaped onto a board, pulling him on behind her. They veered wildly for a moment, Frizz swaying like a littlie on a balance beam.

"Stay close or they'll jam you!" Ren yelled, waving the trick-box as he shot past.

Aya leaned into a hard turn, following Ren and Hiro. She felt Frizz's arms wrap around her, his body pressing close as they gathered speed.

Behind them, the whine of the hovercar rose again, the wind of its fans battering the air. Aya thrust her arms out wide, wishing she hadn't worn platform shoes tonight. At least the last two weeks were paying off: Riding double through a roaring wind wasn't half as tricky as mag-lev surfing.

Frizz's extra weight was a problem, though—Hiro and Ren were pulling away. Aya leaned forward, urging the board faster. If they fell too far behind Ren, they'd drop like the jammed hovercams.

And they weren't even wearing crash bracelets. . . .

"Hold up!" she shouted, but the scream of the pursuing car erased her words.

Luckily, the mansion wasn't far away now. She could see partygoers on its roof watching the chase, probably wondering what sort of publicity stunt this was.

The hovercar roared overhead again, the wash of its fans sending her and Frizz into a series of serpentine curves. Aya twisted her body, barely keeping them onboard.

"Up there!" Frizz shouted.

Two figures had jumped from the open hovercar door, their freakish arms and legs splaying wide as they fell through the air. They hover-bounced, spinning in the whirlwinds beneath the car, but quickly gained control. Aya spotted lifter pads bulging from their thin-limbed bodies.

"They're wearing hoverball rigs!" she shouted. "Not good!"

The figures were zooming toward them now, riding the car's wash like windsurfers in a gale.

"Hold on tight!" she cried, and spun the board into a quick reverse, heading back across the field. Frizz's arms wrapped around her tighter, his weight shifting with hers.

But the inhumans were closing the gap quickly. When Hiro and Ren turned to follow, the spindly figures shot past them without a second glance.

Aya Fuse was who they wanted.

She headed for the nearest trees, trying to urge the board faster. But it was a city toy, nothing like the Sly Girls' high-speed boards.

The trees rose up before them, and Aya twisted from side to side, banking between thick trunks. Beams of light from the hovercar stabbed through the leaves, scattering bright coins across the forest floor.

Frizz's lips pressed against her ear. "Why aren't we crashing?"

Aya blinked—Ren and Hiro had to be fifty meters away.

"Of course!" she cried. "They had to stop jamming to use their rigs, which means . . . Moggle, come here! I need you!"

"Aya!" Frizz shouted. "On the right!"

One of the figures was swooping down at them, long fingers splayed like talons. Frizz dropped down, pulling both of them into a crouch as the figure swept past.

"Ouch!" Frizz flinched behind her. "Something stuck me!"

"What?" Aya stood again, pulling the board into another hard turn. She craned her neck to look at him. "Are you okay?"

"I think so. But I feel a little . . . watch out!"

Aya whipped her head around to find the other inhuman waiting directly ahead, arms out wide, fingertips glistening with needles.

She twisted her whole body to one side, banking the board to a halt. But Frizz's body was going limp, his arms slipping from around her waist.

"Frizz!" she called out, but heard only a groan in response. . . .

And then he was toppling from the board.

"Frizz!"

She reached out to grab him, but he was already tumbling through the air. He flew straight into the waiting inhuman, their bodies colliding with a grim thud. The spindly figure crumpled, its long arms wrapping around Frizz, both of them flying backward into the darkness.

Suddenly free of his weight, the board went into a lopsided spin. Tree trunks whirled around Aya, sharp branches whipping her face and hands. She knelt and clutched the edges, letting the board gyrate its momentum away.

When it had slowed a little, Aya let go and rolled off into the leaves. She stood and ran to where the two figures lay sprawled and unmoving on the forest floor.

Her eyes were drawn to the inhuman's strange face. His skin was pale, his arms thin and weak-looking, but the needles on his fingertips were unambiguous—they were designed to do some damage.

But the strangest thing was the inhuman's feet. Bare and misshapen, they looked almost like hands, their long toes curled up like a dead spider's legs.

She dragged Frizz free of the tangle. "Can you hear me?"

He didn't answer. Then Aya saw the tiny red mark on his neck. One nick from those needle fingers had knocked him unconscious . . . or worse.

She pulled him closer, her head swimming. The hovercar still drifted overhead, spilling a trembling light through the leaves. The shadows slanted as it moved, as though the whole world was swaying.

"Aya!" came a shout. She looked up, and saw Hiro and Ren angling through the trees.

But in front of them flew the other inhuman, zooming straight toward her, arms outstretched and fingers glistening. His pale skin glowed in the darkness.

She pulled Frizz closer, feeling utterly abandoned. Where were the wardens? Where were the half-million others who'd been watching her every move five minutes ago?

He was ten meters away, five . . .

A small dark shape shot from the shadows, barreling into the inhuman's stomach. He crumpled into a ball with a grunt, then whirled past Aya, the hoverball rig keeping him airborne as he spun.

"Moggle," Aya breathed. The hovercam bounced away, crashing through the brush.

The inhuman hung unconscious from his hoverball rig, his handlike feet swinging a meter from the ground. A groan escaped from his lips, and his eyes began to flutter open. . . .

Aya ran toward him, leaping up to grab his shoulders. They glided across the forest floor together, the rig adjusting to her weight.

His hand reached for her, but Aya grabbed his wrist and stuck a handful of needle fingers into his own neck. He sputtered for a moment, eyes widening, then passed out completely.

"Aya!" Hiro banked to a halt. "Are you okay?"

"I'm fine." She jumped down, glancing up at the hovercar. It waited overhead, unmoving, lights probing through the leaves uncertainly. "Help me with Frizz."

Hiro glided to a halt. "He'll be fine, Aya. They don't care about him."

"Yeah, but I do." She ran to Frizz's unconscious body, towing the hoverboard behind her. She knelt and pulled at his arm, trying to get his weight up onto the riding surface.

He let out a groan.

"Are you all right?"

"Feel weird," he murmured. "Heavy."

"Tell me about it!" Aya strained. "If only we had a way to . . ." She glanced at the inhuman lying next to Frizz.

Hiro stepped off his board beside her, staring down at

the inhuman. "Whoa. You left *this* out of your story?"

"Help me get the hoverball rig off this freak." Aya grunted, tugging at the inhuman's shin lifter. "We can put it on Frizz!"

"All right," Hiro said, kneeling. "Here's how you do it."

He loosened the straps with practiced fingers, pulling the lifter pad free and slipping it onto Frizz's leg.

"What happened to him?" Ren asked, joining in the scramble.

"That freak stuck him with those needle fingers." Aya glanced up at the hovercar. Its side door was opening again, light spilling out around two more silhouettes. "Crap. More coming!"

"I'm done." Hiro was strapping the last forearm pad into place. "I've set the rig to neutral. He should be zero-g."

Frizz lifted easily from the ground, suddenly weightless. She wrestled his drifting body onto her board and knelt across him.

Hiro and Ren slipped up on either side and reached out their hands, pulling her forward like a littlie between two parents. Soon they were shooting ahead through a gap in the trees.

"Are they following us?" Aya asked.

Ren looked back. "I don't think so. They're picking up the other two."

"Two freaky bodies are worse than one live witness, I guess," Hiro said. "Speaking of which, you have some explaining to do, Aya."

"When we get to safety."

"Which is back at the party, *right*?"

"No. We're doing what Tally says—we're hiding."

"Where?" Ren asked.

Aya bit her lip, holding tight to keep Frizz's unconscious

form from slipping off the board. "The underground reservoir."

"Cold and wet," Ren said. "But it's the one place in the city with no cams."

"Exactly," Aya said. Something was skimming through the trees in the corner of her eye, and she dared a glance. It was a camo-black hovercam, still wobbly from a recent collision.

It flashed its night-lights happily, and shaky images began to spill across Aya's vision. Whatever the inhuman creatures were, this time they'd been caught by more than just her eyes. She found herself smiling.

Moggle had gotten the shot.

THE WISDOM OF THE CROWD

The new construction site glowed dull orange, the earthmoving machines resting quietly in their foundation pits.

"Check your pings again," Hiro said. "Before we get cut off."

Aya scanned her eyescreen, then shook her head. A few priority pings had come in on the wardens' channel—and maybe ten thousand more asking her what was going on, not to mention a million theories burning up the feeds—but nothing from Tally Youngblood.

"If she's coming on a suborbital, she'll be out of contact for a few hours," Ren said.

Aya sighed. "As long as she gets here fast."

They dropped toward the tunnel below them and slipped inside.

"Hey, am I passing out again?" Frizz groaned, his weight shifting as the darkness closed around them.

"No, we're just going underground." Aya squeezed him tighter. "No lights, Moggle. Too obvious."

"Your dress," Frizz murmured. "Sparkles."

Aya nodded, flexing her fingers, and the party dress sputtered to life. The battery was down to its last dregs, but the flickering embers were enough cut the gloom.

"Told you this was the right dress, Hiro," she said.

"Very funny. Are you going to tell us about what happened back there?"

"Not yet."

They descended, the orange worklights of the surface fading behind them. After long minutes, the echoes of trickling water reached their ears, then the tunnel opened over the reservoir's huge expanse.

Aya brought her board to a halt in midair.

The cavern flickered with the dying lights of her dress, the ceiling shimmering with the water's trembling reflections. Moggle seemed to remember the place, and was soon drifting in nervous circles around the cavern, checking for hidden Sly Girls with lock-down clamps.

Hiro slid to a stop close by, sitting cross-legged on his board. "Great hiding place, Aya. There's no actual ground to stand on, is there?"

"No," Ren said. "But we've got plenty of water."

"It's not exactly Shuffle Mansion." Aya sighed. The apartment Hiro had shown her lingered in her mind's eye—the huge open spaces, the perfect city views. And here she was on her first night of fame, skulking underground.

Frizz's slow breathing echoed from the stone arches. He stirred beneath her, the effects of the needle-stab fading.

She checked the mark on his neck—the redness had almost disappeared.

"Whatever was in those needles was designed to knock you out, Aya," Ren said. "But Frizz is a pretty. He'll be okay."

She nodded. The operation made pretties' bodies stronger and quicker to heal as well as beautiful.

"So who were those people?" Hiro asked.

"I have no idea," she said. "I only saw them once before."

"When you first saw the mountain open up?" Ren asked.

"Yeah. Miki and I were watching over the edge of the train. There were three of them, really skinny and tall. But it was so dark, I thought it was just the crazy shadows . . . at first."

Hiro cleared his throat. "And you didn't bother mentioning this?"

"I didn't have any shots of them! And it was so sense-missing. I thought if I started with those freaks, everybody would think it was just another surge-monkey story. Aliens didn't exactly fit the city-killer theme."

"They didn't *fit the theme*?" Hiro cried. "What are you, some Rusty kicker? That's what the background layer is for!"

"Lecture her later, Hiro," Ren said. "Right now we need to figure out who they are, and why they're after Aya."

Hiro snorted. "We should go back to the surface and kick this! Call the wardens if you want!"

"Do we trust our own city?" Ren asked.

"I trust anyone, as long as there's a few hundred thousand people watching," Hiro muttered. "What I don't get is, how did those surge-monkeys figure out you'd seen them?"

"Maybe there's something in the background layer that explains that," Ren said. "Too bad we're cut off from the feeds down here."

"Moggle's got a copy of everything," Aya said.

"Okay, I'll take a look. Shake me if anything exciting happens." Ren stretched out on his board, his eyescreens flickering a full immersion warning.

Aya swallowed. With Ren shot-scanning and Frizz half-conscious, she was practically alone with Hiro. The last sparkles of her dress were fading, the darkness making his expression look angrier every second.

"How about some light, Moggle?" she said.

The hovercam's night-lights came on, filling the cavern. The deep shadows shifted as Moggle floated restlessly around the reservoir, but Hiro remained stock-still, staring straight at her.

She sighed. "I didn't *mean* to lie."

"No, Aya. But when you pick and choose facts to make your story, you always wind up truth-slanting. That's why good kickers put *everything* up. Save the manipulation for extras who only watch for ten minutes."

"Once more: I didn't have any shots of the freaks!"

"Still, you saw them, and you hid them. That's like lying."

Aya groaned, staring into the water. Its surface grew blacker as her dress's sparkles flickered off one by one. "I messed everything up, didn't I?"

"Not everything." His shoulders slumped. "But if you'd told what you saw, we might already know who those people were."

"How?"

"The wisdom of the crowd, Aya. If a million people look at a puzzle, chances are that one of them knows the answer. Or maybe ten people each know one piece, and that's enough to put it all together."

Aya sighed. "I guess so. I just never thought about the feeds that way."

"That's because all you ever cared about was getting famous," Hiro said. "The feeds are more than that. Like I always say, being a kicker is about making sense of the world."

She rolled her eyes. Just what she needed: a philosophy lesson from her stuck-up older brother. The last sparkles on her dress were sputtering out, the batteries finally expended. "Well, we don't have any crowds down here. So what do *you* think they are? Aliens?"

"No, they're some kind of surge-monkey." The tapping of Hiro's fingers against his board echoed through the cavern. "Sort of like real monkeys, actually."

"How do you mean?" Aya shifted on her board. "I didn't see any fur."

"But you saw their toes, right? They were prehensile, like a monkey's. It's like they have four hands."

"But it doesn't make sense." Aya sighed. "Why be a surge-monkey if you're going to hide all the time?"

"I don't think it's a fashion statement, Aya. It's like my immortal crumblies: The surgery *means* something. There must be some way this all fits together."

"You mean city-killing weapons, hidden bases, and monkey toes?"

Hiro smiled. "I can see why you had trouble fitting all *that* into ten minutes."

They were silent for a while, Aya watching the flicker in Ren's eyes. Maybe by early morning, the flurry of City Killer kick would have faded a little. People had to sleep *sometime*, after all, no matter how big a story was. In a few hours, sneaking up to send Tally Youngblood a ping would be easy.

She remembered the year before in ugly school, learning about the origins of the mind-rain: the Smoke, the Specials, the awful Diego War. One common theme ran through all those lessons: Once Tally-sama arrived, the bad guys didn't stand a chance.

Time passed strangely in the cavern. Cut off from the city interface, the clock in Aya's eyescreen didn't work, but the minutes seemed to crawl. She dozed off once, coming awake in a panic, wondering where she was.

But Frizz was still beside her, sleeping off the effects of the needle. Nestled this close on the board, she could feel his breathing, and his warmth cut the cavern's chill. Whatever Hiro said about fame protecting her, it felt safer next to Frizz than under the eyes of a million people.

Hiro sat cross-legged on his board, eyes closed and head nodding. Ren's eyes were open, his eyescreens shimmering like two red fireflies in the air, but he didn't make a sound.

It seemed like hours later when Frizz began to stir beside her. He sat up halfway and rubbed his neck.

"How do you feel?" she whispered.

"Much better." He looked around sleepily. "Where are we?"

"Underground." She squeezed his hand. "Don't worry. We'll be safe down here till Tally-sama comes."

"You brought me here? How did you manage . . . whoa." For a moment Frizz had started to drift up from the board. "What's going on?"

Aya smiled. "We borrowed a hoverball rig from those freaks. You're almost weightless."

He stopped moving, letting himself settle beside her. "You saved me."

She sighed. "I got you in huge trouble, you mean. If it wasn't for my truth-slanting, you wouldn't be in this mess."

"Truth-slanting?"

"Aya nodded slowly. "Like I said, I saw those freaks ten days ago, but I didn't know what they were. So I sort of . . . left them out of my story."

Frizz didn't say anything, just stared at the black water.

"I think I'm a natural liar," she finally whispered.

He shook his head. "No, you're not."

"I *am*," she hissed. "I can't go ten seconds without slanting the truth. I'm the seventeenth-most-famous person in the city right now, and for what? Tricking a whole clique into thinking I was one of them! And then I couldn't even kick the story without leaving out something. You must hate me."

Frizz took a slow breath. "I never told you how I came up with Radical Honesty, did I?"

"I never asked." Aya sighed. "I pretty much just talked about my own fame obsession."

"Well, I used to lie . . . *constantly*," Frizz said. "Sometimes for a reason, but mostly just for fun. I was always pretending, making up a new Frizz for everyone I met—especially, you know, girls." He shrugged, his manga eyes glistening in the darkness. "But I started to forget who I really was. That probably sounds weird."

"Not really," Aya said. "That's sort of what happened to me with the Sly Girls. I liked being that person—she was braver than me."

He shrugged. "Sometimes it's fun to change yourself. But I wanted to see what it was like without lies. How a relationship works when you can't hide anything." He took her hand, sending a tingle through her skin. "What it's like to do this . . ."

He leaned forward the small distance between their faces, and kissed her.

As they pulled apart, Frizz whispered, "Without lies."

"Dizzy-making," Aya breathed. She felt warmth in her face, like a blush, but not shaming. A ghostly echo of Frizz's lips lingered on hers, and shivers moved across her skin.

"You're right." He smiled. "Dizzy-making is what it is."

"Even with me, the Slime Queen of truth-slanting?"

He shrugged. "But you're also honest, Aya. You put yourself in your stories, one way or another. Even that one about . . ." Frizz paused, looking around the cavern with a thoughtful expression. "Hey, are we close to that graffiti you kicked?"

"Sure, those tunnels all lead down here." She laughed softly. "You want to see them in person?"

He shook his head. "But isn't that story on your feed? Where everyone can see it?"

Aya hesitated. Before tonight, hardly anyone ever looked at her feed. But with a face rank of seventeen, lots more people would be checking her out. And at the same time, everyone was theorizing and debating where Aya Fuse had disappeared to and why.

Maybe only a few thousand would bother to watch her old stories, and most wouldn't notice what a perfect hiding place the graffiti tunnels were. But out of a million people in the city, what if just *one* sent a hovercam down to check?

"Uh-oh. You might be right. Hiro! I think we have to go!"

Her brother jerked awake. "What? Why?"

"The tunnels that lead down here, they're on my feed. That graffiti story I kicked."

"But that was two weeks ago. . . ." Hiro's voice faded.

"What did you call it?" she said. "The wisdom of the crowd?"

Stirred by their voices, Ren sat up, blinking away eye-screen flicker. "What's up?"

"This place is famous from Aya's feed," Frizz said.

Ren got it instantly, groaning, "We're so *brain-missing*."

"Moggle!" Aya hissed. "Lights off!"

The hovercam obeyed, plunging them into total blackness.

Aya blinked away traces of vision, holding Frizz tighter. Gradually her eyes adjusted, and she saw something. . . .

From one of the trickling storm drains, the barest shimmer of light was moving, sending shadows gliding across the dark.

PAPARAZZI

"Follow my voice, Moggle," she called, urging her board toward the nearest wall.

The storm drains on this side of the reservoir hadn't appeared in her graffiti story. Surely there weren't enough Aya-hunters down here to cover every tunnel and conduit in the city.

"Here's the wall," Frizz whispered.

She reached out and touched cool stone, drifting toward the sound of trickling water until a storm drain mouth echoed before them.

"Moggle? Come here," she called softly. A moment later

the hovercam bumped against her. "Go up and see if it's clear. No lights!"

Moggle slipped away.

Over her shoulder, the light from the other storm drain was growing. Aya could make out Hiro and Ren outlined against its glow.

"Can you really jam a hovercam, Ren?" she asked.

"I can try." His face appeared in midair, lit by the glow of his trick-box.

"Aya," Frizz whispered, "if you need to get out of here fast, just leave me behind. I can't ride, and no one's chasing *me*."

"Don't be brain-missing, Frizz," she hissed. "Those freaks know you've seen them. I'm not leaving you down here!"

She booted her eyescreen. In Moggle's point of view, the tunnel stretched out ahead, empty and lightless.

"This drain's clear," she said.

"Let's get moving, then," Hiro whispered. "That light's getting closer."

Aya stretched out flat on the hoverboard, pressed close to Frizz. They slipped into the tunnel, climbing swiftly upward.

Moggle was close to the surface; orange worklights glowed from the storm drain's other end. The feeds were flickering back on in her eyescreen, the city clock showing two hours before dawn.

"Careful, Moggle," she whispered. "Don't let anyone see you!"

The hovercam slowed, peeking up out of the entrance of the drain. Aya watched as it scanned the construction site—nothing but motionless machines and the empty iron frame of an unfinished building.

"Okay, Moggle. Wait for us."

Aya and Frizz climbed toward the surface, until she felt a cold breeze on her face. Moggle's outline appeared, silhouetted by worklights. The feeds came back on line in force, filling her vision with a hundred clamoring arguments: alarm over her disappearance, theories about who'd built the city killer, questions of whether it was all a hoax. Most people thought she'd been kidnapped by the mysterious hovercar. The Nameless One had decreed that the mass driver was the city's secret weapon, and was calling for Aya's arrest as a traitor.

She blinked the commotion away, focusing on the world in front of her. The Slime Queen story had taught her how meaningless the feeds could be.

Sometimes the wisdom of the crowd was just so much noise.

At the storm drain entrance, Aya scanned the construction site with her own eyes. "Okay, it still looks clear. Everyone ready?"

"Just one question," Frizz said. "Where are we going?"

"Oh, right." Aya frowned. If the crowd had managed to find the underground reservoir, where else could she hide? Every interesting place Aya had ever explored had been kicked in some story. Her dorm, all her friend's names, even her favorite color was listed on her feed.

Aya hadn't kept any secrets for herself.

""What about your place, Hiro?"

"*My* place? Could we be more obvious?"

"At least it's got good privacy. It's a big-face mansion, so hovercams can't get close. And the famous part of town isn't too far from here."

"Forget it. You're not bringing this down on . . ." His

voice trailed off. "But you're right about privacy. Why don't we head toward Shuffle Mansion. Remember that apartment I showed you?"

"Sure," Aya said. "But it's not mine."

"But it's open," he said. "Just walk in and declare it. You've got a face rank of . . . whoa! You're down to twelve now!"

"Nothing beats getting abducted by aliens," Ren said.

"What do you think, Frizz?" Aya asked.

He hesitated, then let out a sigh. "Anything sounds better than a hole in the ground."

They rose from the storm drain slowly, shivering in the freezing wind.

Aya looked down at her party dress. It was covered with wet leaves and tunnel trickle: The Return of Slime Queen. But the scent of pine trees and fresh air was a welcome relief after hours of rotting leaves and runoff.

The city looked more awake than usual for the dead of night, the windows flickering, everyone watching the feeds. Anxiety rose in Aya at the sight—the mirror image of obscurity panic.

Suddenly there were *too* many people who knew her name.

They flew back toward the city, straight into Hiro's part of town. The trappings of fame appeared around them—swimming pools drifted overhead, steaming in the cold, and torches lit the paths along the ground.

But no one was out, the windows all glittering with wallscreen light even here. No matter how famous, everyone seemed to be watching the drama unfold.

"Uh-oh," Ren called, glancing up from his trick-box. "We have company."

Aya followed his gaze—a single hovercam was climbing toward them, its lenses catching the torchlight.

"Can you jam it?" she called.

He shook his head. "It's a full-time paparazzi cam, designed to track big faces."

"We're close to Shuffle Mansion. Let's go!" Hiro cried, shooting ahead.

"Hold on tight, Frizz," Aya shouted. She dove toward the ground, picking up speed as they dropped.

Frizz held her close, their bodies twisting and turning as one. He felt more confident than on their first ride, and Aya decided to take a few risks.

She turned hard around a tall, spindly mansion, cutting between two apartments held apart by hoverstruts. The board's lifters shivered, sending them into a series of fish-tails, and Frizz's arms squeezed tighter. A few meters from her shoulder, Moggle shuddered in the strong magnetic currents.

But when she glanced back, the paparazzi cam was still there. Ren was right—this hovercam was designed to chase big faces. A few simple tricks wouldn't get rid of it.

She dropped lower and zoomed down a pleasure garden path, the warmth of burning torches whipping past on either side, the smell of smoke in her nostrils. The cam was tight on their tail now, close enough to recognize their faces.

The last thing she wanted was to show up at Shuffle Mansion with a hundred hovercams in tow.

"At the end of this garden go straight into a climb!" Frizz shouted.

"What are you planning?"

"Just do it!"

The last pair of torches was flying toward them, the secluded garden path spilling open onto a field of pre-Rusty shrines and temples. As they shot out, Aya tipped her weight back, pulling into a hard climb. Moggle followed, happily spinning barrel rolls.

"Come back and pick me up!" Frizz shouted . . . and leaped from the board.

"Frizz!" Aya screamed, spinning around to see him soaring into the air.

Of course—he was still wearing the hoverball rig, still weightless. His momentum carried him up straight in front of the paparazzi cam, and he rolled into a ball. The cam struck him right on his hoverball shin pads, the snap of high-impact plastic ringing like a hand clap.

Frizz spun away from the collision. Aya turned hard, bringing her board across his line of flight.

He hit her with a grunt, knocking Aya from the board. They tumbled through the air together until the rig's lifters compensated for her weight.

"Moggle!" she grunted, Frizz's arms so tight around her that she could hardly breathe. "Bring our board over!"

The abandoned board had come to a confused halt, probably wondering why its riders kept jumping off. Moggle eased up beside it, corralling it toward where they floated, arms wrapped around each other.

"Did I kill it?" Frizz asked.

Aya looked down and saw the paparazzi cam below, bouncing in pieces through the ancient shrines and temples. "Yeah. But that trick was panic-making!"

Moggle eased the hoverboard under their feet, and Frizz let her slide from his grip onto the riding surface.

"Not to mention damaging," Frizz said, reaching

down to rub his shins. The pads were cracked from the collision.

"Serves you right," Aya said, turning the board toward Shuffle Mansion.

She kept low, sneaking under the neighborhood's hovering meditation pool, the starlight filtering down through lily pads and darting koi.

"Aya?" Ren's voice pinged in her ear. "We're here at the mansion. Where are you?"

"Closing in. We lost that cam."

"I think you picked up another one, then. Look at the windows."

Aya frowned. "What windows?"

"*Any* windows," Ren said. "They're all the same!"

"What are you . . . ?" she began, but as they slipped out from beneath the meditation pool, a broad, old-style mansion sprawled out in front of them, its windows glowing with wallscreen light.

All of them were flickering together—hundreds of windows darting from light to shadow in unison, all tuned to the same feed.

"Uh-oh," Frizz said. "Do you see that?"

"Yeah." She swallowed. "Everyone's watching one feed, which almost never happens, unless . . ."

"Either Nana Love just got engaged," Frizz said, "or exactly one hovercam is shooting us."

Aya turned her head, scanning the air around them. Finally she saw it: another paparazzi cam a few meters away, its tiny lens focused directly on her face.

"Crap," she said.

Then she saw the swarm, dozens more hovercams sweeping in from every direction, in every shape and size.

Clouds of them maneuvered together, whipping through turns like schooling fish.

"Just go, Aya!" Frizz shouted.

"Blind them, Moggle!" She leaned forward, shooting straight toward Shuffle Mansion.

Moggle zoomed along behind, its night-lights pointed backward on full, the pursuers' lenses glittering like firework weeping willows across the sky.

By the time they reached Shuffle Mansion, the swarm was catching up, wrapping around them, shooting from every angle as she dropped toward the mansion steps.

"Good job losing them," Hiro said dryly, turning to the door. "Let us in, quick."

"I apologize," the door said. "But Shuffle Mansion is a secure building."

"No kidding," Aya said. "That's why I'm here. I'm declaring . . . um . . ."

"Legal residence," Hiro prompted. "Apartment thirty-nine."

"I'm declaring apartment thirty-nine as my legal residence. And requesting full privacy!" she said. "Oh, and by the way, I'm Aya Fuse. Um, hi."

The door paused a second, ruby jitters of laser flickering across her face and hands. Over her shoulder, a wall of hovercams was gathering, all screeching to a halt at the privacy limit. A few skidded too close and instantly dropped from the sky. Serious privacy was Shuffle Mansion's trademark.

The door opened with a soft shushing sound.

"Declaration accepted," it said. "Welcome to your new home, Aya Fuse."

SHUFFLE MANSION

The windows framed the city's skyline like a painting, gathering vistas of the sea, the mountains, even a glimpse down into the big soccer field. The views were perfect. . . .

Except for all the cams.

There weren't as many now that the chase had ended, but a few dozen still lingered at the fifty-meter limit. Aya could see the curve of the privacy barrier in the way they wrapped across the sky—a literal reputation bubble around the mansion. Even Moggle had to wait outside, because the halls were privacy-monitored as well.

Aya waved, hoping Moggle could see her.

"Close windows," Hiro ordered from where he squatted on the floor.

For a second, Aya wondered why the room didn't obey him—then grinned.

"This is *my* room, Hiro! You can't tell it what to do."

"Rooms," Ren corrected. "Plural."

Aya laughed, turning her platforms frictionless to skate across the apartment. The arm-spreading luxury of space followed her everywhere, especially the walk-in closets waiting to be filled. Aya had already stuffed her slime-spattered party dress into the hole in the wall, and she wore new shoes and a Ranger coverall with internal heating, built-in water filters, and countless pockets.

It was also slime-resistant.

"So you don't mind those freaks looking in at us?" Hiro asked. "They can watch the feeds too, remember?"

"I guess so." She sighed, waving the windows opaque. "Maximize privacy and security."

"Yes, Aya-sensei," the room said.

"Did you hear that?" she said, spinning in place. "The room keeps calling me sensei!"

"You *are* top one thousand," Ren said. He was stretched out on the floor, staring up at the chandeliers, both eye-screens glittering.

"Top twenty," Aya said. In fact, all four of them were sensei now—the others had been swept up in her reputation spiral.

"Let's all agree that Aya's quite famous, shall we?" Hiro said. "Now can we get back to business?"

She skated to a halt and shrugged. "*What* business, Hiro? Tally should be landing soon, then we do what she says."

"You mean you don't want to kick any of this?"

Aya rolled her eyes. The mind-rain had happened after Hiro had left school, so he'd missed all the lessons about Tally Youngblood. He didn't seem to realize that once she got here, everything would be okay.

"We wait for Tally before we decide *anything*," she said. "We're safe here, right?"

"Looks like it." Ren rapped the opaque window. "Hey, room. What's this made out of?"

"A layer of artificial diamond blended with smart matter and electronics," the room said. "Designed to protect residents from fame-stalkers and nano-snoops. Impossible to penetrate."

"We should have come here first," Hiro said. "But you guys had to go sense-missing over doing *exactly* what Tally-sama told you."

Aya snorted. "You wanted to go back to the bash, Hiro! Do you really think a bunch of pixel-heads would have saved me?"

"I would have thought of this place sooner or later," he grumbled.

"Sooner or later usually means *too* late," Frizz said.

Hiro turned to glare at him, but Frizz had already jumped from the spot. He drifted up to inspect the pair of chandeliers hanging from the high ceiling, each made from a million shards of glass suffused with soft blue laser light.

Now that Frizz had recovered, he was experimenting with the hoverball rig, swimming across the huge and furniture-missing apartment with broad sweeps of his arms. Aya found the sight unsettling, too much like the freaks in their lifter rigs.

"Hey, Hiro," Frizz called down. "Why does everyone always say these things are so tricky?"

"Because real flying *is* tricky," Hiro said. "All you're doing is bouncing around in zero-g mode."

"How do I try some real flying?"

"You don't, bubblehead. You'd yank your own arms out!"

"I may have had brain surge," Frizz said. "But I'm not a bubblehead."

"Not *technically*," Hiro muttered.

Aya snorted. "Who's the bubblehead, Hiro? If it wasn't for Frizz, those paparazzi cams would have caught us back in the reservoir."

"Yeah, I guess so." Hiro sighed and sat up straighter, giving Frizz a tiny bow. "Sorry I called you a bubblehead. You're pretty smart, actually."

Frizz returned the bow from midair. "And you're not as big a snob as Aya said you were."

Hiro's jaw dropped. "You said *what*, Aya?"

Ren suddenly sat upright on the bare floor. "I found

something in your background feed, Aya. About when you spotted the freaks."

"Great!" Aya eagerly turned away from her brother's glare. "Can you show it to us?"

"Sure, once I find the wallscreen in here."

"Yeah, where's the . . . ?" Aya began, but the floor-to-ceiling window was already shimmering.

"Whoa," Ren said softly. "Diamond into wallscreen. This place is *so* kick."

An image appeared, shaky and distorted. Aya recognized the view from her button cam. One week ago: Miki studying the mag-lev tunnel wall, looking for the hidden door.

Seeing the Plain Jane face again brought back all the guilt that had been smothered by her sudden fame. Aya wondered what Miki thought of her, now that the whole world could watch the Sly Girls' secret rituals, their private tricks.

Eden Maru's voice came from offscreen, echoing through the tunnel. "This is it. Stand back—there could be anything behind there."

Miki took a slow breath, murmuring, "Or any*one*."

Aya's own voice answered, "Those body-crazy freaks were just storing something down here. Nobody *lives* in this place."

The shot froze, and Hiro grunted. "'Body-crazy freaks'? So that's how they knew you'd seen them. You *told* them in your own background layer!"

Aya shook her head. "But it still doesn't make sense. How did they look through all those shots so fast? There were hours and hours of button cam, and they came after us the moment we left the party."

"What if it was the wisdom of the crowd?" Ren said softly.

Aya frowned. "What do you mean?"

“We don’t know how many of those inhumans there are,” he said. “There could be hundreds. Maybe there’s a mountain full of them somewhere.”

“Or a whole city,” Frizz said. “That mass driver took some serious building.”

A cold finger slid down Aya’s spine. She’d thought of the freaks as a small clique. The notion of an entire *city* of inhumans sent her mind spinning.

“That’s brain-missing,” Hiro said. “Why would a whole city want to—”

“Quiet, Hiro!” Ren closed his eyes. “Does anyone else hear that?”

Aya listened, and her ears caught a faint hum echoing through the room.

Frizz pushed off from the ceiling and floated down. “I think it’s coming from the wallscreen.”

Then Aya tasted it in her mouth: rain and thunderstorms.

“Smart matter,” she said. “The window’s made of smart matter. . . .”

They all spun to face the wallscreen. Its surface was rippling, the frozen image of Miki’s face warping like bad reception. The humming grew dissonant, a chord of incompatible tones fighting one another, causing the air itself to tremble. The taste of rain turned bitter in Aya’s mouth.

“Someone’s hacking your window!” Ren cried, springing to his feet

Shapes began to emerge, three human figures bulging out from the flat expanse. An arm poked through, wrapped in the frozen image of Miki, like a mummy covered in wallscreen.

Frizz grabbed Aya, began to pull her backward toward the door.

"Wait a second!" she cried. "Look at their bodies. . . ."

The figures pulling themselves from the wall weren't misshapen like the freaks; they were tall and strong-looking. They stepped out into the room, strangely faceless and still swathed with the colors of the screen, as if the smart matter had stretched around them.

"Are they pixel-heads?" Aya said softly.

They moved with a predatory grace, colors dulling with every step until they had turned a flat gray.

"No," Ren breathed. "They're wearing sneak suits."

The tallest of the three reached up and pulled the layer of gray from its head, revealing a face of cold, intimidating beauty. Her eyes were coal black and wolflike, her skin swathed in flash tattoos, every feature sharp and cruel.

She was the most famous person in the world.

"My name's Tally Youngblood," she said. "Sorry to disturb you, but this is a special circumstance."

CUTTERS

Of course, Aya had learned all about Specials in school.

A long time ago, Tally Youngblood's city had created a special kind of pretty—cruel, ruthless, and deadly, instead of bubbleheaded. Specials were originally supposed to protect the city, rounding up runaways and keeping order. But gradually they'd become their own secret clique, each generation modifying the next, like weeds growing out of control. They had contempt for everyone who wasn't

Special, and wanted to keep the whole world under control. Ultimately, they'd taken over their own city government and started the Diego War.

Tally and her friends had been Specials too, but a special kind called "Cutters." The Cutters were young and independent, and somehow they'd figured out how to rewire their own brains. They'd rebelled against the evil leader of the Specials, freed their own city, and saved Diego. Then they'd spread the mind-rain across the globe, ending the Prettytime forever.

As Aya stood before Tally, a mammoth reputation shiver went through her. This was the person who had made her world. Feeds, tech-heads, fame—everything important to her had come out of the mind-rain.

It was head-spinning, looking at a face so familiar, yet so strange.

For one thing, in Aya's school lessons Tally-sama had never looked scary. But in person her fingernails were long and sharp, her eyes deep black and penetrating. She was three years older now than during the mind-rain, of course, almost twenty, and she lived in the wild now, guarding it from the expanding cities.

Tally even *looked* wild: her hair long and untamed, her flash tattoos dulled by the sun, her skin darkened.

Aya pulled free of Frizz's grasp and gave a nervous bow, hoping her English wouldn't fail her. "I'm honored to meet you, Tally-sama."

"Um, it's actually Tally *Youngblood*."

Aya bowed again. "I am sorry. *Sama* is a title of respect."

"Great, another cult of me." Tally rolled her eyes. "Just what the world needs."

Aya heard a giggle. The other two Cutters—one boy,

one girl—had pulled off their sneak-suit hoods to reveal faces like Tally's: pretty and cruel, laced with flash tattoos. Their eyes darted around the room with nervous energy, but at the same time smiles played on their faces, as if they were enjoying the excitement.

"My name is Aya Fuse."

Tally didn't bow back, just laughed. "No kidding. Every feed in this city seems to know you. And *stop bowing*!"

"I'm . . . sorry." Aya found herself nodding. She wished somebody else would say something, but Hiro, Ren, and Frizz looked as fame-struck as she was.

The three Cutters were moving through the apartment, checking the other rooms.

"Has anyone else tried to get in here?" Tally called.

"No," Aya said. "This is a very secure building."

"Yeah, we noticed that in the ten seconds it took us to break in," the other Cutter girl said. "Is this what you call *hiding*, by the way? There's about fifty hovercams out there!"

"We tried to hide, but my face rank is recently very high."

The girl looked at her with a blank expression, as if the words had made no sense. "Face rank? Does that mean you're some kind of government official? Aren't you a little young?"

"No. Face is a measure of . . . reputation."

The girl's eyes swept around the vast apartment. "You actually live here? No wonder the cities are expanding. Still an ugly, and she's got five rooms!"

"I live here, but not every ugly gets to . . ." Aya trailed off in frustration with her English. Hiro had been right—no one from outside the city would understand the reputation economy. And this didn't seem like the best time to explain.

"You're Shay-sama!" Frizz said, snapping out of an eye-screen spin. He whispered in Japanese, "Two hundred and fourteen, mostly from mentions in history classes."

Aya nodded, feeling stupid that she hadn't recognized Shay. All the Cutters were famous. Some even had their own cults, but Aya could never keep track of them.

"My apologies, Shay-sama," she said. "Recent history is not my best subject."

Tally and the boy giggled, and one of Shay's eyebrows arched. Aya felt herself turning red, like some littlie asking for an autograph.

"Don't worry about it," Shay said. "And don't do that 'sama' thing with me either."

Tally snorted. "Yeah, she prefers to be called Boss."

"I missed you too, Tally-wa," Shay answered.

"I'm confused," Frizz said.

Aya nodded in agreement, wondering if the Cutters were speaking some dialect her Advanced English class hadn't covered. Hiro and Ren looked like they were having trouble following at all. Foreign languages hadn't been as popular back before the mind-rain, when they'd gone to school.

But Frizz came to her rescue. "We just want to show the proper respect."

"Well, respect this." Tally turned to Aya. "We need to get you out of here, and soon. You've stumbled on something that's bigger than you think."

"Bigger?" Aya said. "Than the *end of the world*?"

"Bigger than this one mass driver. We've been finding them all over the planet."

Aya swallowed, wondering if Ren had been right. Maybe there really were a huge number of the freaks, a whole city somewhere. "Why haven't you told the global feeds?"

"The other mountains were all empty," Tally said. "You're the first person to find the projectiles. And we didn't want anyone looking for the people who built them. They're dangerous."

Aya nodded. "I know, Tally-sama. I've seen them face-to-face."

"We figured that, once they came after you." Tally's eyes narrowed. "People who see them tend to disappear, including a friend of ours. That's why we're here."

"We need to get going, Tally-wa," the boy Cutter said. "The sun's coming up soon."

"Okay, Fausto, but first, two questions." Tally fixed Aya with her dark stare. "You didn't tell anyone we were coming, did you?"

Aya shook her head proudly, suppressing an urge to smirk at Hiro.

Tally smiled. "Good girl. Second question: I know you're great at mag-lev surfing, but have you ever ridden two to a hoverboard?"

"Yes."

"Recently, in fact," Frizz added.

"You can ride with me then." Tally turned to the boy Cutter. "Okay, Fausto. How do we knock those hovercams out?"

He shrugged. "Nanos. Maybe flash-bombs?"

"Definitely flash-bombs," Tally said with a shiver. "Shay and I had a bad experience with nanos once."

"Bombs away, then, Tally-wa," Fausto said. He swung a pack from his shoulder and began to rummage through it.

"Pardon me, Tally . . . -wa?" Aya said, hoping she had the correct title. "My friends have also seen the . . . strange people."

"You've seen them?" Tally turned to the others. "All three of you?"

Hiro, Ren, and Frizz all bowed apologetically, and Tally let out a groan.

"We might be less obvious if there's four of them, Tally-wa," Shay said. "And they'll be safer with us than if they stay here and get kidnapped."

"But we've only got three boards!" Tally said. "That's no good for seven riders."

"This hole in the wall can make big things," Hiro said, his English coming out a little shaky.

"Boards with lifting fans?" Fausto asked. "That work outside the city, off the grid?"

Hiro frowned. "Maybe not."

"Great," Tally said. "We'll have to call David into town, which screws up the whole plan. And you know how much he hates cities."

"Pardon me, Tally-sama," Ren spoke up in halting English. "Hiro has skill with a hoverball rig. If he stays close we can tow him."

Tally hesitated for a moment, glanced at Shay, then nodded. "Okay. That should work."

Hiro began to unstrap Frizz from the hoverball rig and put it on himself, complaining about the cracked shin guards. Ren told the hole in the wall to fabricate some crash bracelets, and reminded everyone to turn their locators off. The Cutters began to slap smart plastic on their faces and hands, hiding the lace of flash tattoos and their cruel pretty features.

Aya wondered why they needed ugly disguises out in the wild.

"Excuse me, Tally-wa, but where are we *going*?"

The Cutters traded glances, and the question hung in the air for a moment.

"We don't know yet," Tally finally said. "But we'll find out soon."

HONORARY CUTTER

Their hoverboards were waiting on the roof.

The three Cutters went ahead, their sneak-suited forms sliding across the darkened expanse like graceful ripples in the air. Aya barely saw the attack unfold—their arms spun almost invisibly, the throwing motions like a sudden breeze stirring dust and leaves across the roof.

It was all so silent and insubstantial . . . until the explosions began.

A spray of bright white flashes filled the night sky, sending jittering shadows across the roof. A cascade of detonations pounded her ears.

"Come on!" Frizz said, grabbing her hand to pull her forward.

A dozen steps away, half-blinded by the flashes, she felt a riding surface under her feet. Someone tall and muscular pressed against her, one arm around her waist.

"Hold on!" Tally shouted, and the board rose hard and fast, the scream of lifting fans filling the air. Tally's body was wiry and hard, like a gymnast full of steel cables. "Didn't we tell you to keep your eyes closed?"

"Sorry." Aya squeezed Tally's waist tightly, blinking away spots. It reminded her of all the times Moggle had blinded her. . . .

Moggle! Her hovercam was out there somewhere, probably battered and confused by the flash-bombs.

"Excuse me, Tally-wa. But can Moggle come too?"

"Who?"

"My hovercam."

"Your . . . wait. You *own* a hovercam?"

Aya blinked again, her vision slowly returning. "Almost everyone here does. How else would we put stuff on our feeds?"

"You mean you all have your own feed channels, too?" Tally laughed. "This city's insane!"

Aya looked over her shoulder. The cams, blinded by the barrage of flash-bombs, were milling around in confusion. The ultrafast Cutter boards had slipped past them in seconds.

"Please? Moggle doesn't like being left alone."

"No way," Tally shouted against the wind. "Have you not noticed we're trying to hide here?"

"Of course . . . but this would be for later. For history."

"Forget it. History's not my favorite subject either. Especially when it's about *me*."

Aya looked up at Tally's disguised face, and for a dizzy-making moment she was reminded of Lai. But the comparison was brain-missing. Tally was the most famous person in the world, and Lai was a deliberate extra—or at least she had been, before Aya had kicked her into unwanted fame.

"Tally-wa? Why are you all disguised as uglies?"

"In case one of those hovercams gets a shot. Can't let anyone know we're in town. Speaking of which . . ." Tally gestured, and her sneak suit began to change, taking on the texture and pattern of a dorm uniform.

Aya nodded with comprehension, but this was still frustrating. Here she was, riding a hoverboard with Tally

Youngblood, and no one could see it. She wasn't even wearing a spy-cam!

She realized how few real pictures of Tally she'd seen. Even in history books all the images were paintings or manga, as if Tally was some pre-Rusty from before the days of cams.

But extras wanted connections with their heroes. That was why Nana Love was always Nana-*chan*, never Nana-sensei, no matter how famous she became. Famous people owed the world images of themselves.

A few shots for history's sake wouldn't hurt anything.

As they zoomed through the new construction site, lifting fans screaming and Rusty iron shooting past, Aya booted her eyescreen. She opened up a tracking signal, whispering a short ping to Moggle in Japanese. . . .

"Follow us as far as you can."

Whatever happened next was going to be very kickable.

They made their way toward the city's edge, screaming past all pursuit.

The predawn air was bitingly cold, but Tally hardly seemed to notice. Aya turned up the heating in her Ranger coverall, thankful that she'd ditched the slime-spattered party dress.

The Cutter boards were amazingly powerful, even carrying two riders each. Of course they'd slow down once they left the grid and had to tow Hiro.

And once out of the city, Moggle wouldn't be able to follow at all.

"Tally-wa?" she ventured. "We could take the mag-lev line out of town. Plenty of metal."

Tally shook her head. "Too much traffic out there. Tons

of wardens are headed out to the mountain, not to mention the Global Concord Committee on its way."

"But they'd be happy to let you through, right? You're Tally Youngblood! You must have stacks of merits."

"Merits?"

"Oh. In my city, merits are . . ." Aya's mind spun for the right English. "Respect from authority. Like fame, but for doing community things. Because you saved everyone from the Prettytime, my city would give you any assistance you needed."

"I'm not interested in their help."

Aya paused, wondering if the Nameless One's groupie had been right after all. "Are you worried that my city built this weapon?"

Tally shrugged. "I wouldn't say *worried*. In fact, that would make things simpler. Governments have been taken down before, after all." She turned around and gave Aya a sharp-toothed smile. "By me."

Dawn began to break, and the wild stretched out before them, black and endless. The factory lights below grew sparser, and Aya's eyescreen began to lose the feeds.

Not that they'd been kicking anything new: Where was Aya Fuse headed off to now? Were all these dramatic disappearances nothing but publicity stunts? Was the mass driver the beginning of a new dark age of warfare?

Nobody had realized yet that Tally Youngblood was in town. Maybe Aya's first night of fame hadn't exactly worked out as she'd planned, but at least she had a big follow-up for the City Killer story.

She smiled. Rescued from aliens by Tally Youngblood!

As they neared the edge of the grid, the formation drew closer, their magnetics interweaving. Aya felt the shudder of

Hiro's rig connecting with the boards.

"Bye, Moggle," Aya whispered in Japanese. *"Get home safe."*

"You ready?" Tally asked. "Things might get a little nervous-making now."

"Don't worry about me. This can't be any worse than mag-lev surfing."

"It might be." Tally looked over her shoulder, eyes narrowing. "When Shay and I watched your feed story and saw all those tricks you pulled—going undercover, mag-lev surfing, flying up the mass driver—we decided you were a pretty tough girl."

Aya bowed a little, feeling herself blushing. "Really?"

"Really. We figured you wouldn't mind having one more adventure, Aya-la, seeing as how saving the world is so high on your list of priorities."

Aya looked into Tally's eyes, trying to read her expression. She was pretty sure that *-la* was a good title. Tally had called her friend *Shay-la* at least once.

"An adventure?"

"That's why we're here, to take you on an adventure."

Aya nodded, but she was still unsure. "But you came to protect me from the . . ." She didn't know the English word for *freaks*. "The strange people. Right?"

"Well, partly." Tally shrugged. "We also want to get to the bottom of all this, and find our friend who disappeared. So we figured a tough girl like you would want to help with that, Aya-la. As a sort of honorary Cutter."

Aya felt a smile spreading across her face, and she had to remind herself not to bow. "Of course. I would be honored."

"Thought you'd say that. I'm just sorry your friends have to come along."

"They must be honored too, Tally-wa."

"Don't be so sure. You know that tracking signal you've been sending to your hovercam?"

"Um, my what?"

"Your hovercam, Aya-la . . . the one that's been conveniently following us." Tally's toothy smile appeared again. "We've been boosting your signal just a little. Not so much that your local wardens will bug us, but enough."

Aya swallowed. "Enough for what?"

Tally turned to face the front of the board. "For that."

Aya stared ahead into the distance. She couldn't see anything but the blackness of the wild, and the glow of dawn beginning to encircle the horizon.

"Let me know when you can see them," Tally said. "I want this to look realistic."

"Realistic?" Aya murmured, and a few moments later her eyes caught a glimmering cluster among the fading stars. She squinted, clearing the last bit of city interface from her eyescreen, and realized what they were.

The running lights of three hovercars.

"Are those friends of yours, Tally-wa?"

"I've never met them. But I think you have."

Aya blinked, her excitement moving in a new and stomach-churning direction. The hovercars were closing fast, the scream of their lifting fans echoing across the wild . . . the inhumans had found her again.

And Tally Youngblood had let it happen.

THE PLAN

"Everyone!" Tally shouted. "Head back toward the city!"

The board whipped around beneath them, and Aya squeezed tight, remembering that her crash bracelets were useless out here in the wild.

"What about my brother?" she cried.

"I got him," Tally said, angling closer to Hiro. She shouted, "Better hang on, just to be safe!"

Tally climbed above Hiro's outstretched arms, and seconds later Aya saw his fingers grasping the board's sides.

The board shot forward, back toward the city. Even with the magnetic connection, Hiro's knuckles turned white as they accelerated.

Aya stared down at the black forest rushing past. This whole towing thing had sounded tricky enough with them all going *slowly*.

"What if Hiro falls out here?" she cried in Tally's ear. "We're all helpless! You were just using us as . . ." Her English faltered.

"*Bait* is the word," Tally yelled. "I'll explain everything later, Aya-la. This is the part where you have to trust me!"

Aya shut her eyes, reminding herself who this was. She was riding with Tally Youngblood—the most famous person in the world—not some crazy-brained Sly Girl.

However panic-making this looked, everything was going to be okay.

She dared a glance over her shoulder. The three hovercars were gaining easily on the overloaded boards. As they grew nearer, the lifter fans began to shake the air.

Tally began to rock the board, and Aya squeezed tighter. "What are you *doing*?"

"They're trying to push us around. We have to make it look like it's working!"

"But why?" Aya cried, trying to keep her balance without shifting her feet. One wrong step, and she'd squash Hiro's fingers!

"Have you not been listening?" Tally yelled. "We don't want to give ourselves away!"

Aya frowned. What was the point of looking helpless? Whatever trap the Cutters had planned, wasn't *now* the time to spring it?

The edge of the city was in sight—maybe that was where they'd make their move. Once they were over the grid, Hiro could fly again, and their crash bracelets would work.

She looked around. Frizz and Fausto were only ten meters away, Frizz's manga eyes wider than ever. Fausto was swaying their board back and forth, an expression of wild delight on his plastic ugly face. Ren and Shay were pulling ahead, riding low and straight.

A car pulled level with Aya and Tally. The side door slid open, revealing two freaks staring at her, lifter rigs strapped on.

"They're waiting until we get back over the grid," Tally yelled. "That means they don't want to kill us."

"Wonderful." Aya swallowed, thinking of all the worse things than death the freaks might have planned.

One of the hovercars swept in closer, and Aya felt a familiar shudder building in the air.

"Shock wave!" she shouted, just as the turbulence hit.

Her ears popped, the wind battering her eyes shut. Then the board hit a pocket of low pressure and dropped.

Her feet lifted from the riding surface, and Aya clutched Tally's waist as hard as she could.

Then the board popped back up, Aya's ankle twisting as her feet slammed down against a bump on the riding surface.

Hiro's fingers . . .

Aya heard his cry as he fell away, the city's edge still in the distance.

"Tally!" she screamed.

"Don't worry." Tally's body twisted in Aya's grip, bringing them around in a heart-stopping turn. For a moment there was nothing below Aya but trees and brush—she was almost upside down, the howling lifter fans pushing her *down* past Hiro's tumbling form.

Aya wanted to scream, but every ounce of her strength went into squeezing Tally's waist.

They fell past Hiro, his panicked cries Dopplering by, then the board twisted again, sweeping up beneath them. Tally reached out and casually grabbed his arm, swinging him onto the board.

His face was pale.

"Sorry to cut that so close, Hiro," Tally said, glancing up at the hovercars. "Didn't want to make it look *too* easy."

The three of them staggered on the unsteady board, arms wrapped around each other. The lifting fans screeched under Hiro's added weight.

Aya's nose caught the scent of burning metal. "Are we overheating?"

"Yeah," Tally said. "The timing's perfect."

They shot across the city's edge just as the fans seized up with metallic shriek. The board shuddered as the magnetics took over.

But they were still descending. . . .

"We're too heavy!" Hiro yelled. "Let me go! I can fly now!"

"Not yet." Tally still had an arm wrapped around him.

Above them six inhumans had jumped out of the cars. Two pursued each of the Cutters' boards, their needle fingers glistening in the dawn light like icicles.

"This is when you get them, right?" Aya asked. She hoped Moggle was close enough to capture the Cutters bursting out of their disguises and surprising the inhumans.

"Not yet," Tally said.

In the distance Aya saw Frizz and Fausto spinning out, their board losing control as two inhumans closed in on them.

Aya looked down. The ground was still rushing up too fast for her liking. Tally guided them toward a narrow alley between two factories, where one of the inhumans waited, all four arms extended.

"Let me go!" Hiro shouted.

Tally nodded. "Okay, in three seconds . . . two . . ."

On *one* she pushed him from the board. Hiro leaped forward, arms outstretched—but something was wrong.

He was spinning wildly out of control, his limbs whirling like a top. An inhuman swept up beside his flailing form and stabbed him with a needle.

"*Hiro!*" Aya screamed. "Tally! Do something!"

"Don't worry, Aya-la. It's all going according to plan."

Tally twisted the board away from the inhuman. But another waited at the alley's other end. They were headed straight toward him.

"Tally! Climb!"

"Quit waving your arms, Aya-la, or this could get messy."

"It's already messy!"

They shot straight into the outspread arms of the

inhuman, and Aya felt a needle jab in her side. Slivers of cold began to spread through her, like tendrils wrapping around her lungs and heart.

"Do something," she whispered, still expecting Tally's smart-plastic disguise to burst away and reveal her fearsome Cutter face.

Then she saw it clutched in Tally's hand—one of Hiro's shoulder pads, its straps undone. Tally had pulled it off on purpose. She dropped it as the hoverboard spun toward the ground.

"Just hang on for a few more seconds, Aya-la. Don't want to bump your head." Tally slumped down toward the riding surface, her eyes fluttering closed. But she sounded totally alert as she hissed, "And wherever you wake up, don't call me Tally. We're just your ugly friends, got that?"

"But why . . . ?"

"Trust me, Aya-la. Sometimes it's a messy business, saving the world."

Aya's brain was spinning from the needle jab, losing its grip on consciousness, but slowly she grasped what the plan had been all along: a way for the disguised Cutters to be captured.

Aya and the others had been nothing but bait. . . .

And Tally Youngblood—architect of the mind-rain, the most famous person in the world—was nothing but a truth-slanting Slime Queen.

Part III

LEAVING HOME

Reputation is an idle and most false imposition;
oft got without merit,
and lost without deserving.
—*Othello* (Iago, Act II, scene iii)

CAPTIVE AUDIENCE

The whole world was dizzy-making.

Everything spun and whirled, dreamlike and unsteady beneath her. A confusion of anger, exhilaration, and terror tumbled through her thoughts, cut with the cold taste of betrayal. All five senses blurred into a constant roar, as if every certainty had tangled.

Then a sudden focus: a mote of pain amid the jumble of sensations. Something fierce stabbing her shoulder, rushing red-hot through her veins . . .

Aya Fuse came suddenly awake.

"No!" She sat bolt upright, the sudden fury roiling through her, but strong hands pushed her back down.

"Don't yell," someone said. "We're supposed to be asleep."

Asleep? But Aya's heart was pounding, her blood sizzling with energy. Her body convulsed, hands flexing and clawing at the hard metal floor beneath her.

A shuddering moment later, her vision finally cleared.

An ugly face looked down at Aya. Two fingers reached out and carefully pulled her eyes wider—checking one, then the other.

"Try to relax. I think I gave you too much."

"Too much what?" Aya asked breathlessly.

"Wake-up juice," the ugly girl said. "You'll be okay in a minute, though."

Aya lay there, her heart pounding, the burning sensation fading in her shoulder. She took steadying breaths, waiting until reality stopped spinning.

But steady was a relative concept. As her body soaked up the mad energy that had possessed her, Aya gradually realized where she was: the cargo hold of a large hovercar that was passing through a violent storm. The frame shuddered, the metal floor bucking beneath her, and rain battered the windows. Lifting fans shrieked as they fought to keep the craft level, adding their cacophony to the howling wind.

In the dim and shifting light, it took Aya a moment to remember that the ugly girl who'd awakened her was in disguise.

"Tally Youngblood," she breathed. "You're a truth-slanting, trust-wrecking waste of gravity!"

Tally chuckled. "I'm glad that was in Japanese, Aya-la. Because it didn't sound very respectful."

Aya squeezed her eyes shut, forcing the sticky gears of her mind to switch to English. "You . . . lied to us."

"I never lied," Tally said calmly. "I just didn't explain the details of our plan."

"You call this a *detail*?" Aya looked around the dark, storm-tossed hold. A windowless metal door separated them from the drivers' cabin. The walls were lined with cargo webbing, which twisted and swung with the rocking of the car. The air was hot and muggy, and Aya felt trickles of sweat inside her heavy coverall. "We trusted you, and you got us captured by those freaks! On *purpose*!"

"Sorry, Aya-la. But explaining our plans to some feed-happy random didn't seem like a very icy idea. This was our one chance to find out where these kidnappers come from. We couldn't risk you turning it into your next big story."

"I never would have done that!"

"That's what you told the Sly Girls."

Aya's mouth opened, but no words came out. Her fury began to rise again, the last dregs of wake-up juice boiling in her blood. Why was Tally twisting everything?

"That was *totally* different!" she finally managed. "I may have misled the Sly Girls, but I didn't use anyone as bait."

"Not as bait, but you did use them, Aya-la. And we had to do the same to you."

"But you *lied* to us!"

Tally shrugged. "What did you say in your interview? 'Sometimes you have to lie to find the truth.'"

Aya found herself speech-missing again, appalled to have her own words used against her. But then she remembered who'd said them first—Frizz. The last she'd seen of him, he'd been spinning toward the ground on Fausto's board.

"My friends . . . are they okay?"

"Relax. Everyone's fine." Tally moved aside.

Aya pulled herself up, leaning back against the shuddering hovercar wall. Shay and Fausto sat cross-legged on the other side of the hold, with Hiro curled between them, still unconscious. Ren's long form stretched down the middle of the cabin, snoring happily.

Frizz lay next to Aya, absolutely still. She rolled closer and squeezed his hand . . . but he didn't respond.

"Are you sure he's all right?" Aya asked. "Frizz got stuck with those needles twice last night."

"I already countered the nanos they stuck you with.

He's just asleep." Tally pulled her sleeve up and glanced at the flash tattoos on her arm. The patterns there were laid out like an interface, not mere decoration. "You've all been out for six hours, which seems a little excessive to me. Do you always sleep till noon?"

The hovercar lurched, setting off Aya's accumulated aches and bruises. Her muscles were sore after the hours of crouching in the reservoir, fleeing paparazzi, and sleeping on a shuddering metal floor.

"No, we don't. We were pretty exhausted after running around all night, waiting for you to *rescue us*." She spat the last two words.

"Listen, Aya-la. Believe it or not, you're safer here with us than back in your city. The freaks would have snatched you sooner or later—they always do. At least this way we're around to protect you."

Aya snorted. "And you've been doing a great job at that so far."

"You look like you're in one piece to me." Tally's eyes narrowed. "So far."

"But how do you think this feels?" Aya cried. "You're the most famous person in the world, and you *used* us!"

"How do I *think* it feels?" Tally leaned in closer, her black eyes glowing with sudden intensity. "I *know* what it's like to be manipulated, Aya-la. And I know what it's like to be in danger. While your city was building you mansions to live in, my friends and I have been protecting this planet. We've spilled more blood than you have flowing in your veins. So don't try to make *me* feel guilty!"

Aya shrank away. For a few terrible seconds, she'd glimpsed the Special face behind the mask, and heard the razors in Tally's voice. She remembered the shudder-making rumors back in school about what the word "Cutters" really meant.

Suddenly, she believed them.

"Stay icy, Tally-wa," Shay said from across the cargo hold. "The randoms are fragile, and we still need their help."

The anger faded from Tally's face, and she slumped back against the cargo webbing, as if exhausted by the outburst. Suddenly she looked like an ordinary ugly again. "Okay, but *you* talk to her. She's making me less than icy."

Shay turned to Aya, spreading her hands. "I understand your annoyance, Aya-la. You know that feeling you're having about Tally right now? Let's just say I've had that feeling before. A few times."

Tally smiled. "You couldn't live without me, Shay-la."

"I *was* living without you," Shay said. "The rest of us Cutters were having a great time in Diego, until you showed up with this brain-missing plan."

"Brain-missing?" Aya looked from Shay to Tally. "But you're friends, I thought."

"Best friends forever," Shay said softly. "It's just that getting captured by a bunch of freaks isn't my idea of fun. How about you, Fausto? You like being stuck in this brain-rattling hovercar?"

"Loving every minute of it," he said absently, shifting his sneak suit through different dorm plaids, as if he didn't want to get involved.

"I don't remember you having a better idea," Tally said.

"I had plenty of ideas." Shay turned back to Aya. "But I've learned that when Tally gets a plan in her head, it's easier just to go along. Otherwise, you'll find out that Tally can be very, very special."

Aya swallowed, wondering if her English had been scrambled by whatever the inhumans had stabbed her with. The conversation had started her head spinning again. The Cutters were so different from how merit-rich, world-saving, famous people were supposed to be.

"By 'special' . . . do you mean something bad or good?" she asked.

"Not bad or good. Just special." Shay shrugged. "Tally's someone who makes things happen, that's all, and the easiest thing is just to play along. So are you going to be a good little random and help us?"

"But you're the Cutters!" Aya said. "You ended the Prettytime, and I'm fifteen. How am I supposed to help *you*?"

Shay smiled. "Well, from the rough translation we saw of your story, you seem to be pretty good at fooling people."

Aya sighed. "Thanks for the reminder."

"You're welcome," Shay said. "All we're asking is for you to lie a little more. Explain to our surge-crazy captors why a bunch of foreign uglies were trying to sneak you out of the city." She pointed at her ugly mask. "These disguises won't hold up if they get suspicious."

Aya frowned, slowly realizing how tricky this was going to be. "But you don't even speak Japanese."

"I'm sure you'll think of some explanation," Shay said, then laughed. "Just imagine the great story you'll get out of it. Honorary Cutter!"

Aya nodded slowly. It would be an amazing story: an ugly drawn into helping the Cutters save the world. Plus, she could show what the famous Tally Youngblood was really like.

"But I don't even have a spycam. Stories don't mean anything without shots."

"Are you sure about that? Check your eyescreen."

Aya flexed her ring finger. The familiar feeds were all missing, but a few signals hovered at the edge of her vision: an unrecognizable language from some passing city, fragments of the hovercar's interface beneath layers of security. And in its corner, her last known face rank captured as they'd shot through the flash-bombed hovercams: eight.

"I made the top ten," she said softly.

Then she saw it: Moggle's signal, its power minimized but steady, coming from only meters away.

Her eyes widened. "Moggle's stuck to the bottom of the car."

"Yep. It snuck under there while they were loading us on," Shay said. "Pretty clever little hovercam you've got there."

Aya looked down at Ren's sleeping form. "It's his mods, not mine."

"Smart boy."

"Okay, you've got a story," Tally said. "So is it worth your time to help us save the world?"

"You promise to protect us?"

"Yeah," Tally said. "I promise."

Aya took a slow breath, remembering Lai's words on the sled.

"Sure, I'll help. I happen to *like* the world, after all."

"That's just bubbly of you, Aya-la," Shay said. "Now what about your friends? Are they going to be a problem?"

"No, I'm sure they'll help too." Aya took Frizz's hand, wondering if she should wake the rest of them up. It was best if they all learned what was going on now, before anyone had a chance to . . .

. . . *give everything away*.

Aya looked down at Frizz, her eyes widening. He was beginning to stir at her touch, a soft moan escaping his lips . . . his beautiful lips that could speak nothing but the truth.

And suddenly Aya realized that now was *not* the best time for Radical Honesty.

ADVANCED ENGLISH

"Aya?" Frizz murmured softly, his eyes fluttering open. "Is that you?"

"Yeah, it's me." She leaned closer. "Are you okay?"

"I think I'm covered in bruises," Frizz answered. "And I *know* I'm very upset with Tally Youngblood."

Aya squeezed his hand, unsure how much to tell him about their situation. After what Shay had said, she wondered what Tally would do to Frizz if she found out that his brain surge threatened her plans.

Knock him out again? Toss him out of the hovercar?

Aya decided that she needed help with this.

She turned to Shay. "Wake those two up, Shay-la? I might as well explain everything at once."

Shay nodded, then nudged Hiro and Ren. They came awake slowly, their eyes sweeping around the shuddering cargo hold in disbelief.

"What happened?" Hiro said, sitting up. His lifter rig had been removed, and his party clothes were rumpled beyond repair.

Aya helped Frizz sit up, then gestured the others closer.

When they were huddled together, she spoke in rapid Japanese.

"They used us as bait, and let us all get captured. So I guess we're headed to wherever those freaks come from."

Ren glanced at Shay. "So that's the real reason they're in disguise."

"Yeah. And now they need our help," Aya said. "They want to sneak into the inhumans' base without anyone knowing who they are. We have to pretend they're friends of ours."

"Are they brain-missing?" Hiro cried. "How dare they drag us into this?"

Aya turned to him and shrugged. "I guess Tally's so famous she thinks she can do anything."

"Well, *I'm* not helping them." Hiro crossed his arms. "Not after they got us kidnapped on purpose!"

"But we wouldn't just be helping *them*," Frizz said. "Tally said there were more mass drivers. Lots. Don't you think that somewhere there might be a cylinder pointed at our city, Hiro? Maybe programmed to take out your mansion?"

"Well, maybe," Hiro mumbled, casting an annoyed look at Tally.

"And don't you think this will make a better story if we help them?" Aya asked. "They want us to be sort of . . . honorary Cutters."

"Honorary Cutters?" Ren whispered. "That *would* be a pretty big story."

Hiro shook his head. "Pretty crappy story without cams."

"Not to worry," Aya said. "Moggle is still with us, stuck to the bottom of this car."

"Moggle did that while we were all knocked out?" Ren laughed. "My mods rule!"

Aya nodded. "So what do you say, Hiro? Do we kick this?"

The hovercar hit a patch of serious turbulence, dropping out from under them for a moment. They all lifted into the air, then came down hard against the metal floor. But Hiro just sat there as though the storm wasn't happening, thinking hard.

Finally he nodded. "Okay, but we all kick our stories at the same time. And everyone gets to use any of Moggle's shots they want."

"Agreed," Aya said.

"You two are very strange sometimes," Frizz said. "Can I point out that how you kick this story is *not* our biggest problem."

Aya sighed. "You're right about that."

Ren's excited expression fell, and he let out a slow breath. "Radical Honesty."

"So what?" Hiro said. "Can't you just keep quiet?"

Frizz shook his head. "I can't even keep a surprise party a secret. How am I supposed to hide the fact that the world's most famous person is standing next to me in disguise?"

"You can't keep a *birthday party* secret?" Hiro said. "Okay, Radical Honesty is officially the most brain-missing clique I've ever heard of!"

"Well, when I came up with it, I wasn't planning on sneaking Tally Youngblood into someplace full of aliens, okay?" Frizz cried. "And neither were you, until you found out you could kick the story!"

"What's your point?" Hiro asked.

"There's one more thing," Aya interrupted. "I think Tally's a little . . . unstable."

Hiro and Ren looked at her like they thought she was kidding, but Frizz nodded. "When I first got the idea for Radical Honesty, I spent some time studying the history of brain surge. Not just the bubbleheads, but everything, including what Tally's city did to Specials." Frizz glanced at the three Cutters. "They could be deadly when people got in their way. Their motto was, 'I don't want to hurt you, but I will if I have to.' And they did. They even killed people."

Hiro gave Aya a sidelong glance. "And you want us to be 'Honorary Cutters'?"

"But I thought they were all cured," she said.

Frizz nodded. "Most of them were completely despecialized. But the Cutters who'd protected Diego in the war were allowed to keep their reflexes and strength, because their brains were cured." He leaned in closer. "But Tally Youngblood never changed at all. She didn't want anyone 'rewiring' her, she said—that's why she disappeared into the wild."

"Crap," Ren said. "They really don't tell it that way on the history feeds."

Aya swallowed. This was much worse than she'd thought.

She turned to Frizz. "So you understand the problem? You can't let Tally know about Radical Honesty. There's no telling what she'll do if she finds out you could ruin her plans."

Frizz's eyebrows rose. "So let me get this straight, Aya-chan. You want me, a person who can't lie, to lie about the fact that I can't lie?"

"We need another plan," Hiro said.

"What about the language barrier?" Ren said. "Maybe you could just tell her everything . . . but in Japanese."

Frizz shook his head. "It doesn't work that way, Ren. Speaking the wrong language is just another way of hiding the truth. I can't deceive people."

"But couldn't you, sort of, *forget* they don't speak Japanese?" Ren asked.

"I can't lie to myself any more than I can to them." Frizz groaned with frustration. "The more we talk about this, the more I'll think about it. And the more I think about it, the more I'll need to let them know we have a secret!"

He groaned again, looking in Tally's direction.

Tally returned his gaze. "So how's that going over there? Coming to any decisions?"

In perfect English, Frizz said, "They don't want me to talk to you!" He choked to a halt, clamping both hands over his mouth.

Tally raised an eyebrow. "What?"

"Nothing!" Aya said in English. "We're still discussing everything, that's all."

Shay gestured with her chin. "Well, you better hurry up. Looks like someone's coming to visit."

Aya looked up and saw that the metal door to the drivers' cabin was swinging open.

Oh, great, she thought. *More people for Frizz to talk to*.

UDZIR

Two of the inhumans floated in.

Even here inside the car, they wore their hoverball rigs. The man glided across the cargo hold over their heads. The other, a woman, waited, hands grasping the edges of the doorway, fingertips glistening with needles. Behind her Aya could see the drivers' cabin, where two more inhumans were seated at the car's controls.

This close, the freakish faces were even more unsettling. The inhumans' eyes were so far apart that they seemed to point in different directions, like the gaze of a fish. The floating man took them all in without turning his head, fixing Aya with one steely eye. He kept himself in place by stirring the hot, muggy air with his hands and strange bare feet.

"I see you are awake," he said. "And no one is injured?"

His Japanese was imperfect—Aya realized that after six hours in flight the hovercar could be anywhere in Asia. She wondered where the inhumans really came from.

"We're all in one piece," she said. "But not very happy."

"We did not expect to have to take seven of you," he answered, performing a little midair bow. "We apologize for any discomfort."

"Discomfort!" Hiro cried. "You kidnapped us!"

The inhuman nodded, an expression of regret passing over his strange features. "It is necessary to hide ourselves for the moment. You have to be silenced."

"Silenced?" Aya said, swallowing. "You mean you're going to *kill* us?"

"No, indeed! And I am sorry for my Japanese," he said. "I only mean you cannot communicate with your home. But very soon there will be no more need for secrecy, and you may return."

"Why can't we go now?" Aya asked.

"We land shortly, then we can explain everything," he said. "In the meantime, my name is Udzir. May I ask yours?"

Aya paused for a moment, then bowed and introduced herself. Ren and Hiro followed suit. The Cutters got the hint, giving false names when Udzir turned to them.

But his stare lingered on Tally.

"You do not seem like the others," he said.

Aya wondered exactly what he meant. Back in the Prettytime, the Global Concord Committee had averaged the different regions of the world, and the crazy surgery since the mind-rain had only further confused the old Rusty genetic categories. But uglies still showed their heritage, and the Cutters' smart-plastic masks didn't look particularly Asian.

But Udzir was singling Tally out—had he glimpsed a hint of uncured Special in her eyes?

"It's true," Frizz said through gritted teeth. "She *isn't* like the rest of us."

Aya snapped out of her silence. "What Frizz means is that our friends are students from another city. They don't speak Japanese very well."

"They don't speak it at all!" Frizz proclaimed. Aya squeezed his hand, willing him to stay silent.

"English, then?" Udzir switched effortlessly.

Tally nodded. "Yes, English is better. Did you say where we're going?"

"You will see soon."

"We've been flying south for hours," Fausto said. "And it's pretty hot. We must be near the equator."

Udzir nodded, smiling. "And you are very *good* students, I see. Let me reward your cleverness: We will soon land on an island that the Rusties called Singapore."

Aya frowned, trying to remember her geography. The name wasn't ringing any bells, but there were hundreds of Rusty cities that had been lost. At least the change in subject had quieted Frizz's need for Radical Honesty.

The hovercar was descending now, the ride growing rougher as clouds darkened the windows. The hold began to pitch from side to side, setting the cargo straps swinging. Aya felt her stomach lurch, and was suddenly glad she hadn't eaten anything since dinner the night before.

Tally, Fausto, and Shay seemed unfazed by the turbulence. They shifted their weight like hoverboard riders, compensating for every movement of the car. It was as if they'd learned to read the storm's howls and anticipate the next assault of the wind.

Udzir, unperturbed in midair, looked down at the Cutters with renewed interest. "You've ridden in a tropical storm before?"

"We travel a lot," Tally said simply.

"I noticed your hoverboards were made to fly in the wild. Most unusual, especially for uglies."

"Really?" Shay said. "They're all the rage where we come from."

Frizz tensed up beside Aya, and she dug her fingernails into his hand.

"Which is where, exactly?" Udzir asked.

"We're from Diego," Shay said, and Aya felt Frizz relaxing a little at the sound of the truth.

"A city known for its forward-looking nature," Udzir said approvingly. "Perhaps you will appreciate our project."

"Which is what?" Tally asked.

"When we land," the man said. The hovercar banked suddenly, and he glanced toward the drivers' cabin. "As you will all realize very soon now. If you wish to take a look at our home, you may."

"Why not?" Tally said. She pulled herself up and peered

down through one of the tiny windows. The other Cutters followed suit.

Moggle was probably shooting from the bottom of the car, but Aya decided to take a look herself. She gulped a deep breath of the dense, muggy air to fight the nausea rising in her stomach, and pulled herself up by the cargo webbing.

"Be careful, Aya," Frizz said.

She nodded, gaining her feet unsteadily. The window was small and streaked with rain, the plastic thick and vision-warping.

The car was passing through a layer of clouds, the window revealing nothing but a dark gray mass and streaks of rain. But gradually the clouds grew thinner, boiling away into tendrils as the car descended.

The view cleared, the hovercar abruptly steadying.

A steely gray ceiling hung just above them, a solid sheet of clouds. Beneath the storm a dense rain forest spread out all the way to a shimmering glimpse of ocean. The mass of jungle was wrapped around the largest ruins she'd ever seen. Clusters of huge towers reared up from the wind-whipped treetops, their metal skeletons disappearing into the clouds.

Even with the storm raging, construction lifters were attached to the ancient Rusty buildings, grasping iron beams like birds of prey, as if waiting for a break in the weather to tear them apart.

The car banked hard, tipping the view in a dizzy-making way, the Rusty towers disappearing. Now Aya could see a broad clearing cut from the jungle. A hoverport sprawled out beneath her—hundreds of cars and heavy lifters arrayed across a landing field, mag-lev lines converging from every direction on a central station.

"This is huge," Tally breathed.

"Yes," Udzir said. "We are very proud of all we've done."

"But you're clear-cutting the jungle!" Tally said, and Aya heard razors in her voice.

"We serve a greater cause," Udzir said. "Once you see more, you will understand the sacrifices we've made."

The car banked harder, gyrating around the port like a tiny boat being sucked into a giant whirlpool, and more structures rotated into Aya's view. Long storehouses, prefab housing, automated factories all jumbled together without rhyme or reason. Figures darted among them, wearing heavy plastic coats against the rain . . . and flying.

None of them walked—they glided from place to place, pushing from poles driven into the ground, gripping with hands and feet to fight the wind.

Aya turned from the window and sank back to the metal floor, her nausea rising again.

"What is it?" Frizz asked.

"You were right, Ren," she said softly. "There really is a whole city of them."

"We're not a city," Udzir said. "We are a movement."

"Sounds bubbly," Tally said. "What kind of movement?"

Udzir spun himself in midair, reaching out a hand to grasp the webbing on the cabin's ceiling. "We're saving the world from humanity. Perhaps you'll want to join us."

Tally smiled. "Maybe we will."

"I doubt that," Frizz muttered.

Aya recognized the pained look from when Frizz had been trying not to blurt out her face rank; he was about to explode! If only Udzir would shut up and go back into the drivers' cabin.

But both inhumans were looking at Frizz curiously now, as if he'd said one radically honest thing too many.

"Your cities are expanding across the wild like a brushfire, young man," Udzir said. "So don't judge us before you know our purposes."

"I'm *not* judging you," he said, squeezing Aya's hand so hard it hurt.

Udzir frowned. "Then what exactly are you doing?"

"He's just airsick," Aya said.

"I'm not airsick!" Frizz's voice was choked. "I'm trying not to tell you everything!"

"What the . . . ?" Shay began.

"*What* are you trying not to tell us?" Udzir said sharply.

Aya saw Frizz's willpower failing, and she reached out to try and stop him. But one of her hands was clenched in his, the other tangled in cargo webbing.

"That this is Tally Youngblood!" Frizz burst out. "And she's here to take you down!"

HARD LANDING

For a moment no one said anything.

Then Shay broke the silence, yelling at Frizz, "You bogus little moron!"

Tally launched herself across the cargo hold, flying beneath Udzir and into the woman hovering at the door. As she flew, her face seemed to explode, the smart-plastic disguise vanishing in an angry puff.

The woman swung her needle-tipped fingers, but Tally snatched her wrists and propelled a shoulder into the woman's stomach. She crumpled instantly, and Tally rolled past her into the drivers' cabin.

Across the hold, Shay rose almost casually to punch Udzir in the face. As he spun in midair, she slipped past his flailing limbs and after Tally.

Fausto stood up, his mask bursting from his face to reveal cruel-pretty features.

"I don't want to hurt you," he announced. "But *nobody* move."

"We're not moving!" Hiro said.

Aya turned to Frizz, whose face was pale. "Are you okay?"

"I'm sorry," he said. "I couldn't stop myself."

Suddenly the hovercar banked, twisting into a violent turn. Udzir's unconscious body crashed against the ceiling, then bounced back into the middle of the hold, spinning in midair. As Aya gripped the cargo webbing, her stomach lurching toward her mouth, she realized that he wasn't really spinning—he was steady in the air, the hovercar spinning *around him*. . . .

Shay appeared at the drivers' cabin door, shoving the crumpled inhuman woman out of her way.

"A quick question," she said, bracing herself in the frame. "Do any of you bubbleheads know how to fly a hovercar?"

"What?" Aya cried. "Don't *you*?"

Shay spread her hands. "What are we supposed to be? Magic?"

The car pitched into a wild climb, and the two weightless inhumans went tumbling again, their limbs flopping like rag dolls. The needle-tipped fingers of the woman whizzed past Aya's face, missing her by a few centimeters.

"Someone grab her!" Aya shouted.

Frizz reached out and snagged the woman's leg, which snapped her body down against the cabin floor with a sickening *thud*.

"Oops, sorry," he said.

"You'd think Tally would have asked *before* she knocked out the drivers," Shay said from the doorway. "But that's Tally for you."

"Get in here and *help* me!" called Tally's voice. Shay turned and disappeared as the hovercar went into another series of wild spins, dropping again.

Fausto leaped across the hold, grabbing the unconscious woman. He guided her into the cargo webbing, making sure her needle fingers weren't exposed.

The car dipped and twisted, the hold spinning all the way around every few seconds. But Fausto gathered and secured Udzir's body easily. He darted across the tumbling surfaces, stepping from wall to floor to ceiling, like a littlie playing in a funhouse.

The lifting fans shrieked unhappily, drowning out the howl of the wind. Aya clutched the cargo webbing with white knuckles, barely keeping her grip. Gravity twisted around her, like some wild animal trying to pry her from the wall.

Then suddenly the car leveled out, the scream of the lifting fans settling into a steady roar. At last the floor of the cargo hold felt like *down* again.

Shay appeared in the doorway. "Everyone okay?"

"More or less," Fausto said. "Took you long enough to find the autopilot."

"I wish we hadn't," Shay said. "It's programmed to take us straight into their hoverport. And it looks like the drivers got off a warning, so they'll be expecting us. We have to jump. Everyone's got crash bracelets, right?"

"Sure, but are we still over their city?" Fausto asked.

"After all that craziness?" Shay said. "Kilometers away. But there's plenty of Rusty metal down there, as far as we can tell."

Fausto's eyes widened. "Are you kidding? Isn't that a little risky?"

Shay shrugged. "Safer than staying in here."

"At this speed, we'll need more than crash bracelets." Fausto knelt and stripped the forearm lifter pads from Udzir, tossing them to Shay.

She strapped them on, turning to Ren. "Come on, you and me first."

"We're jumping out into a storm, with only ruins to catch us?" he cried. "But that's *brain-missing*!"

She laughed. "You'd rather wind up with a bunch of insane surge-monkeys? Are you thinking of joining them?"

Ren groaned, then started to unwind himself from the cargo webbing.

"Open the side door!" Shay called to Tally. "And we'll see you at the usual place!"

The wall behind Aya and Frizz began to move. They scrambled away, suddenly doused by driving rain, the wind tearing at their clothes and hair. As the door opened, the hovercar lost its stability again, shivers passing through its frame, the storm rushing greedily inside.

In the hard gray light that spilled into the cargo hold, Aya saw how close they'd come to crashing—the tops of storm-tossed trees were shooting past, their highest branches whipping the underside of the car.

"Ready?" Shay yelled against the wind.

Ren nodded, and she wrapped her arms around him,

jumping through the sliding door with a wild and wordless cry.

"Our turn, Hiro!" Fausto said as he stood up, the inhuman woman's lifter pads hastily strapped onto his forearms.

"This better work!" Hiro cried, then turned to Aya. "Good luck, and don't forget Moggle."

Fausto grabbed Hiro and yanked him out of the hovercar, the two of them disappearing into the driving rain without a sound.

"But there's two of us left," Frizz said. "And only . . ."

"Me," Tally said. She stood in the doorway of the drivers' cabin, slipping on a hoverball shin pad. "Lucky those freaks all wear these things. I think they can't walk on those feet of theirs."

"You can carry us both?" Aya asked.

Tally scowled. "Why should we take this moron? He betrayed us!"

"But he can't help it!" Aya cried.

"What is he, brain-missing?"

"No," Frizz said. "I just have to tell the truth."

"You have to do *what*?"

"Radical Honesty," Frizz said. "It's a kind of brain surge."

Tally's eyes narrowed. "Wow. Your city is officially the weirdest place on Earth. Why would they do something like that to you?"

Aya tried to think of something distracting to say, but Frizz was already explaining, "I asked for the surge. I designed it, actually."

"You mean you're a voluntary bubblehead? That's it—I'm leaving you behind. Come on, Aya—there's no time to argue!"

Aya struggled out of Tally's grip. "You can't just leave him here! Those freaks will get him!"

"So? He's a freak too. And this is dangerous enough with only two of us!"

"I'm *not* a bubblehead," Frizz said. "But she's right, Aya. You'll be safer without me. Leave me!"

"Crap," Tally growled. "You just *had* to say that!"

She grabbed them both, then jumped.

At this speed the rain felt hard as stones.

"Moggle!" Aya yelled as they tumbled away from the hovercar. "Follow me!"

Then the treetops hit—wet ferns whipping and slapping at her face and hands, branches crunching as they tumbled through the air. Tally's grip around Aya was lung-crushing, the gray light spinning into darkness as they dropped beneath the canopy of jungle.

The roar of the hovercar slipped away, and Tally twisted next to Aya, the borrowed hoverball rig straining to maneuver among tree trunks and shafts of rusty iron. Aya felt magnetic forces wrenching at her crash bracelets—the three of them rose up above the trees again in a shallow hover-bounce, like a speeding rock skipping off water.

They dropped again, tearing through tangled vines and ferns, every obstruction heavy with rain. Aya felt thorns tearing at her clothes and hair—then suddenly the forces in her crash bracelets disappeared, and the Earth itself crashed up against her.

They hit at a shallow angle, tumbling through brush and leaves, skidding across meters of thick, wet mud. She felt her ribs cracking in Tally's grip, her breath forced from her like a punch to the gut.

Finally they slid and rolled to a halt.

Aya took deep, painful breaths, slowly opening her eyes.

Above her, vast flocks of birds were wheeling, scattering away from their wild and unexpected arrival. The jungle was dense down here, the sky almost completely hidden. Aya could actually see the path their sidelong fall had taken, a tunnel of wrecked branches that stretched away into the distance. Water still spilled from the leaves and ferns they had shaken in passing, as if the storm had followed them down.

"You two okay?" Tally asked.

"Uh," Aya managed. It hurt to breathe.

"Let me guess," Frizz said. "We ran out of metal."

"Barely enough," Tally said. "Any less and we would have splatted."

"We *did* splat," Aya grunted. Her soaking hair was tangled around her face, leaves and ferns and mud plastered over every inch of her body.

Tally raised herself into a crouch, pointing up at a towering structure that stretched up beside them. "Yeah, but if we hadn't fallen past that, we'd be paste right now. Whatever those freaks are up to includes salvaging all the ground-level metal from these ruins."

Aya groaned, sitting up slowly. If they'd almost crashed, what about . . . ?

She started to flex her ring finger.

"No pings!" Tally snapped, grabbing her wrist. "You'll give us away. Besides, we must be a few kilometers from the others. Much too far for your skintenna to carry."

"But they could be hurt!"

Frizz took Aya's hand, pulling it gently from Tally's grip.

"Fausto and Shay were only carrying one passenger each. They probably had a softer landing than the three of us."

"Probably? You mean if they didn't fly straight into a tree!" she cried, but resisted the urge to boot her eyescreen. She scanned the jungle, wondering if Moggle had found enough metal to come down soft. "You mind if I yell, at least?"

Tally shrugged. "Go ahead."

Aya sucked in a deep breath and yelled, "Moggle!"

From the depths of the jungle, she spotted an answering flash of night-lights. Through the ferns and hanging vines, she saw the hovercam making its way toward them, weaving from side to side, its lifters grasping whatever metal was left in the ground.

"Did you get that fall?" she called.

The night-lights flashed once more, and Aya smiled.

Ren's mods had pulled through once again.

JUNGLE

Aya had never realized how *annoying* the wild could be.

The jungle was unimaginably hot, snarled, and logic-missing. Every direction was blocked by massive roots that spilled down from the trees. Spiderwebs glistened among the ferns, and the humid air was choked with clouds of insects. Ankle-grabbing vines covered the ground, which the rain had turned into a maze of waterfalls, rivulets, and mudslides. Her Ranger coverall was having trouble staying slime-resistant, and Frizz's clothes—the formals he'd worn to the tech-head bash last night—were threatening to fall apart.

The dense plant life had only one redeeming feature: It made the downpour bearable. Though the rain found its way steadily to the jungle floor, streaming down tree trunks and dripping from saturated leaves, at least it wasn't battering her on the head.

It was amazing that any of the Rusty ruins had survived in this climate, but Aya glimpsed the metal skeletons of ancient buildings among the trees. They were wrapped in vines and ferns, the jungle at work tearing apart their straight lines and right angles.

"Where are we headed, anyway?" Frizz asked. "How do we find the others without pings?"

"Shay said the usual place," Tally said.

"Usual?" Aya waved a mosquito away from her nose. "I thought you'd never been here before."

"She meant the tallest tower in the ruins." A smile played on Tally's lips. "That's where we always met people back in ugly days."

Frizz frowned, and Aya felt a radically honest moment coming on.

"You and Shay are logic-missing," he said. "Sometimes you're like best friends, other times you seem to hate each other."

"Maybe that's because sometimes we're best friends," Tally said. "And other times we hate each other."

"I don't understand," Frizz said.

Tally sighed. "Back in the Prettytime, we kept winding up on opposite sides. It wasn't because we wanted to fight, but people kept rewiring us, manipulating us to betray each other." Her voice grew softer. "I guess we kind of got stuck that way."

"But when the mass driver story kicked, you called

her to help," Frizz said. "So she's your friend, right?"

"Of course she is—she saved me from life as a bubblehead, along with everyone else in the world. But along the way, we had a lot of fights." Tally's eyes narrowed at Frizz. "That's why your brain surge freaks me out. Bad things can happen when other people rewire you. Stuff you can't fix later."

"Maybe you *could* fix things," Frizz said, "if you talked with people instead of running off into the wild."

Tally's eyebrows rose, and Aya said hastily, "Maybe we should figure out where we're going, and leave this for later."

"Let me get this straight," Tally said to Frizz. "You had to get brain surge just so you could *talk about things*?"

"I used to lie all the time," he said. "I couldn't trust myself, so I had to change."

"That's so courage-missing!" Tally said. "Couldn't you just *learn* to tell the truth?"

"Truth-telling *is* what I'm learning, Tally."

"But you aren't making a choice!" Tally pointed at her temple. "I've still got Special wiring in my head, but I fight it every day."

"And sometimes you lose, I've noticed," Frizz said.

Tally's lips curled. "You haven't seen me *really* lose it, bubblehead. You better hope you never do."

"Technically, I'm not a—"

Aya stepped between them. "Maybe instead of comparing brain surge, we should figure out which way to go? The rain's clearing a little."

Tally glared at Frizz for a long moment, then looked up. The steady drumbeat of rain on the leaves above had lessened.

"Fine with me," she spat.

She spun away and bounded toward the nearest tree, launching herself at its trunk and scrambling up toward the treetops. Frizz and Aya watched in silence—it was mesmerizing when Tally moved quickly, slipping through the ferns with deadly grace, scuttling along branches that seemed hardly strong enough to hold her weight.

"I keep upsetting her," Frizz said.

Aya sighed. "I guess Tally and Radical Honesty don't mix. She and Shay have been through a lot. They fought a war when they were our age, after all."

He dropped his eyes from the treetops. "What if she's right? Maybe I'm just too lazy to tell the truth without surge."

"You're not lazy, Frizz. Not everyone starts their own clique."

"Maybe," he said, slapping a mosquito on his arm. "But if it wasn't for my Radical Honesty, we wouldn't be stuck out here in this jungle."

"No, we'd still be captives." Aya turned to him, looking into his manga eyes. "And if it wasn't for your Radical Honesty, you probably wouldn't have stopped me that night to compliment my nose."

"Don't say that," Frizz said, pulling her closer. "Sometimes it scares me, that we met by accident. If you'd left that party a minute earlier, we wouldn't even know each other."

She pulled a wet fern leaf from his hair. "Then you wouldn't be stuck out in this mud-plastering jungle."

"I'd rather be here with you than anywhere else," he said.

Aya wrapped her arms around his shoulders. His jacket was soaked, ripped down the back from their wild landing, and her sore ribs still throbbed, but she squeezed him hard. "I don't care what Tally-wa thinks. When you say stuff like that, I'm glad you can't lie."

He gently pulled her closer, and their lips met in a kiss. For a moment the buzzing gnats and dripping rain faded around Aya, leaving only Frizz's shivering warmth in her arms.

There was a sudden thrashing in the trees above. They glanced up.

It was Tally . . . dropping through the air, hands darting out to catch branches and vines, swinging and tumbling from perch to perch, handhold to handhold.

She alighted a few meters away, landing softly among the ferns. For a moment she stared at them, her Cutter features intense and unguarded.

"What's wrong?" Aya asked, pulling away from Frizz.

"I spotted some inhumans near here."

"Did they see you?"

"Of course not." Tally turned away, her face clouded.

"But you're upset," Frizz said.

"It's nothing."

Aya decided not to ask, but Frizz, of course, had other ideas.

"Our kissing upset you, didn't it?"

Tally turned to him, shifting from wide-eyed surprise to anger, and then to something else. . . .

"Frizz," Aya said softly. "I don't think that Tally-wa cares if we—"

"The last time I kissed someone, I wound up watching him die," Tally said simply. "And I was just thinking: Dying's one of those things that *can't* be fixed. Not by talking about it, not with all the brain surge in the world."

Aya swallowed, holding Frizz tighter, her heart pounding.

"I'm sorry, Tally-wa," he said. "That's sad."

"Tell me about it." She looked away. "I can't believe I

just said that. Is your brain-missing surge contagious or something?"

Aya nodded slowly.

"But you shouldn't give up kissing," Frizz said. "Just because of that."

Tally held his gaze for a moment, then laughed bitterly. "You want to stand here and discuss ancient history?"

"No," Aya said quickly. "I think we've had enough Radical Honesty for the moment."

"Then follow me," Tally said.

She spun around and bounded away into the mass of ferns, trees, and mud. Aya stared after her—and sighed.

Wherever they were going, this was going to be a long walk.

RUIN

Keeping up with Tally wasn't much fun.

Thanks to her Special muscles and reflexes, nothing stopped her—not the giant tangles of brush, the dead trees crumbled into a dozen pieces, or the roaring tumults of rain. She scrambled up trunks to check their route, and leaped across the interlocking web of branches overhead, splayed like a monkey against the sky. As she waited with a bored expression for Aya and Frizz to catch up, the rain and mud slid from her sneak suit, which was camo-mottled into a hundred greens.

Moggle bounced from ruin to ruin, using magnetic fields like stepping-stones. In the few places where the hovercam couldn't find a way, Aya and Frizz had to carry it through the steaming heat. Tally refused, saying she didn't like cams. The amazing thing to Aya was how much a soccer-ball-size hunk of lifters, optics, and electronic brains could weigh.

But the worst part was crawling under tangles of hanging tree roots, slithering through mud, and hacking away spider-webs and vines. Sheets of rotten leaves disintegrated under her hands, and a nest of centipedes scattered from beneath one misplaced foot. The gray light of the cloudy sky barely filtered through the trees, shrouding the jungle floor in constant gloom.

To distract herself, Aya wondered who Tally had been talking about. Lots of people had died in the Diego War, of course, but no Cutters that she could remember. Who else would Tally have been kissing? Everyone else back then was either ugly or a bubblehead. It didn't make sense.

Tally was so different from normal famous people. If some boyfriend of Nana Love's had died, everyone in the city would know his name. But Tally was so closed off—even her outbursts of radical honesty were mysterious.

Aya felt a mosquito biting her arm and smashed it flat—too late. Blood was spattered all over its tiny mangled body. She sighed and flicked it away.

"How can Tally-sama stand to live out here?" she muttered to Frizz. "It's so comfort-missing."

"I don't think she cares about comfort," he grunted. He was carrying Moggle, trying to struggle over a rotting tree trunk without dropping it.

Aya took the hovercam from him. "And apparently she doesn't like her friends much either. So what *does* she care about?"

"Well, the planet for one thing." He dropped back to the muddy earth, and took Moggle back from her. "That's why we're out here, remember?"

"Oh, yeah . . . that." Aya sighed, trudging forward. "I never expected saving the world to be so hot and slime-covering. Are we even going in the right direction? I haven't seen Tally in ages. She must be off scouting again."

"Wherever we're headed, at least there's some metal around." Moggle was rising out of his arms, moving ahead eagerly as its lifters found purchase.

They followed the hovercam until the jungle parted before them. At the center of a recently cut clearing, a pair of ancient Rusty spires stood, their steel girders wrapped in vines.

Aya blinked in the sudden brightness; the downpour must have stopped some time before. It was like two different worlds: Back in the jungle the rain still fell, the trees dripping like wet clothes, but out here in the open, rays of sunshine played across the ferns.

With a soft thud, Tally landed beside them.

"Stay quiet," she said softly, looking up at the towers. "The freaks I saw before are still up there."

Aya took a step back into the shadows, whispering, "You mean you took us right to them?"

"We need to borrow some transportation. Did you think I was going to watch you two *walk* across this jungle?"

"Do you want us to get captured again?" Frizz asked.

Tally sighed. "Not with your bubblehead surge. You'd just give everything away."

"Technically, I'm not a—"

"Just wait here," Tally said, darting across the clearing and into the undergrowth around the base of the ruins.

Aya peered up at the two towers.

One was much taller than the other, but still not as big as some of the spires she'd glimpsed from the hovercar. But like all Rusty buildings, it was big and simple—childlike square angles, no gaps or moving sections, just a huge column thrusting into the air. Vines climbed its girders, wrapped around them tightly, as if the jungle itself were trying to drag down the vast metal skeleton.

At its summit, she saw three inhumans tending a construction lifter. In their hoverball rigs they looked like swimmers, pushing against the muggy air, their long-toed feet waving like extra pairs of hands.

Frizz pointed. "There she goes."

Tally was climbing through the center of the taller tower, through gaps in the ancient rotten floors and invading vegetation. She leaped from level to level, boosting herself with her borrowed hoverball rig, as graceful and silent as a cat slinking toward its prey.

"Follow her, Moggle," Aya whispered. "But stay out of sight."

She pushed the hovercam forward, and it zipped across the clearing and disappeared into the ruin.

Tally had already reached the top, but the inhumans were too intent on their work to notice her approach. They were guiding the construction lifter's claws, setting its cutting blades to tear away a large section of girders.

Moggle rose swiftly through the ruin, lenses glinting in stray beams of sunlight. Aya was aching to watch Tally from the hovercam's point of view, but using her skintenna would give them away.

The construction lifter's blades came to life, wild shrieks erupting as whirring teeth bit metal. Stirred by the sudden commotion, clouds of tiny brown birds—

bats, Aya realized a moment later—swept out from the darkness inside the spires. Waterfalls of sparks showered out in glittering arcs.

As the sound spilled across the jungle, Tally flew from the cover of the vine-choked ruin, ramming straight into one of the inhumans. The figure crumpled, then spun away from the tower, floating limply through the air.

The other two turned to look, but Tally had already disappeared again, bouncing from the collision to slip back into the ruin. The two inhumans made confused gestures at each other, stirring the air frantically, trying to figure out what had happened.

Tally shot from hiding again, barreling into them. Her blows landed swiftly, sending both spinning through the air.

"Uh-oh," Frizz said.

He was pointing at Tally's first victim, who was floating away from the ruins. Drifting farther and farther from the towers' magnetic field, the figure began to descend. . . .

"You think that's going to be a soft landing?" Aya asked.

"I doubt it," Frizz said, stepping out of the shadows and calling upward, "Tally, look!"

But the construction lifter's blades were still grinding away, the shrieks echoing through the jungle, sparks cascading around Tally as she subdued the other two inhumans.

"She can't hear you!" Aya cried. "What do we do?"

"Can Moggle get him?" Frizz asked. "Like back in the city, when you and I fell off your board?"

"But Moggle can't hear us either."

The inhuman was over the jungle now, descending faster, still spinning and unconscious, headed down toward the trees.

"Then use a ping!" Frizz cried.

"But Tally said we shouldn't—"

"You have to!"

Aya swallowed, then flexed her ring finger. "Moggle, go catch the freak who's falling! Quick!"

She cut the connection, hoping the ping hadn't been long enough to track.

Overhead, Moggle's tiny outline shot away from the ruin, rushing out toward the tumbling figure. The two shapes met just at the treetops, disappearing into the dense canopy.

"I hope that wasn't too late," Frizz murmured.

The sound of the metal-eating blades finally cut off, the last echoes fading into the screams of unsettled birds. The construction lifter pulled a few meters away from the ruins, then began to descend, like a huge pair of claws reaching down toward them.

Tally was at the controls, with two unconscious inhumans aboard.

"Brought you some hoverball rigs!" she shouted down. "They must have a magnetic line around here to carry this scrap metal away. No more walking!"

"Um, that's great," Aya called back up. "But did you see what happened with the third one?"

Tally scanned the horizon. "That's funny. Where'd she go?"

Aya waited another few seconds as the lifter descended, unsure how to explain what she'd done.

Frizz's Radical Honesty spared her the trouble.

"She went spinning off," he said. "Past the ruin's magnetic field."

"Did she fall?" Tally asked.

Frizz shook his head. "No. We sent Moggle to catch her."

"Good thinking." Tally smiled. "I guess sometimes you

city kids aren't completely useless."

"There's one problem," Frizz said. "Moggle was up there in the ruins with you, too far away to hear us. We had to send a ping."

"You sent a ping?"

He nodded. "It was that or let her fall."

Aya swallowed, bracing herself for an explosion of Cutter fury.

But Tally's was voice calm and cold. "You had to send your toy after me, didn't you? Did it occur to you that a hovercam might have given me away? Or that I might not *want* everything I do put in some brain-missing feed story?"

"Sorry," Aya squeaked, still expecting a burst of red-hot anger.

Tally only sighed. "Okay, then we better get moving. They'll be on their way here soon."

She knelt and began to strip the hoverball rigs from the two inhumans, tossing a pair of shin pads down to Aya.

"Uh, Tally?" Aya said nervously. "We don't know how to use these."

"Just set them to zero-g," Tally snapped. "I'll tow you."

As they strapped the pads on, Aya glanced at where Moggle and the inhuman had fallen. Nothing moved among the treetops except a few birds settling back after the disruption. Aya wished she could check through Moggle's viewpoint, just to see if the inhuman and her hovercam had survived.

But Tally probably wouldn't find that idea very happy-making.

Once Aya was suited up, Frizz booted the hoverball rig for her. An eerie weightlessness overtook her body, as if invisible spirits had grasped her arms and legs. She took a step and found herself wafting upward, the breeze gently pushing her along.

"Quit playing around!" Tally ordered. "Grab my hand."

"But Moggle's not back yet!"

"Do you think I care? We have to *go*!"

"But can I ping Moggle to follow us? Otherwise it'll just wait here!"

"Don't worry, Aya-la," Tally said, firmly grasping her wrist. "You'll still be real, even with no hovercam watching."

She grabbed Frizz's offered hand and pulled them both away into the air.

METAL

They shot through the air above the treetops, scanning the skies for any sign of pursuit.

Tally had been right: A skein of thick cables stretched across the jungle canopy, magnetic purchase to carry iron salvaged from the ruins—more than enough metal to carry them. Compared to tons of scrap, three people in hoverball rigs were nothing.

But it was nervous-making, flying without a hoverboard. Eden Maru had made it look easy, but Aya felt wobbly in the lifter rig, like balancing on invisible stilts strapped to her limbs.

More disorienting was Moggle's absence. Aya's second set of eyes was lost and alone, probably damaged, falling behind them every second.

And she didn't even have a button cam.

"See those ruins?" Tally said. "That's where Shay and Fausto should meet us."

Ahead and to their right, where a glimpse of ocean glimmered with sunlight, a huge tower rose above the jungle, its summit still lost in the slowly breaking clouds. More skeletal spires clustered around it, all of them in various stages of being dismantled. Even at this distance, Aya could see cascades of sparks spraying out from metal-chewing blades.

Here above the jungle, Aya could see how far the ruins stretched. She remembered that Rusty cities had held populations of ten and twenty million, much bigger than anything in the modern world. And the inhumans were taking it all apart.

"What do they need all this metal for?" Aya said.

Frizz turned to her. "Maybe this is where they make those projectiles you found. They could ship them by mag-lev to their hollowed-out mountains."

"Nice theory, Frizz-la, but I doubt it's that simple," Tally said. "David and I have been all over the planet. Everywhere we go, someone's been secretly tearing into the ruins, salvaging them faster than the cities can."

"And it's always the freaks?" Aya asked.

"As far as we can tell. A friend of ours saw them stripping the big ruins back near my home city. He's the one who told us about them." Tally looked back at Aya. "Then he disappeared, like you would've if we hadn't come along."

"That explains why everyone's scrambling for metal," Frizz said. "Our city was even talking about ripping the earth open to find whatever the Rusties left in their mines."

Tally gave him a cold look. "If they try that, they'll be getting a visit from the new Special Circumstances."

She paused for a moment, then suddenly pulled them to a halt, dragging them lower into the trees. They sank through dense layers of branches, through tangled vines and sticky expanses of spiderweb.

"What's wrong?" Aya whispered.

"Someone heard your ping."

Aya stared up into the fragmented sky, but saw nothing.

The surface of Tally's sneak suit began to stir, its mottled patches of green camouflage shifting and slithering, as if breaking into separate pieces. Slowly the scales began to spread, crawling across Aya's coverall. She looked at Frizz, and saw that he too was being enveloped, the sneak suit spreading out like a pair of scaly wings.

"This will hide your infrared," Tally whispered. "Just don't move."

A shadow moved in the jungle, blocking out the scattered shafts of sunlight filtering through the leaves. Before the sneak suit covered her face, Aya glimpsed its source—a pair of hovercars passing slowly overhead.

A creaking sound filled the jungle, cables sagging as the cars' weight pressed against them. Birds scattered, the air full of fluttering green wings for a moment. Aya could feel her hoverball rig trembling as the magnetic currents built, her hair crackling.

The cars seemed to pause overhead, and Aya heard voices—probably freaks in hoverball rigs gliding alongside, looking down into the jungle. She focused on the ground below, trying not to breathe.

But finally the shadows floated past, the creaking of the jungle slipping into the distance.

Long seconds after the sound had faded, Tally released Aya and Frizz. Her suit folded around her body again, slivers of Tally's skin showing as it restructured itself. Aya glimpsed rows of thin scars lining her arms.

"That's why we can't use pings," Tally said.

"You know, they also might have noticed you beating up their workers," Aya said, taking a painful breath. Tally's grasp had left her feeling like a crumpled piece of paper.

"Good point." Tally smiled. "But they know we're somewhere on this line. We have to stay down here until those cars are out of sight."

They floated there, listening to the constant insect buzz of the jungle. Aya was growing more comfortable in the hoverball rig. She practiced stirring the air like the inhumans did, drifting in the cool treetop breezes.

Up here in the highest layer of the trees, the jungle was much less dismal. The vines sprouted flowers, and shafts of sunlight caught the iridescence of insect wings. A flock of pink-crested birds fluttered just overhead. They squawked and fought over the best branches, baring white bellies inside green wings. One stared suspiciously down at Aya, a bright yellow beak between its beady eyes.

Maybe the jungle wasn't so bad after all—once you could float above the mud and slime. Of course, its magnificence just made Aya feel even more cam-missing.

"Tally-wa," Frizz said softly. "May I ask you a question?"

"Can I stop you?"

"Probably not," he said. "Those cylinders Aya found, what if they weren't really weapons?"

"What else could they be?" Aya asked.

Frizz paused for a moment, staring at the cables strung around them. "What if they were just metal? That's what this is all about, right?"

"But Frizz," Aya said. "They had smart matter in them, remember? That proved they were weapons!"

He shook his head. "That proved they had a guidance system. But what if they were programmed to fly to this island?"

"Why would anyone bomb *themselves*?" Aya asked.

"They wouldn't have to aim for the buildings," he said.

"That's true," Tally said. "This is an island, after all. The cylinders could fall into the ocean. That would cool them off after reentry, then you could salvage the metal."

Frizz spun in midair to face her, his hands stirring the ferns around him. "You said the inhumans were salvaging metal everywhere. So maybe the mass drivers are just a way to get it all here."

"Easier than smuggling it halfway around the world," Tally said. "Maybe all those empty mountains we found had already launched all their metal."

Frizz nodded. "That would explain why they were moving out of the place you found, Aya-chan. They were almost ready to send the cylinders here."

"Frizz!" Aya cried. "Why are you on *her* side?"

"It's not about sides." He shrugged. "It's about what's true."

"What's the matter, Aya-la? Afraid your little story won't hold up?" Tally chuckled. "I wouldn't be surprised if you got it wrong. If you see everything through hovercams and feed stories, you wind up blind to what's right in front of you."

Aya tried to answer, but found herself sputtering. She glared at Frizz.

He cleared his throat. "Well, we still haven't got a clue *why* they want all this metal."

"They're not building anything here," Aya said. "All we've seen is a few factories and some storage buildings."

Tally pondered for a moment.

"You heard what Udzir said about making sacrifices, right?" Aya said. "Didn't that sounded a little *ominous* to you?"

"He said they wanted to save humanity." Tally sighed. "Historically speaking, that can mean anything from solar power to worldwide brain damage."

"*Or* worldwide destruction!" Aya said.

"With the cities expanding like crazy, David and I have been tempted to do a little destruction ourselves." Tally shook her head. "Sometimes it looks like we're headed back to Rusty days."

"But you can't be Rusty without metal," Frizz said quietly.

Tally looked at him. "You think the inhumans are trying to slow down the expansion?"

Frizz shrugged. "You need metal for buildings and mag-levs, after all."

"And without a steel grid, nothing hovers," Tally said. "No cars, no boards, no new fancy floating mansions."

"But wouldn't everyone just start strip-mining again?" Aya asked.

"It's easier to blow up a mining robot than someone's mansion," Tally said softly.

Aya raised an eyebrow.

"If blowing up things was what you were inclined to do . . . in special circumstances." Tally shrugged. "If that's what the freaks are up to, I might even be on their side. Once they stop kidnapping people."

Aya stared through the leaves at the cluster of towering

ruins being taken apart, stunned by the thought that Frizz and Tally could be right.

If the mass drivers weren't weapons, that meant the world wasn't descending into a horrific new age of warfare. If the freaks had figured out a way to stop the cities from ruining the wild, it meant that some human beings really were sane, and that Toshi Banana and his kind could shut up for good.

But unfortunately it also meant one other thing: that a brain-missing fifteen-year-old named Aya Fuse had completely blown the biggest story since the mind-rain.

MAKE LIKE A MONKEY

They flew across the treetops, Aya and Frizz each holding one of Tally's hands.

Brilliant flocks of birds burst up from the jungle as they passed, and wild monkeys screeched at them from below. Tally had to drag them into the trees to hide from hovercars again, down among a shimmering cloud of butterflies whose radiant orange wings were bigger than Aya's hands.

But she hardly saw any of it.

The City Killer story had seemed so logical: a whole mountain hollowed out, like some Rusty command post from three centuries ago. A mass driver pointed at the sky, ready to launch cylinders full of smart matter and steel.

But what if she'd gotten it wrong?

Aya tried to remember the exact moment when she'd become certain that no more proof was needed.

When she'd realized how famous a city-killing weapon would make her?

The greatest outrage was always the biggest story, after all. She'd learned that from Toshi Banana, with his earth-shattering alerts about new cliques and poodle hairstyles. That was why every feed in the city had jumped on her story without question. Of course they'd just as gleefully jump on Aya if she was proven wrong.

Reigning as Slime Queen for a day would be nothing compared to that humiliation. Maybe the city interface didn't care why people were talking about you—because you were talented or merely beautiful, ingenious or just crazy, concerned about the planet or outraged over nothing at all—but Aya cared.

And she didn't want to be famous for a false alarm.

They spent the next few hours navigating the network of cables, hiding from construction lifters and hovercars, backtracking when they reached dead ends.

It wasn't the most happy-making trip. Moggle's absence nagged her like a constant toothache, and the thick, humid air felt like soup in Aya's lungs. Sweat soaked her Ranger coverall.

When Aya complained that she and Frizz hadn't eaten since the night before, Tally produced emergency bars from the pockets of her sneak suit. While they ate, Tally found and munched her way through a bunch of tiny bananas, entirely green and inedible-looking. Apparently her Special stomach could digest anything.

They made gradual progress toward the cluster of skyscrapers. A steady stream of lifters laden with scrap flowed outward from the spires, marking the route.

With only a few kilometers to go, Tally pulled Aya and Frizz down into the jungle.

"We have to stay out of sight the rest of the way."

Aya groaned. "Does that mean we have to walk again?"

"I don't have time for your mud-crawling," Tally said. "Just keep those rigs in zero-g mode, and stay close to the cables."

Tally gave them both a firm push deeper into the jungle, until the slanting afternoon sun disappeared behind the tangle of vines and branches.

"Aren't you going to tow us?" Aya asked.

Tally snorted. "It's a little too crowded down here to hold hands. Just make like a monkey."

To demonstrate, she grabbed a nearby branch and pulled hard, sending herself shooting away through the dense vegetation. Reaching out to snag a passing tree trunk, she swung herself to a halt.

"See? It's easy when you're weightless."

Aya shared a sidelong glance with Frizz, then sighed and looked around for a handhold. A nearby stem of bamboo looked strong enough. But as she air-swam closer, Aya spotted a creature with about a million legs crawling along it. She reached out gingerly, avoiding the crawly thing, and gave the bamboo a tug.

The effort propelled her a few meters before the heavy tropical air eased her to a halt beside a lichen-wrapped tree trunk. She twisted herself sideways and kicked out at it, and was rewarded with a much longer glide through the tangled forest.

It was a strange sensation—though the hoverball rig carried her weight, Aya still had plenty of mass and inertia. Getting herself moving took real effort, especially through the humid air. But once she'd built up speed, coming to a stop—or even changing direction—proved just as tricky.

It didn't help that every surface seemed to be slimy or sticky or covered with insects, or that all the vegetation was still water-laden from the storm. Every time Aya plunged through a growth of ferns, she shook loose a clothes-soaking spray. But gradually she got the hang of it, her brain learning to juggle the tasks of spotting clear paths through the obstacle course, checking ahead for the next object to push off from, and avoiding sticky spiderwebs and water-dumping ferns.

Gliding through the dense canopy, Aya marveled at how rich and intertwined the jungle was, how much more complicated than some ten-minute feed story. She wondered how hard becoming a Ranger would be. At least then she'd be doing something useful, protecting something beautiful instead of stirring up fake calamities for a bunch of bored extras.

After half an hour of pulling herself from vine to trunk to branch, Aya realized she was being watched.

A troop of red-faced monkeys perched in the trees nearby, silently observing as she and Frizz crashed through the ferns and vines. Aya couldn't blame them for their perplexed expressions. She was painfully aware of the eons of evolution that separated her from them, her lack of simian reflexes and . . .

Prehensile toes.

Aya grabbed hold of the next vine to bring herself to a halt.

"You okay?" Frizz asked, sliding to a stop beside her.

She nodded. "Yeah. But I think I just figured out their crazy body mods."

"The inhumans'?" he asked, then laughed. "You mean

you could actually concentrate while swinging along like a . . ." He trailed off, looking at the tiny faces watching them through the leaves. "A monkey."

She nodded again. One of the monkeys dangled from its feet, long toes curled around a branch like fingers.

"Even Hiro noticed," she said. "Back when we were hiding and waiting for Tally-wa . . . the freaks are like *monkeys*."

"What are you two gossiping about?" Tally called impatiently from ahead. "We're almost there!"

Aya realized they'd been talking in Japanese, and she gave a little bow. "Sorry, Tally-wa. But I think we figured out something. If you're getting around in a jungle wearing zero-g rigs, another pair of hands is a lot more useful than feet."

"Like the freaks?" Tally thought for a moment, drifting closer in her rig. "I guess it makes sense having more fingers, if you're never going to touch the ground."

"So maybe they're collecting metal for a huge grid," Aya said. "You think they want people to give up cities and live in jungles, like some sort of hovering *monkeys*?"

"And go backward five million years?" Tally raised an eyebrow. "That's a pretty radical way to get along with nature."

"Radical is what the mind-rain is all about, Tally-wa," Frizz said.

Tally sighed. "Why does everyone always say that like it's *my* fault?"

Frizz looked at her and shrugged. "Well, you started it."

"Don't blame me. I didn't tell everyone in the world to go crazy!"

"But didn't you expect some weird stuff to happen?" Aya asked.

Tally rolled her eyes. "I didn't expect anyone to change their feet into extra hands. Or let hovercams follow them all day. Or get brain surge just so they could tell the truth!"

Frizz shook his head. "But we lost so much in the Prettytime—all the foundations were gone. So we're stuck making it up as we go along!"

Tally laughed. "So what else is new, Frizz? Life doesn't come with an instruction manual. So don't tell me that humanity being logic-missing is *my* fault." She spun herself around and pointed up through the trees. "Anyway, we're almost at those skyscrapers. Shay and Fausto are probably already there."

Above them, the skeletal spires glinted with afternoon sunlight through the trees. The upper reaches were swarmed with construction lifters, and the screech of metal-chewing blades echoed down from them.

"But if we can't use pings, how do we find them?" Aya asked.

Tally shrugged. "We make it up as we go along."

THE PILE

The jungle was clear-cut around the base of the spires, but the ancient Rusty streets were heaped with lattices of salvaged steel.

The pile reminded Aya of a game littlies played: You dropped a bunch of chopsticks onto the floor, then tried to pick up one without moving the others. But instead of chopsticks, these were huge metal beams, encrusted with ancient concrete and rusted cables.

There was no sign of the freaks down here at ground level. The deconstruction crews were all up in the spires, cutting more metal for the pile.

"See the tallest one?" Tally pointed. "Stay under cover till we get there."

"You mean crawl through this?" Aya glanced at Frizz. "But I heard that some ruins have Rusty skeletons in them."

Tally laughed. "That's up north. Down here in the tropics, the jungle eats everything." She pushed off into the pile, threading her way through the rubble and steel.

"Oh, lovely," Aya said, then followed.

Sneaking through the chopped-up buildings was a little like moving through jungle. The rain had left the girders wet and slippery, and lichen grew on their rusty sides.

Hard steel was less forgiving than ferns and bark, though. As they floated after Tally, scraping past girders and jagged chunks of concrete, Aya and Frizz collected scratches like they were crawling through a thornbush.

"Remind me to drink some tetanus meds when we get home," Frizz said, inspecting a bloody scrape across his palm.

"What's tetanus?" Aya asked.

"It's a disease you get from rust."

"Rust gives you diseases?" Aya cried, pulling her hands away from the ancient steel beam before her. "No wonder the Rusties died out."

"Shh!" Tally hissed. "Something's coming."

Shadows flickered around them: a large object passing overhead.

Through the tangle of metal Aya glimpsed its clawed shape—a heavy construction lifter carrying a giant severed piece of skyscraper, like the steel rib cage of some long-dead giant in a predator's jaws. The freshly cut edges sparkled in the sunlight.

"I wonder where they plan to put that down," Frizz said softly.

The lifter came to a halt directly overhead, and Aya felt a shudder pass through the pile. Girders shimmered around her, the magnetic fields straining under tons of ancient metal.

Suddenly the trembling stopped. . . .

"Uh-oh," Frizz said.

The chunk of skyscraper dropped from the lifter's claws.

Aya grabbed the nearest beam and pulled hard, scrambling away.

The falling iron skeleton struck home above her, metal pounding and shrieking, the whole heap ringing with the collision. A shower of rust and pulverized concrete rained down on Aya, clouds of eye-stinging dust billowing from above. She saw steel beams bending around her, twisting under the weight of the new addition.

"Aya!" she heard Frizz call.

She turned—his formal jacket was caught in a cluster of ancient cables, their twisted points like fishhooks through the silk. As he struggled to pull his arms out, the sleeves flipped inside out, trapping his hands inside.

Aya spun around and pushed back toward him, reaching out to grasp his shoulders. She pulled as hard as she could—and with a shredding sound, Frizz ripped free, the jacket tearing into ribbons.

Above, the steel skeleton was still settling, raining debris down on their heads. The iron lattice sagged around them, flakes of ancient rust erupting from ancient beams as they bent into new shapes.

They shot ahead, flying half-blind through the pulverized concrete and rust, the beams squeezing tighter around them. Through the clouds Aya saw Tally waiting, her back braced against a steel bar as long as she was tall—it was set between two girders, like a toothpick holding open a giant's jaw. . . .

And bending slowly under the pressure.

"Come *on*!" Tally cried.

Aya kicked hard at the nearest beam, and she and Frizz flew past Tally.

Tally jumped after them, abandoning the steel bar, which skidded to one side, squealing like fingernails scraping metal. It bent and twisted, then slipped free, bouncing back into the center of the pile.

The whole vast structure crumpled, a host of jagged metal teeth gnashing down on the place Frizz and Aya had just vacated. The new addition slowly rocked itself to a halt on the pile, grinding more concrete dust into the air.

The three of them floated into the ordered lattice of the tallest tower.

"Whoa," Aya murmured. "That was close."

"You're welcome," Tally said, rubbing her shoulders.

Aya remembered the awe she'd felt first laying eyes on Tally. It wasn't just her strength—somehow she'd sensed the dynamics of the pile and braced a piece of iron in just the right place, giving Frizz the long seconds he needed to escape.

Tally really was special, even if Moggle hadn't been here to get the shot.

Aya gave a low bow. "Thank you, Tally-sama."

Frizz just stared into the crumpled pile, stunned into silence. His face was ghost white with dust, like an actor wearing rice powder.

"No problem." Tally nodded approvingly. "You two managed to keep your heads."

"Barely." Aya glanced up at the departing construction lifter. "Were they *trying* to kill us?"

"They didn't even see us," Tally said.

"You saved me, Aya," Frizz said softly.

"It wasn't just me . . . ," she started, but Frizz took her shoulders and pulled her into a kiss. His lips tasted of concrete dust and sweat.

When they pulled apart, Aya glanced at Tally, who rolled her eyes.

"Good to see that you two are okay."

"We're fine." Aya smiled at Frizz, then glanced at a scrape on her elbow. "Except I'm going to get that Rusty disease."

"Relax. Shay's got meds for anything." Tally glanced upward. "And here she comes."

Aya looked up into the reaches of the skeletal tower. The ruin stretched as high as she could see, shafts of sunlight cutting straight through its crumbling walls. She heard the faraway echoes of metal being cut, and heard debris filtering down through the empty, broken floors.

As she stared, shapes began to shimmer against the darkness, like ripples in the air. They took on human form as they descended, surrounding Aya, Tally, and Frizz. They were standing on hoverboards, the riding surfaces wrapped entirely in camouflage.

One shimmering arm pulled a sneak suit hood away, revealing Shay's face.

"Wow. You three look like crap!"

"How'd you get here?" Hiro said, pulling off his own hood. "In a rock grinder?"

"Just about." Aya pointed back at the still groaning pile. "We almost got crushed under that. . . ."

She paused. There were *five* of the sneak-suited figures: Hiro, Ren, Fausto and Shay . . . and someone else.

A boy pulled his hood off, revealing a scarred and ugly face.

"You found us," Tally said softly.

He shrugged. "It was a little tricky, after you escaped earlier than planned. But I figured you'd come to the usual place."

Tally turned to Aya and Frizz, a smile breaking across her face.

"This is David. He's here to rescue us."

THE USUAL PLACE

It was David who'd brought the hoverboards. He'd also brought real city-made food, and the air was already full of slurping sounds and the scent of self-heating meals.

Aya and the others were halfway up the Rusty skyscraper, on a mostly intact floor. The nearest deconstruction crew was a hundred meters above, their metal-chewing blades whining in the background. But there was no chance of being discovered: David's rescue equipment included lots of sneak suits. Aya's felt as smooth as silk pajamas against her skin, though the outer scales were steel-hard to the touch. Everyone was almost invisible from the neck down, bodies blending into the half-missing walls, heads floating eerily as they ate.

"David followed us here," Tally explained between bites

of CurryNoods. "In case we couldn't break out on our own."

Aya looked at David. She remembered him from mind-rain class, of course. His name was mentioned in Tally's famous manifesto, when she'd declared her plan to save the world. During the Prettytime he'd been one of the Smokies, a group who'd lived in the wild, fighting the evil Specials and helping runaways from the cities. So it was natural that Tally would want him around, now that she lived in the wild too. But Aya couldn't figure out why he was wearing an ugly mask.

"Like anyone could keep you three locked up," David said. "My real job was to bring extra equipment and a hovercar."

"Any trouble tracking us?" Tally asked.

David shook his head. "Never more than fifty klicks behind you. The plan would've worked perfectly if you hadn't decided to jump out." He glanced at Frizz.

"It's okay," Hiro said, slurping his own noodles. "I already explained Radical Honesty to them."

"What *is* it with you city kids and surgery?" David muttered.

"But how did you find each other?" Aya asked. "I thought we couldn't use pings."

"When I got into town, these ruins looked like they had burning flares on top." David laughed, looking out through the crumbling wall at sparks falling past. "I thought it was you signaling me!"

"That's how we got in touch with David in the old days," Shay explained.

"After I figured out what the sparks were, I waited here anyway," David said. "Just in case you decided to come to the usual place."

"You always know where to find me," Tally said with a soft smile.

Aya frowned. "One thing I don't get, David. Why are you in disguise?"

"Excuse me?"

"Why are you still wearing . . . ?" Aya began. "Oh, that's not smart plastic? You're really an ugly?"

David rolled his eyes, and Shay said quietly, "David's never had any surge at all. But I wouldn't use the word ugly—Tally might eat you."

"I just figured he was a Cutter, but with . . . ," she began, but found herself silenced by Tally's death-threatening stare.

Aya went back to slurping her PadThai, wishing she'd paid more attention in mind-rain history.

David pointed at a shiny satellite dish on the floor. "We're set up to call in help if you want, Tally. That antenna is focused on a comm satellite, and it transmits as straight as a laser—no one else will hear a thing."

Everyone looked at Tally, who paused, chopsticks halfway to her mouth.

"I don't want any help yet," she said. "We still don't know what the inhumans are up to. And I'm starting to think Aya-la's City Killer story might be a false alarm."

Their stares turned to Aya, who was chewing a mouthful of noodles. She swallowed them slowly, hoping Tally would keep going. It seemed a million times more shaming to explain the mistake herself.

"Yeah," Aya finally said. "The mass drivers might not be weapons."

"What else would they be?" Hiro asked.

"A way to slow down the cities," Tally said. "To strip the

world of metal and send it here. No more cheap metal, no more expansion."

"You've got to be kidding!" Shay cried. "You mean these weirdos are on *our* side?"

"It makes sense," Fausto said. "They could even get rid of the metal permanently—just shoot it into orbit. Those cylinders don't *have* to come down."

Hiro let out a disgusted sigh. "You mean you got this story wrong, Aya?"

"*I* got it wrong?" Aya cried. "You and Ren were the ones who came up with the city killer angle!"

"But it was *your* story, Aya!" Hiro said. "We just gave you an idea!"

"But before you guys started talking about reentry speeds and TNT, I just wanted to kick the Sly Girls mag-lev surfing!"

Frizz frowned. "I thought you said you weren't going to kick that?"

"Would you randoms be *quiet*?" Tally said, her voice suddenly full of razors. "You want those freaks up there to hear us?"

Aya fell silent, glaring at Hiro. It was bad enough that every feed in the city would blame this bogus story on her; she didn't need her own brother piling on. She glanced at Frizz, hoping he understood what she'd meant.

"Don't forget, we aren't sure of anything yet," Tally said. "They could be building a hundred mass drivers right here, getting ready to bombard every city in the world. We may have to blow something up, after all."

"We're almost at the equator," Fausto said.

"The equator?" Tally shook her head. "What does that have to do with it?"

"The closer you are to the equator, the faster the Earth's spinning—more centrifugal force." Fausto made a whirling motion over his head. "Like a pre-Rusty sling—the longer it is, the more momentum it gives the stone. Right here's the best place to shoot something into orbit."

"So maybe there *are* mass drivers here!" Aya said. Maybe her story hadn't been totally truth-missing. . . .

"Don't get too excited, Aya-chan." Ren stood up and crossed to the largest opening in the wall. "I haven't see any mountains on this island."

"The nearest ones I saw were more than a hundred klicks north," David said.

"If you drill a mass driver shaft at sea level, your projectile starts too low," said Ren. "And on a tropical island you'd have to worry about flooding. It'd be a nightmare."

Aya sighed. This island wasn't the best place to destroy the world from, and it was guilty-making how that fact filled her with sadness. If only the inuhmans had been up to *something* world-threatening here . . .

"So why are they salvaging these ruins?" Frizz paused, listening for a moment to the shriek of saws echoing through the ruin. "And why are they on a schedule? In the hovercar, Udzir told us that they'd let us go soon."

"When did he say that?" Tally asked.

"Oh," Frizz said. "I think that was when we were speaking Japanese."

"Thanks for telling me!" Tally shook her head. "Here I've spent all day babysitting you two, while these freaks are getting ready to . . . do whatever!"

She stood up, snapping for her hoverboard. The other Cutters and David scrambled to their feet.

"Good," Shay said. "I've had enough sitting around."

Aya stood. "Yeah, let's go get some answers."

Tally turned to her. "Where do you think you're going?"

"Um, with you?"

"Forget it. You four are staying right here."

"Here?" Aya cried. She had a story to rekick! "But what if you don't come back? Or if the freaks find us?"

"In those sneak suits they'll never see you." David pointed at the satellite dish. "And if we're still gone at sundown tomorrow, you can call for help."

Tally stepped onto her hoverboard. Its riding surface shimmered for a moment, then faded into the background. The four of them pulled on their hoods, and soon they were little more than ripples in the air.

"See you later, randoms!" Shay's voice said from nowhere.

The four shapes rose up, slipping without another word through the gaps in the broken wall.

"Wait, Tally-wa . . ." Aya's cry trailed off.

"They're already gone," Frizz said, putting a hand on her shoulder.

Aya shook him off and went to the crumbling wall of the skyscraper, looking out across the jungle. The sun had set over the trees, and in the distance the inhumans' hoverport was coming alight. The outlines of storehouses and factories glowed against the blackness of the jungle.

All the answers were right there in front of her. All she had to do was go get them.

Aya looked down at her own hand, almost perfectly invisible in her sneak suit glove. . . .

"Aya-chan," Hiro asked, "are you thinking of doing something brain-missing?"

"No." She set her jaw. "I'm thinking that I don't care what Tally Youngblood says. This is still my story."

DO-OVER

"You're nuts," Hiro said.

"Look out there," she said. "The freaks' base isn't that far away. And we've got sneak suits!"

"But the Cutters took all the hoverboards," Ren said. "Are we supposed to *walk* there?"

"Well . . ." Aya frowned, looking at the floor. "We've got enough pieces of hoverball rig for three of us. We can move pretty fast in those."

"You want to float through the jungle at *night*?" Frizz said. "It was tricky enough when we could see!"

Ren nodded. "There are wild animals down there, Aya-chan. And poisonous snakes and spiders."

Aya groaned. Why was everyone suddenly so backbone-missing?

"You're just self-shaming because you got the story wrong," Hiro said.

"That's not why I'm—," Aya started, then glanced at Frizz. "Okay, it's *totally* shaming. But there's still a story here, and we're still kickers, right?"

"I'm actually more of a clique founder," Frizz muttered.

"Doesn't matter how big a story it is," Ren said. "We don't even have a . . ." He paused, staring at her. "Um, where's Moggle?"

"Of course!" Aya cried. "Moggle could tow me in a hoverball rig, maybe two of us. Then we could fly *over* the jungle, above all the vines and poisonous stuff!"

"But it's still back at that ruin," Frizz said.

"You lost Moggle!" Hiro cried. *"Again?"*

Aya shook her head. "Moggle isn't lost, okay? Just

waiting at this ruin we found. We have to send a ping."

"Brain-missing for two reasons," Hiro said. "One, if we send a ping, the freaks will swoop down and capture us. Two, a ping won't travel more than a kilometer here. There's no city interface to repeat it—just jungle."

"He's right, Aya," Ren said, spreading his hands. "There's nothing we can do but wait for Tally."

Aya sighed, sinking to the floor.

If she couldn't rekick the story somehow, she'd be remembered forever as the ugly who'd blown the biggest story since the mind-rain, a useless kicker who'd needed Tally Youngblood to find the real facts.

The name Aya Fuse would forever be synonymous with *truth-missing*.

She looked up. For some reason, Frizz was making a low growling sound through his teeth.

"Are you okay?" she asked.

"It's nothing. . . ." He flinched. "I mean, *practically* nothing."

Aya recognized his pained expression, and smiled. "You've got an idea, haven't you?"

He shook his head, biting his lip. "Too dangerous!"

"Come on!" she pleaded. "Tell me!"

"Linear transmission!" Frizz blurted out, pointing to the satellite dish that David had left behind. He rubbed his temples. "We just need to point that in the right direction."

Ren nodded slowly. "Like David said, the freaks will never hear a thing."

The sun was down, and the horizon was dotted with work-lights and sprays of cutting sparks. The first cool breeze of the day was wafting in from the sea, bringing the smells of salt and brine.

"That looks like the place," Frizz said, pointing into the darkness. "Two towers in a clearing, one twice as tall as the other."

"But the inhumans are there again." Aya watched the sparks tumbling from the taller spire. "Won't they hear us?"

Ren looked at the satellite dish. "The transmission will only hit a small area, and those workers have a building to chop up. Why would they be listening for random radio noise?"

"I guess so." Aya twitched her fingers nervously, playing with her sneak suit's controls. The scales shifted, a texture like tree bark flickering across her body. Her hoverball rig was completely hidden beneath the suit.

"See that heavy lifter?" Ren pointed at a machine leaving the ruin. "If Moggle follows that cable line, then turns there, it'll be here in twenty minutes."

Aya shook her head, remembering all the random twists and turns Tally had taken on the way here. Down in the treetops the network of cables had been invisible. But from this height, the lifters and hovercars flying to and fro revealed its shape, like a glowing, moving map spread across the darkness.

"I'll stay here and guide Moggle while you wait down there." Ren pointed to where the pile of scrap spilled into the jungle. "Take your hoods off, and I'll tell Moggle to look for a couple of heads glowing in infrared."

"There'll be three of us," Hiro said.

Aya turned to face him. "Sorry, Hiro. But Moggle can't tow three people."

"You forget: I actually know how to fly in a hoverball rig.

I don't *need* to be towed." Hiro drifted into the air, spinning around once to demonstrate. "And I'm not going to let my little sister upstage me twice in one week."

She smiled. "Glad to have you along, Hiro."

Ren carried the satellite dish to the outer wall and knelt, balancing it on a pile of rubble. He carefully aimed the metal parabola at the distant ruin.

A flicker of lights blossomed across its controls, but Ren kept his stare focused on the horizon. He adjusted the dish in tiny increments, probing the darkness with its invisible beam.

Long minutes passed that way, Ren's fingers moving the dish as slowly as a minute hand. There was no sound in the room but the metal saws overhead.

"I still can't believe we got the story wrong," Hiro murmured.

Aya smiled. "Thanks for saying *we*, Hiro. But you were right—it was my fault."

He grunted. "You're just lucky to get a do-over."

"Maybe . . ."

"No, definitely," Ren said, staring into the flickering controls. "I finally got an answer!"

"Is Moggle okay?" Aya asked.

"Looks fine from here. The batteries are even recharged—must have found a sunny spot!"

Aya felt a smile growing on her face. She had a hovercam again.

"Let's get moving," Hiro said. He glided to a hole in the floor and dove through, slipping out of sight. Frizz followed, pushing with his hands to propel himself downward.

Before she dropped, Aya turned to Ren. "You'll be okay all alone?"

"Sure. Just don't leave me here too long." He patted the

satellite dish. "If no one makes it back in twenty-four hours, I'm kicking this to the whole world."

NIGHT FLIGHT

They descended through the iron skeleton of the tower, floating past ruined floors in darkness, like divers exploring an ancient shipwreck. The whine of cutting blades faded above, the darkness growing around Aya.

With Moggle on its way here, finally she could make up for all those cam-missing hours flying over the jungle. Not that nature shots were ever famous-making—quite the opposite. Like Miki had said, the point of fame was to be obvious, and so much of the jungle was hidden.

But Aya wanted to remember its quiet magnificence nonetheless.

"Through *there*?" Hiro asked when she landed at ground level. He was pointing to the pile of steel and rubble.

"Yeah, but wait a minute," Aya said. "A lifter's coming down."

They stayed in the shadows, watching until the construction lifter dropped its load of scrap. Metal shrieked and bent, grinding concrete rubble into dust as the new addition settled onto the pile.

"Okay, quick," Frizz said. "Before another one comes."

Hiro was already shooting ahead, slipping into the twisted maze without a glance backward. Aya vowed to learn how to use a hoverball rig properly some day. Floating in zero-g mode was faster than crawling, but way too slow when bone-crushing piles of steel were being thrown around.

It seemed to take forever, making her way through the rubble. As the spires fell behind, stray cables clinging to the girders grabbed at Aya from the darkness—only the sneak suit's armor protected her from countless tetanus-infecting scratches. And she couldn't help imagining another lifter overhead, bringing a giant mass of scrap to squash them all.

Finally the jungle grew closer. Vines had crept into the snarl of metal around her, and the buzz of insects drowned out the distant cutting saws. Aya could barely see, but the shrill cries of birds guided her to the edge of the pile.

"Whoa," Frizz's voice came from absolute blackness. "It's totally different at night."

It was true—the jungle was transformed. The oppressive heat had lifted, and the darkness echoed with a hundred unidentifiable noises. The air was laden with the rich smell of night-flowering plants, and half-glimpsed shadows darted across the stars.

"Pull off your hoods," Hiro said. "Moggle's expecting three of us in infrared."

Aya pulled her hood off, and a buzzing swarm immediately gathered. The cloud was so dense that her first startled breath drew bugs into her mouth. She spat them out. "These mosquitoes are crazy-making!"

A slapping sound came from Frizz's direction. "We'll have to take malaria meds when we get home," he said.

"What's malaria?" Aya asked.

"A disease you get from mosquito bites."

"Gah! Is there anything in this jungle that *doesn't* give you diseases?"

"Hey, Frizz," Hiro's voice called from the darkness. "How do you know all this stuff, anyway?"

"When I was studying brain surge, I took a few medical classes. Maybe I'll be a doctor once Radical Honesty gets old."

"It's *already* old," Hiro said.

"A doctor?" Aya swatted at a buzzing near her ear. "I didn't know that."

Frizz chuckled. "Even with Radical Honesty, there's a lot you don't know about me."

"Wait a second!" Hiro hissed. "Do you hear that?"

They fell silent, and a sound came through the buzzing jungle. Something tentative and wary was slithering among the vines, setting the branches above them creaking.

It slowly grew closer.

"Um . . . hello?" Aya called softly.

Reflected starlight glinted through the tangled vines—Aya recognized the familiar pattern of lenses bobbing happily in the air.

"Hey, for once you didn't blind me!" Aya said, and felt a smile growing on her face.

She finally had a hovercam again.

They flew so fast that even the mosquitoes couldn't catch them.

Aya had one arm wrapped around Moggle and the other around Frizz, their bodies pressed tight together. The hovercam towed them across the treetops, following the cable network toward the inhumans' base. Hiro flew alongside, visible only in the fleeting moments when his sneak suit blotted out stars from the sky.

Suspended above the black sea of the jungle, the fierce wind streaming down her body, the journey was almost like mag-lev surfing. But this was better than any train—

the magnetic currents were invisible and silent, so Aya could hear the calls of birds and bats and unknown creatures whipping past on either side.

She wondered where the Sly Girls were now. Probably still in hiding, waiting for their unwanted fame to fade. She missed them, and in a funny way, Tally Youngblood had reminded her of Lai—or whatever her name was now. Lai was at war with face ranks and merits; Tally struggled with the Special wiring in her head. Both wanted to disappear, yet they kept doing things that were bound to make them famous.

And both of them were borderline sanity-challenged. Aya remembered the death glare she'd received for calling David an ugly. What else was she supposed to call him? Beautiful?

Did Tally *like* him? But she said she hadn't kissed anyone since . . .

"Aya?" Hiro's voice came from beside her. "We're getting close."

Aya scanned the dark horizon, and saw hovercars and heavy lifters in all directions, their lights converging on the inhumans' base.

Hiro flickered momentarily into view, his sky-black hand waving for them to drop down into the canopy.

They descended, Moggle slowing, the darkness of the jungle wrapping around them. Aya tightened her hood as they slid to a halt, not wanting any bugs creeping in.

"See that lifter?" Hiro said.

Behind them, a heavy lifter was approaching, a load of scrap in its jaws. The jungle creaked and moaned, complaining as tons of metal pressed down on the cables strewn across the canopy. Uneasy cries and fluttering wings stirred the humid, scented air.

"It's pretty hard to miss," Aya said. Clouds of insects danced in its skirt of floodlights, and she wondered if Moggle's camo paint was as invisible-making as the sneak suits. "Maybe we should go farther down."

"No," Hiro said. "We should follow it in."

"Follow it?"

"Whatever they're up to, it's about the metal, right? Let's see where they're taking that scrap."

Aya watched the machine's steady approach. Massive girders dangled from its jaws, along with wires and pipes—all the metal guts of Rusty buildings. It looked like some huge beast finishing up a messy meal.

"Okay," Frizz said. "But even in sneak suits, we'll have to be careful."

"No problem," Hiro said. "See how the floodlights are all around the edge, pointing outward? If we float along underneath, we'll be right in the middle of them."

Aya nodded. "And they'll blind anyone who looks up at us."

As the jungle gradually filled with slanting shadows, Aya pulled herself closer to the nearest tree trunk. She felt her sneak suit mimicking the rough bark. The cables sagged around her, branches bending and creaking, Aya's lifter rig trembling in the magnetic currents.

As its jaws passed over their heads, her throat tightened. Concrete dust filtered down, and Aya had to remind herself that the inhumans wouldn't randomly drop scrap into the jungle.

At least, she hoped they wouldn't.

Finally the bank of floodlights was directly above them.

"Now!" Hiro said, shooting upward.

Aya grabbed Moggle. "Come on, Frizz!"

The hovercam pulled them straight up, and for a moment Aya found herself blinded. But seconds later she and Frizz had reached the darkness of the lifter's underside. The floodlights pointed outward in all directions, buzzing with energy and rippling the cool night air with heat.

"Great view, huh?" Hiro said.

Aya looked down into the glowing jungle below them.

Flocks of birds scattered from the lifter's approach; clouds of insects thronged in its path, their wings iridescent blues and oranges; and the gleaming eyes of awestruck nocturnal creatures gazed up at the strange machine flying overhead.

"I hope you're shooting, Moggle," she breathed.

"There it is," Frizz said.

Ahead of them, a bright line on the horizon, the inhumans' base was only a few kilometers away.

MASS PRODUCTION

The jungle fell away, ending in a clear-cut line, the magnetic network coming to an abrupt end.

There was no more need for cables—the hard-packed dirt was spiked with huge pieces of steel. Every few meters, girders had been driven halfway into the ground, like crooked candles in an endless birthday cake.

"Look at that hover grid," Frizz said. "Talk about having metal to waste!"

"It's so crude," Hiro said. "Those girders are still rusty, like they were pulled straight from the ruins."

Aya frowned. So far they'd seen no paths or hovertrails, just drainage ditches half full of runoff from that morning's storm. "This whole place looks like they got here a few days ago."

"Or like they're about to leave," Hiro said.

"Shh!" Frizz pointed down.

An inhuman moved below, pushing herself from one girder to the next, like a bird gliding between branches.

"She must be new," Hiro whispered. "See how she has to push herself around? That's not good hoverball technique. She's in zero-g mode, like you two."

"I don't know," Aya said. The woman's flight looked graceful to her, like some long-practiced piece of choreography. "I saw a bunch of freaks from up in the hovercar, and they were all getting around that way."

Hiro snorted. "Why wear hoverball rigs if you're not going to use them properly?"

"Good question," Frizz said softly.

The heavy lifter turned away, following a row of low buildings, all identical except for the camo patterns mottling their rooftops.

Aya felt warmth rising from them. Their tops were rippling, she realized, billowing like sails.

"They're just big tents," Frizz whispered.

"So this place really is temporary," Hiro said. "It's not a city at all."

The heavy lifter slid to a halt, its jaws directly over a huge pile of scrap. Smaller lifting drones were darting in and out, carrying single girders and tangles of cable away.

At some unheard signal, the little drones all scattered at once.

"Look out below," Frizz said.

The lifter's jaws opened, and the mass of scrap tumbled down onto the pile. Metal crashed against metal in an angry chorus, glinting in the floodlights as it bent and settled. The lifter began to rotate over their heads, facing back toward the jungle.

"This is where we get off," Aya said. "See anyone around?"

"Anything this dangerous is probably automated," Hiro said. "Besides, we're wearing sneak suits. Just set your rigs a little above zero weight, so you stay close to the ground."

He dropped, his outline obvious in the floodlights.

"Hiro, be careful!" Frizz hissed.

Aya adjusted her rig. "Come on, Moggle."

She pushed off from the lifter's underside, floating down to land softly beside the pile. The three of them crouched there, sneak suits blending into the tangle of scrap as the heavy lifter glided back toward the jungle. The edge of its floodlights drifted away, leaving them in darkness.

"See?" Hiro said. "There's no worklights here. It's all automatic."

He started to glide toward the factory buildings.

"Hiro!" Aya called. "Those little ones are coming back!"

The smaller lifting drones they'd seen from above were approaching from all directions, headed toward the pile of scrap. They looked like giant floating hands, each metal finger as long as Aya.

One was coming right for Hiro, the fingers opening. . . .

He shot higher into the air, and it floated right under him, still reaching toward the pile.

"Hey, look," Hiro said. "They can't see me!"

He did a few midair jumping jacks, his sneak suit a hovering whirlwind as another drone passed underneath.

Frizz laughed. "They must only see in infrared. We're totally invisible!"

Aya frowned. Invisible or not, Hiro was enjoying his

sneak suit way too much. The large tents weren't far away, and they'd already seen one inhuman out here in the dark.

Another of the lifting drones glided up beside Aya, ignoring her and reaching into the pile. Moggle jumped away from its grasp, but the drone was too single-minded to notice, picking through the tangle until its huge fingers found a girder. They closed on it and pulled, dragging along a snarl of cables that almost swept Aya from her feet.

"Hey, watch it!" she said. The drone ignored her, hauling the girder away toward the low tents.

"Come on," Frizz said, pulling her away in a bounding, near-zero-g step. "Those things could fly right into you and not even know it."

Aya nodded. "I guess being invisible is sort of dangerous."

Another long leap took them to the edge of the nearest tent, where Hiro and Moggle waited, peering through the gap between canvas and dirt.

The tent covered a pit, about ten meters deep and brightly lit. Rusted girders were everywhere, glinting in the worklights. An inhuman wearing a breathing mask floated overhead, spraying some sort of goo onto a pile of scrap—like the foam from a fire extinguisher, but silvery and seething.

The goo began to bubble, the metal writhing and twisting. Rust and chunks of concrete spat out, clouds of dust hissing into the air.

"Hey, Aya," Hiro whispered. "Remember that really boring story you kicked about recycling a year ago?"

"Yeah." Aya's nose caught a smell like approaching rain. "Those must be nanos—like smart matter, but not as smart.

You can purify old steel with them, or combine it into stronger alloys."

"Nanos can also eat whole buildings if you're not careful," Hiro said. "That's why they're working in a pit, in case they get out of control."

"So the freaks could use nanos as weapons, right?" Aya said.

Hiro snorted. "Whatever makes my little sister happy."

"I'm just saying, they're not exactly making sushi down there," she mumbled. "I hope you're getting some shots, Moggle."

The inhuman air-swam toward a rusted girder that a lifting drone had just dragged in. He gave it a spray of the silvery nanos, and another wave of heat billowed from the tent.

The drone glided away from the wriggling mass, heading toward the pile of scrap that had already been treated. The bubbling nanos were gradually subsiding, leaving a shiny lump of steel. The drone closed its huge fingers around the metal and dragged it out of the tent.

"Let's see what happens next," Hiro said.

Beneath the next tent was another pit, a pile of purified steel lumps at one end. At the other sat a dozen curved shapes made of thin, crisscrossing lines, like skeletons made of wire.

"Nano-frames," Hiro said.

Aya nodded. "Those were in your hole-in-the-wall story, right?"

"Yeah, but I kicked that ages ago." He paused for a second, and they watched a lifting drone drag a lump of metal across the pit. Another hovering inhuman guided its progress, making gestures with his fingers.

"That looks like fun," Aya said, glancing over her shoulder to make sure Moggle was shooting. "See how that drone follows whatever his hand does?"

The nano-frame was glowing now, turning bright white. It was about fifteen meters long, with swelling curves like the hull of a boat.

"Nano-frames are the patterns inside holes in the wall," Hiro explained.

"Huh," Frizz said. "I always wondered about that."

The chunk of metal inside the nano-frame began to turn red, its edges softening like a melting ice cube's. A wave of heat spilled out from the tent.

Aya squinted, her eyes stinging. It felt like standing too close to a fire.

"Whoa," Frizz said. "How come my wall never gets this hot?"

"Because you never made anything that big," Hiro said.

The metal was moving now, flowing across the nano-frame like a viscous liquid, taking on its shape. It filled the spaces between the wires, like skin covering a skeleton. When it had stretched across the entire frame, the steel began to cool back into a solid. The inhuman was already guiding the lifting drone, nudging another lump of metal onto the next nano-frame.

"So here's a question," Frizz said. "What do all these shapes make when you put them together?"

Aya looked at the jumble of pieces. All were gently curved, but she couldn't figure out how they went together.

"They look like boat hulls," she said.

Hiro snorted. "Ah, the popular solid steel canoe."

"I said *like* boats," Aya said.

"There's no point guessing," Frizz said. "Let's keep moving till we get to the end."

The next tent was much larger, as wide as a soccer field.

The pit beneath it was at least forty meters deep, full of finished metal shapes and tangles of circuitry. Several inhumans floated inside, each manipulating a pair of hand-shaped lifting drones. The air was full of clanking and hissing as hot metal collided and fused.

As she crept along the tent, Aya saw how the system worked. Each inhuman added one new piece, then passed it down, hardly pausing before setting to work on the next.

"An assembly line," Frizz said. "Like an old Rusty factory."

"Except much bigger," Hiro said. "Thanks to those drone hands."

Aya nodded, remembering the Rusty term for this: mass production. Instead of making things only when people needed them, like holes in the wall did, Rusty factories had churned out vast quantities of *stuff*—the whole world in a giant competition to use up resources as quickly as possible.

The first hundred years of mass production had created more widgets and toys than the rest of history put together, but had also covered the planet with junk and sucked its resources dry. Worse, it was the ultimate way to turn people into extras—sitting all day performing the same task again and again, each worker a minuscule part of the whole machine. Anonymous and invisible.

As they neared the end of the tent, the shape of the assembled pieces gradually became clear. One finished piece stood there, almost as tall as the pit was deep, with curved sides swelling gently in the middle. It was sleek and aerodynamic, the top tapered to a sharp point. Flight control surfaces stuck out from its sides, like fins on a shark.

Aya remembered this history lesson too—no one could forget it—and realized that the inhumans' plans didn't really need mass drivers, or smart matter, or anything more advanced than classic Rusty technology.

The awful thing that stood before her was a missile—an old-fashioned city killer, pure and simple.

And every few minutes, another one was coming off the assembly line.

MISSILE

"Huh," Aya murmured. "I was actually right."

Hiro nodded slowly. "Somehow, I wish you weren't."

"But this doesn't make any sense," Frizz said. "Why build all those mass drivers and then use old-fashioned missiles?"

"Maybe chunks of falling steel weren't evil enough for them," Hiro said. "Think of all the stuff Rusty missiles carried. Nanos, bio-warfare bugs, even nukes."

Aya swallowed. "So this isn't about using up metal, or even knocking down a few cities. It's about . . ."

"Killing everyone," Hiro finished.

"So they strip the ruins all over the world, shoot the metal here, then launch it right back at us?" Frizz shook his head. "Isn't that a little complicated?"

"You heard Fausto," Hiro said. "The equator's the easiest place to launch from."

Aya nodded, feeling a wave of guilty relief. Her story

was true, except she'd been too optimistic. Nukes, nanos, bugs—whatever these missiles were carrying had to be a hundred times worse than falling metal.

"But it only took a single Rusty missile to kill a whole city," Frizz said. "Why are they building so many?"

"Humanity survived the oil plague," Aya said, shivering. "Maybe they want to make sure they kill everyone this time."

"We have to warn Tally," Hiro said.

"How?" Aya asked. "She's probably more than a kilometer away. And the freaks will catch us if we even try to ping her."

"Then we have to go back to the ruin, use that transmitter to kick this place to the whole world."

"But Tally said to wait!"

"She thought the freaks might be on her side," Hiro said. "But it looks like they're not on *anyone's* side."

Frizz shook his head. "But what if we're wrong? Do you want to make the same mistake twice, Aya?"

He was staring at her, Hiro too, like *she* was responsible for the whole world's safety. But it was still her story, she supposed. Right or wrong, history would remember Aya Fuse as the one who'd kicked it.

She sighed. "Okay. Before we do anything, let's make absolutely sure. We have to take a closer look."

Down in the pit, three lifting drones had gathered around the newly constructed missile. Stretching out their metal fingers, they gently tipped it over onto its side, carrying it out of the factory and into the night.

Aya scanned the darkness, but saw nothing except for the crooked shapes of girders thrusting from the ground. "No one's around."

"Those drones must be automatic," Hiro said. His night-black hand stretched out a finger. "Look where they're headed."

In the distance was a taller building. A lot more solid than the tents, it was shrouded in darkness.

Hiro glided ahead, and Aya and Frizz took hold of Moggle. The hovercam towed them through the girders, staying low to the ground.

"It's kind of weird how few people we've seen," Frizz said.

"Mosquitoes, I guess," Aya said. "If we weren't in these suits, we'd have been eaten right now."

"Maybe so. But you'd think anyone planning to nuke the world wouldn't mind using a little bug spray."

Aya remembered what she'd seen from the hovercar—lots of inhumans braving the wind and rain, pushing their way through the girders. But on this still night no one was outside. Were they all busy making weapons?

As they neared the darkened building, the lifting drones slowly angled the missile upright again. Two huge doors swung open, revealing a vast space within. Orange worklights spilled out across the hard-packed dirt.

The drones carried the missile inside.

The three of them floated to the edge of the huge doorway and peered in.

"Nothing but a bunch of parts," Hiro said softly. "No people, as far as I can see."

The doors began to swing closed.

"What do we do?" Frizz asked.

"We have to get a closer look at that thing," Aya said. She crept along behind one slowly closing door, Frizz and Hiro following. They slipped inside just before the doors met, the *boom* echoing through the building.

"Great," Frizz whispered. "We're stuck in here now."

The missile stood before them, the three lifting drones still attached to it.

Dozens of tiny platforms hovered in the air, like serving drones at a party, but motionless. They carried instruments and tools, electronic parts, and objects that Aya found completely mysterious.

"Shoot those," she told Moggle.

"This must be the next step in the assembly line," Hiro said. "Where they do all the detailed work by hand."

"So where are they?" Frizz asked. "We haven't seen anyone since that last tent."

"I guess that's a little nervous-making," Hiro said.

A hissing noise filled the room.

Frizz nodded. "Definitely nervous-making."

Aya looked up—flakes were falling from the sky, like snow, but softly glowing. Near the ceiling a swarm of tiny drones hovered, spraying out gleaming white clouds.

She caught a snowflake, watching it melt into a softly glowing white spot on her palm. Through the sneak-suit glove, she couldn't tell if it was warm or cold.

"Maybe it's some kind of fire-fighting foam," Hiro said.

Aya frowned. "But nothing's on fire."

"Maybe they're *really* safety conscious," Hiro muttered.

"I don't think it's about safety," Frizz said. "Look at us!"

Aya turned to Frizz, and her eyes widened. Glowing spots had appeared all over his sneak suit. She watched another flake hit his shoulder, melting into a soft white mark. Luminous flecks covered her own arms.

"You're both totally visible." Hiro looked down at himself. "Me too!"

Frizz shook his head. "They knew we were wearing sneak suits!"

"That means they know where we are. . . ." Aya's voice faded. The three lifting drones had drifted away from the missile. They turned as one, floating closer through the air.

Their huge fingers were opening wide. . . .

HANDS

"Moggle," Aya cried. "I need you!"

Hiro was already zooming toward the ceiling. One of the drones swerved to follow him, the other two coming straight for Aya and Frizz.

"Jump!" Frizz grabbed her hand and pushed off hard from the ground.

They shot into the air, spinning wildly around each other, like a pair of hoverballs tied together. The snow swirled around them in a glowing blizzard.

"Let go . . . *now*!" Frizz shouted.

His hand slipped from her grasp, and they shot away in opposite directions—the two drones flew between them, both missing by centimeters.

Tumbling head over heels, Aya saw an expanse of wall coming toward her. She bent her knees, kicking with both feet as hard as she could. The metal boomed and shivered with the impact as she bounced away.

"Moggle, here!" Aya screamed again.

The hovercam twisted through the air below her, its black camo paint speckled with white dots. It wheeled and turned uncertainly, as if the glowing flakes had affected its vision.

"This way!" she shouted. "Follow my voice!"

A lifting drone was headed toward her, its fingers opening, reaching for her. . . .

Moggle barreled into Aya like a punch in the stomach, shoving her out of its grasp.

She doubled over with a grunt, arms wrapping around the hovercam, fingers scrambling for purchase on its smooth sides. The giant hand veered to follow, but its bulk was slow-turning, designed for carrying heavy weights, not chasing people.

"Climb! Quick!" Aya cried.

The hovercam obeyed, jerking her up toward the ceiling. The pursuing drone's fingers crushed the air beneath her dangling feet.

Hiro passed her on the way down, diving with both hands pressed together. His sneak suit was coated with white now, a Hiro-shaped constellation of sparkles. Another of the drones followed close behind him, leaving whirlwinds of glowing snow in its wake.

"Frizz?" she called, looking around. He was somersaulting through the air, a giant hand only meters behind him.

"That way, Moggle!" she cried. The hovercam shuddered in her arms, twisting in random directions, almost pulling itself from her grasp, then headed straight for the ceiling. "No, *not up*!"

She heard Frizz cry out below, and looked down. He'd bounced off a wall, straight into the outstretched fingers of the drone. As he struggled, the hand closed around him.

"Hiro!" she yelled. "You have to help Frizz!"

"I can't!" he called back, his arms and legs twitching wildly. "Something's wrong with my rig!"

"Down, Moggle!" Aya screamed with frustration. "Now!"

Finally the hovercam obeyed, pulling her into a sudden dive. Aya's feet flailed behind her, one ankle clanging against the pursuing drone's metal palm, and spots of red pain washed over her vision. When she could see again, Moggle was still diving, headed right for the floor.

"Not so fast!"

But the hovercam was suddenly a hunk of lifeless metal in her hands. It had lost power completely, pulling her down like an anchor toward the hard dirt floor.

"Moggle!" she shouted. "Wake up!"

There was no response, and Aya let go. She tried to spin around and get her feet under her, readying to kick herself into the air once more. But somehow she wasn't weightless anymore, the pads of her hoverball rig as dead as Moggle.

Momentum carried her down, faster and faster. The ground rose up like a huge fist, and a *thud* went through her body.

And for a long moment Aya was swimming in a sea of blackness. . . .

AN OLD FRIEND

Something hard and huge pressed against her, squashing her lungs—the ground, she realized. She was lying on hard-packed dirt, no longer weightless, every breath hurting like a knife between her ribs.

"Aya?"

She opened her eyes, turned painfully over. A featureless face looked down at her, nothing but gray contours where a mouth and eyes should be, flecked with glowing white dots . . . a sneak-suit mask.

"Frizz?" she said, then let out a gasp. Talking hurt too, it turned out. "What happened?"

"Looks like they caught us."

"Oh, right." The last few minutes came back to Aya as she took a shuddering breath, cataloging all the places she hurt: ribs, shoulders, left ankle. She felt her sneak suit flickering with random textures, damaged from the fall. But its armor had probably saved her from much worse injuries. "Are you two okay?"

"We're fine," Hiro said. "You fell pretty hard, though."

"No kidding," she grunted. "I think something went wrong with Moggle."

Frizz nodded. "Hiro's suit went out too."

"Your hovercam is undamaged," a strange voice said in English.

Aya pulled herself up, looking around for whoever had spoken.

But there was no one in sight but Frizz and Hiro.

From down here on the floor of the huge orange-lit building, the unfinished missile towered overhead like a skyscraper. The three lifting drones lay on the dirt floor around them, their giant fingers in the air like the legs of dead spiders.

The glowing snow had stopped falling, but the ground shimmered softly, as did Frizz's and Hiro's sneak suits and her own arms and hands. They'd gone from invisible to sparkling like fireflies.

"The freaks jammed the magnetics in here," Hiro whispered. "We're not weightless anymore."

"So I noticed," she said. After all day floating in the hoverball rig, Aya felt like she weighed a thousand kilograms.

"Our apologies for any injuries," came the strange voice again. "But we know how dangerous you can be."

Aya blinked, finally discovering the source of the words—it was lying right there on the ground, less than a meter away.

"Moggle?" she said softly.

"Forgive us for making modifications to your hovercam," Moggle said in its weird and unexpected new voice. "We found it damaged in the jungle. While making repairs, we installed this voice chip."

Aya groaned, remembering her reunion with Moggle out by the ruins. For once it hadn't flashed its blinding night-lights, which wasn't like Moggle at all.

"We hoped you would rejoin your hovercam," the voice continued. "And we would have a chance to talk with you directly."

"You've been watching us this whole time!" Aya cried.

"Our apologies for our deception, and for your injuries. It was necessary to disable you temporarily and bring you into a controlled environment."

"Controlled environment?" Aya snorted. "You mean a prison?"

"Of course not!" Moggle's new voice said. "We are honored to have you here. Our colleague offers her profound thanks, by the way. Your hovercam saved her life when she fell from the ruins."

"Yeah, this is some thanks." Aya sat up straighter, pain shooting through her.

"If you allow us to explain, we think you'll discover that our aims and yours are complementary."

Aya laughed. "Sorry, but our aims don't include blowing up the world!"

The voice paused, then answered, "It is unfortunate, but certain foolish children have misled you. Perhaps you'll listen to an old friend."

Aya frowned. An old friend? Who did they think she was? And why were they talking to her in English, anyway?

A rumble passed through the building, the huge doors parting a bare sliver. Through the opening, Aya saw several inhumans hovering nervously, needle fingers at the ready.

In front of them was a strange-looking man, with wild hair and bizarre ragged clothes. He slipped through the doors, which hurriedly closed behind him.

Aya blinked—she'd never seen anyone so *ugly*. His skin was sunburned and his features crooked. The beaming smile he gave her was unbelievably snaggle-toothed.

He laughed and said in English, "I knew you would come for me, Young Blood!"

"Um, I don't think we've met," Aya said. "And *what* did you just call me?"

"Your voice is . . ." He stepped closer, sharp eyes flicking among the three of them. "If you would show your face, Young Blood."

A short, painful laugh escaped Aya. "You think I'm . . . ?"

"She's not Tally Youngblood!" Frizz exploded. He turned to Aya. "The freaks think we're Cutters."

Frizz reached up to pull his hood off. Aya did the same, and after a moment's hesitation, Hiro sighed and followed suit.

The man stared at the three of them, dumbfounded.

"See?" Aya said. "I really don't think we've met." She gave as deep a bow as her injured ribs allowed. "My name is Aya Fuse."

"But you . . . ," the man sputtered, fingering his own

dirty, ragged garment. "You wear the Sayshal clothing, and the floating ones said you had come to rescue me. But your faces are not Sayshal!"

"Indeed," Moggle's new voice agreed. "We seem to have made an error."

Aya nodded slowly. "We aren't Cutters, but we're friends of Tally."

"Young Blood is an old friend of mine as well!" The strange man smiled and clapped her on the shoulder. "My name is Andrew Simpson Smith."

TWO BIRDS WITH ONE STONE

Things were starting to make sense. Sort of.

Soon after their hovercar had limped home on autopilot, the freaks must have realized that Tally Youngblood had arrived. Who else but Specials would have jumped out over the jungle? And Frizz, after all, had announced Tally's name to Udzir. That explained why the inhumans had let Aya, Frizz, and Hiro roam their camp, too afraid to confront them, waiting until they were trapped before attacking. In the sneak suits they'd looked exactly like Cutters.

But there was one thing Aya couldn't figure out. . . .

"How do *you* know Tally? And what are you doing here?"

Andrew Simpson Smith smiled proudly. "Young Blood fell from the sky near my village, three and a half years ago."

"She fell from the sky," Aya repeated. "Near your *village*?"

Andrew nodded. "It is very far from here. Among the little men."

"The little men?" Aya asked, looking closer at him. Had his teeth been surged to be that crooked? His clothing had scruffy bits of fur clinging to it, like something made of dead animals. "Are you in some kind of clique that does pre-Rusty re-creations?"

Confusion clouded his face. "I don't understand. Perhaps you do not speak the gods' language as well as I?" He leaned closer. "Many of the floating ones also speak it poorly."

Aya sighed, deciding to stick to simple English. "Are you from Tally's city?"

"My people live in the wild," Andrew said firmly. "But now we know the ways of magnets and other magic. We help Young Blood watch the cities, to make sure they don't injure the Earth. That is how I met the floating ones."

Aya nodded slowly. "She said she had a friend who got kidnapped by the freaks. That's you, right?"

"Yes." He added softly, "The floating ones don't like to be spied on."

Moggle spoke up again. "Andrew, perhaps you can explain what you've learned about us."

Aya rolled her eyes at the hovercam. Did the inhumans think that this pre-Rusty-looking oddball could convince her of anything?

But the man was nodding sagely. "Do you know about the shape of the world, Aya?"

"Um, pardon me?"

"It is not flat, as it appears. But round, like a ball."

Hiro barked out an astonished laugh, but Frizz bowed and said, "Yes, we've heard this before."

"You are wise, then." Andrew squatted next to where Moggle lay on the ground, placing one dirty finger against its curved, camo-black skin. "All of us live on the surface of this ball. More all the time—more people, more cities, less wild."

"We know." Frizz squatted next to him. "We call that the expansion."

"Expansion." Andrew nodded. "The gods' word for making bigger. But the ball of the world does not get bigger."

"Yeah," Frizz said. "We're kind of stuck with what we've got."

Andrew smiled. "That is where the floating ones are clever. What if we build a new city . . . *here*."

His finger wavered in the air, a few centimeters from Moggle's skin.

Frizz was silent for a few moments, then said, "In space?"

Andrew nodded slowly, spreading out his hands as if warming them over Moggle's surface. "There is a steady place over our heads, called *orbit*. A ring that fits around the world."

"I don't believe it," Hiro said softly.

Andrew chuckled. "It is hard at first, I know. But I learned from Young Blood that the world has no edge, no end. You must learn to see beyond the little men."

"The little *men*?" asked Hiro.

Frizz looked up at the towering metal shape above them. "Turns out you were right, Aya, back when we saw them making this thing. You said it looked like a ship!"

Aya looked up at the missile, or ship, or whatever it was. She shook her head. "But it looks exactly like one of those Rusty weapons!"

"The Rusties had more than one dream," the inhuman voice said.

Aya realized the sound hadn't come from Moggle, and

she turned around. Udzir and two other inhumans floated above her.

"After the first crude city killers were invented," he continued, "they were redesigned to send people into space. Death and hope in one machine."

"That's what this is all about?" she asked softly. "Space?"

"That's why you're all so lame in hoverball rigs!" Hiro cried. "You're not using them to get around quicker—you're using them to practice for zero-g!"

"So you *do* believe in orbit!" Andrew said happily. "It is a place where everyone floats!"

Aya closed her eyes, remembering her own trip through the jungle. "And that's why you're all surged up like freaks. In zero-g there's no point in having feet. So you've all got extra hands."

Udzir frowned, swimming in the air. "We aren't 'freaks,' Aya Fuse. Every change we've made adapts us better to our future home. We're the first extraterrestrial people." He bowed. "We call ourselves Extras."

Aya barely managed to stifle her laughter.

"I assure you," Udzir said firmly, "we are completely serious about our new home."

"Sorry, it's just that in my city 'extra' means . . . well, never mind."

"So you *are* on the same side as Tally," Frizz said. "All that metal's leaving Earth for good."

Udzir nodded. "Two birds with one stone. We can slow the expansion here on Earth and redirect it into space. It's time for humanity to leave our home, before we destroy it."

"You're going to stay in orbit?" Frizz asked. "Not go to some other planet?"

"Permanent orbital habitats," Udzir said. "Close enough

to Earth to lift more supplies with mass drivers, near enough the sun for plenty of solar power. And miniature ecosystems to recycle our water and oxygen."

"The Rusties never managed to save themselves this way," another of the Extras said. "They were overwhelmed by their own numbers and their wars. But humanity is smaller and more united now—we have another chance."

"Unless Tally Youngblood and the Cutters stop us," Udzir added, turning to Aya. "A possibility we have *you* to thank for."

"Me?" Aya said. "Why didn't you just tell everyone what you were doing? If you hadn't been hiding here and kidnapping people, I bet Tally-wa would totally be on your side!"

"We have great respect for Tally Youngblood," Udzir said. "But we couldn't reveal our plans. Do you think the cities would let us strip the old ruins of metal? Or build a fleet of ships that could be easily turned into city killers?"

"You better ping Tally now and explain," Frizz said. "She's probably already here. And if she sees those ships, she'll think the same thing we did!"

"She has not listened to us so far," Udzir said. "We hope that you will try, Aya Fuse."

Aya nodded slowly, her last doubts falling away. The Extras weren't trying to destroy the world; they were trying to save it. The zero-g rigs, their monkey toes, the spaceship towering over her—finally the whole story fit together.

The biggest story since the mind-rain . . .

"I'll try," she said. "But one condition. Give me back my hovercam."

"I should have known," Udzir sighed.

He waved his hand, and Aya felt her limbs lighten, her hoverball rig coming back to life. Hiro floated up into the air, and Moggle rose uncertainly from the floor.

"Is that really you?" she asked.

Moggle's night-lights flashed.

She smiled, blinking away spots and booting her eye-screen. "Tally-wa? Are you around? I've got some news for you."

There was no response.

Aya shook her head. "She must be farther than a klick away. Can you boost my signal?"

"We can try," Udzir said. "But if your ping goes out through our network, Tally may not believe that it's really . . ." His voice faded.

Outside, a low rumbling sound was spilling through the night, like distant thunder. Aya felt it through the soles of her feet, and the walls of the building shivered around them. She heard the squeal of a faraway alarm.

"That sounds like Young Blood," Andrew said softly, and Aya nodded.

Tally was finally blowing something up.

CONFLAGRATION

"Come on, Aya!" Hiro said, reaching down for her. "I'm the fastest person here."

She nodded, grabbing his gloved hand and shouting, "Moggle, bring Frizz!"

The huge doors were already swinging wider, and Hiro pulled her off her feet, shooting toward the opening. Aya's injured ribs burned with pain, her feet flailing behind her.

"Slow down!" she gasped.

"Sorry, little sister," he said. "But we don't have time."

He shot out into the night and through a sweeping turn, leaving Aya gasping as her ribs creaked inside her.

"Maybe you should go ahead," she grunted. "You'll get there faster without me."

"Your English is better than mine. And Tally will listen to you!"

"But she hates me! Or thinks I'm an idiot, anyway."

He laughed. "I doubt that, Aya. And she'll have to believe you on this one—you wouldn't change your mind about the freaks unless you were positive."

"Because it means my story was totally truth-missing?" she cried.

"Exactly," he said, then pointed with his free hand. "Uh-oh."

The horizon before them flickered with a series of flashes, the rumble of detonations arriving several tardy seconds later. Distant clouds of smoke rose into the air, flickering red from fires on the ground below. It looked almost like a party mansion, but the rumbling thunder was much deeper than the crackle of safety fireworks.

"I guess that's where the Extras' ships are," Hiro said.

Aya could only grunt. Hiro was weaving through the floating forms of Extras who'd spilled out into the night, pulling her one way and then the other. Her wrist twisted in his hand, and her ribs screamed with every turn.

Hovercars rose into the air around them. A few flew past overhead, lifting fans stirring the air, screaming toward the flashes on the horizon.

"This could get messy," Hiro said. "It'll turn into a battle if we can't stop her soon."

Aya nodded, flexing her ring finger. "Tally-wa! It's me!"

"We're still too far away," he cried, dropping closer to the girders thrusting up from the ground. Aya could feel them whipping past, the magnets in Hiro's rig pushing off from their metal, each burst of speed threatening to wrench her shoulder from its socket.

The buildings and factory tents fell behind them—Hiro was dragging her across a broad, clear-cut plain, empty except for the girders.

"Look!" Hiro's free hand pointed downward. Huge burn marks darkened the earth, and a charred smell filled Aya's nose.

"They must have tested the rockets here," she yelled.

"I hope that means we're getting close!"

The air itself trembled around them now—Aya felt the explosions rumbling through her body. The flashes threw long shadows from the girders, and half the night sky was shrouded in smoke.

"Aya?" Frizz's voice sounded in her ear. "Moggle and I are right behind you." He paused. "Well, maybe not *right* behind you—Hiro's flying like crazy. But we're coming as fast as we can."

"Okay, Frizz. Just make sure that Moggle gets some good—crap!"

Hiro was pulling her into a sudden climb, wrenching apart her wounded ribs. A black expanse of wall stretched out before them, as wide as Aya could see. They skimmed over its top, then suddenly were flying across what looked like a burning expanse of jungle canopy, treetops waving wildly in the spreading flames. . . .

But this wasn't jungle at all, Aya realized. An endless camouflage net stretched out beneath them, textured with vines and flowering ferns, as detailed as a vast sneak suit. The flames were real, though—sheets of them roared across the dark expanse, an eye-watering windstorm of heat and smoke spilling up into the air.

Where the camouflage had already burned away, Aya saw the tops of the Extras' ships thrusting through the camouflage, as black as ashes, the needle sharpness of their nose cones melted.

She and Hiro soared higher above the nearest flames, carried for long seconds by the momentum of their climb—but soon began to fall.

"Sneak suit!" she cried, scrambling with her free hand to pull on her hood. She saw Hiro reaching up to do the same.

They descended into the fire, skimming among the metal ships in a shallow dive, clouds of smoke churning in their wake. The boiling air burned Aya's lungs, and she smelled her own stray hairs bursting into flame. Even through the sneak suit's armor, her skin blistered from the heat.

But Hiro was already pulling her out again, hover-bouncing up from the forest of steel and flame. She looked around—there were *hundreds* of them, a vast fleet of ships stretching in all directions.

A dozen of the Extras' cars hovered over the conflagration, spraying fire-fighting foam in all directions. But new fires were bursting into life much faster than they could put them out.

A *boom* thundered across the field, shuddering through Aya's body. She saw the shock wave spreading, a growing circle of roiling smoke and flame. At its center was the wreckage of one ship, a tower of steel ripped and twisted from within, slowly tipping over. . . .

It crashed to the ground with a metal shriek, spilling a fresh sheet of flame across the ground. The burning rocket fuel wrapped around the base of the next ship, traveling up its side like a lit and crawling fuse.

Aya tore her eyes away and flexed her finger, shouting, "Tally!"

The name rasped from her smoke-filled lungs, barely audible. But a moment later a faint answer came through the roaring tumult. . . . "Aya?"

"Tally-wa!" she croaked. "It's me!"

"Why aren't you back at the ruin? It's dangerous here!"

Aya coughed. "I noticed!"

Hiro and she were descending again, like a rock skipping across water, plunging back down into the sea of smoke and flame.

"You have to stop!" she said quickly. "I was wrong about—"

The fire enveloped Aya again, setting her coughing. She could see nothing but smoke and the dark shapes of the Extras' ships surrounding them. Her sneak suit was stiffening around her skin, its armored surface breaking down in the heat.

"Where *are* you, Aya?" Tally's voice said, the signal stronger now.

Aya felt Hiro's grip tighten, and he pulled her up out of the smoke once more.

"Flying over the ships!"

"What ships?"

Aya coughed again, cursing herself for being brain-missing. "The *missiles*! I'm right over them. But they're not really missiles!"

"Are you sanity-challenged?" Tally shouted. "Get out of there!"

"I think she's this way," Hiro said, yanking Aya into a shoulder-wrenching turn. They wheeled just above the nose cones of the ships, level and steady, Hiro's hover-bouncing finally under control.

Another deafening *boom* erupted, closer this time, knocking Aya's breath out of her. She lost her grip on Hiro's hand, and shot away from him into an aimless, weaving course in zero-g, buffeted by the windstorms of the raging inferno and the ships' magnetic fields.

"You have to stop, Tally!" Aya yelled, angling her hands like a mag-lev-surfing Sly Girl, guiding herself back toward Hiro. "Wait until we reach you, and I'll explain."

"Some of these missiles are already fueled!" Tally said. "They could start launching the moment we let up!"

"But they're not missiles! They're ships! Stop blowing things up and let me explain!"

"Forget it!" Tally shouted. "If even *one* of those missiles launches, a whole city dies. Get out of there *now*!"

Hiro came sweeping toward Aya, reaching for her, but she twisted away and he shot past empty-handed.

"If you don't promise to stop, I'm staying right here," she said flatly. "And you can blow us up too!"

"I can't sacrifice whole cities for you," Tally said. "And I know you, Aya-la—you'll save your own skin. You have ten seconds."

"I'm not budging!" she yelled.

"I doubt that."

Hiro had turned around and was cutting back toward her,

reaching out his hand again. Aya sobbed with frustration—who would believe that a truth-slanting ugly like her would sacrifice herself?

"I'm here too," came another voice. "And I'm not leaving."

"Frizz?" Tally said. "Have you *all* gone brain-missing?"

"The Extras aren't trying to kill anyone," he said firmly.

"But what if you're wrong?" Tally yelled.

"I'm *certain*," Frizz said. "And you know I can't lie, Tally."

Hiro grabbed Aya's hand, pulling her up and away from the flames. She twisted in his grasp, searching for Frizz. There he was—clutching Moggle near the center of the field, his glowing sneak suit barely visible against the inferno.

"Tally, please," she sobbed. "He means it!"

Tally let out a long sigh, then said, "Start moving, Aya-la. You have two minutes to convince me."

A single flare rose on the horizon, and Hiro headed toward it.

REKICKING IT

Two sneak-suited forms were waiting at the jungle's edge, perched on the high wall that surrounded the Extras' fleet.

Tally pulled off her hood as they landed, her black eyes glistening in the light of the inferno. "Fausto and Shay are waiting for a signal from us. Ninety seconds from now they'll launch more bombs, unless I tell them otherwise. So start explaining."

Aya swallowed. "The Extras . . . I mean the freaks, aren't what we thought."

"Then what are all those missiles for?" David said, pulling off his own hood.

"They aren't missiles," Aya said. "They're ships."

Tally frowned. *"Ships?"*

"It all fits, Tally-wa. You just have to listen! Them taking the metal from the whole world! And they float in the air! Their extra hands . . . because they don't need feet up there!"

Hiro grabbed her hand and muttered, "Aya, slow down."

"Or at least make sense," Tally said. "You've only got seventy seconds left."

Aya closed her eyes, trying to put the story together in her head. More pieces were coming together now, all the threads she'd been following since her first steps into the hollow mountain back at home.

"When I tested that cylinder for my story, the smart matter was programmed to guide it up . . . but not back down. And remember what Fausto said? How mass drivers would be perfect to shoot the cylinders into orbit permanently? That's exactly what the freaks are doing. Except they don't want to get rid of the world's resources—they want to *use* them up there."

"Use them for what?" Tally asked.

"To live. Your friend Andrew explained it to us! They're going to build orbital habitats out of all that metal and smart matter. The whole point of the mass drivers is to launch their raw materials."

"All the mountains we found were empty," David said slowly. "Because the metal's already gone up?"

Aya nodded, pointing out across the burning field. "And these are all ships, rockets to take people up. Mass drivers would kill you if you tried to ride one at full speed—the Sly Girls said so. That's why this base is here at the equator, the easiest place to get into orbit."

"And the hoverball rigs they wear," Hiro said in maddeningly slow English. "They are practicing for zero-g."

"In orbit, where an extra pair of hands are more useful than feet," David said. He turned to Tally. "Twenty-five seconds left."

Aya watched suspicion settle on Tally's cruel pretty features. According to Frizz, Tally had never fixed the wiring in her head. She'd been *designed* to have contempt for anyone who wasn't Special, to think that humanity was always trying to destroy the world. What if her brain surge wouldn't allow her to see what the Extras were really planning?

Like Udzir had said, rockets were death and hope in one machine—it was all how you saw them. Aya wasn't even Special, and she'd been confused before Andrew had explained, convinced by her upbringing and her own story-slanting that the Extras threatened the world.

Once you'd told yourself a story enough times, it was so easy to keep on believing it.

Tally shook her head, her eyes shut tight. "If we let up, even for a few minutes, they could launch enough of these things to wreck the planet."

David put a hand on her shoulder. "But why would they? Even the Rusties managed not to do that. Maybe they built the missiles and aimed them . . ."

Tally opened her eyes. "But they never pushed the button. Shay! Fausto!"

"Yeah, we heard," Shay's voice pinged. "No more bombs today."

Aya let out a long, shuddering breath.

Tally turned to look out across the Extras' fleet, her features softening. The camouflage netting was still burning, and every ship looked charred and blackened. But only a handful had been completely destroyed, toppled on their sides, burning rocket fuel spilling from them like rivers of fire in the darkness.

There were still hundreds of the ships standing, maybe thousands. Enough to lift a whole city into the sky.

"Okay, Cutters," Tally said, exhaustion in her voice. "Maybe we should give them a hand with these fires."

"Why not?" Shay said. "Fighting fires is almost as fun as starting them!"

Tally pulled her hood back over her face, then stepped onto her waiting board. Her sneak suit switched to bright orange, like a firefighter's coverall, and she shot out across the burning field.

Aya saw two more hoverboards rising from the forest of metal shapes. They joined the Extras' hovercars, attacking the burning leftovers of camouflage netting with bursts of foam, spraying any ships that were dangerously close to the blazing spills of rocket fuel.

"They cleared the jungle here," David said. "Once that camo netting's gone, the fire won't have much fuel." He pulled his hood from his face. "Still, you two stay here. You look fried enough for one night."

Aya nodded wordlessly. Her sneak suit crackled when she moved, the scales fused solid, and its coloring was stuck for good on the red-tinged gray of smoke and flame.

"Tell Tally this wasn't her fault," Aya said to David. "We thought the same thing."

He turned toward her, and shrugged. "It's no wonder. We were all brought up in the world the Rusties almost destroyed. It's hard to remember that they did more than fight each other. But thanks."

"For what? For slanting the truth, so you all came here expecting world-killing monsters?"

"No. For helping Tally rewire herself a little more." David lifted into the air, his hoverboard shooting out across the firestorm.

"You did pretty good, Aya-chan," Hiro said.

She looked up at her brother. "Are you kidding?"

He shook his head. "I'm serious. You finally learned how to kick a story without going over time."

Aya let out a short laugh, which sent a fresh wave of pain rippling across her ribs. She groaned, rubbing her sides. Her right shoulder was sprained and twisted from being towed here at hoverball speeds, and her wrist felt like someone had squashed it in a sushi maker.

"Look," Hiro said.

Moggle was making its way across the smoldering ruin of the camo netting with Frizz in tow, the smoke swirling around them.

"Are you okay?" she pinged.

"A little singed," Frizz said. "But we got some awesome shots."

Aya shook her head, for once not caring if any of this was recorded. At last all the threads of the last two weeks made sense, the truth assembling itself like an Extras' ship out of scattered bits of scrap. It was a relief, no longer having to struggle with unwieldy facts and her own total lack of Radical Honesty.

As Frizz landed and took her gently into his arms, a

brain-calming hum traveled through Aya's battered body, like a perfect edit falling into place.

She'd finally gotten this story right.

THOUSAND FACES

"Remind me again why I'm doing this."

"To show your support." Aya adjusted the sparkles on Tally's gown, then took a step back to admire them. "You're the most famous person in the world, Tally-wa. If you tell everyone you're behind the Extras, they'll get a lot more recruits."

"And less hassle for all that metal they grabbed," Fausto added. He adjusted his necktie. "And for kidnapping everyone who saw them."

"Plus, Tally-wa," Shay said, straightening her hair. "We haven't been to a party in *ages*!"

Tally just grunted, looking at herself doubtfully in Aya's huge wallscreen. Her ball gown was rippling smart matter and velvet, as black as night and shimmering like starlight. Perfect for the Thousand Faces Party.

"Don't look so glum," Shay said. "You used to wear stuff like that all the time."

"Yeah, back when I was a bubblehead."

Aya tried to picture Tally perpetually happy and clueless, and shook her head. Even in the ball gown, Tally was still a total Cutter, her face and bare arms laced with flash tattoos and scars.

"You know," Aya said softly, "there's still time to fix those if you want."

"No chance." Tally ran one finger down her arm. "They remind me of things I don't want to forget."

"You look beautiful," David said. He was wearing one of Hiro's antique silk jackets, having proclaimed that anything from a hole in the wall made him nervous. He'd been jumpy since he and Tally had arrived from Singapore that afternoon, as if the city was too cramped for him.

Aya's apartment *was* a little crowded tonight. All nine of them were here—Aya, Frizz, Hiro, and Ren; Andrew, David, and the three Cutters—everyone who'd featured in the Leaving Home story. It had kicked two days ago, and all of them were in the top one thousand. Nowhere but Shuffle Mansion had enough security to keep the paparazzi cams at bay.

At least there was room for everyone here. Upon her return home, Aya had found her apartment twice as big as when she'd left, expanding in proportion to her fame. Maybe face rank wasn't everything, but there were some advantages to being the third-most-famous person in the city.

"I still don't see why we have to go to this stupid party," Tally said. "Couldn't I do some kind of feed announcement?"

Aya frowned. "That won't be any fun. And it won't help the Extras nearly as much."

"Plus," David said, "we sort of owe them for a couple of dozen spaceships."

"I guess." Tally gave her ball gown one last glum stare.

Shay chuckled. "They're just lucky we didn't use nanos."

When they stepped outside, swarms of hovercams were waiting.

"Okay," Tally said. "I officially hate this city."

Aya took a deep breath, but couldn't find it in herself to argue. It was getting annoying, being followed everywhere, constantly pinged and cam-swarmed, her hairstyle imitated by littlies, her nose mocked on slammer feeds. Sometimes Aya wondered if she'd ever get any privacy again.

Even her own hovercam made her a little nervous these days. Ren had taken it apart and removed the Extras' mods, but Aya still had nightmares full of betrayal and swarms of talking Moggles.

But it was useless pretending not to enjoy her single-digit face rank. After all, here she was with her famous friends, all headed toward Nana Love's party, a smile on her face and Moggle in tow to capture every second.

"So how do we get through those things?" Tally asked.

"Glitter bombs?" Fausto suggested.

"Nanos!" Shay cried.

"None of the above!" Aya said. "You don't always have to blow stuff up, Tally-wa. In this city you've got a reputation bubble."

"A what?"

"Just start walking, and they'll give you room."

Tally took a few steps forward, and the wall of hovercams curved away from Shuffle Mansion's fifty-meter boundary. David took her arm and pulled Tally farther along, and soon they were headed into the night, an almost perfect sphere of hovercams surrounding them.

"This is very strange," Andrew Simpson Smith said. "Are all cities like this?"

"Not really," Tally answered. "After the mind-rain, this one went particularly brain-missing."

"The reputation economy isn't brain-missing!" Hiro

said. He'd been practicing English with Andrew Simpson Smith over the last few days, and enjoyed spouting long sentences. "Wanting to be famous motivates people, which makes the world more interesting!"

Tally snorted. "I've seen that motivation at work, Hiro. It leads to some truth-slanting, too."

Aya sighed, wondering when Tally was going to let it go. Most of the feeds had already gotten over the mistakes in her City Killer story. They had better things to kick, now that Aya Fuse had given them a new future to speculate about, a whole new kind of Extra.

And, unlike certain people, she hadn't blown anything up.

Nana Love's mansion was filled with astonishing sights.

The NeoFoodies were there in force, showing off their new aerogel, both edible and smart. It floated overhead, changing forms and flavors as the night went on, contesting with the hovercams for valuable airspace.

The surge-monkeys were all playing Extra, with wide eyes and pale skin, though most stopped short of prehensile toes. Hoverball rigs set to zero-g were fashion-making too, though Hiro kept muttering about how everyone could use some training.

Glittercams, newly invented for this party, were everywhere. Hovering at eye level like nosey fireflies, each recorded only a few pixels, from which city interface assembled a continuous image—everyone in the city could navigate through the party as if they'd sent their own invisible hovercam.

Of course, it wasn't long before the glittercams had annoyed Tally. She swatted a handful to the ground, and the rest retreated into a respectful reputation bubble. Before long Tally had vanished into the recesses of Nana Love's mansion, the other Cutters in tow.

"Good evening, Aya," a familiar voice said in English.

Aya looked up to find Udzir floating next to Moggle, dressed in a formal sari and holding a champagne glass in one set of curved toes.

She bowed, hiding her expression. The Extras still gave her the creeps, even after Udzir had explained their surge in detail. The Extras' pale skin was to help produce vitamin D from the barest sliver of sunlight. Even the wide-set eyes made sense—the first orbital habitats would be so cramped that normal depth perception wasn't necessary.

Still, the overall effect was unsettling.

"I hope you're enjoying the party," she said.

"Indeed. It was kind of you to arrange an invitation."

"It wasn't me," Aya said. As the new face of extraterrestrial humanity, Udzir's fame was top one hundred. Everyone joked that he was the only Extra who wasn't, strictly speaking, an extra at all.

"One way or another, Aya, my presence here is thanks to your story." He performed a little midair bow. "You have helped our cause immensely."

"I'm just glad things got cleared up before Tally-sama toasted your whole fleet."

"As are we," he said. "Though as it turns out, the drama of our rescue has proved more valuable than the ships we lost. A strange thing, fame."

"That's for sure. Getting many recruits?"

"Indeed." He glanced over Aya's shoulder. "Even a few tonight."

"Hey, Nosey."

Aya turned, and her mouth fell open. "Lai? How did you . . . ?"

"Get in here?" Lai asked, then smiled. "Same as you: with an invitation."

Aya blinked. She hadn't thought to check the Sly Girls' face ranks lately, but of course with a whole new version of the story kicking . . .

"Nine hundred and fifty-seven," Lai supplied. "Since you were about to ask."

"Oh. You must be hating that."

Lai shrugged. "It won't matter much in orbit." She glanced up at Udzir, who had turned to talk to someone else. "I just hope Mr. Big Face Alien realizes that there's no time for fame on the new frontier."

Aya laughed, then pictured Lai with four hands and fish eyes. She shuddered, banishing the image from her mind. "I'm still sorry about sneaking all those shots of you."

"And I'm sorry for shooting you out of a mass driver." Lai paused. "Wait a minute—no, I'm not. That was *fun*."

Aya laughed again. "I guess it was. So how are the Sly Girls?"

"Probably all watching this party on their wallscreens."

Aya frowned. "Really? But the Thousand Faces doesn't exactly seem like a Sly Girl kind of thing."

Lai shrugged, then glanced up at Moggle and leaned in closer. "So, you want a lead on a story?"

"A story?" Aya asked. She hadn't thought much about what to kick next. After the end of the world and the birth of a new frontier, everything seemed anticlimactic. She still wondered sometimes about becoming a Ranger. "I guess."

"Okay, but you have to promise you won't tell anyone before they cut the cake."

Aya raised an eyebrow. One of the traditions of the Thousand Faces Party was Nana Love serving a huge pink cake at the stroke of midnight. All the big faces gathered around it when she did, sharing their slices of fame.

"Um, okay."

Lai waved away a few glittercams, then pressed her lips almost against Aya's ear, her voice dropping to the barest whisper. "I injected the cake with this smart matter that Eden cooked up. It's spreading as we speak, making the sugar kind of . . . unstable."

"Unstable?"

"Shh!" Lai giggled. "When Nana cuts it, it'll sort of explode. Not in a lethal way . . . just in a cake-spreading way."

Aya's jaw dropped as she tried to imagine the city's illustrious faces covered with pink frosting. "But that's . . ."

"Pure genius? I agree," Lai said, turning away with a smile. "Just remember that you promised, Nosey. You owe me one kept secret."

Aya pinged for Frizz's location, then went to find him on the upstairs balcony. He was alone, looking out over the darkened privacy gardens.

"I have an ethical question for you, Frizz."

He turned to her, his manga eyes glittering with the safety fireworks overhead. "An ethical dilemma? At *this* party?"

She looked around: no glittercams sparkled in the air, and Moggle was the only hovercam in sight. Nana Love's garden was off-limits to cams tonight, which was probably why the balcony was empty.

"What if you were a kicker, Frizz, and you knew something was going to happen at, say, a party? And it might be host-shaming—definitely shaming—but you'd promised not to tell anyone?"

"Hmm," he said. "It's only embarrassment we're talking about, right?"

"Yeah, but quite a lot."

He shrugged. "Probably I'd keep my promise."

She sighed, staring across the city at the windows flickering with feed light—everyone watching the Thousand Faces on their wallscreens. "Sometimes I wish I could tell you secrets."

"Maybe you can soon."

Aya frowned. "What do you mean?"

"I've been thinking about what Tally said, how I'm a wimp for not telling the truth on my own." He pointed as his temple. "Maybe Radical Honesty *is* getting a little old."

"But the clique's bigger than ever now!" she said.

"Exactly. They don't need me anymore."

Aya blinked, trying to imagine Frizz without his mortifying outbursts. "I don't know, Frizz-chan. I kind of need you around to keep me honest."

His arm wrapped around her shoulders, drawing her closer. "Don't worry. I'll still be here. And I'm not giving up on honesty, just *Radical* Honesty."

She leaned her weight against him. "But if you're not compelled to tell the truth, how will I know you still like my big nose? I'm not fixing it, you know. Tally-wa made me promise."

"Yeah, she told me about that. But don't worry, a little brain surge won't change my mind. Not about you."

They stayed there on the balcony for a long time, listening to the ebb and flow of laughter and music inside.

It was strange, hovering at the edges of the party. As long as she could remember, Aya had watched the Thousand Faces unfolding on the feeds, imagining herself as one of the anointed few. But now that she was really here, all she wanted was to be alone with Frizz, staring at the city over the empty expanse of Nana Love's cam-missing gardens, immensely happy that no one else wanted privacy tonight.

The tumult behind her was just a party, after all. Generations of bubbleheads had occupied this very mansion, wearing pretty much the same clothes, mostly saying the same things. Glittercams and face ranks didn't change that. . . .

A soft *thump* came from below, and Aya looked down.

It was David, rolling to his feet. He must have jumped out of one of the windows.

Tally Youngblood was right behind him, descending as gracefully as a cherry blossom, her hands and feet darting out and catching windowsills and sashes to slow her fall. She landed softly, slipped her arm through David's, and they made their way into the garden.

Frizz leaned closer. "I was wondering about those two."

"You heard what she said, though," Aya whispered. "No one since . . ."

But Tally was leaning against David, pulling him deeper into the darkness, their shoulders pressed together in the cool night air.

"Moggle, are you getting this?" Aya began, then shook her head. "Never mind."

She turned to Frizz, leading him from the balcony with a smile.

"Come on, it's almost midnight. Let's go watch them cut the cake."

Scott Westerfeld is the acclaimed author of numerous best-selling novels for teens, including the UGLIES sequence; *Uglies*, *Pretties*, *Specials* and *Extras* published by Simon and Schuster. His other teen novels include *The Midnighters Trilogy*, *Parasite Positive*, *Last Days* and *So Yesterday* which was named an ALA Best Book for Young Adults.

Scott was born in Texas and now he and his wife, Justine, alternate summers between Sydney, Australia and New York City. Visit Scott's website at www.scottwesterfeld.com.